SAVAGE SKIES

THE FOURTH EMPIRE
BOOK 1

KAT ROSS

SAVAGE SKIES

First Edition

Map by the author.
Cover by Atraluna.

ISBN-13: 978-1-957358-09-3 (Ebook)
ISBN-13: 978-1-957358-13-0 (Paperback)

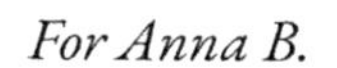

For Anna B.

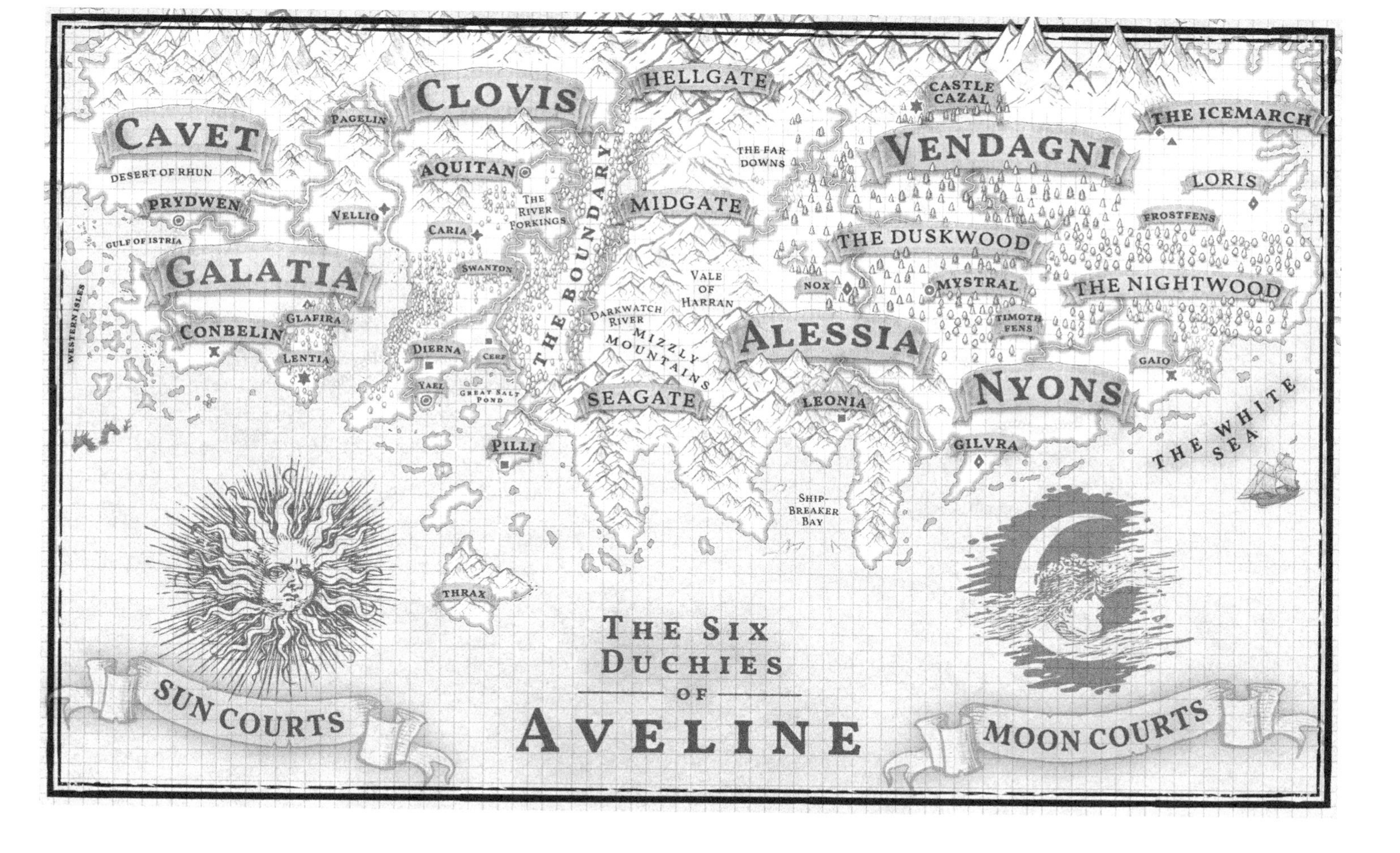
The Six Duchies of Aveline
Cavet
Desert of Rhun
Prydwen
Gulf of Istria
Western Isles
Galatia
Conbelin
Glafira
Lentia
Pagelin
Vellio
Clovis
Aquitan
Caria
Swanton
The River Forkings
Dierna
Yael
Cerf
Great Salt Pond
Pilli
Thrax
The Boundary
Hellgate
Midgate
The Far Downs
Darkwatch River
Mizzly Mountains
Vale of Harran
Seagate
Alessia
Leonia
Ship-Breaker Bay
Nox
Castle Cazal
Vendagni
The Duskwood
Mystral
Timoth Fens
Nyons
Gilvra
The Icemarch
Loris
Frostfens
The Nightwood
Gaio
The White Sea
Sun Courts
Moon Courts

A History of Aveline, Volume I

The Advance of the Vatras

As flaming cinders rained from the heavens, and birds fell dead, and smoke from the pyres turned day into night, thus did thirty ships sail forth from the Bay of Farewell, that fairest of seaports at the northwestern tip of Eddyn. Each carried nobles and retainers of the six great houses: Marcel and Redvayne, Cazal and Courtenay, Scalici and Do Santillan.

The crossing of the White Sea brought such hardships that only half the fleet reached the shores of the new world. Not long after they made land, the Avas Vatras, the fire daemons whose wrath they had fled, conspired to drive Bel from His chariot and halt the sun in the sky. The realm was severed down the spine of the mountains — west graced by eternal Light, east cursed by eternal Darkness.

But that was merely the first blow. Under a blood moon of that same year, the Greater Gates to the underworld were sundered by the feckless ambitions of Jaskin Cazal, disrupting the passage of souls into the Dominion of the Drowned Woman.

These twin cataclysms would bring profound cultural, economic, and political consequences for centuries to come.

— By Brother Hunfrei de Farnfold,
Astrologer to the Damiata of Conbelin,
Year 684 of the lunar calendar

Chapter 1

It was a bad year for fever.

Even out on the Boundary, Castelio knew it was a bad year. His parents were woodwards, practitioners of green lore. When the fever came with the rains, they would gather moss and bark in the misty glens and cross the river to minister to the villagers on the far bank. Sometimes they let Cas come along to help, but not this year.

It was a killing fever this year.

Burning fierce and unquenchable like spilled lamp oil. Those who lived were frail and trembling for weeks. Those who died were buried with iron coins on their tongues and silver bells sewn to their sleeves.

Still, some came back.

Cas heard his Da talking about it with Gui Harcourt when he arrived at the farm on his black charger. Gui was a Quietus, which was like a soldier except that instead of fighting the living, he banished the dead. Gui was tall and broad, with kind eyes and a mild voice. The two men sat at the trestle table under the old lightning-scarred oak where the family took all their meals now.

The homestead sat in a forested valley with the Forkings River on one side and the fog-cloaked Mizzly Mountains on the other.

Cas knew Boundary folk were considered queer. They lived in the shadow of the Greater Gates of the high passes, where the Ducissa's border guards kept watch with pikes of iron and made sure nothing came through that didn't belong in the living world. The Boundary had no noonday sun like the duchies of the west, nor was it always midnight like the east.

No, the Boundary was a middling place, forever at the edge of dusk. On a clear day, if all three moons were aloft, the light had a bright, silvery quality. Now, dark clouds mounded on the horizon, leaving a gloomy half-light. Cas needed to fetch wood for supper, but the storm wouldn't arrive for a while and he wanted to know what tidings Gui had brought. So he took a bucket to the well and dropped it down, turning the winch slowly so he could listen without being too obvious.

The men spoke in low, troubled voices.

". . . more than a dozen risen in Caria . . . reinforcements at the border . . . locked inside the houses for quarantine . . ."

Cas stared into the mossy mouth of the well, ears pricked. It was nothing new, the dead returning. That's why they needed men like Gui Harcourt. Why corpses were buried with coin to pay the Drowned Woman. Some folk were too poor to afford the charms, but that was a problem in the villages, not here.

The Boundary had a dangerous reputation, being next to the mountains, but Cas had lived there all his life and never seen a single Low Dead, let alone—

He looked up and found Da staring at him. A strong, calloused hand beckoned. Cas drew up the bucket and walked over, wondering if he was in for a scolding for eavesdropping.

"How old are you now, lad?" Gui asked.

"Twelve," he replied, meeting the man's gray-blue eyes. "Almost thirteen."

Cas had known Gui since . . . always, really. The Quietus ranged up and down the Boundary, stopping at the Nerides farm several times a year. Cas held him in awe. He couldn't imagine facing the risen dead.

Gui's staff leaned between his knees. It was made of ancient, yellowed wood with sigils carved along the length. A dozen small pouches hung from his belt.

"Let's hear you whistle," Gui said.

Cas wet his lips and mimicked the tune he'd heard Gui whistling when he rode up the lane.

"Well done. A strong, clear whistle is as good as chimes and bells. Sometimes better." Gui cast a look at Da that Cas didn't entirely understand. "Maybe you heard what I was saying to your father, but there's been trouble across the river. More than usual."

"I wasn't trying to," Cas said, cheeks pinking. "But aye, I heard."

Gui's gaze drifted to the youngest members of the Nerides family. Teo was seven, bare-chested and scrawny, with scratches on his arms from picking gooseberries. He perched on a stool, shelling peas, while four-year-old Filippa played with little people Cas had made from twists of straw. They both had Ma's flaxen hair and freckles.

"Nothing close to here, mind," Gui said. "But you're near a man now, you should know."

Cas nodded and looked at Da. "The risen can't cross the river though, can they?"

"No," Gui answered. "They can't."

And then the Quietus glanced at the farmhouse and Cas felt a trickle of ice. Ma was inside, upstairs abed, and he hadn't been allowed to see her in more than a week. She was the reason they ate their meals under the oak instead of in the kitchen. Why all of them except Da were sleeping in the barn.

Cas knew she was locked inside their bedroom. The fever made its victims so restless they'd leave their beds and wander, which is why some called it the walking plague. Da said the fever was smart because if people moved around, they could pass the bad humors to others.

"Are you here to take us away?" Cas asked tightly.

Gui frowned. "No, lad. Why would I do that?"

A knot loosened in his chest. "Never mind. Are you staying for supper?"

Gui grinned. "Is that an invitation?"

THEY HAD FRIED duck eggs and bread toasted on long forks, and peas in sweet butter. The rain held off until dessert, which was apple tarts that Cas had baked that afternoon from Ma's recipe. They weren't as good as hers — the middle of the crust was soggy and the edges burnt — but Da made a show of eating two and praised Cas's cooking.

Gui told them stories about the court at Aquitan that had Teo spellbound, but Cas kept looking up at Ma's bedroom window and wishing she were well enough to come down. Lippa missed her, too. His little sister was clingier than usual, climbing into his lap while he was eating. Da offered to take her, but Lippa didn't want him, she wanted Cas, so he held her warm, drowsy weight, her hair smelling like hay, until the drizzle began and he carried her into the barn.

Once Cas got her up the ladder into the loft, he left Teo watching her and went back down. The sheep were peaceful in their pen, snuggled together in wooly humps. Rain drummed on the roof as the two men stepped through the barn doors. Gui had donned his long oilskin coat. Da wore a broad-brimmed felt hat and carried his own hickory walking stick. Cas looked most like him, slender and chestnut-haired, though Da had threads of white at his temples.

"I need to gather nettles and rowan," Da said, "for the poultice. They've got to be fresh."

Cas lowered his voice. "How is she?"

"The same, but that's a good sign. The seventh day is usually the worst. Then the fever breaks."

Cas counted back in his head. "And the seventh day was . . . yesterday?"

Da nodded. "Gui offered to come with me. Can you mind your brother and sister?"

Cas glanced up at the loft. "Sure."

The Quietus stepped up. He held out a small glass vial stoppered with a bit of cork.

"Keep that with you, lad. Just in case. It's Kaethe's Tears."

A nine-pointed star was tattooed on the webbing of Gui's hand between thumb and forefinger. The sign of Kaethe, the Drowned Woman. Patron of the dead.

"Go on," Gui said gently. "Take it."

Cas regarded the vial, wary. But why . . . ?

His mind went blank for a moment, unwilling to finish the thought.

"Do as he says," Da said quietly.

Cas took the vial. It felt cold against his palm.

"We'll be back in an hour or two." Da laid a hand on his shoulder, gave it a brief squeeze.

Cas watched them ride down the lane on Gui's black charger, Da behind with a cloth satchel slung across his back. The trees bent and swayed, sending eddies of dry leaves whirling into the twilight. He gripped the vial in his fist. For the first time, it came home to Cas just how isolated their farm was. The closest neighbors were an hour's brisk walk. An old couple whose children had grown up and moved across the river. Before she got sick, Ma would visit them every week—

"Whatcha got?"

Teo hung over the edge of the hayloft, peering down.

Cas slid his hand behind his back. "Nothing."

"Don't lie, I *saw*. Gui gave you something."

He sighed and showed him. "Kaethe's Tears."

His brother's eyes widened. "Can I see?"

Cas felt suddenly angry. At Gui for thinking he'd need protection. At Da for allowing it. The dead couldn't cross swift-running water. Couldn't reach the farm. And they had iron horseshoes above all the doors, including the one leading into the barn. Cas had nailed them up himself.

A recklessness seized him. "You can keep it," he said.

He tossed the vial into the air, a long, looping arc. Teo groped for it, almost had it, and then the vial slipped through his fingers. Time seemed to slow as Cas watched it fall back to earth and shatter on the warped floorboards.

"What did you do that for?" Teo demanded.

Heat flooded his cheeks. He grabbed a broom and whisked the glass into a pile, feeling stupid. "Just forget it."

"What if Gui wants it back?"

"He won't."

"How do you know?"

"It was a gift. Now come down and clean your teeth."

Cas ran through the rain to the well and fetched the bucket. They squatted at the open doors, rubbed salt on their teeth, rinsed and spat. As they walked back to the ladder, Teo paused next to the damp patch. "What's Kaethe's Tears again, Cas?"

"Just water."

Teo's ginger brows wrinkled. "Must be more than that."

"Well, I s'pose it is," he conceded. "It comes from the source of the Forkings River, way up north, and it's blessed by a priest of Bel."

The notch in his brother's forehead deepened, as it did when he was trying to work something out. "But if it's blessed by a priest of the sun god, why's it called Kaethe's Tears?"

Cas laughed and ruffled his hair. "I've no idea. You'll have to ask Gui."

He left the pile of glass in a dark corner, meaning to sneak off and bury it in the woods the next day. If Lippa found it — and she would, *of course* she would — she'd cut herself. Besides which, he didn't want Da to know what he'd done. Or Gui.

Cas climbed the ladder after Teo, wishing he hadn't acted so rashly. So *childishly*. It seemed an ill omen. An insult to the Drowned Woman.

"Let's say prayers," he said once they were settled up in the loft.

He lit a lantern and hung it carefully on a hook. Fire was a much greater threat than the risen dead, especially in a barn. The light burnished Lippa's hair to a golden flame. Dark lashes fanned across her round, rosy cheeks. She'd burrowed into the nest of blankets, thumb stuck in her mouth. Cas gently shook her shoulder.

"Wake up, Lip."

She made a soft noise but didn't rouse.

Teo shot him a worried glance. Cas knew what he was thinking, but Lippa's forehead felt cool when he touched it.

"No fever," he said.

"I guess she's just tired," Teo said with relief.

For some reason, Cas had a twinge of unease at letting his sister skip the bedtime prayer. Ma said it was a special catechism of Boundary folk handed down by her grandparents and *their* grandparents, all the way back for hundreds of years. Cas had repeated it so many times, he'd stopped hearing the words. It was what you did after cleaning teeth and before lights out.

But tonight felt different. He listened to the wind muttering in the eaves, the rain pattering on the roof, the wet slap of branches through the half-open barn doors. The river was too far away to hear, but he fancied he could anyway — a ribbon of rushing whitewater that started up in the mountains and ran the length of the Boundary down to the Great Salt Pond.

Yes, between Lippa's soft exhalations, he could hear the river now, and the creak of the ferry rope going taut, and the bump of the raft as it touched the shore. Hear the shambling footsteps of some fell thing as it staggered up the muddy bank . . .

Cas grabbed his brother's hand, too hard.

"Ow," Teo protested.

"Sorry," Cas mumbled, loosening his grip.

Stop playing the fool, he told himself sternly. *Gui said you're almost a man. It's time you start acting like it.*

He cleared his throat. "We'll say it without Lip."

Teo nodded, swallowing, and Cas could see he felt it, too, the faint sense of something off. The boys squeezed their eyes shut, whispering the words together.

Bless us, Kaethe
Guide us through the thickets of night
Let our feet not lose the path
And at the last hour
When your cold hand beckons
Lend us courage to cross the stormless sea

Bless us, Kaethe
Seal gate and tomb against us
Let us not rise again

They pulled their clammy palms apart. Teo punched his wool-stuffed pillow. Lay down with his back to Cas.

"When's Da coming back?" he asked softly.

"Soon."

Cas twisted the wick on the lantern. The flame shrank and darkness rushed in. Not absolute — it was never full night on the Boundary — but the heavy clouds left a twilight that was deeper up in the hayloft. He lay back with his hands laced behind his head and thought about the chores that needed doing tomorrow, and how he'd manage them all with Lip and Teo to watch. He desperately missed Ma, though he knew they all had to be strong and do their part until she was better.

And she *would* get better. Da said so. She was past the seven-day mark. Ma was young and strong. Full of jokes and song and good cheer. Kaethe wouldn't take her yet.

He slipped into a doze and woke to Lippa tugging at his hand. He sat up, instantly alert. "What is it?"

"I had an accident." Her voice was small. "I'm sorry."

His heartbeat slowed. Lippa had started wetting the bed again since Ma got sick. He usually took her to the privy right before she went to sleep, so really it was his own fault.

"Don't worry," he said, "I'll get you some dry clothes."

"Please don't tell," she begged.

Da wouldn't be mad. He wasn't that sort of man. But it seemed to be a point of pride with Lip, and so far, Cas had covered for her.

"I won't," he promised.

Lippa nodded in the half-light. "I'm thirsty, too, Cas."

"Then I'll bring you a cup of water. Do you need to pee again now?"

She shook her head.

"Stay up here. I'll be right back."

He knuckled grit from his eyes and climbed down the ladder, hoping to see a light through the kitchen window that meant the men had returned, but the farmhouse was dark. Hadn't it been more than two hours by now?

What was taking them so long?

Chapter 2

The rain had eased and Cas crossed the yard quickly, wishing he'd remembered to bring the lantern.

Laundry was at the top of tomorrow's list of chores. All their clothes were waiting in a basket to be carried down to the river, but he'd left a few of Lippa's things in the chest at the foot of her bed.

Upstairs. Where he wasn't supposed to go.

Cas fixed his gaze on the lane, hoping to spot Da's broad-brimmed hat and Gui's black charger. The wind was high, lashing the trees. Shreds of cloud scudded across the face of Selene, the brightest moon. Shadows pooled in the woods and around the sides of the house.

He paused at the door, then plunged inside. Da had let him bake the tarts in the oven and the kitchen smelled like cinnamon and sugared apples. He scurried up the cramped staircase, stepping over the seventh creaky step, and went straight to Lippa's nursery. Wind chimes hung above her window, but the sash was shut tight and they dangled unmoving in the still air. Cas thrust a hand into the maple hope chest, grabbed the first thing he found, and quietly closed it. He told himself that if Ma was sleeping, he didn't want to wake her up, but some unacknowledged part of him also thought it might be wise to stay quiet as a mouse pilfering crumbs.

He went back out to the hall. The room he shared with Teo came next, and lastly, his parents' bedroom at the far end. Cas squinted. The door looked ever so slightly ajar.

He felt a jolt of surprise. Did Da unlock it because she was doing better? He hadn't actually *said* she wasn't contagious anymore, but maybe that's what he meant about the seven days being past. Cas turned for the stairs, then paused. What if Ma was thirsty, too? What if she needed something? Had been calling for help and gotten no answer?

Da hadn't come back. What if, what if . . .

Before he could think too hard about it, Cas crept to the end of the hall. He eyed the dark crack between the door and the jamb. A stale, musty smell wafted out. He couldn't see anything beyond and didn't want to open it wider, not yet. Da would kill him.

"Ma?" he whispered.

No answer came. Just the settling of the house around him, the blood pounding in his ears.

"It's me," he said softly. "I . . ." All the unspoken words he'd saved up for the last week dried in his throat. "Lippa misses you, Ma."

The silence beyond was deep and absolute.

Cas backed away. He sucked in a shaky breath and took the stairs down two at a time, the soles of his feet tingling and Lippa's clothes balled up in one hand.

She's sleeping, that's all. In a few days, she'll be downstairs, weak but hugging us all and asking for tea, and I'll make her promise not to cross the river again, not when it's such a bad year—

Halfway across the yard, he heard the sheep bleating in their pen.

Terror gripped him. He ran flat out for the barn, bursting through the doors. Everything looked normal, though the sheep were milling about, bleating and bleating. Cas tore up the ladder so fast he skinned his knuckles. He felt dizzy with relief when he saw Lip sitting there, her white-blonde hair sticking up like milkweed fluff. He pressed a finger to his lips. Then he covered Teo's mouth with a hand. His brother gave a muffled exclamation, eyes flying open. When Cas saw he understood to keep quiet, he let Teo go.

What's happening? Teo mouthed.

Cas shook his head. He crawled to the edge of the loft and peered down. Patches of light and shadow skimmed across the floor of the barn. The sheep had gone quiet, though he could hear them bumping against the slats of the pen. Restless. There were still a few wolves along the Boundary. Maybe they smelled one.

Maybe it was all a big fat nothing. Just his imagination running wild.

But if it wasn't, he could think of only one place they could go that might be safe.

The ferry, he mouthed at Teo, jerking his chin toward the barn doors.

His brother nodded, eyes so big Cas could see the whites all around.

There wasn't a single bridge for the hundreds of leagues of the Forkings River. Some of the High Dead could cross those, or so he'd heard. But they couldn't do it by boat, not over water so deep and swift. That's why there were only ferry crossings and building any kind of bridge was punishable by death — an irony even a twelve-year-old could appreciate.

"Where's my breeches?" Lippa demanded, covering a yawn.

"Right here," Cas whispered, groping through the straw for the bundle. "But we're going to climb down now, and you'll be very quiet."

"Why?" she asked, so loudly it made him wince.

"Because he says so," Teo hissed.

Lip wailed when she saw what he'd brought her. "Don't want a dress!"

For months, she'd only wanted to wear Teo's old clothes. Ma thought it was funny.

"Well, that's all I could find," Cas whispered.

She stuck her bottom lip out — a habit that had earned the nickname.

"Don't wear it then," Cas muttered in exasperation. "I don't care."

She scowled. "But I'm all wet."

"Lip," Teo said softly, with a desperate gleam in his eye, "I'll let you have my wagon tomorrow."

"Want you to pull me."

"I'll pull you, I promise."

She gave a brisk, satisfied nod like Ma did when she got her way. Then she held her arms up and let Cas take off the dirty tunic and pull the clean dress over her head. He did it careful and smiling so she wouldn't get scared, even as the voice in his head urged him to hurry hurry hurry.

"I'll go first," he said, lifting the shuttered lantern from its hook. Cas clambered down the ladder and looked around. "Come on," he called softly.

Teo scrambled down next, followed by Lippa. Cas stood underneath and watched her make her way, short legs stretching for each rung. He was reaching for her waist when he felt Teo stiffen next to him, heard his brother's quick inhale. Cas turned, heart pounding.

A dark silhouette stood in the open doors. He twisted the wick on the lantern. Light bloomed and he saw it was Ma, her white cotton nightgown wet on the bottom from dragging through the grass. Her feet were bare and dirty. She stepped inside the barn.

"Cas?" Teo said uncertainly.

"It's okay." He looked up. The two horseshoes above the doors were still there. A charm of protection. "You're supposed to be in bed, Ma. You'll catch a chill."

She looked thin and pale, but his spirits lifted to see her. She'd heard him calling through the crack in the bedroom door and come down. Now she crouched and held out her hands. Teo hesitated, then started forward. Cas grabbed his arm.

She still hadn't said a word.

"Hold on," he said, pulse ticking up a notch.

Lippa stood at the bottom of the ladder, blinking in the light. Cas handed Teo the lantern. He started to walk toward Ma. He was halfway across the big open space between the loft and the doors when he realized two things. One, the sheep were jammed up against the far wall of the pen, milling and pushing in a panic. Two, Ma cast no shadow even though she stood full in the lantern light.

The spit dried in his mouth. At that moment, Lippa flew past.

"Mama!" she cried.

Cas caught his little sister in three strides, yanking her back as those white arms reached to enfold her. Ma's eyes glittered like blue stones. He cast about and saw a rusty old hoe in a bracket. Pried it loose and thrust the iron head at her. She shrank away.

He felt it now, the bitter cold filling the barn, like a wind from the high peaks. Gooseflesh dimpled his arms. His breath streamed out in white shreds. Lip let out a whimper of fear. He pushed her behind him and jabbed out with the hoe again. Ma moved fast this time, a hungry look on her hollowed-out face. He backed away. Tried to whistle the tune Gui had taught him.

His mouth was too parched to make more than a breathy wheeze.

Then his gaze caught on a jar of nails. The same ones he'd used to mount the horseshoes and forgotten to put in the toolshed afterward.

Cas grabbed the jar and upended it. Iron nails rolled helter-skelter across the floor. Ma stopped moving as if she'd stepped into a peat bog. She stared at him, gaze burning. He gripped the hoe, which was the only thing keeping his hands from quaking like an aspen. The risen's touch could stop your heart.

Her lips moved. She was trying to speak.

A strange thing happened then. The knee-buckling fear lessened. Mainly, he felt grief and pity. Because it wasn't some infernal thing, it was *her*. She'd died but she wasn't doing what you were supposed to do, which was to cross the stormless sea and face what waited on the other side.

"You'd never hurt Lip, I know you wouldn't." He glanced at Teo, who clung to his little sister, their faces pinched. "So why are you here, Ma?"

A tear ran from her eye. It turned to frost on her cheek. She opened her mouth and sounds spilled out, but it wasn't words. Only meaningless gibberish.

"I'll help you if I can," he stammered. "But I don't understand—"

Cas suddenly felt sick. Sicker than he'd ever been in his whole life. His neck flushed with roaring heat. Sweat broke across his brow. An instant later, a convulsive shiver took him. The muscles in his legs twitched and bucked. The coarse russet camicia was agony against his tender skin. He braced himself on the hoe with his right hand and traced the sign of Kaethe with his left. Three triangles, each tilted to form a nine-pointed star like the one inked on Gui's hand.

It seemed to shimmer in the air for a moment. He felt the power in it.

"Go," he stammered, holding Ma's blistering gaze. "We'll be all right, I promise. I'll look after Teo and Lip."

Waves of emotion slammed into him, so powerful he saw flashing colors. Red anger. Gray despair. Festering yellow regret. They tried to drag him down into the depths.

But he remembered Kaethe's sign. Clung to it like a piece of driftwood on a storm-tossed ocean.

He remembered his promise, too.

I'll help you, Ma. Help you . . .

He was an empty vessel taking in all her fear and fury. Cas thought it would break him, break his mind, but somehow it didn't. He let it all wash over him, like a stone in the riverbed. The scent of primroses filled his nose. The lantern flared, then guttered. Shadows writhed and leapt, and when he looked up, Ma was gone.

For a long moment, no one moved or spoke.

"I want Da," Teo said at last, his voice small and shaky.

Cas could see her muddy footprints on the boards. Proof it was real. Part of him felt numb, unwilling to face what had happened, what it meant. But his brother and sister needed him, so he gathered the two of them close and made himself think.

Maybe Ma was gone, and maybe she wasn't.

"We're leaving," he said. "We stick with the plan and go to the ferry—"

A quiet scuff made him jerk around. A tall figure stood in the gloom beyond the barn doors. Not Ma.

A stranger.

He wore soft knee-high boots and a fine blue cloak over a leather jerkin. It wasn't one of the Ducissa's soldiers. Cas often saw them on the main road, marching up to the mountain passes. They wore conical helmets and red surcoats with a golden phoenix.

A merchant, then. One from the east, from the darklands, because his skin was chalk white as if he'd never seen the sun—

The man raised a hand as if in greeting. The hoe was wrenched from Cas's fingers. It flew through the air and clattered against the far wall. The man smiled and his lips were bloodless too, his teeth white and gleaming.

A sudden warmth between his legs told Cas he'd pissed himself for the first time since he was Lip's age, but he was too terrified to care.

A mortifex.

One of the High Dead.

A flick of its finger and his feet left the ground. Cas flew clear across the barn. He landed on one hip and skidded into the wooden slats of the sheep pen. Something banged his head so hard he saw stars. Then a new pain, sharp enough to slice through the dizziness. Cas looked down, still half-stunned. Blood welled from a deep cut on his palm. He plucked out a large shard of glass.

The broken vial of Lady's Tears.

His gaze snapped back to the mortifex. Its soft boots made hardly a sound as it crossed the barn, stepping over the nails. Teo's mouth gaped. One skinny arm still held the lantern high. He was shaking so bad, the light swung crazily. Shadows scurried across the thing's face. Cas's gut roiled as it loomed over Teo, but it passed his brother by without a glance.

"Come, child," it rasped at Lippa.

Her eyes were bright with terror, like a mouse under the spell of a snake. Bare feet whispered against the boards as she walked towards it.

"No, Lip!" he cried hoarsely.

It stooped and lifted her into its arms. Bent its head to her face.

The sight of his little sister in its clutches drove Cas to his feet. He sketched a wobbly nine-pointed star in the air with his bleeding hand. Begged Kaethe to save them.

The mortifex turned. It was no longer so pale. An obscene blush colored its blade-sharp cheeks.

"Your lady exercises no power over me," it said, and returned to its feeding.

Bile rose in his throat. He spun around, searching for the iron hoe. Panic bubbled up when he couldn't see it. Then a loud crash made him jump. Teo had dropped the lantern. The light dimmed. An instant later, the oil caught some bits of straw and hungry flames rose up.

The sheep were bleating frantically. Cas stood next to the gate to the pen. Without thought, he unlatched it, hoping the stampede would distract the mortifex. They rushed out the gate, giving it a wide berth. But not even the burning barn seemed to have any effect on the monster.

His eyes darted around, frantic. Where was the hoe?

There!

He limped across the barn. Gripped the wooden handle and swung it as hard as he could.

The iron struck its face with a sickening crunch. The mortifex hissed and dropped Lip. Cas threw the hoe down. Leapt through billows of black smoke and scooped her up.

"Run!" he screamed at his brother. "For feck's sake *move*!"

Flames were racing up the ladder now. Teo blinked. For some reason, the bad word broke his trance. They sprinted outside. Heavy clouds swirled above. Cas smashed a shin into Teo's wagon, which sat carelessly in the middle of the yard, and then they were hurtling down the lane. When he looked back, the mortifex followed behind, a flitting shadow beneath the trees.

Lippa lay limp in his arms. He couldn't tell if she lived, but Cas had room for only one thought in his head.

Get them all across the Forkings.

He took a shortcut through the pine woods, angling for the river. If the ferry was on the far bank, they were done. He crested a low hill, heart in his throat, and saw the boat's square stern poking out of the mist, bobbing in a backwater. When he glanced over his shoulder again, the mortifex had halved the distance.

It was impossibly fast, racing from shadow to shadow. With a thrill of fresh terror, he knew it would catch them before they left the trees.

"Go on ahead!" he panted at Teo. "Untie the boat! I'll catch up!"

His brother took off running flat out, arms and legs pumping. Cas's shoulder blades itched as he ran behind. He kept his eyes on Teo, praying his brother would get away, but after a minute he couldn't help looking back again.

The mortifex had vanished.

Then, a shout. Relief flooded him as his father and Gui galloped up on the black charger. Da slid from the saddle.

"What happened to Filippa?" he asked, face tight with concern. "Is she sick?"

"There's a mortifex," Cas gasped. "It tried to take her—"

"Mortifex?" Gui dismounted. "Slow down, lad."

Cas looked around wildly. "It's *here*. We all have to get to the ferry!"

"I'm sure you saw something, lad, but are you certain it was High Dead?" Gui asked.

There was a skeptical edge to his voice.

"It threw me across the barn," Cas said, holding up his bloody hand.

Da thumbed Lippa's eyes open. He pressed his cheek to her little chest. Teo stood there shivering, eyes blank and arms wrapped around himself. Gui laid a hand on his shoulder.

Cas fought a wave of nausea. *It's all my fault. I broke the vial. I—*

"Kaethe has not embraced her," Da said at last, his voice raw.

Cas felt tears welling and swallowed a hard lump in his throat. "It did something to her, Da."

Gui looked at Teo, who nodded. The expression on Gui's face made Cas even more scared. Because the Quietus was afraid now, too, and he had never known Gui to fear anything.

"Take the ferry out to the place where the deep water starts," Da said. "Hold it there while we fetch your mother."

A new vise of grief tightened across Cas's chest. "Da, she's gone." His voice cracked. "I . . . I *saw* her—"

Da shook his head. There was a funny look in his eye. "You're wrong," he said flatly. "You must be. The fever had broken. She was resting."

Gui looked between them with a frown. "What happened, lad?"

Cas looked around. No sign of the fex. He licked dry lips. "She came to the barn first, before the mortifex. She cast no shadow. The sheep . . . I spilled some iron nails and they held her fast. Then . . ." He looked away, unable to meet Da's eyes. "I made the sign of Kaethe and she went away."

Gui eyed him as if he knew there was more to the story but said nothing as he wrapped Cas's hand in a square of linen.

"She was confused," Da said stubbornly. "Wandering. The fever does that. I want the three of you to go across to Swanton. Wait for me there."

"She wasn't *wandering*," Cas protested. "She was—"

"Enough!" Da snapped. "There's a blue house with yellow flowers in the yard four streets up from the ferry. They'll help you."

"Da, please," Cas begged. "Come with us. You can't go back—"

"Just do as I say." His father took off at a jog for the farmhouse.

"Gui," Cas said in a low voice. "You have to believe me. Don't let him go back there!"

"I do, lad." His face softened. "And I'm sorry. But first let's get you—"

A wind rose, whipping the pine boughs. The horse gave a nervous whinny.

"Run to the ferry!" Gui gave Cas a shove. "Now!"

Cas staggered off again, cradling Lippa in his arms. Teo ran next to him. The river rushed along its narrow bed a short distance away, a silver serpent winding between rocky banks. Mist rose from the water, dense and damp.

"Take hold of my cami," Cas hissed and Teo knotted his fingers in the rough-spun cloth.

They ran blindly, aiming for the bank. A shadow loomed ahead and his heart leapt into his throat, but it was the stone landing. The ferry had a flat bottom with ramps at either end for loading horses and cargo. It was operated by pulling on two chains suspended across the river. When the ferry was docked, the chains would sink to the riverbed so as not to interfere with other boats.

Cas carefully lay Lippa down on the bottom of the ferry. She looked so pale he could see the fine blue veins beneath her eyes. "Hang on, Lip," he whispered, smoothing her hair back. He started to untie the mooring rope. It should have been simple, but in his haste, he pulled the wrong line and cinched it tighter.

"Cas," Teo squeaked.

His gaze sliced to the trees. Through shreds of mist, he saw Gui standing with his back to them, staff planted in the earth. He had a funny bald spot shaped like a heart. Cas had never noticed it before. The mortifex walked toward him, graceful and unhurried, its cloak billowing out. A sword hung at its hip, white like bone. The fex drew it from the scabbard in one fluid motion. Gui's staff met its assault with a crackle like sheet lightning.

Cas tore his gaze away. He picked at the knot in the mooring rope, heedless of the blood soaking his bandage. When he looked again, the fex flung Gui away like one of Lippa's straw people. He bounced off a tree and lay still.

"Hurry!" Teo cried.

A nail tore. Cas hardly felt it. From the corner of his eye, he could see the mortifex striding in their direction. With a curse, he tried using his teeth. The feckin' knot finally gave. The rope slithered through the cleats and the ferry swung free. Cas and Teo each took a side and started hauling it hand-over-hand along the chains through the shallows. Ten paces out, the current caught them, bobbing the boat up and down. Cas pulled harder, muscles straining taut, head twisted around so he could watch the fex.

It stopped at the edge of the riverbank. An angry red weal marked its cheek where the iron had struck it. Even from a distance, Cas could see the twin flames of its eyes fixed on him as the boat glided away.

Chapter 3

"Get in there, boy."

The reeve gave him a hard push. Castelio stumbled into the dim cell. The door slammed shut, the heavy key clanking in the lock. He blew out a breath and looked around. Half a dozen men hunched in the filthy straw. He knew them all by sight, if not by name.

Shouldn't have stolen those apples.

But they'd been so hungry. And it was only windfalls.

Shouldn't have gotten caught, he amended.

Cas decided not to sit. The others were all scratching away and he'd just rid himself of the last round of lice. A few of the younger men looked him over speculatively, but at fifteen he'd hit his growth. They dropped their gazes at the challenge in his eyes.

He wondered what they'd do to him for stealing from the margrave's orchard. A whipping for certain. Maybe the stocks. If it was a fine, he'd never get out. At least only murderers merited the gallows anymore. The village had enough problems with the dead as it was.

He whistled a tuneless ditty as he thought it over. He'd never been in trouble before. With luck they'd settle for a whipping before the whole village. But he couldn't afford to stay locked up for long. Not with Da's drinking.

"Yer that necromancer, aintcha?"

Cas realized a toothless old geezer was staring at him. The name came to him: Herf Aubrey.

He stiffened. "What's it to you?"

"Nothing, son." The geezer winked with one clouded eye.

His fellow prisoners exchanged nervous glances.

"I'm no necromancer," Cas muttered. "They call the dead, don't they? I do the opposite."

As soon as he said it, he realized his mistake.

A board creaked outside the door. The red-veined face of the reeve appeared in the grill.

"What's this about necromancy?" he demanded.

There was a long silence.

"Speak, you villains," the reeve growled. "Or I'll have the lot of you flogged."

"It's that young fellow," the geezer said at last, with a note of reluctance. "The one been banishing spirits. He did for my Maizy when she came back. Kept his hood up, but I recognize the scar on his hand."

"You've got it wrong," Cas said hastily.

The door swung open. "Turn out your pockets," the reeve ordered.

"I already did—"

"Search him, boys."

Cas narrowed his eyes and balled his fists. No one moved.

"First one finds something gets to go home."

That did the trick. All but the geezer surged to their feet. Knowing he was beaten, Cas raised his hands and let them paw through his clothes. A bearded man who reeked of sour ale tore the small cloth pouch from his belt and opened it.

"Found some nails," he declared, handing it over to the reeve. "Looks like iron."

"Where'd you get these, boy?" the reeve demanded, spilling the nails into his palm. "You steal 'em?"

Cold iron was worth more than silver in Swanton these days.

"No! They're for my own protection."

The reeve eyed him in a considering way. "Maybe you summon the dead so you can take coin to banish 'em again."

Cas gave a hollow laugh. He knew he shouldn't dig himself deeper, but he hadn't eaten a thing in two days besides half a wormy apple and wasn't thinking straight.

"Coin?" he echoed in amazement. "Who's got coin round here? I'm lucky to get a loaf of week-old bread for . . ." He trailed off at the triumphant look on the reeve's face. "It's only nails," he finished lamely.

The reeve spat on the ground. "That sounded like a confession to me."

The men nodded eagerly — the same people, Cas thought with bitterness, who begged for his help when their dearly departed shuffled down from the lichyard and came rapping on the window.

"How was that a confession?" he wondered. "And I haven't done anything wrong. Besides the apples, I mean."

"We'll see." The reeve's eyes glinted. "There's a bounty on necromancers. If the charge is true, I'll summon a judge from Aquitan to pass sentence on you, boy." His lips curled in an ugly smile. "And they don't go easy on your kind."

Cas's heart sank. He felt a surge of hatred for this miserable village, for the margrave and his sheriff — but most of all for himself. What would Teo and Lip do now?

Stupid! Da had warned him to be careful. To keep his mouth shut. He might have gotten off with a whipping. Now . . .

"You're well and truly fecked," someone remarked.

The door slammed shut. The one who'd found the nails banged on it. "Milord! You said I could go home!"

A chuckle drifted through the grille. "Keep the necromancer out of trouble and I might consider it."

The boards creaked under his weight as the reeve walked away.

All but Herf stared at him with open hostility. Cas wasn't really afraid of them. They looked as thin and wretched as he did. The margrave's hand was heavy in these parts. Most likely they'd fallen behind in the rent.

But mob justice wasn't unheard of, either. Better they feared him, or he might not live long enough to face the judge.

Cas straightened his jerkin. "Touch me again," he said coldly, "and you'll see what happens."

A vague remark, but as he hoped, they took it as a threat to work the dark arts. The men sketched Kaethe's nine-pointed star and scooted back, giving him a wide berth.

"Yonder scum," one muttered.

Yonder, Cas had learned, meant anyone not from Swanton.

He took the far corner, sinking down to the filthy straw. Three years he'd lived in the village, but he'd never be one of them. His accent was, apparently, pure Boundary. Before coming there, Cas didn't know he even *had* an accent.

Outsiders. That's what him and Teo would always be. Even little Lippa. And Da . . . Well, he'd given up, hadn't he? Cas wanted to blame him but couldn't quite do it. Da was a gentle man. He wasn't made to survive in a place like this.

Cas did his best to provide for them all, but he'd soon discovered there was no honest work to be had if you were a yonder. He never spoke to any of the villagers except when they furtively sought his services. With his temper and loose tongue, it was probably all that had saved him from the noose.

Of course he remembered Maizy. He remembered them all. She was Herf's daughter. A pretty lass who always had a smile for Lippa. Sometimes she'd leave a little pile of potatoes or whatever she could spare on their doorstep. Maizy had drowned herself in the river when she got with child out of wedlock. It had been the margrave's bastard. She'd told Cas so herself before he helped her cross the Veil.

I'm better with the dead than the living, he thought darkly. *And, all things considered, I prefer their company.*

TWO DAYS PASSED. Only Herf would speak to him. His rheumy eyes held pity when he crawled over and offered Cas his bowl of pottage.

"I'm sorry, son." There was shame in his voice. "I spoke out of turn."

Cas eyed the bowl. Not even the acid dread in his throat could quench the endless, gnawing hunger. But Herf looked like a stiff breeze might knock him over. He shook his head. "It's all right. It was my own fault."

"I'll tell 'em I was mistaken," Herf whispered.

He nodded and chewed a fingernail instead.

Teo appeared late that night, calling his name softly through the grille. His brother's face was so thin, it made Cas's chest hurt.

"What are people saying?" Cas asked. "The reeve won't tell me anything."

Teo looked bleak. "He's found a dozen witnesses willing to speak against you. All you ever did was help them! It's not fair!"

Cas glanced over his shoulder at the huddled forms of the other prisoners. They watched him warily.

"Keep your voice down," he whispered. "Do they say I summoned the spirits? Or just sent them away?"

"Both."

Cas's heart sank. "Why would I do that? It makes no sense."

But he thought of what the reeve had said. *Maybe you summon the dead so you can take coin to banish 'em again.*

His brother scowled. "Doesn't matter, does it? They want someone to blame and they've always hated us." He paused, voice hitching as he fought back tears. "What'll happen to you, Cas?"

They twined their fingers together through the bars. He forced a smile. "Don't worry, I'll talk my way out of it."

Teo wasn't stupid. He knew how the world worked. "And if you don't?"

Cas sighed. "How's Lippa?"

"Worried sick. Da, too." His brother bit his lip. "Maybe I can steal the key from the reeve's house while he's sleeping. Get you out. We can all run away—"

"No! If he catches you, and he *will*, he'll put you in the stocks or worse. And Lip needs you, Teo." He swallowed. "If they do take me away, you'll have to watch out for them as best you can."

Now the tears spilled over. "But—"

A clout sent his little brother staggering. The reeve stuck his red face in the grille. "No visitors," he snapped, banging his cudgel against the bars so Cas had to snatch his fingers back before they were broken.

After that, the reeve set a watch outside the jail.

Cas returned to his corner and pulled his knees to his chest. He tried to remember their lives on the farm before everything changed. The peaceful evenings when they'd gather in the yard, his parents sorting through the day's gathering and brewing their healing elixirs while Cas finished his chores and Lip and Teo played *huckle-buckle-beanstalk* in the tall, rippling switchgrass. The clean smell of the mountain air, so different from smoky, dirty Swanton, where people dumped nightsoil out the windows.

Ma had tried to teach him woodward lore, but he'd never loved it as she did. What he liked best was hiking alone through the vales. Swimming in the secret lakes and climbing the tallest trees so he could look out over the Boundary and see it grow brighter in one direction and darker in the other, like straddling the seam of the world.

"You're a wanderer, Cas," she'd told him with a smile. "When you're older, you should go visit my cousins in the west. Have an adventure. I've been meaning to write to them. You can carry a letter for me."

"I want to stay here," he'd said with a frown.

"You'll come back. And then you'll be ready to learn." Ma

ruffled his hair. "But you lack the discipline now. Don't worry, it can wait."

Of course, it didn't. She was dead within the year.

Thinking of Ma still twisted a blade in his heart. So he remembered the first time he held Lip in his arms, wrinkled and squalling, and the feel of her tiny fingers gripping his thumb, how strong they were for such a tiny thing. The time Teo went missing for hours, and they were all at wit's end until they found him curled up sleeping with the new lambs like he was one of them.

Cas clutched these memories tight, yet they weren't enough to keep the despair at bay. He wasn't sure what they did with necromancers, but it was the vilest crime in the duchy. Worse than murder.

Dark thoughts crowded his head as he drifted into an uneasy slumber. If they did hang him, Da couldn't pay for a proper burial with the nuns. Cas's greatest fear wasn't even the noose.

It was that he'd come back.

He had nightmares about it, that night and the next. Sometimes Teo swung a hoe against him. Sometimes he chased a screaming Lippa through a house with endless halls and doors. The dreams left him drenched in icy sweat, shaking like he had the fever.

Then, on the morning of the fourth day, he saw a cloaked rider gallop past wearing the Redvayne colors, red and gold.

The judge from Aquitan.

By then, he'd settled into a state of grim resignation. It would be his word against a dozen witnesses, maybe more now. He planned to tell the truth — that he'd banished spirits who already haunted the village — but with the current mood, he doubted the judge would listen.

If the Ducissa's justice was anything like the margrave's, the only question was whether they'd hang him here or in the capital. He hoped it was Aquitan so his family wouldn't have to watch.

Cas had lost the war with the lice by the time he was taken, blinking and scratching, to the reeve's house. It was the biggest one in the village, though that wasn't saying much.

"Keep your mouth shut 'til you're spoken to," the reeve said sternly, prodding him through the door. "And mind your manners. Sir isn't to be trifled with."

A large man stood at the window, looking out, hands clasped behind him. He had a bald spot on the back of his head that Cas half-recognized, but his hair was snow white . . . Then he turned around and Cas saw it *was* Gui Harcourt. A welter of emotions took him, relief and joy foremost among them. He'd assumed Gui was dead. Cas swiped his eyes with one grimy hand. Surely, Gui would help him.

But the Quietus gave no acknowledgment that they knew each other.

"This the one?" he asked gruffly.

"Aye, Sir Harcourt." The reeve knuckled his forehead and bowed.

"Doesn't look like much." Gui frowned. "Young to be a necromancer, don't you think?"

"Well, I can't say what age has to do with it. I leave that for you to decide. But he's been trafficking with the risen. That much is certain. I can call those who'd offer testimony—"

"That won't be necessary," Gui interrupted. "We have tests to determine such things. I'll take custody of him."

"Of course, of course." The reeve licked his lips. "And the bounty, milord?"

"I'm not a lord." Gui tossed him a purse. The reeve caught it and quickly suppressed a smile at the clinking within.

"Thank you, mi— . . . er, Sir Harcourt."

Gui nodded brusquely. "Guard your tongue about this. I won't have rumors spreading."

"As you say." The reeve bowed again, deeper this time.

"Let's go," Gui said to Cas, sweeping past without a second glance.

Cas trailed him out to the yard, where Gui's black charger

waited. Was it a lucky chance? Or did Gui mean to punish him? The expression on his face was impossible to read.

"Where's your house?" Gui asked from the corner of his mouth as he untied the horse and led it away.

"That way, sir." Cas pointed.

He glanced back as they started down the lane. The reeve was watching from the window. Once they rounded a bend and were out of sight, Gui turned to him. His bluff face softened. "I regret giving him a single copper pyre, but it greases the wheels of justice. The sooner you're gone, the better."

For days, Cas had been certain of his own death. He knew he should be grateful. Should fall to his knees and thank Kaethe for this miracle. But his relief at seeing a familiar face was giving way to something else. Something ugly that had been simmering for the last three years.

"Where have you been, Gui?" he asked at last.

Alive all this time and he'd never come to check on them. Not once.

"Up to my ears in the dead," Gui replied, giving him an appraising look. "Same as you, I reckon." He shook his head. "Why'd you do it, lad? Don't you know better?"

"Know better," Cas repeated slowly. "That's a funny way of putting it. Well, I guess I did it so we'd have food on the table."

Gui frowned. "What about your Da?"

"The villagers burned the ferry, if you hadn't noticed," he said tightly. "After the fex came. There's no way across the Forkings now, not for leagues. How's he supposed to be a woodward when he can't get the plants he needs? Most grow only in the Boundary." He gave a bitter laugh. "We didn't know that until we couldn't go back."

Gui stared into space for a long moment. "I'm sorry," he said at last, and the deep remorse in his voice softened Cas a bit. "I spent weeks tracking the mortifex back to the border. It went over the mountains. Heading east into the dark, which was no surprise. They can't abide sunlight. Then I was summoned back to Aquitan." He rubbed his bald spot. "I kept meaning to come . . . Should have done it. How's Filippa?"

"You'll see when we get there," Cas said. He stumbled on a rock and would have fallen if Gui hadn't gripped his arm.

"You're naught but bones," Gui exclaimed. "Didn't the reeve feed you in there?"

"Pottage," Cas said, swaying on his feet. "It had worms but it was filling."

Gui muttered an oath. "You ride the rest of the way."

He protested that he could walk, but Gui wouldn't hear it. They passed clusters of thatched cottages with skinny pigs rooting in the dirt and gaggles of children who were scarcely cleaner. Most had knots of willow catkins above the door, the only charm they could afford. In Cas's experience, these knots were useless against the dead, but they seemed to make people feel better.

On the way, he recounted what had happened after they'd crossed the Forkings. Cas carried Lippa up the hill to the blue house with yellow flowers. A woman with frightened eyes opened the door a crack. At first she thought Lip had the fever and wouldn't let them in, but Cas stammered an explanation and she finally agreed to take his brother and sister. He begged some of the men to go back for Da with him, but no one would.

Cas had stood on the landing for a long while, gathering his courage. When the clouds broke and the sun came out, he took the ferry over himself.

There'd been no sign of Gui or the mortifex. The barn had burned to the ground, but the rain kept the fire from spreading. He found Da upstairs in the house, sitting with Ma. She lay on top of the covers, her feet caked with dried mud and bits of grass. She looked like she was sleeping.

He'd tried not to remember the way she'd crouched down and held her white arms out. The hungry look on her face.

They buried her by a young willow at the edge of the river. Da put an iron coin in her mouth and mumbled some choked words. When it was done, they rounded up the animals and any valuables they could carry back across on the ferry. After word got round what had happened, the villagers burned it. Cas couldn't blame them.

The tired-looking woman at the blue house laid out straw pallets for them in a spare room. Her name was Nomi. Ma had healed her oldest boy a few years before, though she hadn't been so lucky this year. Her sister was dead, and two of her sister's children. They'd all been buried with silver bells in hallowed ground up at the convent of Kaethe.

None came back.

The rest was quickly told. Nomi let them stay for a spell, but she had her own family to feed. So Da sold off the animals, one by one, and leased a patch of land from the margrave. Lippa cried about it, she loved those sheep, but Da said they couldn't go home again, not even if the ferry had been running. The Boundary was too dangerous now.

"Aye," Gui interjected at this point. "He's right about that. No one lives there anymore. It's been bad these last years. Worse even than you know." He cast him a sharp look. "When a messenger came and said the reeve caught a necromancer in Swanton, I had a funny feeling it might be you."

"I'm not a necromancer!"

"Easy, I know that. But I also know what you did with your Ma."

Cas had glossed over that part of the story. He drew a steadying breath. "I'll never do it again, I swear. Just let me go and—"

"Let you go?" Gui gave a dry chuckle. "I don't think so, lad."

He swallowed hard. "So you're taking me to Aquitan?"

"Aye."

Cas remembered his ominous words. *We have tests to determine such things.*

"Can't you . . . I don't know, say I ran off? Teo and Lip need me—"

"And the Ducissa needs you more," Gui said firmly. "I mean to make you a Quietus, lad. A proper one."

He absorbed this in silence for a minute. "Does it pay? Real coin?"

The nuns of Kaethe dispensed iron coins for the dead, but he hadn't seen silver in years.

Gui laughed. "Aye. More than you'd earn in a year in Swanton."

The solution to all his problems. It sounded too good to be true. "Do you really think I can . . . be like you?" he asked, fresh doubts crowding his mind.

Besides Da, Gui Harcourt was the man he'd most looked up to all his life. Brave and steadfast. He remembered how Gui had stood calmly, feet planted, as the mortifex came on with its bone-white blade.

After Cas had pissed himself at first sight.

That was something he didn't plan to share.

Gui clapped a hand on his shoulder. "You already are," he said. "We'll talk more about it later. Is this the place?"

He nodded at the smoke drifting from a ramshackle chimney up ahead. Cas nodded, still struggling to accept this new turn of fortune.

"Let's talk to your Da," Gui said.

Chapter 4

The house was one room with a dirt floor and leaky thatched roof that Cas had been meaning to mend. He did his best to keep it clean, but warmth rose to his cheeks as they stepped through the door. He'd gotten used to living as they did, but he wondered what Gui thought, coming from the Ducissa's court.

Most of their old belongings had been traded away in that first year. What remained was the bare necessities: sleeping pallets, a table and four rickety chairs, some cracked pottery, and an iron cauldron for soup — by far their most valuable possession. Lippa was tending it now, golden hair hanging in a long braid over one shoulder. Teo must have snared a rabbit for Cas smelled it in the pot, a meaty aroma that made his stomach twist. He couldn't eat animals anymore. Another thing that made him a yonder.

But every beast had a soul. Cas knew it because he'd seen them. Silvery wisps that drifted away when the body died. For some reason, animals didn't fight the end like people did. They crossed without a fuss.

He didn't begrudge fresh meat to his siblings, though. They'd have starved long before without Teo's poaching. He didn't try it often — poachers were punished even harder than apple thieves — but Teo was a shadow's shadow when he wanted to be. Cas had long ago given up trying to forbid him. And it made Teo feel like he contributed to the household. That was an important thing.

"Filippa!" Gui boomed, sweeping her up into his big arms. He leaned back to study her face, his own beaming in a broad smile. "Look at you, a right beauty now."

A knot loosened in Cas's gut as she laughed in delight, slender arms hugging him tight.

Lippa was seven, almost eight, though you wouldn't know it. She was a tiny thing, hardly bigger than she'd been when they arrived. It had taken her two days to wake from the trance, and when she did, Cas had wept and thanked Kaethe for bringing her back. He'd thought it was over. That by some miracle she'd survived unscathed.

Lip was the same girl inside, but her body didn't want to grow. Whatever the mortifex had done to her — the *feeding* — it took something away. Cas kept hoping it was temporary, that she'd catch up, but she never did.

She was smart as a whip, though, and had a sweet, wistful kindness in her that, in Cas's opinion, more than made up for her small stature. But if the grownups in Swanton were clannish, the children were worse. Cas had never told the full story, but somehow they knew. It was why Lippa never went into the village anymore.

Gui set her on her feet as Teo banged in the door. Unlike his sister, at eleven he was already filling out the frame of the man he'd become. His hair had darkened to a sandy brown; it curled in a mop around his ears. "I saw your horse!" he cried. "I hoped it was you!"

Another difference between them, Cas thought ruefully. Teo never held a grudge for long.

An instant later, Teo barreled into him. He pressed his cheek to Cas's chest, shoulders shaking, and Cas knew that Teo had given him up for dead. Gui cleared his throat. "What's in the pot, Filippa?"

The Quietus turned his back, listening to Lip's chatter about the stew. After a minute, Cas gently disentangled himself.

"Watch out," he whispered. "I got lice again."

Teo gave a choked laugh and wiped his nose with a sleeve. Cas wondered how on earth he was going to leave them behind.

Then Da appeared, hickory stick in hand, and Teo stepped away, pulling himself together. Da looked sober, Cas was relieved to see. And he'd been gathering. The battered satchel hung across his back, bulging with roots and herbs.

"Harcourt?" Da squinted in the smoky gloom. "Is that really you?" His gaze shifted to Cas, gaunt face sagging with relief. "Blessed Bel, you got him out."

"Castelio is safe in my custody now," Gui said. "And I was just telling your son I'm sorry I didn't come sooner."

Da stood up a little straighter. "We're not your responsibility."

Gui held his gaze. "Never said you were. I can see you've done the best you could. Life dealt you a hard hand, Willem. Worse than any of you deserved." He sighed. "I can't make right what happened. But I might be able to help if you'll hear me out."

Da seemed to relax. "Make yourself at home, old friend. I'm just glad to see you again."

Gui smiled and sank onto a stool, which creaked alarmingly under his weight. Da unslung the satchel and gave Lip some wild thyme for the rabbit stew. Cas was used to doing for himself on these occasions, and his sister steered him to some withered turnips that he roasted in the coals. Mugs of water from the spring were passed around, Teo and Lip sharing since they only owned three. Once everyone had eaten, Gui put his proposal to Da.

"There's a reward for every new Quietus I bring the Ducissa," Gui said. "A purse of gold."

Teo's jaw dropped open. He shared a stunned look with Lippa.

"And I'll send more," Cas put in. "I won't need much to live on."

"I told the reeve to keep quiet," Gui said wryly, "but I imagine the whole village already knows what Castelio is accused of. You'll find it hard to stay here. Better you all move on, Will."

Da nodded slowly. "Starting again . . ." His eyes grew vacant. Cas noticed that there was more silver than brown in his hair now. Da had always been thin, insisting on the smallest portions, but he looked frail, like an old man. It came as an unpleasant jolt. Cas had half expected him to stay the same forever.

"I suppose we have no choice," Da said at last. He rubbed his stubbled jaw. "Your Ma has a cousin in Prydwen. The sun might be good for . . ." He glanced at Lippa and trailed off, clearing his throat. "For all of us."

"Prydwen?" Cas and Teo exclaimed at the same time.

He'd assumed they would all go to Aquitan together. That he could see them whenever he wanted.

"But that's . . . *far*, isn't it?" Cas objected.

His knowledge of the world was limited to the Boundary, Swanton, and its immediate vicinity, but he had an idea that Prydwen was somewhere in the distant west.

"The capital of Cavet," Gui agreed. "A long journey. But I could arrange it." He winked at Lip. "Have you ever traveled in a fancy coach?"

Her delicate, elfin features lit up. Cas was less thrilled. It was all happening much too fast. The Quietus part was one thing. He thought he could do it. Like Gui said, he'd already *been* doing it. But to lose the only family he had left? He'd cared for them for so long . . . Who would make them wash every day, like Ma had? It was a sore point with Teo, who hated cold water, but Cas had dutifully kept up the routine from when they lived on the farm, even on the bitterest days. Another yonder custom the villagers frowned upon.

No one, not even the margrave himself, bathed more than twice a year.

"Why not Aquitan?" he asked, looking at Da. "I'll be there—"

"You won't," Gui said gently. "Not for long. A Quietus roams all over, lad. Wherever he or she is needed."

"Girls can be a Quietus, too?" Lippa asked with a note of skepticism.

Gui nodded gravely. "Some of the best are women. But there's not many of us. Not enough." A quick look at Cas. "That's why your brother is special."

"Special how?' she persisted.

Gui opened his mouth to reply, but Cas wasn't ready to take a side road — not until he settled the matter at hand.

"Could I go all the way to Prydwen?" he interrupted. "To see them?"

"You'll have leave," Gui said with a nod. "And your own horse. Where you go with it is your business."

He shut his mouth, slightly mollified. Teo was still frowning, but Lippa was already pestering Gui about Prydwen and what it was like there.

"It's so far, Da," he said.

His father was watching Lippa.

"Do you really think the sun might help her grow?" Cas whispered.

"I don't know." Da shook his head wearily. "Maybe it . . . left something inside her. Some dark magic. If so, Bel will burn it away."

The sadness in his eyes withered the last of Cas's objections. And that, it seemed, was that. Gui said he and Cas had to leave right away — before the reeve could tell the margrave, who might insist, as was his right, that Cas take his whipping for the apples before departing.

"There's an inn half a day north that has coaches for hire," Gui said. "I'll send one back for you. Write a letter when you get settled. Send it to me at the Ducissa's court, I'll see it delivered."

He handed Da a purse twice the size of the one he'd given the margrave. Da opened it and blinked in shock.

"All this for my boy?" He gave a nervous laugh. "I'm not selling him into indenture, am I?"

"A bounty, nothing more," Gui promised.

"A single Quietus is worth so much?" Da asked in wonder, spilling heavy gold coronets across the table. They gleamed in the light of the embers, each bearing Bel's chariot on one side and the Ducissa Orlaith's regal profile on the other.

Teo's eyes went huge. None of them had seen so much gold coin in their lives. Not even close.

"The true worth of a Quietus is ten times that," Gui said softly.

Da looked at Cas like he'd never seen him before.

Cas wasn't sure he liked it.

HE HAD LITTLE TO PACK. It didn't even fill a small meal sack.

A feeling of unreality washed over him as he bent down to hug Lippa.

"Buy a new dress with that money," he whispered.

"I'd rather have parchment," she said with a happy laugh. "And an inkwell!"

The mistress at the schoolhouse had taken pity and let Lip come to her house for lessons. She was one of the kinder souls in Swanton. That's how Cas knew Lip was smart. Ma had taught them all some letters, but he'd been an indifferent student then, and hadn't gone back to the village school after getting beaten bloody by a gang of boys on his second day. He could make out most common words, a bit laboriously, but Lip knew how to *spell* them — without looking. Even ones she hadn't been taught. It was a game they played sometimes.

"Quietus," he said proudly. "Show Gui."

She nodded and drew a breath. "Q. Then U. It always has a U

after. That's the rule. I. E. T. That spells quiet." She bit her lip. "U . . . S . . . Am I right?"

Gui grinned. "As rain. You'll go far, Filippa."

She blushed.

Cas hugged Teo next, who looked mutinous but dry-eyed, and then Da. His father no longer regarded him like he was a stranger, but his gaze held a new distance.

"Mind Gui," he said gruffly. "Don't do anything foolish."

The unspoken words *Like stealing* hung between them. Da had refrained from a tongue-lashing, but Cas knew his thoughts on the matter. It wasn't something decent folk did. Not even to survive.

But then, Da had been too sotted to hear Lip moaning from an empty belly.

"I'll see you all soon," he promised with a smile.

Cas didn't look back. If he had, he might have wept.

Chapter 5

"Tell me about the first time," Gui said, as they rode up the northern road.

Cas had almost drifted off in the saddle, leaning against his broad back. He'd hardly slept in days, between the nightmares and fretting about what awaited him when the judge from Aquitan came.

"Ma, you mean?" he asked.

A bubble of dread rose in his chest. He didn't like revisiting that night. It, too, haunted his dreams.

"No," Gui replied, seeming to sense his discomfort. "The next one. In the village."

Cas relaxed. He didn't mind telling that story quite as much. "It was about a year after we came. I'd hiked up to the sisters at the convent, begging for a crust. Anything."

He felt a surge of shame, remembering that day. It was the lowest point of his life. They'd had nothing to eat for days besides some green berries that made Lippa sick. She was already so small and weak. He'd watched her, curled up on her pallet in a dark corner, and known with cold certainty that they'd all starve to death unless he did something.

Fever season had returned and half the village was quarantined. The ones who weren't sick drove him off with rocks when he tried to approach. So he'd climbed the winding road to the convent of Kaethe.

"The nuns offered me work digging graves," he said. "No one else wanted to do it, but I fair jumped at the chance. They had no coin to spare, but they paid me in barley."

"How much?"

"Half a short sack for twelve graves."

"That's paltry." Gui made a tsking sound. "The nuns of Kaethe used to be more open-handed."

"It was a poor harvest. Too much rain." He spotted a pair of riders coming from the opposite direction and slouched in the saddle, but they passed with a nod at Gui and kept going.

As bad as things were now, they'd been worse at the end of that first year. He'd had to tie a bit of rope around his breeches to keep them from falling to his ankles.

"The fever came back," he explained. "Not as bad as before, but still . . . there were plenty of graves to be dug. And the sisters were hard-pressed to keep up with preparing the bodies for burial. They were falling sick, too." He cleared his throat. "When I saw old Serle Tirrel standing in the lichyard, I could tell right away he was risen."

"How?"

Cas shrugged. "Just could. I made the sign of Kaethe and then I . . ." He trailed off. He couldn't see Gui's face, but he sensed him listening closely.

"You what?" Gui prompted.

"I opened the door." He felt foolish saying it out loud. "That's what I call it. Most people scream and carry on, but that only riles them. I said I'd help and then I let him . . . "

"Give you the pain," Gui finished softly.

"Aye. I smelled roses and he went away. I didn't tell the sisters. But when I heard about . . . other people's troubles, I offered my services. They'd pay me in eggs and whatnot."

"Do you understand the dead when they speak to you?"

That was the part that had worried him the most. "I didn't at first," he said slowly, remembering the nonsense Ma had gabbled at him. "But then, after a while, I started to." He lowered his voice, though there was no one around. "I feared it *was* some kind of necromancy, though I wasn't doing it on purpose."

Gui nodded. "It's called tongues. Takes most of us much longer to grasp. Necromancers speak it, too, but it's not a black art. Not exactly." He glanced over his shoulder. "Did you ever get in trouble?"

Cas knew he didn't mean with the reeve.

"Once or twice. But I wasn't stupid. I carried a pocketful of nails."

Gui shook his head. "A pocketful of nails? That's it?"

"You know how much cold iron goes for these days?" Cas asked with a laugh. "You might scoff, but those nails served me well."

"I'm not scoffing. Where'd you get them?"

"Dug 'em out of the loose boards in the privy."

Gui grunted. "So you ran your own little Quietus business. Well, you got lucky, Castelio."

"I suppose I did," he replied contemplatively. "But you get hungry enough, the dead don't seem so scary anymore."

They took rooms at a large inn called the Iron Bell, halfway to Aquitan. It was the furthest he'd ever been from home. While Gui arranged the coach to Prydwen, Cas asked a serving girl for a cake of yellow soap and a bucket of water. He scrubbed himself pink and changed into the only other clothes he owned, a russet cami and patched breeches. Then he snuck out and threw the lice-ridden garments onto the dung heap.

In the common room, he got by with a vegetable pottage. Gui ordered mugs of weak ale and they fell into quiet conversation.

"You know the basics already," Gui said. "That's something a person's born to. Most run from the dead. We don't."

"Never?" Cas asked warily.

He'd found that being fleet of foot was a definite asset when all else failed.

Gui gave him a hard look. "You see a mortifex, you run. I'm talking run-of-the-mill risen."

"You didn't run," Cas pointed out.

"And look where it got me." He pulled up his sleeve and showed Cas a deep, winding scar on his forearm. "Turned my hair white, too."

Cas thought it made a dramatic contrast to Gui's dark skin and youthful features.

"I like it," he said, with a shy grin.

The Quietus laughed. "Well, thank Bel, the High Dead are few and far between. Most are bound to a necromancer." His smile faded. "But the one that attacked your farm wasn't. Made it even more dangerous."

"How can you tell the difference?"

"It didn't wear the *menotte*."

Cas was starting to realize how little he knew about his new trade. "What's that?"

"An iron band around the wrist. It binds them to obey a living will."

"So you fought an unbound fex?" Cas asked, even more impressed.

"You fought it, too," Gui pointed out.

"Not really. I just whacked it with a hoe and ran away." He met Gui's eyes. "Did it kill Ma?"

The thought tormented him. Had the mortifex been inside her room when he stood at the door? He remembered that terrible silence when he called her name. The nameless dread that sent him scurrying down the stairs.

"I can't say for certain," Gui replied. He cleared his throat. "But it's likely."

"The iron horseshoes didn't stop it," Cas said bitterly. "Didn't stop her, neither."

"Because they weren't pure." He looked angry. "I went back to the barn to take a look. Found one in the ashes and tested it with a lodestone. Whoever sold them to you broke the law. They were an alloy. My guess would be nickel."

"How'd the fex get through the Veil?" Cas stared into his ale, the pottage souring in his stomach. "That's what I've always wondered."

"It came through Midgate and killed a lot of the Ducissa's soldiers when it did," Gui replied. "Then it must have stumbled across the farm."

There were three Greater Gates in the Mizzly Mountains, all portals to the spirit realm of the Drowned Woman. Hellgate on the northern border with Vendagni. Midgate and Seagate on the border with Alessia. The Boundary sat in the foothills and was protected from the gates by a second river called the Darkwatch.

"But how?" Cas pressed. "How did it cross the river? How'd it even escape Midgate?"

Gui looked troubled. "No one knows. The men who were guarding it that day are all dead."

They were both quiet for a minute.

"My point," Gui said at last, "and to answer Filippa's question earlier, is that you're special, but there's no magic in what we do. Anyone could, if they had the strength. But that's not the most important part. A Quietus must have compassion. Mercy." His gaze was piercing. "Do you feel the last minutes, too?"

Cas nodded, relieved he wasn't the only one. "The first time was with Ma," he confessed. "I felt like I was burning up."

He prayed Gui wouldn't ask about the vial of Kaethe's Tears he'd broken.

"Some of us find that's the hardest part," Gui said.

"But not you?" Cas prompted, eager to change the subject.

"No." He downed his ale. "It's the regret."

"What about your staff?" Cas eyed the rune-covered stick

propped against the wall. He remembered the crackling light when Gui battled the mortifex.

"An old and powerful talisman. It dampens a mortifex's magic. Likely the only reason I'm alive."

Gui signaled for another ale. Only one. Well, Cas hadn't even finished his first. When it came, Gui rose to his feet. He gave off a natural authority, and the lively buzz of conversation faded as he looked around.

"To the Ducissa Orlaith!" he rumbled, lifting his cup.

Cas shot to his feet, raising his own tankard. The crowd, mostly farmers and finely dressed merchants, also stood, though not with great enthusiasm. Most eyed Gui with mingled fear and respect. A few wore sour expressions. Cas didn't blame them. Until Gui rode into Swanton, he hadn't seen a single Quietus in the three years since he came there.

And everyone knew the problem was getting worse. On the road, they had passed abandoned villages, the houses standing but the people gone. Dead of the walking plague, Gui said, or driven off by the spirits of its victims.

"To the Ducissa," the men echoed, burying their faces in the foamy ale.

"A fine woman," Gui said as he settled his bulk onto the bench again. "She still wears mourning garb though it's been six years since the Duc died."

"How did it happen?" asked Cas, who knew little about anything more than ten leagues from where he'd been born.

"The Courtenays of Nyons," Gui replied with a scowl. "Wickedness incarnate, they are. It was at the Battle of Hellgate. The Duc's mortifex was badly injured trying to save him."

Cas choked on his ale. Gui slapped his back.

"Did you say . . . his *mortifex*?" Cas stammered.

The men at the next bench looked over for a moment, then resumed their conversation.

"I forgot you never had much schooling, lad," Gui said in a low voice. "It's no secret, though the Ducissa doesn't encourage loose talk. Yes, the Redvaynes have their own mortifex. Bound for centuries. His name is Lucius."

"But . . . they're evil!"

"Is a sword evil? Or is it the hand that wields it?" Gui drained his mug. "If the eastern necromancers have High Dead to serve them, then we must, too. Lucius is bound to the Ducissa now, and someday to her son and heir. The boy's only six now. Too young for the responsibility. Poor lad never met his father. He was still in his mother's belly when the Duc fell." He covered a belch. "Enough history lessons for tonight, Castelio. We have a long day on the road tomorrow."

Gui took the bed, while Cas curled up on a pallet in the corner. Within minutes, Gui was snoring like a rasp, but Cas tossed and turned, doubts swirling. Was a bound mortifex really safe? Gui said it had served for centuries and not slaughtered them all.

But his flesh crawled when he remembered the fex on the riverbank, how it stood at the ferry landing and watched them cross the Forkings, holding perfectly still like a wolf watching sheep reach the safety of the pen.

Until that moment, becoming a Quietus had felt almost like a game — or at least an adventure. He was glad to have Swanton at his back, and even happier that his family would be well provided for. On the road, he'd listened when Gui told him things, but sometimes he daydreamed, too, about what Aquitan would be like, and if there were pretty girls at the Ducissa's keep.

But it wasn't a game.

He resolved to pay closer attention from now on. To learn all he could and ask questions if he didn't understand. It might end up saving his life someday.

They ate a quick breakfast at dawn. Gui carried on with his lecture as they rode north through a warm drizzle.

"Mostly you'll be called to deal with Low Dead. Some are folks buried without an iron coin in the mouth. You've met those already. Others are called up by necromancers to carry out some task."

"Why are mortifexes called High Dead?"

Cas couldn't stop dwelling on it.

"They're intelligent and think independently of their masters. Near impossible to put down. They wield the elements. Earth, air, fire, and water. And they can have a beating heart for a period after they consume someone's spirit."

Cas thought of Lippa and felt cold.

"As close to true life as a demon can get," Gui went on. "It lets them bypass all the charms and wards and nine-pointed stars and walk beneath the sun like it's nothing to them. Cross running water, too. But only for a brief time, thank Bel."

"What if you cut a fex's head off?"

"It would slow it down," Gui replied absently. "But they can come back from most anything."

The sun grew higher and hotter as they veered west. The traffic on the road thickened. Carts and wagons laden with produce, a few lacquered coaches with the curtains drawn tight. They passed a group of nuns on foot, all in white with their hair shorn almost to the scalp.

"Is there a convent nearby?" Cas asked.

Gui chuckled. "Just wait, lad."

They were several leagues from the city wall when Gui's charger topped a rise and Cas saw it. His jaw slowly hinged open. Gui reined up.

"The Drowned Woman," he said, sketching her sign in the air. "Kaethe, Lady of Pilgrims."

"May she seal gate and tomb against us," Cas murmured, finishing the catechism.

The high gray walls of Aquitan sat below, surrounded by green fields. Rising above them was a stone statue as tall as the hills beyond. Hooded, faceless, with a torrent of water spilling ceaselessly from her open mouth. The cataract plunged downward from such a great height that a fine mist hung in the air, dazzling his eyes with shimmering rainbows.

A weight slipped from his shoulders as he gazed down at her, cloak falling in granite folds, one hand raised in benediction. He'd prayed to Kaethe often, called on her power when he needed to, but until that moment, he'd never truly felt her presence.

Tears pricked his eyes and he was glad Gui couldn't see. It seemed to him that she stood watch over the city, protecting its inhabitants from harm. And for the first time in three years, Cas felt safe.

Chapter 6

A stone convent nestled along the shallow pool at Kaethe's feet, wreathed in white vapor from the waterfall flowing out of the statue's hooded visage far above. Supplicants streamed in and out of the open doors. Great iron bells tolled the hour, four o'clock by Selene's lunar circuit.

As Gui rode past, Cas ceased his neck-craning long enough to notice the glint of silver ferries and copper pyres at the bottom of the pool — even a few gold coronets.

"Doesn't anyone steal the coins?" he asked. "There's a fortune down there!"

"And risk the Drowned Woman's wrath?" Gui snorted. "Would you chance it?"

Cas shook his head — though he couldn't help but think of what that money would do for the families living in the shantytown outside the walls.

Gui rode on, joining the river of people in the streets. The buildings were tall and narrow, fronted with shops of every description. Spicemongers and apothecaries, wool merchants and bladesmiths. The busiest sold silver bells and iron charms against the dead, while cheaper stalls hawked knots of willow and river reeds. Children with feral eyes slipped through the crowds, evading the mounted patrols in red and gold livery. They aimed their pitches at the latest arrivals to Aquitan, who were still slapping off dust from the road.

"Looking for lodging and a hot meal?"

"Need protection?"

"A silver ferry for the Drowned Woman's blessing! Guaranteed to stop the risen in their tracks!"

Cas saw vials of Kaethe's Tears change hands, along with other metal charms.

"Are those real?" he asked.

"Rainwater and pig iron," Gui replied. "Or lead dipped in lampblack. But it's no use trying to stop the little rascals." His face softened. "Plague orphans, most of 'em."

The deep voice drew the attention of a dirty-looking, painfully scrawny girl, who stared hard at the tattoo on Gui's hand. She whistled at a confederate who was pocketing coins from some gullible rustic. Within seconds, the pair had melted away into the throngs.

The city seemed to go on for leagues. They passed fragrant flower markets and clangorous foundries, bustling guesthouses and stinking cattle markets. The poor wore plain russet dyed with woad and madder, while the rich decked themselves out in red, yellow, and blue doublets under traveling cloaks. Wagons clogged the streets, along with groups of pilgrims who sang and chanted in strange accents. There were many nuns of Kaethe about, and even a few Sons of Bel. Cas had never seen a priest of the sun god before, though he'd overheard villagers in Swanton talking about them. Bel's devotees wore sandals and pleated knee-length skirts of dark wool, with a red sash across their bare chests. Each had a stripe of hair shaved above his left ear. They looked strong and fit as soldiers.

But what made Cas's nape prickle was the masks. Painted gold with holes cut for the eyes, the rigid faces identical and blandly handsome. It was supposed to be a likeness of Bel. Cas noticed people crossing the street to avoid them, and Gui gave a quiet snort as he rode past.

"Does Bel have a temple here, too?" Cas asked.

"Just a chapter house and a few shrines." His voice was flat. "This is Kaethe's city."

Aquitan was such a riot of noise and smells — some pleasant, most less so — that it was a relief when they left the busy area near the gates behind and entered a quieter district of manor houses and offices with signs advertising lawyers and notaries. Presently, a second wall and a second gate appeared, this one smaller but heavily guarded. A banner with the Redvayne phoenix hung over the gate. They rode through and Cas gaped in surprise. The city was gone. In its place, a country estate stretched into the distance. A big house perched on a hill at the end of a dirt lane lined with cypress trees.

"The Redvayne vineyards," Gui remarked, pointing to the terraced rows of grapes on one hillside, where workers toiled to fill woven baskets. "They make a fine claret here."

Olive groves occupied the south side of the estate, their trunks low and gnarled. The leaves were light green on top and silvery beneath, making them shimmer when the wind rustled their boughs.

"Those are nearly a thousand years old," Gui said proudly. "Planted by the first Redvaynes when they landed on these shores."

Cas nodded. He'd expected a dark, intimidating stone keep, but the Ducissa's estate was peaceful and rustic. It was like stepping into the magical fairyland of Ma's tales, where there was no fever or hunger — and the dead stayed that way. The only grim reminder of reality was the picket line of stakes along the wall, spaced about two paces apart. All he could think was how much they must have cost, with the price of iron sky-high, and how nice it would be to fall asleep knowing nothing would shamble up to the edge of your bed and wake you with an icy touch.

The manor itself was a hodgepodge of styles that gave the

impression of several different buildings mortared together. Gui explained that the central axis had been the first convent of Kaethe long ago. After the giant statue of the Drowned Woman was raised, the sisters moved into the city, and the Duc took over the property. Over the years, later generations of Redvaynes had added bits and pieces to it. The result was a jumble, but Cas rather liked all the odd turrets and chimneys and sprawling wings, some of wood, others of stone.

They left the horse with a page. A servant with broad hips and hair covered by a white wimple ushered them inside the house, eying Cas with curiosity. He bowed, then flushed at her look of amusement.

"I'll inform the Ducissa of your arrival, Sir Harcourt," she said, chuckling as she waddled off.

Cas looked around at the stark, elegant chamber, then down at the dirty toe poking from a hole in his left boot. He thumbed the scar across his palm. It was a nervous habit he couldn't seem to break, but he felt terribly out of place. His coarse russet cami was more patches than cloth. His breeches sagged dangerously.

What if he didn't live up to the Ducissa's expectations? Said something to accidentally offend? He'd never met a noble, but he'd heard stories — not all from the living. Everyone in Swanton feared the margrave's wrath. A Ducissa must be even worse.

"Steady, lad," Gui said, sensing his discomfort. "Let's wash off the dust of the road."

Gui led him to a stone trough of water, where they rinsed their faces and hands. Cas dried his palms on a scrap of cloth. They immediately began to sweat again.

"Will Lucius be there?" he asked in a low voice.

The thought of facing a mortifex on top of all the rest was more than he could bear.

"No, Castelio. And I told you, you needn't fear him."

Easier said than done, Cas thought.

"So she's expecting us?"

Gui nodded. "I sent a message from the inn last moonrise. A

soldier I knew was heading for Aquitan." He clapped Cas on the shoulder. "Don't worry, you'll do fine. Remember what I told you."

By the time the servant returned, Cas was in an agony of terror. It wasn't just his own future at stake. If he put a foot wrong, Orlaith would take back the bounty. Maybe lock him up again. Where would his family go then?

He barely saw his surroundings as he followed Gui through a series of halls, some wide and hung with tapestries, others dim and cramped. At last, they paused in front of a plain wooden door. The servant in the white wimple knocked. A woman's voice bade them to enter.

Later, he would have no memory of stepping through the door. Only of a sudden burst of sunlight and the sweet, earthy smell of grapevines. The first thing he saw was a small boy playing with a pup on the carpet. The child reminded him of Teo when his brother was younger. He had a sturdy build and reddish-blond hair. The dog had hold of the edge of his tunic and was growling and tugging with its teeth. The boy laughed.

"No, Jak, let go!" he cried.

The boy noticed Gui and jumped to his feet. The dog, a terrier with a bonny black spot on one eye, hung on bravely for a moment, then dropped to the carpet. "Sir Harcourt!"

Gui smiled. "My Lord," he said with a bow.

Cas followed his lead. When he rose, the boy was looking him over in frank appraisal.

"You must be Castelio," a rich, cultured voice said from his left.

He didn't dare look at her. Instead, he quickly sank to one knee and bowed his head, as Gui had taught him. "Your Grace."

The silence seemed to stretch for a lifetime. Blood rushed in his ears.

"I'm sorry for your loss," Orlaith said at last, as if it hadn't been three years since Ma died.

He raised his head and met her gaze. She stood in front of an open window overlooking the vineyards. Like Gui said, she wore a long-sleeved dress of black bombazine laced tight to the throat, and a black hood from which a few bright gold strands had escaped. It was the exact shade of his mother's hair.

She was younger than he'd expected, around the age Ma had been when she died. They weren't alike otherwise. Orlaith looked like a rich noblewoman, and Ma had looked like a daughter of the mountain glens, always windblown and with black dirt under her nails. Yet there was a sadness in Orlaith's blue eyes, and Cas fell half in love with her right there.

"Thank you, Your Grace," he said. Adding impulsively, "And I for yours."

Orlaith blinked in surprise. Cas shriveled under Gui's look of reprimand. *Too forward.*

He was saved by the pup, which let out a merry bark. The Ducissa turned to the boy. "I think it best if you take Jak outside."

His face fell. "But I want to stay! Please, can't I?"

She eyed him indulgently. "Very well. But I won't have him disrupting. Give him to Esme."

The boy — who must be Orlaith's son, Enrigo — darted out the door. Cas tried not to fidget as a different servant appeared to take charge of Jak. The dog squirmed in her arms, yapping for its master, and Enrigo scratched it behind the ears.

"Go on," he said. "Have a runabout. I'll come soon, I promise."

Cas had found in Swanton that much could be learned about a person by the way they treated their animals. He liked the boy already.

"Oh!" Esme exclaimed, as Jak nearly broke free. She had freckles and a pert nose. Her gaze rested on Cas for a moment, then slid away, cheeks going pink. "Come on, you little devil," she scolded, as Enrigo helped her carry the wriggling pup to the door.

Cas was still down on one knee. Most of Gui's detailed instructions had flown straight out of his head. Uncertain if he was supposed to stand yet, and fearing another mistake, he took a moment to look around. All the furniture had gilt and brocade. He couldn't imagine sitting on any of it. But the thing that impressed him was all the books. Dozens of them. Lining shelves and piled haphazard on the floor. Maybe someday he could buy a book for Lip, to have as her own. She'd be over the moons.

When things had settled down, the Ducissa regarded him seriously. She did not tell him to rise and he was relieved he'd guessed right.

"Your apprenticeship begins tomorrow," she said. "You could not ask for a finer master than Gui Harcourt. But, by tradition, I will administer the oaths now. As you might already have deduced" — a brief pause that made him wonder how much she knew — "becoming a Quietus is learned primarily by doing. It is a dangerous vocation. If you die in the performance of your duties, your next of kin will be entitled to a pension regardless of how long you've been in my service, even if it is only a single hour."

She said this matter-of-factly. Cas wondered if that had ever happened.

"I understand, Your Grace," he replied, amazed at the steadiness of his voice.

Orlaith walked toward him. As she came near, he noticed the thick iron band around her wrist. A chill touched his nape. It was stamped with the Redvayne phoenix. A talisman of binding. The same *menotte* that her husband the Duc had worn until he fell at Hellgate. It had been passed down through the family for generations. He tore his eyes away and stared down at the carpet.

She placed a light palm on his head. "Castelio zah Nerides, I charge you with carrying out the Drowned Woman's will not only in Clovis but throughout the lands of Aveline. Do you accept?"

Aveline was the name of the old empire. It had collapsed like the others before it, leaving the six duchies — three to the west and three to the east — as independent sovereign states. That much he'd learned from Gui's brief history lessons on the road.

"I accept, Your Grace," he said.

"If the dead defy Her will, you have the authority to compel them. If any living person should ask for aid on matters of the risen, you will not refuse. If any of the Low Dead shall cause plague or pestilence, or kill any living person, you will hunt them down and send them through the Veil. Do you accept this charge?"

"I accept, Your Grace."

"The practice of necromancy in my domain is punished by exile across the mountains. If you encounter a necromancer, you shall endeavor to arrest them and bring them to the nearest border crossing. If that is not possible, you shall alert the nearest garrison."

"I understand, Your Grace."

"The term Low Dead encompasses wraiths, liches, ghouls, revenants, and regular spirits. You will learn the difference between them and the methods related to their disposal. You will carry these weapons on your person at all times, without exception."

His head spun trying to absorb the long sentences. Gui had mentioned all that, but in a way that was easier to grasp.

"I accept, Your Grace."

"If any hostile High Dead cross your path, you shall exercise sound judgment in the defense of the citizenry and endeavor to alert the nearest garrison."

No mention of compelling a mortifex. Cas almost expected her to add, "And when those tasks are duly accomplished, you shall run like hell."

He fixed his eyes on her black slippers and swore the last oath, which was to make sure he always carried an iron coin for himself if he took a mortal wound. The little heir, Enrigo, presented this token to Cas. The coin was blackened with age. It had a rosette on one side and Kaethe's nine-pointed star on the other. Enrigo tried to look serious and dignified, but he had Teo's mischief, Cas could see that, and they shared a furtive grin.

Then it was, mercifully, done.

The Ducissa did not smile at him, but she brushed his cheek

with her cool fingertips before stepping back. The sensation lingered as he rose and gave a low bow.

"I will not fail you, Your Grace."

He felt flush with triumph. It had all gone off without a hitch. And the Ducissa was someone he would gladly serve, even at the cost of his own life. Gui looked pleased, too. Cas was eager to begin his apprenticeship. Oddly enough, it felt like the hardest part was behind him now. The dead were no trouble.

It was the living that scared him.

As they strode shoulder to shoulder from the library, Cas chanced to glance down a crossing corridor. It had no windows and was lit by smoky torches in brackets. A man stood at the end, looking down the length of the gallery. His copper hair caught the torchlight, and he wore a long cloak clasped at the neck. The face was too far to be more than a blur.

Perhaps it was the way he held himself unnaturally still. Or perhaps it was the singular whiteness of his skin. But Cas knew right away who he was.

Orlaith's mortifex, Lucius.

Hatred boiled up from the depths of his being. The iron coin dug into his fist, pressing tight against the scar on his palm. They stared at each other for a long moment. He knew it had to be imagination, Lucius was too far away, but he fancied he could see twin pinpoints of flame dancing in his eyes.

Cas finally broke the contact. He turned to Gui and found the older man ten steps ahead.

"You coming, lad?" he called over one shoulder. "There's much to show you. We'll start at the armory."

When Cas looked back, the mortifex was gone.

Chapter 7

The storm rode into the harbor on clouds black as midnight, sending mountainous swells crashing against the stone jetty. Three dozen ships at anchor dipped up and down on the whitecaps, their square sails furled. Nothing else moved on the horizon.

Cas swept the spyglass across the upturned roofs of the city below. Silken banners on shops and teahouses rippled and snapped in the wind. The usually busy streets had emptied.

The first raindrops pattered down and he tucked the glass into his coat, leaning his forearms on the thick rope bridge. The best vantage point on the isle of Tjanjin was at the emperor's aquarium. A network of pools joined by islands and bridges, it sat high in the hills and was open to the public. Ten paces below, long shadows circled the artificial lagoon, tails lashing. Every now and then, a fin sheared the surface. Cas had watched the black-eyed, razor-toothed fish every day for weeks. They were agitated.

He felt the same way about storms. No matter that eight years had passed since the night Ma came back. That he'd been an official Quietus for five of those years, sending hundreds of restless souls through the Veil. When he heard the rumble of thunder, part of him still felt like that frightened boy up in the hayloft.

This storm was the worst Cas had ever seen. A real monster, blowing up out of nowhere. Just a short while ago, the skies had been clear, the sea calm. He sighed and rubbed a thumb over the old scar crossing his palm. Another day gone and nothing to show for it.

When the Ducissa sent him here, he'd been unsure what to expect. He knew almost nothing about the lands south of Aveline. Only that there had been a war a long time ago among mortals and demons, and he was descended from the people who fled on ships across the White Sea.

As it turned out, Chang'un was much like Aquitan. Crowded and noisy, if not quite as dirty. Beyond a few stares, no one bothered him. At first, he'd taken cheap lodgings in a sailors' hostel near the port. When his money ran out, he asked around until he found a tavern so sleazy and disreputable no one else wanted to work there.

The owner smelled desperation. She refused to pay him a wage but let him sleep in the attic and gave him two meager meals a day in exchange for mopping up the various fluids spilled across the floor at the end of each night. He had accepted. It was that or starve, and he'd vowed never to go hungry again if he could help it. He was too able-bodied to beg, which left thieving . . . and he'd learned his lesson with the apples.

"Send me a sign, Kaethe," he muttered. "How long must I stay here?"

Lightning forked low on the horizon. A kittiwake darted past in a flash of yellow bill, fleeing the thunderheads that raced toward the harbor. Cas watched them devour the last scrap of blue sky. He was turning to leave when movement caught his eye. He dried the spyglass on his coat and raised it again, the nine-pointed star tattooed in the webbing between thumb and forefinger stretching taut.

"Mother of Pilgrims," he whispered, pulse quickening.

A ship dropped from the belly of the leading cloudbank. It moved so fast, he could scarcely track it. Two masts with white sails taut against the gale. Cas didn't know much about wind ships, but it had to be the one he was waiting for.

It rolled hard to one side and his gut tightened. Surely it would fall into the raging sea far below. But the ship righted itself, coasting up and down on the air currents like a raft navigating rapids. He expected it to land down by the port, but it headed straight for the aquarium.

He tracked its progress with the spyglass. A figure stood alone on the deck, long hair whipping in the wind. The slender build suggested a woman. Even at a distance, she gave off a brash confidence he found intriguing.

Cas tilted his face up, squinting against the downpour as the ship passed directly overhead, canvas crackling. The whole sky was dark, but lightning flared again and he made out the words emblazoned on the back as it soared away.

Wind-Witch.

"Thank you, Kaethe," he said with a fierce grin.

A howling gust rocked the rope bridge. The ship plummeted abruptly, a near vertical drop, and cleared the palace wall by a handspan. Cas stared at the spot where the vessel had vanished, rain stinging his eyes.

He'd hardened over the last five years. Faced walking nightmares of every stripe. But a ship that sailed through the clouds? In the teeth of a tempest?

The figure he'd seen on deck was either a powerful necromancer or one of the High Dead.

He wasn't sure which was worse — but Orlaith had commanded him to bring the ship back to Aquitan.

Heart pounding, he took off running for his attic room.

Chapter 8

Lo gripped the rail, squinting through curtains of rain.

The aquarium came and went in seconds. It was empty of visitors besides a man on one of the bridges who flashed past before she could register more than the fact that he was watching the ship descend. Then the wall loomed ahead and she put him from her mind. It had been six months since she last visited Tjanjin, but there should be a koi pond on the far side of that wood . . .

A ferocious gust batted the *Wind-Witch*. It listed to starboard and dropped in a sickening plunge, then righted again. Her rope harness jerked tight, saving her from a tumble over the side, but her concentration didn't waver. She floated in an eye of calm amid the raging storm.

Her father called it the Nexus, the source of all elemental magic. You could only find it by surrendering your own will — which is why her mother had always struggled to master it.

Lo twitched the air currents, relying on instinct and past experience to guide the ship's landing path. There was no room for error. At this speed, the smallest miscalculation would lead to disaster. It was like holding the reins of a stallion that bucked and fought, but she'd landed in gales worse than this.

She'd also crashed — more than once. Walked away from wind ships that were smashed to splinters.

It was the reason she stood alone on deck. No one at Falcon Couriers would fly with her anymore. Her birth name was Delilah, but she went by Lola, or simply Lo, and back at the Abicari in Samarqand, "Lo's Luck" had come to mean a double-edged sword. An ironic mixture of good and ill fortune in which one canceled the other out.

When she was younger and new to piloting, Lo felt like a pariah. Wherever she went, whispers and stares followed. Sailors in general were a superstitious bunch, and wind ship crews were the worst. Some she'd counted as friends started to surreptitiously fork their fingers at her until Javid, the owner of Falcon Couriers, noticed and put a stop to it.

Now, at twenty years of age, she embraced the freedoms of solitude. She had her cat Thistle for company. And she hadn't crashed in more than a year.

A personal record.

The red pagoda-style imperial palace loomed closer, and about a league beyond, the koi pond. She sprang into action, lowering the mainsail by hand while simultaneously tweaking a dozen air currents. The dark tops of fir trees blurred by under the hull, almost close enough to touch. Lo fixed her gaze on the pond, her mind one with the ship, the salt wind, and the earth rushing up to meet her.

The last of the canvas dropped, flapping wildly, as the *Wind-Witch* hit the rain-dappled surface of the pond. Momentum propelled it forward at a brisk clip, so she increased the drag of the water at the bow. The *Wind-Witch* skimmed to a stop among the lily pads, rocking hard.

Lo unbuckled her harness. A moment later, six palace guards in knee-length belted black tunics appeared from the trees. They shouted a greeting. She was expected, though overdue since she'd been traveling and hadn't received Princess Pingyang's message until a few days before.

She furled the sails and lashed them to the boom, then hurried below. The captain's cabin was spacious, with railed shelves built into the bulkheads, a thick carpet from Susa with a motif of palm leaves, a writing desk, and a large bunk.

Lo peeled off her soaked shirt and trousers and flung open a wardrobe. The doing-business-with-rich-people clothes.

Every garment had long sleeves and modest necklines to hide the scars that ran down both arms and across her back. They resembled the fronds of a fern or the branching limbs of a tree. She was self-conscious about the scars, though few would recognize the source — lightning strikes, which she had survived twice and had no memory of beyond waking up afterwards with painful etchings on her body.

After some consideration, she chose a dark green gown with slashes up the skirts for ease of movement. It was a simple cut but well-made and suited to her stark looks. Delilah Dessarian had inherited her grandmother's raven hair, her father's blue eyes, and her mother's penchant for moral outrage, though not her explosive temper. Lo was more a shrewd and calculating sort. This had served her well at Falcon Couriers, which served clients in both the darklands controlled by daēvas and the sunlands where the mortals reigned.

Thanks to Javid's tutoring, she felt equally at ease conversing with kings and farmers, prosperous merchants and dissolute gamblers. In recent years, she had negotiated contracts with the Matrium of the forest-dwelling Danai daēva clan, the Five of the seafaring Marakai, the fire-workers in Pompeii, and even the new Oracle of Delphi. Her success brought certain liberties, not to mention Javid's indulgence when she destroyed one of his costly wind ships. Falcon Couriers was thriving, and she had earned grudging respect from the other captains — even if they did walk the other way when they saw her coming.

This particular mission, however, had nothing to do with profits.

Lo smoothed her skirts and kissed the coin that hung on a

silver chain around her neck — her own superstitious ritual. One side bore an image of the moon, the other the sun. A maker of talismans named Nicodemus had given it to her mother. It protected the wearer from injury and illness. When Lo was born, her mother had put it around her neck and she'd never taken it off since.

Considering the company she kept, the talisman had saved her life more than once.

The wardrobe had mirrors set into its inner doors. Her gaze shifted to the cabin behind, where a cat the same color as the storm clouds outside was washing its paws. The cat was impressively fat, pillow-shaped with impassive green eyes that glowed brighter with each flash of lightning, as though lit by infernal fires from within.

"Do you think it will amount to anything?" she asked.

The cat stared at her. It blinked once, slowly. Then it returned to its washing.

"You're right," Lo muttered. "I won't get my hopes up again. That would be foolish. But if there's a new lead, we have to look into it."

She strode to her desk and took a ledger down from a shelf. It held records of every whisper, every alleged sighting and rumor about her parents. Eight years ago, they'd vanished without a trace. Javid and his husband Katsu had taken her in, raising her as their own. Both were close family friends and she couldn't have asked for kinder foster parents.

She flipped through the stiff vellum pages, crammed with lines of precise handwriting. Lists of acquaintances she'd spoken to; maps and places her parents might have gone. She'd spent a fortune on mystics and soothsayers, even visiting the Oracle herself. As the years passed, it became clear that they had gone into the Dominion, into the shadowlands of the Drowned Lady, and they hadn't come back out.

Her parents were well-loved by many people, mortals and daēvas alike. Exhaustive searches had turned up nothing. The trail went cold. Yet Lo refused to give up hope. Most likely this trip to Tjanjin was another wild goose chase, but Princess Pingyang had found someone who claimed to have seen them only a few weeks ago.

The back of the ledger held a single piece of loose parchment. Lo carefully unfolded the page. It was coming apart along the creases, but she couldn't help reading it now and again. She always heard her mother's voice, serious but with a hint of laughter.

> Mouseling,
> If Javid gave you this, it means we are late coming home to Susa. Do not wory, we will be home for your birth-day. I think we should get more gotes. Papa says we have two many gotes already, but he is wrong. Love to Thissel. Do not wory. Yours faithfully, Mama

Lo studied the childish block lettering. In her more desperate moments, she'd wondered if they were a code she was meant to decipher. "Gotes" sounded like "gates," as in the gates to the shadowlands.

Then again, her mother was barely literate.

Mama had grown up in the mountains, the child of nomadic herders. When she and Papa settled down in Susa and had Lo, she had bought several goats to keep as pets. The cat, Thistle, was named after a goat Mama had known when she was a little girl. Thistle (the cat) did not like to be reminded of this fact; he found it insulting. But the reference to "gotes" made sense. Her mother was very fond of them.

Lo tucked the page into the ledger. She slung a cloak over her shoulders and dug out another smaller one for the cat, who, ironically, hated to get wet. He eyed her with feline disdain but allowed her to settle the cape on his back and tie the strings of the hood beneath his chin. Despite his size, Thistle sprang easily to her shoulder. Lo climbed up the ladder to the deck. She lowered a dinghy and rowed for shore, Thistle perched on the facing bench.

"Try to behave," she said. "Don't shred any tapestries. And no knocking over priceless vases, either."

The cat affected not to hear. He blinked from the depths of his hood.

"I suppose you're hungry," she continued. "Don't worry, we'll find you something."

Once on shore, he again leapt to her shoulder, sinking needle claws into her cloak. Lo followed the guards along a wooded path and across a wide plaza of crushed pink and white seashells to the pair of bronze dragons flanking the palace entrance. More guards waved them through, and she was given to a steward who led her through halls of polished wood to an audience chamber. Princess Pingyang waited on a dais, her attendant and bodyguard Feng Mian at her side.

"Your Highness," Lo said, bending a knee.

Fine lines etching the corners of Pingyang's eyes were the only sign of age, though Lo knew her to be in her late thirties. She wore several stiff, embroidered robes on top of each other, with the outer garments cut away to reveal colorful layers underneath. Shining black hair was piled atop her head and held in place with ivory combs. She was a small woman, yet she gave off an aura of confidence and command.

The princess made a gracious greeting and waved the guards away. When they had gone, she clasped Lo's hands. "It's wonderful to see you." She smiled at the cat, who was following an ant across the floor. "And dear Thistle."

She sank down and held out a hand. After a moment, Thistle wandered over and allowed her to scratch his chin.

Lo bowed to Feng Mian, who bowed back. Roughly the same age as her mistress, Feng Mian's features were sharper, her dark eyes warier. Her hair was long and loose, cut in a fringe above her thick brows. She wore a simple black tunic and trousers.

On previous visits, they had sparred together for fun. Lo had been trained to fight with a staff by a cult of fierce Greek women who worshipped the sun god Apollo, and with her hands and feet by Katsu, who taught her a technique called the Hard and the Soft that he'd learned at the Temple of the Four Winds in Tjanjin.

Feng Mian was formidable, and they had forged a friendship over the years.

Rain drummed on the roof as they took seats by the window, which overlooked a garden. The sweet fragrance of jasmine drifted through the open window, mingled with the scent of damp earth.

"How fares your father, the emperor?" Lo asked.

"He's taken to his bed," the princess replied sadly. "His mind remains sharp, but his body grows frail. I fear he might never return to the throne."

"I am sorry. But he is fortunate to have such a wise and devoted daughter. I'm sure it sets his mind at ease."

Pingyang gave a grim smile. "There are always those who seek to take advantage of a succession to promote their own interests. Even to seize power themselves. But I'll keep them in line."

Lo nodded slowly. "I'm sure you will, Your Highness."

Pingyang was known as the Jade Dragon. She would handle the court, Lo didn't doubt it.

"But you have not come to speak of politics," Pingyang said.

Lo waited, heart sinking as a look of regret crossed the princess's face.

"I wish I had happier news to give you," she said. "I sent a second message to the Abicari. It must have passed you on the way here." She glanced at her bodyguard. "I'm afraid the man we found was lying. Feng Mian investigated his claim. With the reward, we have many false reports. It seems this was another."

Lo had half-expected it, yet as always, the news left her frustrated. Javid had posted a generous bounty for any useful information about her parents. Before he fell ill, the emperor agreed to spread the word in Tjanjin. They knew it would encourage unscrupulous claims, but if there was a chance it might unearth a fresh lead, Lo was willing to chance it.

"We have the man in custody. I knew you would want to question him yourself." She frowned. "He is lying, I'm sure of it. But he also knows more than he's ready to admit."

The princess nodded at Feng Mian, who strode from the room. He must already have been brought up from the cells, for she returned moments later with guards gripping a young man between them, shackled hand and foot. He looked disheveled and scared, eyes darting about the room.

"Tell the story again," the princess commanded.

"It was all a mistake!" he cried. "A misunderstanding!"

"You approached the palace guards and tried to claim the reward," Pingyang said sternly. "You said you saw two people matching the descriptions from the poster at the octopus pagoda. Based on that information, I summoned this young woman all the way from Samarqand. But when we located others who were there that day, not one could confirm your tale."

"I interviewed two dozen people," Feng Mian growled. "No one else saw them. Yet you knew that one of those we seek is missing a hand. And it wasn't mentioned in the poster."

That was Lo's mother, Nazafareen. A feature not easily overlooked, and which had proven invaluable in winnowing out false claims. She felt a spark of interest.

He sank to his knees. "Please, Your Highness, have mercy! I meant no harm!"

Lo turned to the princess. "May I have permission to question him privately? Perhaps I can persuade him to tell me more."

She cracked her knuckles. Feng Mian gave her a small, wicked smile.

Pingyang nodded. "Of course. He is yours to dispose of as you see fit." She eyed him with contempt. "I do not think he is dangerous, just greedy and foolish."

The guards released him. He remained on his knees, staring at the carpet. The princess directed her men to wait outside the door, then nodded at Lo and swept out with Feng Mian.

The man looked up with sullen defiance. "Who are you?"

"An interested party." She stood up and walked to the window, leaning against the sill. "How did you know about the missing hand?"

He glared at the floor. "Lucky guess."

Thistle padded across the room. With each step, his shadow grew blacker, monstrous and misshapen, until it engulfed the quaking prisoner in a pool of utter darkness.

"What do you know?" he hissed, eyes glowing like hellish forges. "Tell me or I'll eat you up."

It wasn't a single voice but many overlapping at once. Beneath the words, other voices wept and growled over the lonely shriek of the wind. Lo was used to it, but the young man's eyes widened to the size of teacups.

"Someone paid me!" he gasped.

"Who?" Lo demanded softly. "Give me a name."

"I don't know! A foreigner! He . . . he had a strange accent. Said there would be more gold after I went to the palace and made my report, but I'd better keep my mouth shut about our deal or he'd come find me." The man swallowed hard. "He never threatened me. Not in so many words. But there was something hard about him. He meant business, if you get my drift."

"Where did you meet?"

"Down by the docks. Only the one time." A sigh. "I got arrested before I could see him again."

"What did he look like?"

"Tall. Dark hair."

"Young or old?"

"Young."

Lo considered the story. "If you never saw him again, how were you supposed to get the money?"

"He gave me half first. Said I'd get the other half after I made the report. That he knew how to find me."

"And you trusted this stranger," she said flatly.

"No. I followed him back to his lodgings."

She felt a flicker of excitement. "Where?"

"A tavern called The Two-Fisted Wife."

"Did he tell you why he didn't claim the reward himself?"

The man shook his head. "I swear I don't know. I thought it was a prank." His shoulders slumped. "I never expected to get in this much trouble!"

She studied him for a minute. "What's your trade?"

"I'm a fisherman." Chains clanked as he held his hands up. "Please, mistress! I have a family to think about!"

Thistle had returned to following the ant, tail lashing. The man watched him warily.

"Where is The Two-Fisted Wife?"

"At the bottom of Plum Blossom Lane, near the wharves. But you mustn't go there alone, mistress. It's a bad area."

Lo pushed off the sill. "I'll take that under advisement. For now, you'll keep quiet about all this."

He nodded fervently. "Whatever you say."

"This foreigner. How would I recognize him?"

The man thought. "He wore his hair tied back. I couldn't see much of his clothes. It was dark."

"Thistle?" she called.

He shrank away from the cat's glowing eyes. "Wait! There is something . . . when he gave me the gold, I saw a tattoo on his hand. A blue star."

Now *that* was useful.

"Watch him," she said to Thistle.

The cat gave no sign of hearing, but the fisherman blanched and scooted back as far as he could get. She went into the hall and found Princess Pingyang and Feng Mian.

"This man knows nothing," she said in a low voice. "I think he was used. He said a foreigner paid him to invent the tale, but he has no idea where to find him. No doubt the accomplice was hoping they'd split the bounty."

"A foreigner?" Feng Mian's eyes narrowed. "Give me a few days. I'll bring you this man."

Lo shook her head. "It's a waste of time. That was a month ago. Surely, the fellow has left Tjanjin by now. But you have my thanks."

"For what?" the princess wondered. "Wasting your time?"

"It is never a waste of time to see you, Your Highness," Lo said with a smile. "If you agree, I think he has been punished enough. He said he had a family."

"That part is true," Feng Mian said. "I've been to his home to tell his wife and children what happened to him."

The princess frowned. "Are you certain, Delilah? His actions were not harmless. You came all this way—"

"I bear him no ill will," Lo said. "And I pity his children. Perhaps a month in the cells is enough?"

"I suppose he has learned his lesson." She nodded at Feng Mian, who went to inform the guards. "You must stay at the palace and dine with me tonight. I've had rooms prepared."

Lo made a regretful face. She hated to lie to the princess, but if Pingyang sent guards to raid the tavern, the man might slip through her fingers. If he wasn't already gone.

"I wish I could. But I'm afraid this trip has already put me behind schedule. It's why I was late in responding to your message. I've been traveling nearly without pause for the last six months." That much was true, at least. "Will you forgive me if I decline? It is not by desire but necessity."

The princess took it in stride. "Of course. With my father unwell, there has been little joy in these halls anyway. But you must come again. And stay longer next time."

"I will," Lo promised, adding casually, "Oh, and with your permission, I will go down to the city before I depart. I have messages to deliver from Javid."

Pingyang looked like she suspected a ruse, but she simply nodded. "The guards at the gate will be alerted. You are free to come and go as you wish."

Lo bent a knee again. Thistle leapt to her shoulder. The steward appeared and escorted them both out. As she strode past the twin dragons, Lo hesitated. She knew Plum Blossom Lane, if only by reputation. The fisherman was right. It was a rough part of town. Better she retrieved her quarterstaff from the *Wind-Witch* before seeking out this foreigner.

It was unlikely he knew anything. He'd probably sought to use the fisherman to collect the reward, thus avoiding risk himself. But the story *was* rather odd. Worth investigating, at least.

Chapter 9

The alley behind The Two-Fisted Wife reeked of garbage, urine, and a miasma of decay that reminded Cas of a freshly opened grave.

The tavern was named after a local woman who became famous for hunting down her wastrel husband and dragging him by the scruff from whichever wine sink he was hiding in, often blackening his eyes in the process. But that was many years ago, according to the story he'd heard. Cas doubted the men who frequented the place now even had wives, or anyone who cared enough to come looking.

He skirted a dead rat the length of his forearm and slipped through the side door. The proprietor eyed him from her post behind the bar. She was a tiny, shriveled woman who sampled her own wares all day long. Considering the quality, it was a wonder she still had her sight.

"Where have you been?" she demanded. "The evening rush is about to start. And the place is filthy!"

Cas bowed and glanced around the empty room. "Ah well, it's always filthy, mistress."

She cackled. "True enough. With this weather, the usual scum will probably be passed out under a bridge. But we must keep up appearances, eh?"

He smiled, thinking he would not miss working here in the least. "Can I change out of my wet clothes first? It won't take long."

She seemed about to object, but then her features softened. "Go on. I'll have a hot meal for you when you get back."

Her "hot meals" consisted of a thin broth with noodles and strange rubbery weeds floating on top — not that he wasn't glad to get them. He hadn't eaten since moonset the night before and his belly felt hollow as a rotten tree, but any appetite withered as he made his way up the stairs.

The attic room was tucked under slanting eaves in a space so cramped he could only stand upright in the middle of the floor where the roofline peaked. A straw pallet and moth-eaten blanket were pushed into one corner. The other held a stub of candle. He moved to the window and cracked it open, breathing deeply. Gusts of rain blew inside, wetting the floor with fat drops.

"Almost home," he said softly, resting his forehead against the glass. A few people hurried along the street below, blurred shapes in the downpour. "Just get it over with."

Death held no terrors for him anymore. It was simply the other side of the coin. Both an end and a beginning.

It was natural.

But this . . .

He swallowed the bitter taste and unsheathed an iron knife from his belt, drawing it across the old scar on his palm. For a moment, he felt a shard of glass gouging his flesh. Saw bloodless lips and gleaming teeth in the darkness.

Cas shoved the memory down. That was a different mortifex. This one wouldn't try to kill him.

Probably.

Dipping a finger in the blood, he sketched a nine-pointed star on the wooden boards, about two paces in breadth. Then he sat back on his heels, stomach knotting. He'd banished hundreds of spirits, but this was the first time he'd summoned one.

Lightning flashed through the window as he emptied his pockets of charms. Two pouches of iron nails. Eight vials of Kaethe's Tears. Hidden inside his coat, the twin of the knife he'd used to cut himself. Interlocking iron daggers that nestled in the same sheath; one to attack, the other to parry with his off-hand. He piled it all on the pallet. Then he stared at the nine-pointed star.

It felt utterly wrong. He exorcised demons — he didn't conjure them up. But there was no way around it. He couldn't fly a wind ship back to Aquitan alone.

The Ducissa trusts him. And I trust Her Grace.

Cas wouldn't have done it for anyone else. But Orlaith had always treated him with kindness and respect despite his low status. Almost like a son, though she was only a decade older. And their duchy was under siege from both the risen dead and the necromancers across the mountains. They needed the wind ship to study. To replicate. With a fleet of such ships, the realm might be saved.

Thunder rumbled outside. Cas steadied his nerves and whispered a name, a secret name known only to a very, *very* few.

A sudden gust snuffed the candle. The wind died, grew heavy and still. He could feel it in his ears, a subtle shift in the air, the kind that sets dogs to howling. He held his bleeding hand over the center of the star. The droplets shimmered and began to jump like grease on a hot griddle. They multiplied into a rippling crimson pool. He rose to his feet and stepped back, every muscle rigid. Lightning flickered again. The room went pitch dark.

When it grew light again, a man stood inside the nine-pointed star.

He was clean-shaven with hair that shone like beaten copper. At first glance, he would be mistaken for a noble, or at least a prosperous merchant. His clothing was the latest fashion at court, a slashed doublet and snug fawn-colored breeches tucked into knee-high leather boots, with a cloak of blue woad clasped at the throat by a gold pin. An iron menotte circled his right wrist, the metal stamped with a phoenix, the sigil of the Redvaynes.

That is where any resemblance to a living human ended.

The mortifex's complexion was as pale as whey — too pale for a denizen of the Sun Courts. His irises were the green of mossy stones along a riverbed. Pinpricks of flame danced at the center of each pupil.

"You called me," he said dryly. "Do you intend to let me out?"

His posture was relaxed, as though they spoke over wine at one of Orlaith's suppers. Not that either were invited to mingle with the nobility at such affairs. In fact, Cas had seen little of Lucius in his five years serving the Ducissa. His work as a Quietus kept him on the road most of the time. Even on those occasions when he returned to Aquitan, he seldom encountered the Ducissa's mortifex. Gossip said Lucius avoided mortal company — or had been ordered to.

Besides which, he couldn't tolerate the sun, and in the duchies west of the mountains it never set. Lucius's personal apartments were deep beneath the manor. Needless to say, Cas had never visited them.

Now the fex waited with the perfect stillness of its kind, like a coiled serpent. The room felt suddenly even smaller. Airless.

Overriding every instinct for self-preservation, Cas scrubbed a gap in the star with the toe of his boot. Lucius stepped across the red smear. He looked around the dusty attic, with its tiny crooked window and mouse droppings.

"Are these the best lodgings you could find?"

Cas quickly bound his hand in a strip of cloth. He forced himself to keep a measured pace as he crossed the attic and retrieved his iron knives. The vials of Kaethe's Tears and bags of nails. None would do him much good against Lucius, but he felt better having them.

"The *Wind-Witch* is here," he said. "But there's a problem. It landed inside the palace walls."

Flames flickered in the depths of Lucius's eyes. "How is that a problem?"

His voice was soft, but it held an undercurrent of menace.

"Because I won't let you slaughter the guards to get us aboard that ship."

"What will you do?" He tilted his head. "Banish me?"

"Aye. I know your true name now."

The mortifex laughed. "But I'm not inside your star anymore. You'll find it's a bit harder to put me back in than to let me out."

Cas was opening his mouth to reply when a hard knock sounded on the door.

"Open up!"

It was the proprietress. Cas glanced at the bloody star, then at Lucius, who looked faintly amused — but also like a cat who'd just noticed a small furry thing scurry past.

"I'll be right down!" Cas called, stuffing his belongings into the pack.

"Is someone with you? I heard voices."

"Don't worry, there's no one."

"Well, you're late for your shift. I found a spider big as my left tit living in the privy. And the floor needs mopping."

"I'm . . . changing my breeches. Down in a minute!"

He waited for her to leave, but there was no sound of footsteps.

"You have someone in there, don't you? A girl?"

Cas didn't reply.

"A boy, then." She coughed, then spat. "I don't care who you tumble, but you know the rules. No visitors. Not unless they pay room and board."

In the blink of an eye, Lucius stepped forward and opened the door. Cas's breath caught. He readied a vial of Kaethe's Tears.

"It's a kind offer," Lucius said, "but I don't sleep much."

The landlady had poor eyesight and the attic was dim. She peered up at him, mouth twisted in annoyance. Then her watery gaze caught on the gold clasp of his cloak. "Ah. You look like the paying type," she said in a milder tone. "I run a respectable business here. Not a brothel." Her lips spread in a grin, revealing the yellowing stubs of teeth. "But I'm sure we can reach an accommodation. Cut me in on the action and I won't make trouble. Let's say a 15 percent commission?"

Lucius snapped his fingers and the wick of the candle ignited. Its light fell on the sharp white angles of his face. Her eyes widened. She shrank away into the hall.

"Do as you will," she gasped, stabbing a finger. "Just go and don't come back!"

The last was directed at Cas.

"Wait until she finds the blood," Lucius remarked as they fled down the stairs. "You definitely won't be getting a reference."

A single patron hunched over the bar. He eyed them blearily as they raised their hoods and stepped outside, hurrying through the windswept streets back to the aquarium. The eaves of the narrow buildings had turned into waterfalls, the gutters to streams that rushed downhill. It wasn't enough to stop the mortifex in his tracks, but it pained him to cross swift-running water. Cas could see it in the tight line of his mouth.

"Did you have to announce yourself?" Cas demanded when they were a few blocks away. "She might summon the city watch."

Lucius eyed him sidelong. "In this weather, I very much doubt it. And I left her alive, didn't I?" A cluck of his tongue as Cas flipped his collar up. "Still wearing peasants' russet? Really, Quietus, you could try to blend in."

Cas snorted. "Like you? Might as well wear a sign that says *bash me in the back of the head and rob me.*"

Lucius gave him a wolfish grin. "You're assuming the thieves can read."

The city of Chang'un fell away behind as they climbed up into the hills. Cas wondered what he would do if Lucius defied his order to refrain from murder. The Low Dead could be banished with cold iron, but it was merely an annoyance to a mortifex.

Lucius was right about the nine-pointed star. He had to be

standing inside it to be bound again, and Cas doubted the fex would wait around while he made another one. Only Orlaith, who wore the match of the iron menotte, could control him.

The gates of the aquarium were open, though its exhibits sat deserted. They crossed the swaying rope bridges, now wreathed in mist, and Cas pointed to the place where the wind ship had gone over the wall.

"I saw the pilot," Cas said. "It looked like a woman. Do you know who she is?"

Lucius shrugged. "No idea."

"You knew enough to lure her to Tjanjin."

"I've heard rumors. Nothing more."

"Who are these people she seeks? The man and woman with one hand?"

"My sources never said. Only that there was a bounty on their heads. And the owner of the *Wind-Witch* would be eager to deliver it personally."

If he was lying, Cas couldn't tell. Lucius's face was impossible to read.

"You're sure you can fly the wind ship back to Aquitan?" Cas asked.

"I need to examine it first."

"And if you can't?"

Lucius's gaze was distant, fixed beyond the wall. "Then we bring the necromancer with us."

Cas rubbed his forehead. This was getting worse and worse. "Here's the bargain. If you can get us into the palace grounds without killing anyone, I'll show you which way the ship went."

Lucius turned to him. "Do you think I enjoy needless bloodshed?"

"I don't know what you *enjoy*," Cas replied. "But I do know how you feed."

A flash of anger, there and gone in an instant. Lucius gave him a crooked smile. "Fortunate for them I'm not hungry."

The wall was high and sheer, but the mortifex scaled it with ease. A long minute passed.

"*Sanglant*," Cas swore softly. "The bastard left me—"

He bit back a yell as invisible tentacles hoisted him aloft and over the wall, dumping him on the wet earth below. Lucius sat on his haunches nearby, scanning the wooded grounds.

"You could have warned me," Cas muttered, brushing dirt from his breeches.

"Next time I'll send an engraved invitation," Lucius replied. "Get down. They haven't seen us yet, but they will in a moment."

He dropped behind a bush as a patrol appeared in the distance. The guards strode along a pathway, swords strapped across their backs. The flat roof of the palace rose above the trees about half a league away. Once they were past, Cas checked to make sure his charms were intact. Then he crept with Lucius through the gardens, crouching in the foliage when patrols passed. Most were focused around the palace. Cas had marked the ship's direction and a short time later he spotted it, floating in the middle of a pond. They studied the ship from the shelter of the trees. No lights shone from the vessel.

"Can you cross?" Cas asked.

Lucius studied the interlocking circles of rain on the pond's surface. "Stagnant water I can abide," he said.

They waded into the pond. It turned out to be thigh-deep with a muddy bottom. A rope ladder dangled over the side. Lucius went first, then Cas. He'd never been on a boat bigger than the Forkings ferry. This one had ropes running everywhere. It looked complicated. Doubt stirred that Lucius would be up to the task.

"I'll go below," Lucius whispered. "Make sure there's no one else aboard. You wait here."

"And if she comes back?"

"That's why you'll be standing guard."

"So can you fly it?" He was eager to be gone.

"Perhaps. I need to determine how much lift it requires."

Lucius trailed a finger along the rail. "This wood . . . It's strange. I've never seen the like."

"Is that good or bad?"

The mortifex inclined his head, considering. "Well, it's very light. That should help."

"Just tell me, can you fly it or not?"

Cas was used to working alone. Relying on himself. He despised being beholden to Lucius. The fex was too cagey.

"Patience, Quietus. I will return with the answer."

Lucius stepped away, blending with the shadows. In an instant, he vanished down the hatch. Cas sighed and dragged a hand through his sodden hair. Rubbed the scar on his palm.

"Well, hurry the feck up," he muttered, settling in to wait.

CHAPTER 10

With every step, Lo's mood grew darker.

She refused to give up hope but keeping it alive only brought despair when the latest lead petered out.

They'd all been so happy together. But ever since Lo could remember, her parents had traveled for half the year. They ran a small shop in the seaside town of Susa that sold religious trinkets. Her father, Darius, was a master carpenter. He was also a daēva, with the ability to wield three of the elements — earth, air, and water. Papa was especially strong in earth. He used both his hands and the power to shape marvelous things from wood.

Her mother, Nazafareen, was mortal. Once, she'd had a unique talent — to break the magic of others — but she'd lost the ability before Lo was born. Why, Mama never said.

When they went on their buying trips, they would leave her with various friends. The Maenads who had taught her the quarterstaff. Javid and Katsu. Even an old woman who lived in a funny house with lots of doorways, though Lo had been too young to remember much else.

She knew they'd had all sorts of adventures before she was born, but she'd thought that her parents had finally settled down.

Ha.

It was only long after they vanished that Javid told her the truth. For six months of each year, they hunted in the Dominion. The shadowlands beyond the gates. The way Javid explained it, the Dominion was a between-place. Across the Veil between life and death, but not the final destination. Souls might linger there for a spell, but they eventually boarded boats and crossed the Cold Sea. What lay beyond *that*, no one knew.

But some souls refused to cross. And if they stayed in the Dominion long enough, they grew dangerous. Her parents, it seemed, were tasked with rounding them up and sending them on their way.

They'd always returned home — until the day they didn't.

She was twelve when Javid and Katsu took her in. Sixteen when Javid deemed her old enough to know what they'd really been up to. Mama's obsession with keeping her old sword sharp suddenly made sense.

"It was a bargain, Lo," he said gently. "They had no choice."

"But *why?*" she'd demanded. "Why would they agree to take such a risk?"

And leave me behind.

"I'm sorry, but that's not my secret to tell," he replied. "You'll have to ask your mother when we find her."

That was eight years ago.

She reached up to stroke Thistle's tail, which wrapped around her neck like a muffler. They'd been together since he was a wee ball of gray fluff. He was the only constant in her life. The only one she knew would never leave her.

"You are a true friend," she said softly.

He sank his claws through her cloak in agreement.

She was nearing the pond when she realized how quiet it was. The chorus of frogs had gone silent. Not a single insect chirped.

Her steps slowed. She crept the last part of the way, crouching in the reeds. The *Wind-Witch* was there. So was the dinghy on the shore. But she was half daēva, and her heightened senses detected something amiss. Thistle's claws sank into her shoulder again, deeper. He sprang to the muddy ground.

Lo knew every inch of her ship. It took moments to spot a shadow at the bow that didn't belong. She held still and considered the problem. She could fetch the guards. But instinct told her it was no coincidence that a stranger had boarded her ship uninvited.

Perhaps he'd saved her the trouble of a visit to Plum Blossom Lane.

Wait here, she mouthed at Thistle.

He blinked slowly, eyes like yellow moons in the darkness. Lo drew a deep breath and slipped into the water.

Chapter 11

Cas hunched in the rain, waiting Lucius to return. Finally, he crawled to the dark hole leading down below.

"Lucius," he hissed.

No answer.

It had been at least two hours since the ship landed. Every minute they remained, discovery grew more likely. What was taking the fex so long? He did a slow turn, scanning the pond and the high cattails at the edge.

Nothing moved.

It was as silent as an iron-bound coffin in hallowed ground.

Cas idly rubbed his scar, tracing the jagged line with his thumb. It curved from the joint of his first finger to the heel of his palm. An old woman had once told him that if it had crossed his lifeline, he would have died young. Instead, they ran in an eerie parallel next to each other, never quite touching.

She said it meant he was destined to become a Quietus. She also told him he would have many children, which is how he knew she was a fraud.

"I'm already wed," he'd said, paying her with two copper

pyres that she tucked into a leather pouch. "To the Drowned Woman."

The seer had laughed, though her gaze held pity. "That's a cold marriage bed, Quietus."

He was about to go below and find Lucius himself when a faint noise made him turn.

It was the necromancer.

She wore a cloak with the hood thrown back and held a staff marked with sinister runes. Long black hair coiled across her shoulders like serpents.

"The guards will be here any moment," she said, her face hard as frost. "Tell me what you're looking for, and it will go easier for you."

When he didn't reply, her blue eyes narrowed. The wooden planks bucked beneath his feet. He stumbled and caught a rope, mind racing.

Necromancy used blood and grave dirt and ground-up bones. Rituals and incantations to summon the dead.

That was a clear display of elemental magic.

Not a necromancer, then. Which left one other possibility. His gut tightened.

She was one of the High Dead.

"Well?" she demanded. "What do you want with me?"

Cas tore a vial of Kaethe's Tears from his braces. He flicked the cork off with a thumb and hurled the contents in her face. The woman spluttered in surprise, but her flesh didn't blister.

She only looked more annoyed.

What under Bel's Blessed Light was he dealing with?

The staff blurred. He saw the blow coming from the corner of his eye, but she was too fast. The next thing Cas knew, he was lying on his back, staring up at her. The tip lifted his chin. It had sprouted a wicked-looking blade.

"Where do you come from?" she snapped. "Speak!"

"North! Across the sea," he said quickly, trying to calculate his next move.

"The *White Sea*?" she echoed with stark disbelief.

"Aye. I mean you no harm."

She clearly doubted the truth of this. "What did you throw at me?"

"Kaethe's Tears."

"What does it do?"

He eyed her smooth, unblemished skin. "Nothing, apparently."

She scowled. "You're the foreigner who put that fisherman up to collecting the reward. Why?"

Cas was saved from answering by the arrival of reinforcements.

The staff flew from her hand and hurtled into the darkness like a javelin, splashing into the pond. The woman spun around. Lucius stood behind her. He held an enormous cat by the scruff. It dangled limply, teeth bared in a snarl. Flames engulfed his other hand, flowing down his arm like water.

Rain lashed the desk but didn't dampen the mortifex's magical flames. They rose higher, crackling and hissing in the downpour. The woman stepped back, then yelped as Lucius bound her in coils of air and lifted her off the deck.

"Let me go!" she growled.

"*Make me.*" Lucius watched her with an intent expression, as though waiting for something. She struggled wildly, legs kicking. At last, he released her. She dropped to the deck, landing with far more grace than Cas had when Lucius dumped him over the wall.

"What do you want?" she demanded.

"This ship."

Her chin lifted. "Give me my cat and it's yours."

That surprised Cas. She'd trade her wind ship for a cat?

"It's not that simple." Lucius stepped closer. "I need you to fly it."

Shouts sounded in the trees. A dozen palace guards appeared, running for the pond.

"Take off," Lucius rasped, flames gathering in his hand. "Right now, or they all die!"

Lo stared at the creature who held her beloved Thistle by the scruff.

At first, she'd assumed he was a Vatra daēva — a child of fire. He had their look, with his coppery red hair. She knew most of them, but she'd never seen him before. And what would a Vatra from the western desert be doing on the distant isle of Tjanjin? The clan made a fortune selling talismans. Surely he could afford to buy his own wind ship.

Then he stepped closer.

Close enough to see the yellow pinpricks dancing at the center of each pupil, like candles in a black void. To see the parchment-white skin. Feel the bitter cold rolling off him in waves.

Gooseflesh pricked her. Her fingertips tingled and went numb.

But most disturbing of all was the wide band around his wrist, forged from some dull black metal. It had an emblem she couldn't quite make out through the flames licking up his arm.

Lo's parents wore similar cuffs made of gold. A magical bond linking mortal and daēva together. She glanced at the one with brown hair. His wrists were hidden in his sleeves. Perhaps he wore the match . . . though he looked more like the first man's servant. His coat was coarse drab cloth, his boots scuffed. The creature who held Thistle was richly dressed.

Lo took a step back, heart hammering. But . . . he was no fire daēva. Their blood ran hot — hotter even than mortals.

This was something new. Something she had never encountered before.

She met Thistle's eyes, glassy with terror, and knew what she had to do.

"If you want to leave before the guards board us," she snapped, "I'll need help."

"I'll do it," the brown-haired one offered.

He clambered to his feet. He had a heavy-lidded look about him, as if he'd tumbled out of bed after a night of carousing. His hair was carelessly pulled back and tied with a ribbon at his nape. But she had a feeling his wits were quicker than he let on.

"Watch her," the fire-wielder said. "No tricks."

The flames in his hand withered. He pressed Thistle to his chest and leapt tiger-like down into the hatch.

"Haul up the anchor," Lo said. "That." She pointed at the rope when he looked around cluelessly.

Sleepy-eyes dragged up the sandbag while she hoisted the mainsail. The wind caught the canvas, drawing it taut. The ship started plowing across the pond at a rapid clip. Lo waved at the shouting guards on shore, signaling that everything was fine. She couldn't make out their expressions, but they didn't seem to believe it. Three waded out to intercept the ship. Behind them, the trees bent double and the gale screamed like a tortured animal.

Thistle.

She tamped down her fury. Get aloft. That's all that mattered now.

But anger marred her concentration, and she miscalculated the angle of ascent. The prow lurched from the water, deck tilting. Sleepy-eyes had just let go of the anchor. He staggered straight into her arms. Luckily, Lo had her back braced against the mast. He blinked in surprise, so close she felt his breath on her cheek.

Warm breath, at least.

She planted a firm hand on his chest, but he was already scrambling away, grabbing desperately for the webbing of ropes, his eyes not so sleepy now.

"Not that one," she snapped, tearing the mainsheet from his grasp as the sails luffed and the ship rolled hard to starboard. "I *need* that one!"

He settled for clinging to the mast with arms and legs like it was a long-lost lover.

"Just stay out of my way," she muttered, and put all her attention on gaining enough altitude to clear the wall.

It loomed ahead, coming on fast.

"Climb," she whispered to the *Wind-Witch*. "Climb!"

Normally, Thistle would direct the wind to suit their navigational purpose. But he was mad with fear, and wild cross-currents buffeted the ship.

Clear the wall. That's all I'm asking.

Being only half-daēva, she wasn't strong in the elements. Only enough to tweak things a bit. Lo worried they wouldn't make it, but then a powerful gust came from below. She fancied she heard a faint scraping sound at the stern.

The pagodas and rope bridges of the aquarium blurred past below.

They'd cleared the wall.

"Can I do anything?" Sleepy-eyes shouted.

Lo ignored him. She eyed her harness but didn't buckle in.

Whatever the creature below was, he had power. When he'd wrapped her up in flows of air, she'd felt like poor Thistle, dangling helplessly.

Make me, he'd taunted.

Oh, how she'd tried! It was clear within seconds that he was many orders of magnitude stronger than she was. Lo knew she couldn't best him with magic. But she could crash the *Wind-Witch* into the sea. Let these would-be pirates swim to shore or go to a watery death, she didn't care which.

She'd survive. She always did.

Now, she used her meager power to make the air beneath the ship denser so it could be guided with the keel, as if they sailed through water. That was the real trick of a wind ship — steering. The aquarium fell behind and the long wharves of the port of Tjanjin appeared. Up and up the *Wind-Witch* climbed, into the flickering belly of the storm.

She turned. The man was watching her. His knuckles were white where he gripped the mast. Between the thumb and forefinger of his right hand, she saw a blue star.

Lo didn't ask his name. She didn't want to know it. But she did want to learn what she could about them in the few minutes they had left.

"What do you want my ship for?"

She willed him to answer quickly. With each second, they drew farther from shore.

He stared at her for a long moment. "Do the dead rise in your land?"

"What do you mean, *rise*?"

"Come back."

Lo blinked. "No."

"They do where I come from. I don't know why. They say its because our gates are broken."

He had a rapid manner of speech, with a lilting cadence that blurred the words together like a scroll left out in the rain.

"Is your friend . . . *dead*?" she asked cautiously.

A brief nod. "But he's not my friend."

Lo glanced down at the heaving, white-crested sea far below. *Now. Do it now.*

"Things are bad in my homeland," he said. "Your ship might save us."

She didn't look at him, reluctant to meet his eyes. "How?"

"Ask the Ducissa. She's a good woman and means you no harm."

Of course she doesn't. She just sent an Undead something-or-other to kidnap me and steal my ship.

Lo firmed her resolve. She'd never killed anyone before and didn't want to start now. The Undead one was . . . already dead. But she'd give the live one a fighting chance.

Lo gave him a raw look. "Can you swim?"

"Can I . . .?" He trailed off, studying her face. Tore one hand from the mast in a beseeching gesture. "No! Please don't—"

She released the web of denser air beneath the hull. Once Thistle was free of the Undead, he would fend for himself. He might not like water, but it didn't hurt him.

"What are you doing?" the man shouted.

An all-too-familiar weightlessness twisted her gut as the *Wind-Witch* dropped like a stone down a well. Lo twined her fingers in the rigging. The other hand held fast to the protective talisman on a chain around her neck. She readied herself to dive off at the last instant.

"Please, listen! I risked my life to find you! I came through the Dominion—"

She managed to lift the bow seconds before it plunged into the waves. The ship skimmed above the surface, so low that swells dashed against the hull, drenching them both in frigid saltwater. She rubbed her stinging eyes and twitched the reins of Air. They began to climb again. He sagged against the mast in relief.

"Did you say the Dominion?" she demanded.

He managed a nod. "Through a gate at the aquarium," he gasped.

She chewed her lip, watching the island of Tjanjin recede to the south. There *was* a gate in the aquarium, though few people knew that. He might be telling the truth.

Could a wind ship even cross the White Sea? It was uncharted territory.

But her parents had disappeared in the Dominion. Might they somehow have ended up in this strange land where the dead returned? She'd already looked everywhere else. In her heart, Lo knew that if she didn't find them soon, she never would.

"This problem," she said with a thoughtful frown. "Tell me more."

Chapter 12

"Lucius?"

Cas rapped on the door. There was no answer.

"I'm coming in," he said loudly.

He'd left the whatever-she-was up on deck. She'd questioned him for the last hour, asking about the dead and why so many of them rose again. When he mentioned necromancers, she looked more intrigued than horrified. Clearly she'd never met one.

Cas tried to answer her questions honestly. He told her that Lucius was a mortifex, one of the High Dead, but that he was bound to the Ducissa and did her bidding. When he tried to pose a few queries of his own, such as what her interest might be, she gave him a flat stare.

"Not until I get my cat," she said, and turned her back.

"I'll go check on it," he offered.

After nearly meeting the Drowned Woman himself, Cas was happy to go below. Thick clouds smothered the ship so he couldn't see how far it was down, a small mercy. But the unspoken threat that she would crash them into the sea again loomed over him. The woman didn't seem to care that she would die, too.

He pushed the door open.

"Lucius?"

"Leave me be," came the weak response.

Cas stepped inside the room. It was pitch black.

"Can you make a light?" he whispered.

"Go away."

"Do you still have the cat?"

Lucius gave another low moan. "That wretched creature—"

Cas startled as something brushed past his leg and shot down the corridor.

"There it goes," he said.

"Catch it," Lucius snapped.

Cas knew he ought to try. The cat seemed to be the one thing she cared about. He had no intention of letting Lucius harm it, but at least it gave them something to hold over her. But he hated the mortifex, ally or no, and wasn't about to follow his orders.

Besides which, he didn't think she'd turn back now. She was after something. Probably the people she'd come looking for in Tjanjin — though he had no idea why she wanted them, or why she thought they'd be in Aveline.

"No," he said. "Let her have it."

A lantern hanging from a hook burst into flame. Cas blinked in the sudden light. It must be the woman's room. Wet clothes hung over the back of a chair. The furnishings reminded him of the Ducissa's manor. Costly and rich. Was she a noble of some sort? The thought made him even more uneasy. Like any sane person, he had a healthy fear of angering the titled.

A hump at the edge of the bed must be the mortifex. Cas made his way over.

Lucius lay on his side, curled into a tight ball. His skin looked even more bloodless than usual.

"What do you want, Quietus?" he whispered, raising his head an inch from the pillow.

No flames burned in his eyes now. They were a clear emerald green, like the one who had killed Ma.

Cas's heart beat faster. For a moment, he was tempted to drag the fex from his lair and throw him over the rail. Could Lucius stop him? Maybe not. He looked terrible. It had to be all that raging water far below. He could tell the Ducissa it was an accident.

One less High Dead in the world to worry about.

But even the White Sea might not finish him. Orlaith would only summon him back. And then Cas would be in for a world of pain.

"I want to know what she is," he said. "She works magic like yours. But she's living. How?"

"I don't know."

As usual, he couldn't tell if Lucius was lying. The fex had centuries of practice at concealing his true emotions.

"She sure isn't human," Cas said.

The fex licked his lips. "I have a boon to ask, Quietus."

He turned away, walking to her writing desk. It was covered with ledgers with weights on top so they wouldn't slide around. He opened one and saw rows of numbers and what appeared to be cargo manifests. So she could read and write.

He set the ledger down and investigated a wardrobe. It was jammed with expensive-looking garments, though of a peculiar cut. His own reflection stared back from the inset mirrors. He leaned in, rubbing the stubble on his cheeks.

"And what would that be?" he asked.

The ship gave a sudden dip. He caught the door to steady himself. Lucius groaned.

"Banish me back to Aquitan," he begged.

Cas turned. "So *now* you want me to banish you?"

A sickly nod.

"I could." He smiled. "But I don't care to be left alone with her. Not when I don't know what she is."

The lantern flared, then sank low.

"Some kind of sorceress, obviously," Lucius rasped. "But I'm sure you can manage her."

"Sorceress," he repeated slowly. "Well, there's only two kinds of sorcery that I know of. *Your* kind." He glanced at the iron menotte. "And necromancy. But I see no signs of it. None of the usual trappings. Skulls and bones. Black mirrors. Poisonous herbs. Strange, don't you think?"

Lucius didn't reply.

"And here's another strange thing," he said conversationally, sinking into a chair and stretching his legs out. "If the sea makes you this sick, even leagues below, there's no way you could have flown this ship. I think you knew that all along. I think you deliberately waited for her to come back. But you didn't warn me. Why not?"

Lucius lay his head back down. He closed his eyes. "If you won't banish me, then go away."

The fex refused to speak again. Cas returned to the deck, making sure he had a firm grip on something with each step. The woman sat cross-legged at the bow. Her immense cat filled her lap. She was stroking its neck. It hissed when it saw him.

"Thank you," she said without looking at him.

"Don't thank me," he said. "It escaped on its own."

She did turn then. Her face was more relaxed, if unsmiling. It was stupid, but he couldn't help himself. He found her appealing. Not just the deep blue eyes and black hair, which he'd always had a weakness for. It was the air of mystery.

And the utter competence.

"How do you fly the wind ship?" he asked.

"If you don't need me anymore," she replied evenly, "who's to say you won't toss me overboard?"

Cas frowned. "I would never do that—"

"I know nothing about you." She looked away. "But I'm not telling you how my ship works."

"It's magic, isn't it? Like when you made the deck move."

She made a scoffing noise. "I did nothing of the sort. If I knew magic, do you really think I'd be sitting here as your hostage?"

He gave her a hard stare. "I didn't imagine it."

"You mean when I used my quarterstaff?" she asked innocently.

"No. Just before that."

"I have no idea what you're referring to."

He studied her profile. She had a long nose with high cheekbones and a firm chin. Her brows were straight and dark, and she had a cleft at the center of her upper lip that made it poke out the littlest bit.

He decided to let it lie for the moment. "Will you tell me your name at least?"

A long pause. "Delilah."

"Mine is Castelio."

No sign she'd even heard. They were moving with the wind, at exactly the same speed, and it felt like the ship stood still, or drifted in the doldrums of a dark ocean. It made him think of the stormless sea in the prayer to Kaethe that he whispered every night before he slept. Clouds billowed around them, leaving a coating of dew on every surface. It made the deck even more treacherous.

"Do you need to sleep?" he asked, after the silence grew unbearable.

"I catch my rest here and there," she replied vaguely.

"Lucius is in your bedchamber, but I could kick him out if you want it back."

"It's called a cabin. You might as well learn something about the ship you've stolen. And yes, I would like it back."

He smiled and swept a bow. "As you command, captain."

That was one order he'd be happy to carry out.

"Wait!" she called as he moved away. "You said you came through the Dominion."

He nodded. "I passed through Seagate. Lucius told me the route through the shadowlands to the gate that led back out to Tjanjin."

"So you have no idea how far it is on this side to Aveline?"

"Not really," he admitted. "But I do know it's due north from Tjanjin. A straight line."

She propped her chin on one fist and returned to stroking the cat.

As Cas was about to leave, he thought he saw lightning flicker in the depths of its yellow eyes.

Chapter 13

Five days later, Lo sighted the blue haze of mountains in the distance.

She was up in the crow's nest with Thistle, who had allowed the storm to disperse so she could watch for land. Their stores were nearly gone. The mortifex didn't eat but Castelio did. Never more than his fair share, but Lo hadn't planned for a long sea journey with extra passengers. She was starting to worry when the rugged coastline came into view.

The other side of the world! She felt a thrill of victory, followed by trepidation. Castelio insisted that his mistress meant her no harm, but Lo didn't believe him. If the dead rose in Aveline — and the mortifex was clear evidence that they did — it must be a grim place.

"When we land, you must tell them that you are the Khamoun of Samarqand," Thistle hissed in her ear.

"Khamoun?" she repeated. "What does that mean?"

"An old title, no longer in use. But I crept down to the hold and overheard them talking. They hold great store by such things here. If they think you are important, they will treat you better. Out of fear, if nothing else."

"This Ducissa Orlaith, you mean?"

"Yes. They know little about the Greeks or Persians. Tell them your uncle is the king."

"But why would they believe me?"

He sank his claws into her leg. "Has Javid not taught you the ways of royalty?"

The Persian court practiced a nearly infinite number of rules governing decorum. Lo knew them all. As Javid's trade emissary, she had to.

"Perhaps I should have begun the ruse a bit earlier," she said dryly.

She had shunned Castelio's attempts at conversation. He was the enemy. He had lured her on false pretenses. Threatened that foolish fisherman. But he had such an easy way about him, she'd found herself sharing a meal on several occasions. He'd done all the cooking. Did anything she told him to without complaint.

And those sleepy eyes *had* concealed a keen intelligence. It didn't take him long to learn his way around the ship and the proper names for things. He still blanched when he looked down but so did every passenger. It's why captains and crew earned a premium wage.

"What Castelio thinks does not matter," Thistle growled. "The mortifex is a far greater concern. But he has not seen you nor spoken to you since we left."

Lucius was somewhere in the hold. By unspoken agreement, only Castelio went in there to fetch supplies. She felt a queasy sensation when the mortifex was near. A tingling chill in her left hand.

Now, Lo turned the idea over in her mind. If it didn't work, she would be no worse off. But if she managed to pull off the imposture, she might keep her ship. Castelio claimed they only wished to study the design.

What troubled her most was the iron cuff she had seen around the mortifex's wrist. The thing Castelio called a *menotte*. Long before she was born, similar cuffs had been used to trap and enslave daēvas. It was how her parents met each other. After her father was freed, they had chosen to keep their own cuffs. They called it their *bond*.

Which was very close to what he'd said about Lucius.

That he was *bound* to the Ducissa.

It was obvious Castelio didn't know she was part daēva. He seemed bewildered by her ability to fly the ship. So there were no daēvas in Aveline.

But if they learned the truth about her, and they already had the means to control her power . . .

Well, she might never leave this place.

Lo knew it was a risk. A big one. But she'd never been averse to risk. Not when so much was at stake.

"That is sound advice," she said, stroking the cat's ears. "I will try my best."

"And I will make myself scarce," Thistle replied, licking his lips. "Every keep has mice."

She smiled faintly and climbed down through the rigging to forge letters from her dear uncle, the king of Samarqand.

THE *WIND-WITCH* KEPT to the Umbra for the first part of the journey overland — what Castelio called the Boundary. The twilight lands between light and dark. This was for Lucius's benefit. The sun would burn his skin, even a single ray through the small portholes of the hold.

With Castelio's guidance, she turned west at the last minute, crossing a wide river he named the Forkings. From the air, the enormous statue of the goddess they called Kaethe was a sight to behold — before rainclouds enveloped the ship again.

Lo landed in a fallow field behind the manor house. She hauled up the keel at the last moment, but the vessel still dug a deep furrow in the black soil. Like her father, she was strongest in earth. It had been easy to increase the drag at the bow and stop the *Wind-Witch* before it struck the curtain wall.

They'd hardly ground to a listing halt when Lucius appeared. The hood of his cloak was raised. Lo caught a flash of white skin before he vaulted over the side and took off in a blur for the manor house. Moments later, people appeared from the same direction, both servants and soldiers in conical helmets.

Castelio helped to lower the sails. His cheeks were flushed with triumph — and relief to be on solid ground again, no doubt. He turned to her with a boyish grin.

"That was quite the landing, Delilah," he exclaimed. "Her Grace will surely fete you with a banquet tonight!"

Her lips started to curl in an answering smile before she remembered herself.

I am the haughty Khamoun of Samarqand.

"You may fetch my baggage," she said, lifting her chin. "It's in my cabin."

His smile faltered and she felt a moment's regret, but then he simply nodded and ducked into the hatch.

She smoothed her skirts and descended the rope ladder. Her best gown was plum velvet with a snug bodice and long, tight sleeves. The gold-mesh belt around her waist was echoed by threads of gold embroidery at her neckline. It was nothing like the royal costumes worn at the court in Samarqand, which were loose and flowing, but Orlaith couldn't know that.

The air of normalcy reassured her. Workers toiled in lush vineyards, straw hats pulled low against the drizzle. Lo marched off to meet the approaching soldiers without a backward glance. Castelio caught up before she reached them, puffing under the burden of a large trunk.

"I require a horse at once!" she called out in an imperious tone. "The mud is ruining my slippers!"

Castelio shot her a confused look. He'd seen her moving barefoot about the deck in a shirt and trousers only a few hours before.

"Do as she asks," he said to the soldiers. "Is Her Grace in residence?"

They'd paused to goggle at the *Wind-Witch.*

"Ah, yes, Quietus," one said, gathering his wits. "She's been informed of your arrival."

"Take this luggage, will you?"

The men took charge of her trunk, then passed it to the servants — young girls, Lo noticed with a frown — who began to lug it back to the house, each taking a side. She stood straight-backed in the rain, gazing into the middle distance, while one of the soldiers left to find a horse. The rest beelined for the ship.

"No one is to board without permission," she called after them sternly. "It's my private vessel. A gift from my uncle."

They looked at Castelio, who nodded.

"Can we look at the outside?" one asked.

She gave him the thousand-yard stare the real king of Samarqand deployed when a courtier displeased him. The man visibly withered. She might have a talent for this.

"You may look," she said, enunciating each word with icy precision. "Not touch."

He knuckled his forehead and trotted off.

"Where's your cat?" Castelio asked, looking around.

"You know cats." She waved a hand. "Always off somewhere."

Silence descended. She gazed at the house, tapping one toe impatiently.

"It's not a long walk," he began. "We could—"

"I'll wait," she interrupted.

He shrugged. "Personally, I'd be glad to stretch my legs after days of confinement. But have it your way." He pointed. "Those are the vineyards. You'll taste the wine they make at the Ducissa's table. I'm not much of a drinking man, but I hear it's very—"

"You needn't wait with me," she said brusquely. "I am certain you have things to attend to."

His gaze narrowed. "Then I won't," he said. "Enjoy your ride."

Lo watched him stride off, dark hair caught in a horsetail at his nape. He paused to pluck a flower, sniff it, and tuck it behind one ear. She caught the whistled notes of a cheerful tune, sharp and clear.

What Castelio thinks doesn't matter.

Well, it didn't, did it? With luck, she'd never see him again.

An instant later, Thistle leapt to her shoulder.

"You did well," he hissed in her ear.

"Thus far," she agreed. "Now I must handle the Ducissa. And I doubt she will be so easily cowed."

THE MANOR WAS MUCH LARGER than it appeared from a distance. Lo had seen only one angle of it from the field, but other wings sprawled out in different directions like the hive of some giant insect. The main stone structure occupied a hilltop, with tiered additions attached to the central axis.

Some parts looked ancient, with thick walls broken only by tiny slits that spoke of wars past. But the newer parts had rows of broad windows, all shining with warm yellow lamplight.

Two mounted soldiers escorted her to the front doors. Lo almost slid from the saddle herself before she remembered that a noblewoman would demand assistance.

"Fetch a block," she snapped.

This was brought, and one of the soldiers offered his hand.

"Lady?" he asked respectfully.

She swallowed a laugh. There was no real difference between them. Only her demeanor and manner of speech. But that was enough to give her a title, even though she'd yet to play her trump card.

She accepted the aid without comment and was given to a steward, who bowed and led her into the manor, where the Ducissa Orlaith herself stood waiting.

With Lucius.

A thin, gray daylight spilled into the antechamber, but heavy clouds obscured the sun and he seemed untroubled by it. Lo had hoped the mortifex would be too exhausted from the journey to attend his mistress.

"I am afraid you have the better of me," the Ducissa said in a polite but neutral tone. "I don't know your name."

So Castelio hadn't told either of them. She felt a flicker of surprise, then made herself focus.

This was the tricky part. First impressions mattered a great deal. Giving offense could be fatal. The woman didn't know her rank — supposed rank — yet. Some degree of deference was required. But a khamoun was near on par with a princess.

Lo settled for a slight curtsy. She wondered where Castelio had gotten to.

"Delilah of House Dessarian," she replied in her best regal tone. "Guardian of the Nine Seals, Daughter of the West Wind, the Khamoun of Samarqand."

Silence greeted this statement.

Orlaith glanced at Lucius. He had changed into dark silks and velvets that made his pallor even more extreme. A spark lit in his eyes. Not an actual flame — no, something else.

Amusement.

Her throat dried.

The mortifex *knew*. Of course he did.

Castelio admitted that Lucius was the one who'd invented the story to claim the reward. Who had known exactly how to lure her to Tjanjin. Castelio did the dirty work, but it was the mortifex who fed him the information. Clearly, he knew a great deal about her.

How could she possibly have overlooked that?

But five days with little rest had scattered her wits. Lo gathered power, ready to unleash her worst and make a run for the *Wind-Witch*, when Lucius dropped to one knee, head bowed.

"Khamoun," he said softly. "It shames me that I did not realize your rank. But I was . . . indisposed. Please forgive any liberties I might have taken, Princess."

Shock twitched one of Lo's eyebrows before she composed her face to stillness.

Not only was he playing along — he knew what the word meant.

How?

Thistle might know. She would ask him when he showed up.

"There is nothing to forgive," she said graciously.

Orlaith's eyes widened a fraction, but she was quick to find her feet.

"You do us an honor then," she said quickly, making a brief curtsy. "Let us speak more in private, my lady."

She turned and made a sharp gesture at the servants standing behind her.

"See that the khamoun's baggage is taken to our finest guest chamber."

"Yes, Your Grace," a chorus echoed.

They hurried off. Lo released a slow breath as Lucius rose to his feet. He held her gaze for a long moment. She read volumes in it and didn't much like the message.

I owe him now.

A smile touched the corner of his thin lips. It faded when the Ducissa turned to him.

They spoke quietly for a moment, heads bent together in such an intimate fashion that Lo wondered . . . but no. Would she really bed such a creature? Even now, the chill emanating from his skin was palpable. Orlaith wore black from head to toe, including a loose hood that covered her hair, though Lo could see golden strands framing her face. The only adornment was the iron cuff around her wrist. Just like the one Lucius wore.

Her gut twisted looking at it.

Then he bowed and withdrew, and she accompanied the Ducissa to a study down the hall. It was bright and airy, with pale wood and white walls. Delilah paused to admire a large standing clock that judged the hour by the position of the three moons moving across its face, each a different size and traced in gold and silver.

"That has been in the Redvayne family for centuries," Orlaith said, as a servant poured chalices of wine.

"It's beautiful," Lo said, moving closer to examine it. "In my land, we call the moons Selene, Artemis, and Hecate."

The servant withdrew. They sat down opposite each other, quietly assessing.

"The names are the same here," Orlaith replied.

"How could that be?" Lo asked, surprised. "I had not heard of Aveline before. There is no trade between us."

The Ducissa smiled. "And yet we speak the same tongue."

Lo had already considered that, of course. The Ducissa's accent was different from Castelio's. Softer and more easily understood. Sometimes his words tumbled out so fast, Lo could barely follow them.

"We derive from a common root," she said with a frown. "But who came first?"

"Yours," Orlaith said. She leaned forward, curiosity in her eyes. "Our blood comes from those who fled here in ships a thousand years ago. I can only assume by your presence that the demons lost the war?"

"Demons?" Lo repeated uncertainly.

"Those who sought to burn the world."

"Ah. *Those* demons."

She knew Orlaith meant the Vatra daēvas. Their descendants lived in the desert now. Once, long before, their mad king had gone to war against the other daēva clans. Even the mortal cities were swept up in it. The conflict had only ended when a great magic was worked that stopped the sun in the sky and divided the land between light and dark. The king and his followers were walled away in a prison called the Kiln.

"I feared Lucius was one of them," she admitted.

Orlaith blinked. "But he is."

The truth landed with a clunk in her thick brain.

He *was* a daēva. A dead one.

Lo gave a little gasp. "And you don't fear him?" she asked innocently, widening her eyes.

"You misunderstand. He is loyal. But you never answered my question. What became of the demons?"

No mention of the menotte. Lo sipped her wine, washing away the sour taste.

"Oh, they killed each other off." She waved her chalice. "They're all gone now. Tales to frighten children."

Orlaith frowned. "Is that so? I am glad then. Our ancestors hailed from the kingdom of Eddyn. Have you heard of it?"

Lo shook her head. "Where was this realm?"

"In the northwest. Near the demons' capital."

"I'm sorry. That land is barren desert since the war."

The Ducissa did not seem surprised. "But your home is also severed in twain, I assume?" she asked. "Between night and day?"

"Naturally. We call the two sides Nocturne and Solis. Samarqand lies in the latter."

Orlaith nodded and cleared her throat. "Forgive my ignorance, but I have not yet seen Castelio. He found you at my bidding. I hope . . . er . . ." She faltered.

Lo let her dangle for a moment. "That I have not taken offense at being boarded by reavers and kidnapped to a strange land?"

Orlaith took a hasty gulp of wine. "That was not my intent, khamoun. I hoped to procure a wind ship, yes, but—"

"Sometimes our loyal servants take matters into their own hands and go too far to please us," Lo interrupted. "But that is their error of judgment, not ours."

The Ducissa nodded fervently. "I see you understand."

"The *Wind-Witch* was a gift from my uncle, the king. If it can aid you, I am happy to allow carpenters to examine the design."

"Thank you," Orlaith said quietly.

Lo smiled. She held up her chalice. "This is a robust vintage.

From your own vineyards, I understand. A toast to new friendship between our realms!"

"I would welcome that," the Ducissa said, raising her own cup. "We are beset."

"So I heard." She formed her lips into a moue of distaste. "By the risen dead? Truly?"

"I see your land does not share this affliction," the Ducissa said with bitterness. "It is the fault of the necromancers across the mountains. They're the ones who broke the gates and angered Kaethe. Always, it has been so, but in recent years the problem has worsened."

"And you believe my ship could help you? How?"

"Not *your* ship, khamoun, but a fleet of wind ships." Her face shone with determination. "I weary of doing nothing while they punish us with hordes of spirits. If I had a force capable of crossing the mountains . . . well, I would finish the work my late husband, the Duc, began. Rout them from their foul keeps and restore peace and prosperity to my land. The people suffer greatly. I do what I can, but it is never enough."

Lo made a noise of sympathy. "And I imagine you take the blame."

Orlaith sat back. She looked weary. "I don't care what they think of me. I only want an end to this plague."

A noble sentiment, thought Lo. And one that rang false. She had yet to meet a ruler who didn't secretly fear being deposed.

"But enough of our difficulties," Orlaith said with a forced smile. "Tell me more of Samarqand. Is it normal for a khamoun to travel without a retinue of servants?"

The question was asked in a light tone, but it felt like a test.

"No, but I do as I please," Lo replied carelessly.

"Surely, they must worry for your safety."

"Yes, of course. But none dare to question me. I have taken jaunts alone on many occasions." She heaved a little sigh. "To be frank, Your Grace, sometimes I weary of the endless audiences and petitioners. The court can be dreadfully dull."

She launched into a lengthy explanation of the various customs and rules of etiquette, the different ranks housed within the inner and outer royal households, and all the duties expected of a khamoun. By the time she finished, Orlaith's polite smile had grown fixed. She kept glancing discreetly at the clock.

"That does sound tedious," she said.

"I escaped to visit my dear friend, Princess Pingyang of Tjanjin." Lo gave a rueful smile. "It was within the grounds of the palace that I encountered your agents."

She prayed Orlaith wouldn't press her about the details of the trap they'd set, but the Ducissa seemed eager to move on.

"If I may ask, how is the ship carried aloft? It would be of no use to me to replicate the design if I lack the means of propulsion."

Her eyes grew sharper. But Lo had expected this question.

"The secret," she said, lowering her voice to a conspiratorial whisper, "is in the wood. A special resin that makes it as light as the bones of a bird. Of course, there are various other mechanisms. Ballast and counterweights. It is a complex vessel."

She only needed to buy a little time. Learn what she could about these necromancers — and then pay them a visit herself. If her parents were held captive somewhere in Aveline, Lo doubted it would be in this manor house.

"It is a marvelous contraption," Orlaith said. "You must show me—"

She broke off at a rap on the door. It opened before she could speak, and a boy entered the study. He had dark blond hair and wore a doublet of red and gold. The resemblance between them was obvious.

His eyes widened when he saw Lo. "Caino said she was in here!"

"Enrigo," his mother said sternly. "Mind your manners."

He reddened and gave a bow. "Apologies, my lady," he said in such a formal tone, Lo couldn't help but smile. "I have intruded."

A stout older man with a white beard bustled in behind him, cheeks puffing. "Your Grace! The boy got away from me."

Orlaith rose. After a moment, Lo followed suit.

"Lady Dessarian, allow me to present Duc Caino Scalici of Alessia."

She inclined her head.

"A great pleasure indeed," he said warmly.

"And my son, Enrigo." She eyed him with maternal forbearance. "Whom you have already met."

"And where is Alessia?" Lo asked. "You must forgive my ignorance, Duc. I am a stranger to these parts."

"First duchy east of the mountains," he replied. "I will find you a map, khamoun, so you might acquaint yourself with Aveline."

She didn't need to feign confusion. "But I was under the impression that the eastern duchies were the source of . . . the troubles."

"Not Alessia," Orlaith said. "The Duc is our stalwart ally." Her face darkened. "It is those beyond his borders who practice the black arts."

The Duc gave a weak smile. "Let us not speak of politics. I am sure the khamoun would like to rest from her journey."

"May I have permission to view the wind ship?" Enrigo asked hopefully.

No doubt that was the reason he'd come barging in.

"The khamoun has requested that we do not board it—" his mother began.

"Which means I will have to lead the tour myself," Lo said with a smile, eager to be gone from the study.

Enrigo looked delighted. "That is very kind," Orlaith said. "Are you certain you're up to it? He can wait until tomorrow . . ."

"Not at all. It would be my pleasure."

And I will be sure they see the letters from my "uncle" that I left strewn across my desk.

The Duc offered her his arm. Lo took it. "I have always

dreamt of flying," he confided as they walked to the door, "but I tend to fall at the last moment and wake with a terrible start."

"I can assure you," she replied, "my vessel would keep you snug as a babe in arms."

He laughed and she found herself liking him. When she glanced back, the Ducissa was watching her with a considering look.

"Will you join us, Your Grace?" Lo asked.

Orlaith's smile didn't touch her blue eyes. "I wish I could. But I'm afraid I have other matters to attend to."

Chapter 14

Cas read the letter for the third time.

Esme had presented him with it when he came in through the kitchens. "I've been saving it for you, Cas," she said, then blushed furiously when he grinned and arched a brow. She was a comely lass, but he'd sworn not to sire bastards and that's all he could ever give her.

Esme knew this, but a little flirting never hurt anyone.

"Why is there a flower in your hair?" She pretended a pout. "Are you courting someone?"

He'd colored himself and plucked it out, having forgotten it was there. "For you," he'd said with a formal bow. "The rose of Aquitan."

Esme gave him a playful swat and returned to her mending.

He'd hurried to the soldiers' barracks in the old south wing, where he kept a chamber. It had little besides a bed and washbasin since he was almost never there. Then he eagerly broke the seal and took it to the narrow window where the light was better.

Dearest brother,

I have exciting news to impart. The seneschal of the new Duc of Cavet has offered me a position in the scriptorium

of his household. He promised to find places for Da and Teo, too. This good fortune came about through the aid of our cousin, who is third steward to the Earl of Davalos. Brother, I can scarcely believe it! When next you come to Prydwen, you will find us at the Duc's palace. I hope that day is not far off. All of us are well, though we miss you sorely.
Your Loving Sister,
Filippa

Cas folded the letter, wishing she'd written more. The script was flowing and perfect, with none of the inky blots of his own scrawled missives. He was not surprised that Lippa was rising in station. She'd devoted herself single-mindedly to her letters. It was only a matter of time before someone important noticed how clever she was.

A full year had passed since he saw his family last — the longest gap yet. Things had gotten too bad for him to be spared from his duties. Sometimes he felt like he was trying to hold back a crumbling dam with leaks in a dozen places. Every time a hole was plugged, a new one broke open.

He feared the day the whole thing collapsed.

At first, he'd visited Prydwen every few months, though it was a long journey. The gold from the bounty saw his family settled in a nice little cottage, with enough left over to hire a tutor for both Lippa and Teo. Everything seemed ideal, until he learned that Da was still drinking — and dicing, too. Cas had been shocked to the core at that. He would never have imagined it of his father.

Da's debts eventually cost them the house, and they'd been living on what Cas could send. He prayed Da wouldn't muck up this new opportunity. But it wasn't his father he blamed the most.

Every evil that had befallen them could be traced back to that one night.

Back to the mortifex who'd killed Ma.

Cas remembered its face. He'd encountered a few since but not that one.

Someday, he hoped to cross paths with it again. The creature would not find him such easy prey next time.

He tucked the letter away with all the others she'd sent. Then he changed the dressing on his hand, which was healing cleanly, laced up a clean cami, and went in search of the Ducissa. By the time he found her steward, he was told that Orlaith was in her study with the foreigner and couldn't be disturbed.

So he grabbed a bite to eat in the kitchens, where he caught up with the latest news. It was dire. A Quietus named Edgard had died the week before, touched by a lich. That left eleven of them to patrol the entire duchy, from the mountains to the sea.

He pushed the broth away, appetite gone. Edgard had been seventeen.

He'd hoped to see Gui, but he was out in the field, along with the rest of them. Cas returned to his room to wait for a summons. It came not long after.

"Your Grace." He bent a knee.

Age had only increased her pale beauty. For the first two years, he'd been dumbstruck in her presence, stammering replies on those rare occasions she inquired about his progress. She had never given a hint that she noticed his awkwardness and he finally got over it.

Cas knew this was partly due to his work. Mastering fear was an essential part of being a Quietus. He realized now how lucky he'd been not to have died in Swanton, with his boyish swagger and pocketful of nails. If anything more serious than a regular spirit had passed through, he would have been, as the wit in the reeve's jail had put it, well and truly fecked.

"Castelio," she said warmly. "I am relieved to have you back. It is a great thing you have done for the realm."

"Thank you, Your Grace. I am pleased to be of service."

Orlaith seemed restless. She moved aimlessly about the study, black skirts rustling.

"Tell me, how does the ship work?"

"I'm not sure, Your Grace. It uses sails and a keel, like a regular seafaring vessel."

The Ducissa paused and eyed him frankly. "Is she a necromancer?"

He hesitated, choosing his words with care. "I don't believe she is. I searched every inch of the ship. There was naught but supplies and regular cargo."

Delilah claimed it was his imagination when the planks of the deck had bucked and made him lose his balance. He knew it wasn't, but he hadn't seen her repeat the trick. If he accused her of necromancy . . . Well, that was never a charge he made lightly.

He considered mentioning the cat. There was something odd about the creature. Perhaps it was the feline equivalent of a mortifex? But animals never returned from beyond the Veil. And how would she bind it? It wore no collar, and she didn't wear a menotte.

"She claims to be the Khamoun of Samarqand," Orlaith said, dragging him back to the present.

"Khamoun?" His brow furrowed.

"So she never mentioned it to you."

"No, Your Grace. She barely spoke to me."

Orlaith tapped her fingers. "Perhaps she feared being ransomed."

Ransomed? He felt a prickle of unease. "What is a khamoun? Some kind of merchant?"

"A princess, apparently. She says her uncle is the king."

The ground tilted under his feet. "The king?" he echoed faintly.

"She could be telling the truth," Orlaith said, speaking half to herself now. "I'm certain she's highborn. She knew a great deal about the court." Her lips thinned. "Of course, it could all be a clever ruse. But if it isn't, Samarqand would make a valuable ally. I can't risk making an error. We will treat her as if she is indeed a princess until proven otherwise."

He nodded, mind racing. Highborn? Delilah was educated, certainly, and rich. But he'd never known a noble to scramble barefoot through rigging or break their fast with a commoner. Her manner had been cool but not high-handed. Not until they arrived. Then she was a different person.

"I want you to watch her closely," Orlaith said. "Her rooms are in the old astronomy tower. Ensure she doesn't leave them."

He bowed. "Aye, Your Grace."

"That's all, Castelio." She gave him a taut smile. "We'll learn the truth soon enough, I'm sure."

Chapter 15

Delilah's chambers were large and luxurious, with heavy fustian brocade and gold candelabras.

They were also tucked away high in one of the old turrets. It was quite inconvenient for escaping.

She stood at the narrow window, gazing at the *Wind-Witch*. It sat in the field about half a league distant. Her keen eyes picked out a dozen of Orlaith's soldiers watching the ship.

How she longed to be alone on deck again, listening to the crisp snap of the sails. She was adept at dealing with others — that was all Javid's tutoring — but she preferred solitude. Lo was happiest in the sky, with none but Thistle for company. He only spoke when he had something worthwhile to say. She wished more people would follow his example.

Now, a light touch brushed her leg. "There you are," she exclaimed.

Thistle gave her an affectionate butt with his head, then leapt to the bed and began to wash himself.

"Would you like to know what I've learned?" she asked.

A slow blink.

"Oh, the intrigues," she said dryly, sitting on the stone sill.

"They make the cutthroat court at Samarqand seem tame by comparison."

Orlaith had feted her at a six-course supper with all her minor nobles. No Lucius, no Castelio. Lo stuck to one cup of wine. Conversation centered on complaints about the dead and the related topic of the wicked necromancers across the Mizzly Mountains.

Duc Caino Scalici, she gathered, was on amicable terms with all the duchies. As promised, he'd presented her with a map, which gave a better picture of the various alliances. There were two duchies east of his own — Vendagni and Nyons. Orlaith despised them both. They openly practiced necromancy and she blamed them for inflicting the dead on her own realm.

Lo suspected she would have invaded already save for the fact that Caino Scalici's duchy stood in her way. It stretched the length of the Boundary east of the mountains and he wouldn't permit foreign troops to march across his borders. This was understandable, since the poor Duc was sandwiched between hostile realms and walked a fine line keeping them both from his throat.

All this she learned from a minor earl on his fifth cup of wine.

"And what are the names of these dread necromancers of Nyons?" Lo had asked breathlessly, leaning into a cloud of stale breath.

"Chaos and Caul Courtenay," the earl replied, his accent so thickened by drink she was forced to read his lips, another skill Javid had taught her. "Twin sisters and scarcely past girlhood" — he waggled a bejeweled finger — "but no less depraved for it. Their parents fell at the Battle of Hellgate, the same day the good Duc Redvayne did. They've been plotting their revenge ever since."

"Oh, they sound *awful*," she whispered. "Are there many necromancers in Nyons?"

"Well, the black arts are legal there." His chins wobbled with disapproval. "The capital Mystral is a haven for every traitor and hedge necromancer cast out of the Sun Courts."

"What of Vendagni?"

"Nathan Ouvrard holds sway there. Another young upstart. He comes from a long line of sorcerers. All the way back to the founding of Aveline. T'was his distant ancestor who bound the first mortifex."

"Fascinating," Lo murmured. "How did he manage it?"

The earl's eyes dropped to her bosom, then reluctantly climbed to her face again.

"Went through one of the gates. Came back with the menotte and a fex wearing its match. It still serves the family."

"Do they all have mortifexes?"

"Aye, my lady. Their magic is the lifeblood of the Moon Courts. Naught would grow there without it."

"So it is not a frozen wasteland?"

"I've never been there myself, but I hear tell it's forested. Teeming with all manner of infernal creatures." His bleary eyes shone with righteous conviction. "But one day, Bel will return and burn them all to ash, mark my words. The Ducissa will see it done."

After spilling this juicy gossip, the earl had clumsily fondled her knee under the tablecloth, at which point she stood and announced that she was exhausted from her travels and wished to retire.

"We must leave tonight," she said to Thistle. "Before this Ducissa discovers what I am. She's a clever woman. I think she is only playing along to hedge her bets. But if Lucius tells her what he knows, we're done for."

Thistle leapt down from the bed and sauntered to the door. He began pawing at it.

"Will you go to Mystral with me?" Lo asked. "I thought we could hire one of these hedge necromancers. A reputable one. We still have the reward that was never collected in Tjanjin." She patted the lacy front of her gown, where the silver talisman was hidden. "And this. I'm willing to trade it if the information is solid."

"How will you know?" Thistle growled.

"I'm not sure yet. But if it seems they're trying to take advantage, you can do your trick with the shadow. I think even a necromancer would think twice."

The cat said nothing, but he seemed to be smiling.

Lo abandoned the trunk of fancy clothes without a backward glance. Her usual attire of shirt and trousers was aboard the *Wind-Witch*, and all she wanted at the moment was to change and be gone from Aquitan.

"We'll need cover," she said. "Could you . . . ?"

Lightning flared through the window, followed by a deep cannonade of thunder. An instant later, the heavens opened in a deluge.

Thistle switched his tail. Lightning flashed again, mirrored in his yellow eyes.

No one had approached the chamber since she entered and the door swung open freely. She slipped down the winding turret stairs, Thistle a shadow at her heels. It was an old part of the keep and the steps were worn to a slope in the middle. The bottom held a chapel to the Drowned Woman that Lo found unsettling. It had a miniature of the icon they had passed in the town, except that whatever mechanism made the water flow seemed to be broken, so her mouth gaped in a silent scream.

Halfway down, Lo stopped next to a funny little door. She'd noticed it when the servant led her up the stairs.

"What is this?" she'd asked, tracing a fingertip across the age-blackened wood.

"A bolt hole for the nuns, milady," the girl had replied. "T'was their convent once."

"What were they running from?" Lo asked.

"The sons of Bel. There were many raids in those days."

"Bel is the sun god?"

"Aye, milady."

She'd tried the handle and found it locked.

"That leads into the main keep," the girl had said.

"Do you have the key?"

"No, milady."

Now she pressed her ear to the wood. Hearing nothing, she used a thread of earth power to open it.

"I'm sure the Ducissa has a guard posted below," she whispered to Thistle. "We'll go this way. Find another route out."

The bolt hole was tucked into a shallow ell so it would be invisible from the main passage. A wide gallery lay around the corner, with tapestries along one side and broad windows on the other. It was quiet save for the drumming of rain against the glass. She peered through one of the windows. A muddy courtyard sat below. Beyond lay the stables. It was a full three stories down, too far to jump—

"Going somewhere, my lady?"

She nearly jumped out of her skin. Lo spun around and bit back a vile sailor's oath. How on earth had he managed to sneak up on her? She was still wearing the tight-bodiced velvet gown from supper and wished she'd taken the time to change into something looser. Something easier to fight in.

"Do you make it a habit of creeping about?" she asked imperiously.

Castelio swept a low bow. "Just keeping you safe, khamoun."

He was a head taller, but she did her best to stare down her nose at him. "The Ducissa sent you to shadow me, didn't she?"

"It *is* her manor, my lady."

"Am I a prisoner here?" she demanded.

The slight pause was answer enough. "Of course not. But fell things can walk in a storm like this."

Right on cue, a powerful gust rattled the windowpanes.

"I thought the manor was protected."

"It is. Are you looking for something?" His tone was all innocence.

"My cat. He seems to have disappeared."

Castelio glanced around. "Then I'll help you find him."

She suppressed a sigh. "He's shy of people he doesn't know. And he doesn't like you. You'll only be a hindrance."

He gazed at her, implacable. "Nonetheless—"

Lo heard soft footsteps approaching from the crossing corridor. Her left hand began to tingle. She felt the powerful sensation of something wrong.

Lucius.

She grabbed Castelio by the arm and dragged him into the alcove, pushing him against the bolt hole door. He'd shaved his beard and smelled of soap. Those drowsy brown eyes widened in surprise. He had thick brows and even thicker lashes.

"Begging your pardon, my lady," he stammered, "but I'm already wed to the Drowned Woman—"

"I don't want a *tryst*, you oaf," she hissed. "Can't you feel it?" Lo stepped away and rubbed her arms. "The chill?"

He shook his head, but he looked wary now.

They peeked around the corner. It was not Lucius but three of Orlaith's guards. One carried a squirming sack. A muffled sob came from within. It sounded like a child. He gave the sack a vicious cuff and it fell silent.

Fury stirred. She opened her mouth to confront them, but Castelio gripped her arm and pressed a finger to his lips. He looked so calm, the next word came as a shock.

Wraiths, he mouthed.

Then she saw their solid black eyes, like chips of obsidian.

Lo had heard of such creatures, though her mother called them wights. Spirits strong enough to possess a living body. One had taken Mama's sister when she was a little girl.

Castelio silently drew a pair of iron knives from his belt.

She sensed the gathering of power, though it didn't feel like magic — not the way most people understood the word. But she recognized the look in his eyes, both detached and intensely focused. Lo felt the same when she was in the midst of a complex aerial maneuver with a thunderstorm raging all around. Castelio had gone to his own Nexus.

The footsteps drew closer, then stopped. Deep in the shadows of the ell, Lo watched them untie the sack. A head popped out, gasping for air. Dark blond. The heir, Enrigo Redvayne.

"Where's the cart?" one of the wraiths growled.

"It will come."

The boy sniffled and the soldier gripped his chin. "Not another peep."

He nodded, terrified.

Castelio stepped out to the gallery. Three heads turned.

"Unhand the boy," he said. "In Kaethe's name!"

He sketched a symbol in the air, a nine-pointed star traced in blue light like the tattoo on his hand. The wraiths shrank away from it. Then the symbol faded and chaos erupted.

"Castelio!" Enrigo cried. He leapt from the sack. For a moment, it tangled around his feet, and then he was running like a jackrabbit down the gallery in the opposite direction. One of the soldiers took off after him. The other two ran at Castelio. The first to arrive got a vial of Kaethe's Tears in his face. The wraith screamed, clawing at its skin. The second drew a pale dagger and lunged. Castelio got his own blade up just in time to parry it.

Their forms blurred together. Lo was about to help him when a sudden dizziness buckled her knees. The walls shimmered. She was gripped by the idea that they were a flimsy stage setting, like the dramatic performances at the agora in Delphi, and something else waited beyond. Close enough to see, if she only reached out a hand and tugged the curtain aside . . .

The talisman around her neck went cold, searing the skin between her breasts. Through a long tunnel, she saw Castelio dodge a thrust and press the flat of his blade against the wraith's neck. It gave a guttural howl. An inky substance poured from its eyes, trailing away like smoke.

The other one had caught Enrigo. It held the boy clamped under one arm, kicking wildly. Without an instant's hesitation, it hurled itself at a broad window. Glass shattered. The last one, whose face he'd burned, managed to stagger to the jagged gap and tumble through.

Castelio ran to the sill and leaned out.

Her terrible weakness faded as quickly as it had come. Lo pushed off the wall and hurried to join him, heart pounding. *Three stories down*.

The courtyard below was empty. Castelio slapped the sill in frustration. Warm rain blew through the gap, clearing her head. He turned to her. "Are you all right?"

"Fine," she said.

"Then let's alert the guards." His long legs took off at a sprint down the gallery.

The body of the possessed soldier lay sprawled on the stone floor. Lo crouched down and thumbed his eyes open. The irises were hazel now. She found a pulse.

Castelio could have killed him quickly, she realized. But he'd tried to save the man inside. And this mercy had cost him the heir.

Lo followed, stopping to retrieve the knife the wraith had dropped. Pale wood shaped like a claw, with a strange emblem on the hilt. Some kind of bird.

She frowned and lifted her skirts to run.

Chapter 16

"How could this happen?" the Ducissa demanded.

No one spoke. The assembled nobles exchanged worried glances.

"We'll get the boy back," Duc Scalici said grimly. "But we must act immediately."

They'd gathered in Orlaith's formal audience chamber. It was a stark room, with a great cold hearth and barrel-vaulted ceilings. Lucius stood behind her, impassive. The dark blue woad of his cloak blended with the shadows, making his pale face seem to float in darkness.

A search of the grounds had turned up nothing — nothing except for a gap in the iron stakes surrounding the wall. The soldier who survived remembered only taking his supper in the barracks and going on his customary rounds.

No one seemed to blame *him*.

"We all know who did this," Orlaith said tightly. "The Courtenays!"

She held up the dagger Lo had retrieved from the gallery. The bird on the hilt turned out to be a stooping Nightjar. The twin Ducissas' device.

"I heard they dine on children's flesh," a woman near Lo

whispered to her companion. "The younger the better. It is a great delicacy in the Moon Courts."

Her voice was pitched too low for mortal ears, but Lo turned and caught her eye with a frown. The woman — a margrave's wife — blanched and looked away.

"We do not know that for certain," Duc Scalici said in a conciliatory tone. "It appears that way, but why would Ladies Chaos and Caul wish to provoke you?"

"Why?" Orlaith gave a brittle laugh. "I thought it would be obvious. To destroy the last heir of House Redvayne!"

Then why not simply kill him in his bed? Lo wondered. She did not voice this aloud, but she suspected Scalici was thinking the same thing.

"Regardless of whose hand guides these wraiths," Lucius said, "our first task is to get him back alive. The best course of action would be to cut them off before they cross the border. We know they're mounted."

Two horses were missing from the stables.

Orlaith turned to her mortifex. They shared a look and she nodded briefly. But before she could speak, Castelio stepped forward. "I'll go," he said. "Let me leave at once, Your Grace. If I gallop to the pass—"

"You will not catch them in time," Delilah interrupted. "I would offer my own ship to carry a force to the border. It is the swiftest way."

Castelio shot her a look of surprise. Murmurs rolled through the chamber. A slight frown creased Lucius's pallid brow.

"That is a generous offer, but I could never ask such a thing, khamoun," Orlaith said. "It will be far too dangerous."

"It is only to the border," Lo replied. "Which I understand is well-guarded. I have studied the map Duc Scalici gave me. We could be there in two hours. Perhaps less, if the winds favor us."

The crisis presented a perfect opportunity to escape the Ducissa's gilded cage, but Lo would have offered anyway. It sickened her to think of the boy with those creatures.

Orlaith met her gaze. "Thank you, khamoun. With my son's life at stake, I can hardly refuse. Lucius, you will go with them."

Lo had half expected this, but the news was still unwelcome. He might be one of her kind, but the gulf between them was vast. As wide as the gulf between the living and the dead. She had not forgiven his treatment of Thistle — and knew the cat hadn't, either.

Lucius leapt down from the dais, cloak billowing. "Then let us ready the ship immediately, my lady." He bowed to her. When he rose, pinpoints of flame danced in his eyes. "Wraiths travel fast."

Fog wreathed the green slopes and valleys of the Mizzly Mountains as the *Wind-Witch* ascended into the higher passes. The skies had grown darker with every league they travelled eastward. The border was not fully on the night side but in the twilit zone between the Sun Courts and Moon Courts.

Thistle had appeared at the last minute, leaping to her shoulder in the rain as she was about to clamber up the rope ladder. She'd known he would, but it was a relief to feel his warm body curled up at her feet.

Lucius waited below with six of the Ducissa's soldiers. Lo had insisted on it. She didn't want them watching her while she flew the ship. After brief consideration, she had allowed Castelio to remain on deck. He knew enough to be helpful, and he hadn't betrayed her to Orlaith. Why, she didn't know. But it made her like him better — if not trust him.

There were three routes through the mountains. Riders had been dispatched to Hellgate and Seagate, but everyone agreed that since Midgate was closest, it was there that the wraiths would attempt to cross.

A road wound through the mountains up to the pass. It was this that the *Wind-Witch* followed, carving a serpentine route through the foothills. From the air, the rivers were misty silver ribbons. Granite boulders thrust from the earth, carpeted in deep green moss. A curious falcon trailed them for a spell, then broke away with a piercing cry.

"This is a beautiful place," Lo remarked.

"It is, my lady," Castelio agreed with a wistful note. "Though I've never seen it this way before."

"Have you spent much time in the Boundary?"

"I was born here," he said shortly.

Something in his voice forbade further questions on the topic.

"Of course you know it," she said quickly. "You went through one of the gates. We have them, too."

He turned to her in surprise. "But nothing comes through?"

She shook her head, thinking of her parents. "Nothing dead, if that's what you mean. Our gates are quiet."

"They say ours are broken," he muttered.

"I wonder why?"

"Jaskin Cazal did it."

"The Duc who bound the first mortifex?"

He shot her a sharp glance. "*You've* learned an awful lot . . . ah, my lady." Another quick look, worried this time. "No offense intended."

He seemed to be having trouble remembering that she was supposed to be a khamoun. But Lo was weary of playing the part of a spoiled noble. She'd be free of them all soon enough, anyway.

"The earl of Caria told me," she confided. "He was deep in his cups and in a mood to gossip."

Cas seemed familiar with the name. He cast her a wry look. "I hope he did not overstep himself, my lady."

"It was like dining with a tank of live eels, but I managed to escape with all my clothes intact."

He looked shocked for a moment, then burst into laughter. "I am glad to hear it," he said, rubbing the back of his neck and staring out at the mountains.

"What do your gates look like?" she asked.

"You'll see it in a moment," he replied. "We're nearly there."

Her breath grew shallower as they passed over a peak. It fell steeply on the other side, revealing a forested vale. At the center sat a lake. Perfectly circular like a mirror and surrounded by tall iron stakes. Shreds of mist hovered above the still surface. From within, a faint greenish glow.

She gripped the rail. Stared down at it spellbound. Thistle rose to his feet, tail swishing.

"The gate is at the bottom," Castelio said.

Lo pictured him wading into that dark water alone. She tore her gaze away. He was watching her. "Don't land there, my lady."

Lo swallowed. "I won't."

She studied the terrain. There were two wooden garrisons, one on either side of the lake. The road skirted it to pass by each garrison. Soldiers stood outside both buildings, heads tipped back to watch the ship.

"That one belongs to Alessia," Castelio said, pointing to the farther garrison, where a yellow banner flapped from a pole. "The rosette and lion passant of House Scalici."

"Passant?"

He walked his fingers along the rail. "In motion. Dexter forepaw raised."

Dexter must mean *righthand*. She filed this away.

"The red and gold phoenix is House Redvayne," he clarified, glancing at the closer flag.

"I gathered that," she said with a smile. "It's everywhere in the keep."

She circled around to come in for a second pass. Castelio followed her orders, lowering the jib while she dealt with the mainsail. In minutes, they were coasting to a stop in a meadow behind the Redvayne garrison. Lo felt pleased. It was one of her smoother landings.

"Now let us hope we have overtaken them," Castelio said.

He slid down the rope ladder, leaping off before his feet

touched the earth. He met the soldiers halfway. Within seconds, Lucius and the rest had joined him.

"Well, Thistle," she said, crouching to stroke his chin. "We've done our good deed."

The relieved expression on Castelio's face told her that they had indeed reached the border ahead of the wraiths. A runner broke off for the camp on the other side, presumably to inform Duc Scalici's men what had transpired.

She exhaled, glad to be out of the Ducissa's reach. No doubt the men had bows, but she could be gone in a trice when she chose. As long as Lucius didn't set her alight . . .

She didn't know where the mortifex stood. Or exactly what this *binding* did to him.

"We will wait until we know the boy is safe," she said to Thistle.

"That is foolish," he growled. "We should go now, while they are distracted."

The mortifex had climbed atop a spur of rock that looked over the road. He stood perfectly still, cloak gathered about him like a raven's wing. She almost pitied the wraiths.

"Not yet," she said. "I want to see this gate first."

His tail switched back and forth. "That, too, is foolish."

"You go wherever you please," she pointed out.

"Because I am a cat."

She shook her head with a smile and climbed down the ladder.

Someone had cut down all the trees around the lake for a hundred paces, leaving barren ground. She could see traces of ancient, petrified stumps. Other than the distant voices of the border guards, the vale was silent. No birdsong. No rustle of squirrels in the underbrush. Just the soft hiss of raindrops on the water. Low clouds drifted above, but they cast no reflection.

Lo walked to the line of iron staves. The sharp points angled inward, toward the lake.

She'd found a gate once, in the darklands of Nocturne. That

one had the shape of a door, though with the same watery, mirrored surface. The same greenish glow. When she tried to pass through it, a buzzing had roared in her ears, like a swam of maddened flies.

She'd had a sudden impulse to take off her talisman of protection. To—

"Khamoun?"

A warm hand took her arm, gently pulling her back from the picket.

"You should not stand so close," Castelio said. "It's not safe."

The heat of his palm seeped through her dress, leaching away the sudden chill.

"Do they come through?" she asked. Her voice sounded heavy and slow. "The dead?"

"Sometimes." He eyed her with concern. "Are you well? You look pale, my lady."

Lo shook off the languor. She drew a steadying breath. "Perfectly." A glance at the hand holding her arm and he hastily withdrew it. She found herself wishing he hadn't. *Stupid*. "What do the border guards say?"

"That no one has passed this way in two days."

"So there is travel permitted between the duchies?"

"Yes. With the proper papers." The corner of his mouth curved. "Though smugglers earn a good living bringing goods through from Nyons and Vendagni."

"How?"

A shrug. "They forge the documents."

"And the guards look the other way?"

He regarded her seriously. "Are all men honest where you come from?"

She laughed. "No."

"Then it is another thing we have in common. Come, I will escort you back to your ship."

"Not yet." She gazed at him squarely. "What was it like to pass through the gate?"

He glanced at the dark lake. "Cold. At first, I felt I was drowning. I held my breath until I saw stars."

"And then?"

"Lucius had sworn it wouldn't kill me. I don't trust him, but I had vowed to find you. So I kept going. It is not water. I don't know what it is, but I soon learned that I could breathe it well enough. There is a forest of tall reeds at the bottom. Within them lies another gate."

His words tumbled out like a stream in flood, but Lo was getting better at deciphering his accent.

"Into the Dominion," she said.

Castelio nodded solemnly. "It is a fey place, my lady. There is neither sun nor moon, only a gray sky. The rest is much like this world. Rivers and lakes. Deep woods. I followed the route I'd been given."

"Did you encounter any souls?"

"From a distance. I steered clear of them." He gave an uneasy laugh. "Here, I can banish the dead. But since the Dominion is where I send them, my charms would do me little good."

She shook her head. "I've heard there are worse things than spirits. Those who linger become corrupted. Powerful. Weren't you afraid?"

For a moment, she feared she'd given too much away. What would a pampered khamoun know of the Dominion? But his gaze was distant.

"Every minute," he agreed softly, "of every hour. I prayed often to the Drowned Woman, asking for safe passage. Fearsome hounds roam the Dominion, called Shepherds. They harry the dead to the ships so they may cross the stormless sea. And the living, too, if they are stupid enough to enter a gate."

He had no idea about her parents, but Lo bristled. "Perhaps some of them have good reason to. Like you."

"Perhaps." He looked unconvinced. "Well, the Shepherds didn't bother me."

Lo suddenly understood. "That's why Orlaith sent a Quietus to Tjanjin. You have the favor of Kaethe."

Castelio nodded. "I wouldn't usually carry out such a task. But none of our ships can cross the White Sea. The gates were the only way."

"And you found the one to Tjanjin with no trouble?"

"My parents were woodwards. I grew up gathering and tracking in the Boundary. My mother taught me . . ." Castelio trailed off and cleared his throat. Dark brows drew together in a slight frown. "How did you know—"

"Riders!" Lucius called, leaping down from the outcrop.

"Wraiths *do* travel fast," Lo said, as they shared a tense look.

"Return to the ship," Castelio called over his shoulder, running to join the mortifex. "Wait for us there."

The mist on the lake was thickening. Fine tendrils of it had nearly reached the stakes.

"Hide yourselves," Lucius snapped at the milling border guards. "All must appear normal or they'll turn tail and ride back down the road. We wait to strike until we have them trapped."

Lo strode for the *Wind-Witch*. Now, she thought. He'll never risk giving himself away.

Yet her steps slowed as she watched Castelio draw his iron daggers. He would think her a coward, abandoning them as the wraiths arrived. And despite his obvious skill . . . Well, he might need her help.

Of course he did have Lucius, who was ten times stronger than she was.

The mortifex leaned against a tree, out of sight of the road. All she could see of him was a glint of copper hair.

The guards had scattered, but her sharp ears caught the scrape of arrows to bowstrings. By a lucky chance, her ship was blocked from view of the road by the Redvayne garrison. The mainmast stuck up above the roofline, but the wraiths might not notice until it was too late.

She climbed up to the crow's nest, which gave a perfect

vantage point. Thistle watched her go with luminous eyes. He said nothing.

The minutes stretched out. She peered into the mist, eyes locked on the bend in the road.

Then two mounted figures appeared, galloping hard for the pass.

"Keep going," she whispered. "Closer. That's it."

They wore the Redvayne colors since the wraiths had possessed Orlaith's own soldiers. The first had the sack tied behind his saddle. It was not moving. Lo whispered a silent prayer that the child was only unconscious.

The riders slowed. A guard strolled out of the garrison. He gave a salute. They mimicked the gesture — but stayed too far back to reveal their black eyes.

"Dismount and present your papers," he called casually.

"We are on a mission of the Ducissa."

"Are you?" His face hardened. "Then I'm sure you have an order bearing her seal."

The wraiths turned to each other. An instant later, a circle of flames erupted around them. Lucius strode from the trees, dark blue cloak billowing behind. If not for their hostage, she knew he would have burned them to ash on the spot. The horses reared in alarm and the wraiths struggled to rein them in.

"Dismount," Lucius grated.

"Or what?" A hollow laugh. "You'll kill us? We are the same, brother."

Lucius scowled. The wraiths looked amused, until Castelio appeared at his side.

"The dead can't banish the dead," he said grimly. "But I can."

"Ah, a reaper." Swift as a serpent, it opened the sack and displayed the limp form of Enrigo. The boy's eyes fluttered as it pressed a blade to his throat. "He is alive. If you want to keep him that way, you will let us pass."

An agonizing moment slid by. She could see Castelio's frustration. He cast a furious glance at Lucius and she knew what he was thinking. The mortifex had struck too soon. The flames held them fast, but they also prevented Castelio from getting close. Now they were at an impasse.

One she feared the wraiths would win.

Then she realized that he was not looking at them but at the lake. He spoke a single word. She read it on his lips clear as a bell.

Feck.

The dead were rising from its depths. A score of them. Some wore the garb of beggars, others of farmers and nobles. Their eyes shone in the gloom like silver coins. She felt their hatred of the living like a bitter wind.

Soldiers poured from both garrisons, carrying long iron lances. The bodies of their foes were shimmery and translucent like the mist. They swarmed up to the stakes. Those who brushed against the iron gave eerie keening cries and subsided into the water, but there were so many. With mounting horror, Lo watched several break through, squeezing between their less fortunate brethren.

One reached out to touch a guard. Its finger was a trail of smoke, but the man collapsed, clutching his shoulder, face contorted in pain. The mist above the lake was boiling now. She felt a sudden weightless sensation and realized she'd nearly slipped from her perch at the top of the mast. She clung to the wooden spar, breath coming fast and hard.

He left arm had gone numb. She looked up in time to see the wraith with Enrigo force his mount through the flames and gallop for the far pass. Toward the nightlands. Its back was pincushioned with arrows by the time it vanished, but that didn't seem to slow it down.

Lucius had drawn his own pale blade and was using it to cut a swath through the spirits.

"We must depart," Thistle growled in her ear. Somehow, the cat had leapt to her shoulder. "Now!"

Chapter 17

Lo nodded and clumsily scrambled down from the rigging. On the way, she saw Castelio fling a handful of nails at a cluster of spirits about to overwhelm some guards. The iron sliced through their gauzy forms and the spirits dispersed. But other guards had fallen from both garrisons, writhing in agony.

Castelio strode through the carnage for the last wraith. *Reaper*, it had named him. He looked the part, his face as stern as an avenging angel, his mouth set in an unyielding line. Without breaking stride, he sketched the sign of Kaethe. It flared like blue lightning. Then one of his daggers found the wraith's throat. It tumbled from its horse. An inky stain trailed into the sky.

The dead surged forward, a horde of silver eyes and grasping hands. For some reason, they seemed drawn to the ship. Lo tried to hoist the mainsail, but her left arm wouldn't work right. Pain ripped through her chest. She braced herself on the rail, panting. Afraid.

What's wrong with me?

"I've got it." Castelio took the line from her hand. She hadn't even seen him board. In seconds, the sail was raised, the boom tied off. Crosswinds luffed the canvas. "Can you fly?"

She nodded, unable to speak. Thistle twined between her legs. The next moment, a huge gust came, lifting the hull. Unsure of her footing for the first time in years, Lo buckled into her harness with shaking hands.

As they rose up, something caught the rope ladder. The ship listed slightly to port. Lucius vaulted to the deck.

"We're going after them," he snarled, eyes like banked coals.

It wasn't a request.

Castelio stepped up between them. "It's the khamoun's vessel," he said firmly. "She decides."

They glared at each other. But Lo knew which direction he would choose.

That's what I wanted anyway, she thought.

"We go on," she said.

Lucius gave a brisk nod, as if he'd expected no less of her. "There's only one now. And yet another border it must cross before Nyons. We will catch them there."

Thistle summoned a strong, steady wind from the west. Lo fussed with the rigging and discreetly used her own power to guide the ship aloft, but without the cat's aid, the *Wind-Witch* would have been grounded — and swamped with the dead. She felt guilty fleeing the chaos below, but at last glance, the tide seemed to be turning in the guards' favor. Now that the wraith with Enrigo was through the border, the lake had gone still again.

"The attack must have been planned," Castelio said, echoing her thoughts. "We should have been ready for it."

He didn't sound angry, just resigned. When she looked at him, he had that drowsy, heavy-lidded aspect again. Sometimes, like now, he seemed close to her own age. But when he'd crossed the battlefield, stony gaze fixed on the wraith, he had seemed much older.

She found the Nexus and let it soothe her racing thoughts. Let the wind cool her flushed skin. The gate dropped away behind them. With each passing league, she felt its hold over her loosen. She wiggled the fingers of her left hand, which was a bit numb but serviceable. She lifted her hair to coil it into a knot and winced as a strand caught in the chain around her neck.

Her hand went to her breast, feeling the slight lump of the coin hidden beneath her dress.

It must be the talisman my mother gave me, she realized with a rush of relief. The gates ignite its protective magic. The disk had gone cold back at the keep, too, when the wraiths appeared.

And yet the talisman never reacted this way before, a small voice in her head whispered. *Not all those times you crashed your ship. Not even when you were struck by lightning.*

Lo frowned and pushed the thought away. She set a course due east. Into the darkness.

If the dead have this effect on me, I must be mad to leap into the lion's den.

And yet.

The lions might have some answers for her.

"How long have you been doing this?" she asked Castelio.

"I've served the Ducissa for five years," he replied — which, she noticed, was not precisely the same thing.

"It must be a dangerous profession. Does she pay you well?"

He frowned. "Yes, but that's not why I do it."

"Why then? Were you conscripted?" Better to know where his loyalties lie.

"Against my will, you mean? No. At first, it *was* the promise of gold," he admitted. "Perhaps you've never known true hunger, my lady, but it is hard to endure. You find yourself willing to do almost anything to stay alive." A shadow crossed his face. "But that has not been the case for a long time now. I am a Quietus of Clovis because Her Grace is a beacon of light in the dark. I trust her judgment in all things and am grateful to carry out her bidding."

His voice held an almost religious reverence. *Well, that's one question answered*, Lo thought dryly. *But is Lucius the same?*

"I would like to rest, if you have no objection," Castelio said.

"I may not have another chance and I'd rather be fresh when we land."

"By all means. But what is my destination?"

"Keep heading due east. I'll wake before we're at the border." He curled up on the deck and wrapped his coat around himself. The garment was hard-used, patched many times and faded to a grayish-brown. She looked away, but he'd already caught her staring.

"You wonder why I don't buy myself a new coat with my generous allowance," he remarked with a note of amusement. "Perhaps even a fine wool cloak like Lucius."

"It's not my business."

A shrug. "I happen to like russet. It's what I grew up wearing. My mother used to gather the lake madder herself and mix the pigment. I see no need to put on airs because I work for the Ducissa now, my lady. Besides which, I spend most of my time alone on the road." A wry smile. "Pretty clothes are an invitation to robbery."

Put on airs. Was that a subtle accusation? Or her own guilty conscience?

Lo smiled back. "That I can well believe. But it's chilly on deck. Don't you want to go below? You can rest in any of the empty passengers' cabins."

Castelio glanced toward the stern, where a tall form stood in the mist. "I prefer the fresh air."

So they don't trust each other. Well, he told me as much already.

She stood at the wheel, pretending to steer, until she felt sure he'd slipped into a doze. Then she headed aft.

"Khamoun," Lucius said without turning.

He stood at the stern rail, tall and straight-backed, the copper of his hair softened to a rich mahogany in the twilight. She drew close enough to feel the chill from his body and stopped. As usual, close proximity to the mortifex numbed the fingers of her left hand, but she'd grown used to it.

"I would like to know more about Chaos and Caul Courtenay," she said. "Since it seems I will be flying perilously near to their duchy."

"What do you want to know?"

"So they are twin sisters. And necromancers." She paused. "But I don't really understand what that word means. What are their powers?"

He turned to face her, leaning back against the rail. He looked like an ordinary man now, handsome although uncommonly pale. "They use blood magic to summon the dead. Bind them. Speak to them. Force answers if the spirit is unwilling. Let's see . . . They also dabble in poisons. Employ certain animals as their eyes and ears. Some claim they can change their own shapes, but I doubt this is true."

"And they are locked in a feud with your Ducissa?"

"Not only them, the entire bloodline. Ever the Courtenays and Redvaynes have hated each other."

"But Orlaith is not a Redvayne. She married into the family."

"And the Courtenays killed her husband, the Duc," Lucius pointed out.

"At the Battle of Hellgate. What were they fighting about?"

"The usual." He sounded bored. "Land. Power. Old grievances."

"What do Chaos and Caul want now? Why have they taken the heir? If they mean to hold him hostage, they must have demands."

There were always two sides to every story. Perhaps the Redvaynes had started the whole thing.

"I cannot say, khamoun."

Was there a hint of mockery in the last word?

"Surely you have some idea."

"Perhaps they will eat him," Lucius drawled, "as Lady Voisin suggested."

So he'd caught the whispered remark, too.

"You don't seem troubled by that prospect," Lo said.

"Unlike the Quietus, I do not serve by choice. But I also do not believe the Ducissas are quite that wicked." He studied her. "And what is it that *you* seek in the Moon Courts, my lady?"

"Enrigo's safe return, of course."

An ironic pause. "Of course."

"Have you ever met the Courtenays?"

"The current ones? No. I have not crossed the mountains in a long time."

"I heard they are young."

A nod. "Seventeen, I believe."

"So who raised them? After their parents died at Hellgate?"

"I haven't a clue. But they are the last of their line."

"How did you know I would come to Tjanjin?"

The abrupt change of subject caught him off guard. Lucius went very still. He seemed to be weighing his response. "I have heard of your mother," he admitted at last.

Lo's heart thudded in her chest. "What," she managed, "did you hear?"

"That she wields negatory magic. That she is a Breaker."

She suddenly remembered the intent way Lucius had stared at her as she struggled in coils of air, shouting for him to let her go.

Make me, he'd taunted.

"You believed I might have the same ability," she said softly.

The mortifex didn't reply, but the look on his face was confirmation enough. Her gaze flicked to the iron menotte around his wrist. It must be a talisman.

Lucius thought I might be able to free him. That is the true reason he sought out the Wind-Witch.

"The talent does not pass down that way," she said. "Why didn't you tell Orlaith that I am part daēva?"

"And see her try to do the same to you? I might be a monster, but I am not so callous as that." Lucius met her gaze. "I kept your secret. I ask that you keep mine. Orlaith believes me to be loyal. If she learned otherwise . . . "

He trailed off, leaving the consequences unspoken, but Lo

wondered what the extent of Orlaith's control was. "Can she cause you physical pain?"

Lucius blinked once, then lifted a brow sardonically. "That's a forward question. We barely know each other."

"Yet you already know far more about me than I do about you." She studied the menotte around his wrist. It had no seam or joint. "If that is similar to others I've seen, the mortal wearing its match can sever your power at whim. Even if you found a way to remove the actual talisman, it would not break the bond contained within it. Not unless the talisman itself is destroyed."

He barked a startled laugh. "So you're familiar with the poor bargain I made."

"And there is one more thing. The mortal can inflict punishment on the daēva. In the mind only, but it feels real."

Her mother had never used the bond with her father in such a vile fashion — though she could have if she chose to.

Lucius let out a sigh. "All that is true, though Orlaith is softer than her husband was. Duc Robert Redvayne never hesitated to wield his authority to the fullest." Green eyes glittered with dark amusement. "Needless to say, I do not mourn him. Nor do I fear pain. That brand of suffering always ends at some point. But Orlaith could also exile me to the Dominion."

Lo frowned. "At least you'd be rid of her."

"Rid of her — and at the mercy of others who are worse. Trust me when I say I prefer Orlaith's wrath."

She stepped closer, into the deeper chill of his presence. "I would help you if I could. My mother would, too. But she vanished in the Dominion eight years ago, as you must know. My father Darius, too. Do you have any idea—"

"No," he interrupted. "Else I would have sought her out directly." Lucius seemed to decide he'd said enough. "Excuse me, *khamoun*." He brushed past her and strode for the hatch leading below. She watched him go, thoughts spinning.

How had he heard about her parents? From whom?

A gentle pressure against her leg announced Thistle. She bent down and met his fierce yellow eyes. "What do you make of all that?"

His tail switched. "The mortifex knows more than he's admitting."

"Naturally. But how do I drag the truth from him?"

"He has no better nature to appeal to," the cat growled. "Only self-interest. But perhaps you can make common cause. You both seek the same thing — Nazafareen."

Delilah nodded thoughtfully. "He doesn't know she lost the ability to break talismans, and I don't plan to tell him."

She was about to pursue Lucius into the hold when she saw Castelio standing amidships. He stared at her with a grim expression. She bit back an oath. Had he heard Thistle's dreadful overlapping voices? Or worse, the whole conversation with the mortifex?

No, she decided quickly, Lucius would have noticed him if he'd been there for long. Which meant he'd just arrived. The cat, then. Well, let him goggle. It was *her* ship.

"Is something wrong?" she asked in a casual tone. "I thought you were napping—"

"Don't move," he said softly. "Not an inch."

Then she saw it. A solid patch of darkness hovering in the air to her left. It had wispy edges like a raincloud. Her left hand began to tingle again. Thistle hissed and backed away, fur rising.

"What is that?" she whispered, eyes widening.

"A lich." He held out a hand. The other had a vial of Kaethe's Tears, already unstoppered. "Come to me. Slowly, now."

She vented a quiet breath. Took a single step—

The lich struck, wrapping around her wrist like a snake.

Icy cold sank into her flesh. She staggered against the rail. A vise squeezed her chest, tighter and tighter. Then, the sensation of a nail being methodically pounded straight into her heart. Her back bowed. Her head sank back.

Then she was falling.

Chapter 18

Cas knew she was dead the instant it touched her flesh.

No one survived a lich. They were what remained of mortal souls that lingered in the Dominion until the last spark of humanity was gone. The briefest contact with one was invariably fatal.

His own heart stopped beating as he stared at the place where she'd gone over the rail. At the tattered patch of soot that now drifted towards him.

It had to have come aboard at the gate. Lurked in the shadows. I should have seen it before—

Lucius flashed across the deck. He seized the lich with his bare hands. It whipped in his grasp, screeching.

"Destroy it!" Lucius shouted.

Moving without conscious thought, Cas hurled the contents of the vial. The lich hissed and blew apart. A few drops of Kaethe's Tears struck Lucius, raising red blisters on the backs of his hands. It must have hurt, but he allowed no sign of pain. He merely wiped his palms on his cloak with a look of distaste. Cas ran to the rail.

Delilah had been buckled into her harness when she fell. Her body swung to and fro beneath the hull like a pendulum.

"Help me pull her up," he cried, distraught.

"Forget her," Lucius snapped. "She's gone."

"I won't let her hang there!"

The mortifex stepped closer. "We have bigger problems, don't you think?"

His stomach rose to his throat as the *Wind-Witch* pitched and started to dive. Not quite free-fall but close enough. Cas grabbed a rope.

"Do something!" he shouted.

"Like what?" Lucius didn't look especially worried. Of course, he was already dead.

"Fly it!"

"I already told you, I can't. Air is not my talent."

"I saw you use it before!"

"On a small scale. But this . . ." He waved a hand at the flapping sails and groaning timbers. "It requires a defter touch, I'm afraid."

"Just try!"

Lucius sighed. "Very well."

His eyes narrowed. After a long, agonizing minute, the ship pulled out of its steep dive, though it kept descending rapidly.

"Whatever you're doing, keep it up!" Cas shouted, staggering to the rail again. The treetops rushed past, closer with each passing second. Delilah swung below, her body twisting in circles. The thought of her corpse being battered by branches was more than he could bear. No matter that he was about to join her.

Grunting with effort, he began to haul her up. The grim task was made harder by the careening of the ship. The *Wind-Witch* was fully at the mercy of the winds now, with no firm hand to guide it. Sweat broke across his brow.

"Curse you, you *sanglant* bastard," Cas snarled. "Help me!"

Lucius crossed the heaving deck and seized the rope. With the mortifex's strength added to his own, they dragged Delilah over the rail. Her eyes were closed, her black hair damp from the rain. She was still warm.

But not as warm as she should be. Kaethe had already embraced her.

His hand stole to the iron coin in his pocket. "I don't want to have to banish you," he whispered.

The coin was supposed to be for himself, if he took a mortal wound. But he had others in his pack. Cas gently placed it on her tongue and closed her mouth. The sweet notch in her upper lip made his chest ache.

"Goodbye, khamoun," he said shakily. "May Kaethe bar gate and tomb against you. May you cross the stormless sea in peace."

Most of those who came back had unfinished business. Delilah struck him as one of those. She kept secrets.

"Brace yourself," Lucius informed him. "I might be able to slow us enough that you make it through, Quietus."

He looked up and nodded. To his surprise, the fex's harsh face softened as he gazed at Delilah.

"I am sorry she was taken so young," Lucius said. "If I had been closer—"

The ship dropped abruptly. "We're going down too fast," Cas said through gritted teeth.

Lucius closed his eyes. An expression of serenity settled over his face.

"How will that help?" Cas exclaimed. "You can't even see where the feck we're going!"

"Be *quiet*," the mortifex said. "You can do that, can't you?"

Too fast. They were still coming down too fast. The highest peaks lay behind and the sky had grown darker, but not dark enough. The horizon tilted. The earth rushed up to meet them. No clearings or level ground in sight. Not a single place to land—

They hit the first trees with a jolt. There was a horrific sound from the hull, like an ogre grinding the planks between its teeth. Another jolt, harder this time. Cas flew through the air, limbs akimbo. He hit more branches, slithered through them, and looked up in time to see the ship smashing its way down on top of him.

He must have lost consciousness, for when his eyes opened, it was quiet. He groaned and tried to move. Something heavy pinned his waist. Sounds gradually came to his ears. The drip of rainwater. The distant warble of a wood thrush.

He managed to push up to his elbows. The mast had crashed down across his hips. His legs felt wooden, but he managed to wiggle his toes. Nothing broken. Kaethe had stayed her hand. She must have a use for him yet.

"Lucius?' he called weakly.

His vision slowly cleared. The *Wind-Witch* had come to rest on her side. There was a long breach in the hull and the mainmast had snapped. The part lying across him was wedged at an angle, with one side jammed against the ship, the other against a tree. He tried with all his might, but it wouldn't budge.

"Help me, Lucius," he shouted. "I'm stuck!"

For a moment, Cas feared the mortifex had abandoned him. Then a flicker of movement caught his eye. Lucius was crouched over something. There was a furtiveness in his posture that made Cas's nape prickle.

"What are you doing?"

Lucius's head turned. There was a deep gash on his forehead. It wasn't bleeding. His kind didn't. They had no beating heart to make the blood flow. Most people didn't understand how the organ worked, but Cas had seen a great deal of death. The body held few mysteries anymore.

"I'm hurt," Lucius whispered.

The mortifex had always worn the masque of a courtier, with his fine clothes and refined manners. Even when his back was against the wall, he had an icy self-control. Now Cas saw the feral creature that lurked beneath. His lips were slightly parted and his teeth gleamed white in the twilight. Then he realized what Lucius had found.

Delilah's body.

"Leave her be," he growled, struggling to free himself.

"She's dead, farm boy. She won't care. But her blood is warm."

His voice was thick with barely restrained hunger.

There were several ways a fex could feed. Blood was one. It healed them.

Cas held out a hand. "Please. Don't defile her that way. She never troubled you when you lay helpless on her vessel."

For a moment, he thought he might have gotten through. Lucius hesitated. Then he shook his head. "There's no other way. Don't be sentimental." He looked around the gloomy forest. "I cannot afford to be weak in the Moon Courts. I have enemies here."

And I hope they find you, Cas thought savagely.

"She has an iron coin on her tongue," he warned, praying it was still there.

Lucius only laughed. "I don't mean to kiss her."

Nausea twisted his stomach. He redoubled his efforts to shift the mast. "Bel blind you, come over here and free me, I'll give you mine—"

Lucius ignored him. He started to bend over her again, then rocked back on his heels. Never had Cas seen the mortifex so completely and utterly shocked.

His own breath caught as Delilah sat up with a gasp. She choked for a moment, then spat out the coin.

"Gah!" she said, wiping her lips. "That tastes awful."

They stared at her in frozen silence.

She gave a nervous laugh. "Castelio? You look like you've just seen a spirit."

Then she looked around and noticed the ship. Her face fell. "I crashed again?"

Again? Cas blinked, trying to catch up. She wasn't speaking tongues. Only wraiths and fexes could use the language of the living. And her eyes weren't black.

All his misgivings came rushing back. Not a necromancer. Not High Dead. Not Low Dead.

Not human either.

Lucius was the first to recover. He rose gracefully to his feet and offered her a hand, as if he hadn't been seconds from draining her blood. Delilah accepted it, wincing at the chill of his flesh.

"Khamoun," he said. "A lich came aboard. You . . . fell."

She frowned and unbuckled the harness. "I'm so sorry. I lost control." She eyed the ship appraisingly. "It could have been worse. Did you cushion the landing?"

"I did my best."

She turned back to Cas. "You're injured!"

Once, the concern on her face would have warmed him, but he couldn't meet her eyes. "Lucius," he said. "Help me."

The mortifex limped over and heaved the mast aside. His hands trembled. When he saw Cas looking, he gave a chilly smile. "Does your offer still stand, Quietus?"

Delilah was wandering through the wreckage, calling for her cat. She didn't seem to have so much as a scratch. Cas leaned in close.

"Touch her again," he said, softly so she wouldn't hear, "and I'll banish you straight to the ninth hell of the Abyss. Understand?"

Pinpoints of flame flickered in Lucius's pupils. He turned away.

They filled packs with whatever they could salvage. Food and water, blankets, and a change of clothing. Lucius needed none of these things and waited with obvious impatience. Cas feared she'd find the body of her beloved Thistle in the wreckage, but the cat had vanished. It had a habit of doing that, he'd noticed.

"Nine lives," she'd said brightly, when he remarked on it. "He'll turn up, I'm sure."

The khamoun shouldered her own pack. She'd changed into snug breeches and a cotton cami, both black, and wound her hair into a knot atop her head. Gone were the delicate slippers. She wore stout boots. When he offered to carry the pack for her, she frowned.

"You're not a beast of burden, Castelio."

He scratched his head. "I'm not, my lady? I seem to remember a heavy trunk—"

"That was before," she said, cheeks flushing. "You're injured."

"True," he said with a grimace. "It's a good thing you have a strong back, khamoun."

Pins and needles pricked his flesh where the mast pinned him, but the tree had saved him from two broken legs. Other than some bruises and a scrape on his cheek, Cas wasn't hurt. Which was good, since they had a long walk out.

The skies cleared and Artemis shone above as they gathered beneath the listing bow of the *Wind-Witch*. Delilah rummaged through her bag and unrolled a map.

"Do you know where we are?" she asked.

"Roughly," Cas said. He was forced to move closer to see. The warmth of her body was both a relief and a burden. He couldn't stop seeing that lich wrapped around her wrist. Couldn't stop feeling her soft lips as he pressed the coin to her tongue.

"There's Midgate. We didn't make more than thirty leagues before we crashed. Which puts us here." He tapped the map. "The Vale of Harran."

"I suppose we'll never catch them now."

"Not necessarily," Lucius said, all business now. "We flew over the highest mountains, but those passes are a hard journey, even mounted. The wraith will have to make camp and rest its horse. There's no doubt we're well ahead of it now. And we're not too far off course."

"So we find the road and wait?" Cas asked.

Lucius shook his head. "It will expect that and cut through the forest. The best place to catch it is the bridge at Nox. It's on the border of Nyons. The only crossing for leagues. If the wraith is heading for its mistresses, it will cross there."

"Chaos and Caul Courtenay," Delilah said.

Lucius nodded. "Their seat is in Mystral, across the Castor River."

"We'll need horses," Cas said. "It's too far afoot."

"I saw a spark of light when we were coming down," Lucius said. "That way."

He pointed to some hills rising up ahead.

"There's nothing out here," Cas said. "It's wilderness."

A shrug. "I know what I saw. If there's a village, we might be able to buy horses. Unless you have a better idea?"

Cas sighed. "No. It's in the right direction anyway. Lead on."

After a while, the cat slunk out of the undergrowth. It leapt to Delilah's shoulder. She absently stroked its tail and kept walking.

The woods were pine and spruce, open enough that they had little trouble finding a path. It was cooler than he was accustomed to. This was the start of the Duskwood, a vast forest that ran from the mountains, across Duc Scalici's duchy, to Nyons and beyond, at which point any hint of sun faded over the horizon and it became the Nightwood.

They'd walked several leagues when Lucius stopped and held up a hand, his face taut.

"What is it?" Cas whispered. He gripped the hilts of his iron knives.

Delilah had gone still, waiting.

"I think we're being followed," Lucius said. "Wait here. I'll circle around and check the backtrail."

"No," Cas said firmly. "You're not leaving us to—"

The mortifex tilted his head, listening. Before Cas could stop him, he'd slipped into the twilight.

Feck.

Chapter 19

They climbed a longleaf pine and hid in the upper branches until the cold white crescent of Hecate set and buttery yellow Selene took her place. Nearly an hour, by Lo's reckoning.

Lucius did not return.

"Do you think something happened to him?" she whispered.

Castelio seemed lost in dark thoughts. He'd hardly spoken a word.

"I hope so," he muttered.

"Why do you hate him so much?" she asked softly. "Has he wronged you?"

"Lucius is a wolf on a leash," he replied. "Never forget that, *my lady*."

The last words had a mocking ring.

"Have *I* wronged you?" she persisted.

Castelio's anger faded. He looked weary. "No. I'm sorry. It's been a trying day."

"For me, as well. I lost my ship." She gave him a sad smile. "It isn't the first one I've wrecked. But it *was* my favorite."

"How many times have you gone down?" he asked.

"Oh, a few," she said vaguely. In truth, she'd lost count. "Do you think Lucius was lying about hearing something?" She shifted on the branch. Her bottom had gone numb. "We can't stay here forever."

"If he's in trouble, you can be sure he'll find his way out of it. Lucius always lands on his feet."

Castelio glanced at Thistle. The cat crouched on the opposite branch, staring back at him unblinking.

Lo covered a yawn. "Then let's go on. If we don't find this light soon, I propose we find someplace to make camp."

"I hate to lose time, but we won't make Nox without rest," he agreed.

They climbed down, hoisted their packs, and set off through the woods.

"If Lucius thought he had a better chance of finding Enrigo alone, he'd abandon us for certain," Castelio said. "I expect that's what happened. Fexes are inhumanly fast runners. We'd only slow him down."

"But?" she prompted.

He scanned the trees. "*But* . . . Lucius told me he has enemies here."

"Aren't the necromancers your enemies, too?"

"Yes, but the way he said it sounded personal."

"Then perhaps it's better he left us," Lo said.

They walked in silence. She heard no furtive sounds of pursuit. Just the wind sighing in the pines and the lonely hoot of an owl. Finally, Castelio stopped at a stream. Boulders formed a rough semicircle on the opposite side. Beyond it, the land rose again in a steep hillside.

"This might be the best spot we find," he said.

She gave a tired nod. They waded across and dropped their packs. Thistle prowled off to hunt his own supper. Lo took out a hunk of barley bread and goat cheese from her pack, courtesy of Orlaith's kitchen, along with grapes from the vineyards.

She sat against the boulders and watched Castelio use his knife to trim branches from a pine and lay them out for pallets. It had begun to drizzle and he wove others together to form a roof above their heads.

"Is it safe to have a fire?" she asked hopefully.

Her clothes were damp, but it was the light she craved most.

He hesitated. "Well, it might deter unwanted visitors. The dead don't like fire."

"But Lucius wields it."

"High Dead are different. The rest, the ones we call Low Dead, will only pass through flames if they have to."

"Like the wraith that took Enrigo." She felt a pang thinking of the poor boy.

"Yes. That's why they fear mortifexes."

"So that's one point for a fire," she said. "But now you'll tell me that it attracts something else even worse."

He smiled. "Only bandits, and I doubt there are any around here. They'll be watching the main road. I suppose the rain will dampen the smoke. If we position it right, it won't be visible."

Leaves and twigs had drifted beneath an overhang. They proved dry enough to catch when he struck a flint. Within minutes, a small blaze crackled. She parceled out the food, then stuck a piece of bread on a fork and held it to the flames. For the first time since Tjanjin, she felt herself relax. Lucius was gone, Orlaith far away. If the dead did appear, she trusted Castelio — and her own instincts — to keep them safe.

"My mother used to make me toast when I was little," she said. "It tastes so much nicer that way. Too bad we don't have any butter."

When she looked up, he was staring at her bare forearms. She'd pushed up her sleeves to keep them away from the fire. Now she cursed her thoughtlessness.

"What happened to you?" he asked. "I've never seen marks like that. Like . . . someone painted trees on your skin."

She studied him from beneath her lashes. He didn't look repulsed, just curious. And his tone was so gentle, she relented.

"Lightning," she said.

His sleepy eyes widened a little. "You've been hit by lightning?"

"Twice. They go all the way down my back, and both arms."

He was silent for a moment. "I think you have more lives than the cat."

Lo smiled. It faltered when he didn't smile back.

"How did you do it?" he asked quietly.

"Do what?"

"Survive the lich's touch."

She froze with the bread halfway to her lips. "It touched me? I thought . . ."

"You were dead," he said flatly. "I saw it happen. You fell overboard and I hauled you back up. Your body was already cooling. That's why I put the coin on your tongue."

In the fog of waking up and finding her ship destroyed, she'd forgotten about that part. Then, the sickening realization that he did it so she wouldn't come back. Lo swallowed and lowered the fork. He hadn't pulled out an iron weapon, but his shoulders were taut. *Tell him the truth.* Or part of it at least.

"I have a talisman," she said quickly. "My mother gave it to me."

He blinked. "A talisman?"

"I'll show it to you." She pulled the silver disk from her shirt. "See? It has the sun on one side and the moon on the other."

He leaned closer to examine it.

"I'm not immune to cuts and bruises," she explained. "Scars, even. But it protects me from the most severe injuries."

Relief flashed across his face. This explanation seemed to make sense to him.

"The man who trained me as a Quietus had a talisman. A staff that repels the power of a mortifex. They are rare." He frowned. "So . . . you cannot die?"

"I doubt that," she said wryly. "I haven't tested the limits."

"But you have," he insisted. "What do you remember after the lich touched you? Did you go beyond the Veil?"

She shook her head, flustered. "I don't know. I don't remember anything! I never do—"

A twig cracked. They both leapt up, but it was too late. Six figures in green cloaks materialized out of the trees. They carried bows with black-fletched arrows at the ready. Lo couldn't see their faces. Or their eyes.

I won't be taken, she thought wildly. *Not by wraiths.*

She slid into the Nexus, power pulsing at her fingertips, but felt none of the tingling or weakness. Necromancers? She held her power in check, waiting as the leader approached. He pushed his hood back. He had pale eyes and dark auburn hair, worn long. Ginger stubble roughened his cheeks.

"Drop the knives," he snapped.

Bowstrings creaked. After a moment, Castelio shrugged and tossed them down. "We're just travelers passing through," he said. "Take our packs. You won't find much of value."

The man turned to Lo, gaze knowing. "Don't," he warned.

A shock ran through her. Could he know? She slid out of the Nexus and threw the fork into the bushes — as if that's what he meant. A twitch of amusement crossed his face, but he merely nodded.

Their camp was broken, the fire doused. They were led on a long trek through the Vale, up into the same hills Lucius had mentioned. Perhaps he'd seen something after all.

Castelio pestered them with questions they refused to answer. He finally fell silent.

The path grew steeper and narrower, taking rocky tracks a goat would be hard-pressed to navigate. She waited for a chance to strike, but they were alert and armed, and she feared she'd get Castelio killed. Lo was dead on her feet by the time they reached a cliff wall and passed through a narrow crevice. It was thick with brush and easy to miss. Thorns caught at her trousers, but after a short way, the crevice opened onto a shallow bowl in the mountains.

Lights glimmered below. They would only be visible from the

air. She shared a quick look with Castelio. So Lucius *had* been telling the truth.

A dozen rough stone dwellings were nestled on the eastern side of the declivity. Her heart sank further when they were separated. Three of the men led Castelio away. He cast her a worried look, but they'd bound his arms behind his back. The rest dragged her to the largest dwelling.

"If you mean to make me a gift to your leader," Lo said coldly, "you're making a grave error."

Clouds gathered above, dark and ominous. They hadn't caught Thistle. He would summon a storm such as they'd never seen. Tear the thatched roofs from their houses and destroy what remained with hail. She could shake the earth a little. Scare them enough to send them running.

Her pulse beat swiftly as she stepped through the door. A large man lounged in a wooden chair, legs stretched out before him. Lo recognized the quality of its craft. It looked like something her father would make. Simple, clean lines and built to outlast empires.

The bandit king was ruggedly handsome, with short silver hair and bright green eyes. They moved about the room like a dragonfly, never settling on anything for long. A small, dark woman, quite beautiful, sat at his side.

"My scouts saw your wind ship go down," he said in a sardonic tone. "If you behave, we won't kill you, but you will not leave this place. It's a shame, but that's how it is."

The woman gazed at her directly, but the man stared at a point off to her left. Lo had a sudden inkling of who he might be. Was it possible? She gave a pretty curtsy, though she suspected he couldn't see it.

"I am sorry to have disturbed your peace, Culach Kafsnjor, formerly of Val Moraine. But as I am the granddaughter of Victor Dessarian, and the daughter of Darius and Nazafareen, I hope you will offer us your hospitality."

Chapter 20

The man gripped the arms of his chair and leaned forward. "You are . . .?"

"Delilah Dessarian."

He looked astonished, then scowled deeply.

"Leave us," he said to the daēvas who had brought her there.

Lo should have seen it right away. The lithe, prowling grace of their movements. The way the leader had known she was holding her power. But on the surface, daēvas looked the same as mortals, and she had not expected to find her own kind here. Not living, at least.

She had never met Culach Kafsnjor, but her mother had always spoken of him fondly. He had left Nocturne before Lo was born. His wife, Mina, had gone with him, along with many of the fire daēvas. They'd set off across the White Sea and no one had ever heard from them again.

"And why should I believe you?" he growled.

"Peace, Culach," Mina said, laying a hand on his arm. "She does have the Dessarian look. And she arrived on a wind ship."

"Still . . ."

"You gave my mother a sword called *Nemesis*," Lo said. "It once belonged to your mother, Ygraine. When you presented

Nazafareen with the blade, you said . . . " A surge of emotion tightened her throat. "You told her that there were things worth dying for, but hatred isn't one of them. I always remembered that. It is a noble sentiment."

The suspicion on his face faded to wonder. "She told you about *Nemesis*?"

"She told me many things about you."

"What else did she say?" he asked with a warm smile that did much to soften his imposing looks.

"He's fishing for compliments," Mina said, elbowing his ribs.

Lo laughed. "Then I'm happy to oblige. She said you are brave and true. Nothing like . . . ah . . ."

"My father?" he finished. "I sincerely hope that's true. Who is your companion?"

"He is from this land. Quietus to the Ducissa Orlaith of Clovis. Her son was abducted by wraiths. We pursued them over the mountains."

Culach absorbed this for a moment. "By what chance," he said slowly, "does Nazafareen's daughter find herself keeping company with a Quietus of Clovis?"

"It's a long story," she said. "And I will tell you all of it. But will you make sure Castelio is fed and treated well? I can vouch for him."

"I'll see to it," Mina said, rising. She touched Culach's cheek. "This is a strange turn, my love," she whispered. "But it will be good to have news of home." She approached Lo. "I trust *you*, but we must set a guard over the Quietus."

"He doesn't know I'm part daēva," Lo said, cheeks flushing.

Castelio had stopped calling her "my lady," and she had stopped behaving like one, but that was a minor deceit. She could not let him discover what she really was. Not when he believed daēvas were all wolves to be leashed.

"I don't plan to tell him anything," Mina replied evenly. "Not about you — or us." Her lovely face hardened. "You were right to conceal your power." An exasperated shake of the head. "These people are crazy. Culach will tell you."

She surprised Lo by kissing her cheek. "We are cousins, if distant ones. You are welcome here, Delilah." Mina glided for the door, long dark hair rippling to her waist.

"Oh, and he doesn't eat meat," Lo called after her. "I don't know why, but he always refuses it. So if you have something else . . ."

She trailed off. Mina wore a half smile that was too amused for Lo's taste. "I'm sure we do," she murmured.

Lo gave a brisk nod and thanked her. Well, of course she noticed what Castelio ate. They'd been confined together for days. She'd have to be blind not to—

She cleared her throat and approached the chair. Culach held out his big hands.

"May I?" he asked.

She realized he wanted to touch her face. "Of course," she said, kneeling at his feet.

His calloused fingers were surprisingly delicate, tracing her cheekbones, chin, lips, and brows. It felt intimate, but she understood that this was how he saw.

"You're beautiful," he said at last with a smile, withdrawing his hands. "Like your mother. Tell me, how is she?"

His kindness shattered her composure. To her horror, she started to cry. He stood without a word and drew her to his chest. Lo hadn't wept about her parents in years — certainly not in front of a perfect stranger. She'd believed her tears were all spent, leaving nothing but a hard kernel of loss.

She was wrong.

"Nazafareen is gone, Culach," she sobbed. "Darius, too."

Memories flooded her, of laughter and gentle teasing and love. So much of it. She'd never realized how lucky she'd been until it was gone. And afterwards, the nagging fear that this "bargain" Javid spoke of had something to do with her. That she was the reason they were forced to hunt restless souls in the Dominion.

Culach Kafsnjor was solid as an oak tree. He made soothing noises and patted her back. At length, she wiped her face and let out a ragged laugh.

"I'm sorry."

"Tell me." There was an edge to his voice. "Are they dead?"

"No! That is, I don't know. But I won't believe it until I know for certain."

He blew out a breath. "Bloody hells, you scared me. I expect that long story is about to come, and I seem to remember you mentioning something about hospitality. Wait here."

He ambled to the pantry and returned with a cup of water and plate of stew. He clearly knew every inch of his own home and had no trouble getting around.

They sat down at a long trestle table. Lo dug in, famished. Between bites, she studied him more closely. A winding scar crossed his jaw, but it only made him more attractive. He was a Valkirin daēva of the frozen mountain holdfasts of Nocturne and looked every inch of it, with his silver-white hair and jade eyes. Now, his face tilted to the window. It was framed by pretty white curtains — Mina's touch, no doubt.

"What's the weather doing out there?" he asked. "I smelled a thunderstorm, but I hear no rain."

She swallowed a bite of stew. "The stars have come out."

"How odd. I could have sworn we were in for a big storm."

"Hmmm, well, the weather in the Umbra is always unpredictable."

He sat patiently while she finished the stew — and gathered her thoughts. At last, she pushed her plate back. "My mother was carrying me when you left, Culach, though she didn't know it yet. They moved to Susa and bought a little house." Lo smiled. "It had blue shutters and a red roof and it always smelled of the sea. That's my first memory. The cries of gulls and Mama . . . Nazafareen singing to me."

His eyes went misty. "Go on."

"All was well until a week before my twelfth birthday. They'd left me with friends. They always came home on the same day. Always. But this time, they didn't."

She told him the whole story from start to finish, all except for the way she was affected by the dead. Lo didn't understand it herself and felt reluctant to share it with anyone until she did. Her throat was hoarse by the time she reached their capture at the clearing. Saying it all aloud dredged up the anguish she'd kept buried, but it was a relief to trust someone.

Culach was quiet for a minute. "I rashly promised not to kill this Quietus of Clovis," he growled, "but that was before I knew he stole your ship."

"Only because I allowed it."

"That hardly matters—"

"I don't want him harmed," she said quickly. "He was just following the Ducissa's orders. He believed the ship was their salvation."

A silver brow arched. "You know him so well after less than a week?"

"I'm a good judge of character." She leaned her arms on the table and bent closer. "Do you know anything about this bargain?"

Culach shook his head. "I'm sorry, Delilah. They never mentioned it. Perhaps it happened after I left."

She swallowed her disappointment. "Now, it's your turn. How did you come to the Vale of Harran?"

He gave a slow nod. "We tried to land on Orlaith's shores twenty years ago. Her soldiers welcomed us with flaming arrows. Half the ships burned before we escaped."

"No!" Lo exclaimed. "Why?"

"Fear, I imagine. You know who they are? Where they came from?"

Lo nodded, then remembered he couldn't see her. "Yes. Orlaith said her descendants fled the first daēva war."

"They assumed the Vatras won," Culach said. "They want nothing to do with anyone from across the sea."

"Orlaith thinks I'm a mortal. That must be the reason she let me live." Lo paused. "So you've heard of the creature they call a mortifex?"

He frowned. "Not until now. We avoid contact. What is it?"

"A powerful spirit."

"And this Lucius is one?"

"I think he is a fire daēva. A dead one. Bonded to the Ducissa with an iron cuff."

Culach leaned forward. "Are you sure?"

"Here, they call it 'bound.' But it amounts to the same thing. She controls him."

His mouth twisted. "That is repellant. So Lucius is her slave?"

Lo had already considered this question.

"I get the feeling it's more complicated. From what I saw, she treats him with respect. And the link gives him a semblance of life. He implied that he chose it as a way to return to the living world. But he is weary of the menotte now, that I'm sure of. He hoped I could break the talisman that binds him."

"And you don't know where he went?"

"Castelio thinks he abandoned us to rescue Enrigo himself."

"Well, if an undead Vatra is on the loose," Culach replied, "I appreciate the warning. But he is not here, Delilah."

She knew that was true. Had Lucius been nearby, she would have sensed him. "What about this plague of the dead? Do you know the reason for it?"

He considered for a moment. "Divine punishment for being assholes?"

"Then the nobility should suffer the most," she replied sardonically, "but they seem well-protected."

"Wraiths stole Orlaith's son," he pointed out.

"There was a gap in the iron stakes around the manor. That suggests a living accomplice."

Culach gave a shrug. "Mortal betrayals are no concern of ours. But you're safe here. There are no villages for leagues and these spirits don't seem to wander far from the place they died." He sounded dismissive. "When they do, they're easily dispatched with iron."

"What about the forest? An earl told me it was, quote, teeming with all manner of infernal creatures."

He laughed. "If so, they know we're here and keep well away."

"That's reassuring." She covered a yawn. "I don't mean to stay long, though if you are able to repair the ship, I'll retrieve it when I return."

"Return? From where?"

"Mystral. The seat of Chaos and Caul Courtenay."

A chuckle. "Are you mad?"

"Well, first I must rescue the boy. When that is accomplished, I will hire one of these hedge necromancers to make inquiries about my parents."

"Now I am certain you are who you say. You sound like Nazafareen. Leap into the pot first, then look to see if the water is boiling."

It was a backhanded compliment, but Lo warmed at the words.

"I'll be careful," she promised. "But communing with the dead is their area of expertise. My parents vanished in the Dominion. If someone does know something, it won't be the living."

He shook his head. "Your mother would murder me if I let you do this."

"Let me? I'm a grown woman, Culach."

He scrubbed a hand through his thick silver hair. "I suppose you are. Forgive me, but time passes differently for me. I am very old."

He didn't look a day over thirty-five, but that meant nothing. Daēvas lived for hundreds of years before showing any signs of age.

"We will be leaving here soon," Culach continued. "I have had enough of hiding like an old badger in its den. There are Marakai among us. It took them a little while, but they finally found the right wood to build new ships and a safe place to launch them. The vessels are almost finished."

"A little while?" she said with a laugh. "Twenty years, you mean."

He brushed this away. "My point is that I can take you home with us, Delilah. And then, once we are back in Nocturne . . . well, I've traveled through the Dominion before."

A shadow crossed his face. She knew the loss of his sight had something to do with it, though her mother had balked at telling her that part of the story.

"I will take a force of daēvas through a gate to search for them," Culach said. "But not here. They are too heavily guarded by the mortals." He groped for her hand and gave it a squeeze. "Come with us. This is no place for our kind."

She squeezed his hand back, then gently withdrew her own. "I cannot. But I thank you for the offer."

He scowled. "Why not?"

"I already told you. Others have searched the shadowlands. My grandfather Victor—"

"So the bastard is still alive," Culach interrupted fondly.

"Very much so. Do you think he did nothing when his son and daughter-in-law vanished?"

Culach rose and poured two cups of wine. "No, Victor would lose his mind. Rant and rave and threaten every god he could think of. Then, once he calmed down, he would strap on a blade and go after them alone if he had to."

"I see you do know him," she said dryly. "That is precisely what happened. He was gone for weeks and came back empty-handed."

"And why won't the same thing happen to you?" He held out a cup. She accepted it but set it on the table without drinking.

"It might," she conceded. "But I must try. This is the last lead I have, Culach. With each year that passes, the trail grows colder. I fear there will be no others."

He sat down. "Very well. But what about the Quietus? I cannot let him leave here."

"Then I'll go alone."

Her words had the effect she hoped for.

"Don't be ridiculous. I will send some of our kin with you."

"I thought you were in hiding."

He opened his mouth, then closed it again.

"Give me Castelio," she coaxed. "He is best equipped to deal with both the dead and their masters. He is the logical choice and you know it."

"I know nothing of the sort. He'll report everything to his Ducissa the moment he returns to Aquitan. I can't risk discovery."

"Hmm. Do you remember the mortifex I mentioned? Lucius? He saw the lights of your houses. He already knows you're here. So the cat's out of the bag." She grinned. "Ah, there you are!"

"There who is?" Culach demanded. "I didn't hear anyone."

She stroked Thistle's soft fur. "My best friend and stalwart travel companion. Give me your hand."

Culach seemed to know his way around cats. He unerringly found the favored spot beneath Thistle's left ear. A deep rumble filled the room.

"Where did he come from?" Culach wondered.

She laughed. "Now this is a tale about you I know well. I believe you met his mother, Anuketmatma."

"The Mother of Storms!" Culach exclaimed. "Truly, this is her offspring? I must tell the Marakai. They will be beside themselves."

Anuketmatma was one of the Marakai deities. She took the form of a small striped cat and brought fair weather to their vessels when pleased — and the opposite if they neglected to pamper her.

"He was a gift from Queen Meb," she said. "We've been together since I was born."

Culach's face softened. "Ah, Meb. I have longed to see her again."

"She is a grown woman now and a fine ruler. Her people love her."

"Of course they do," he said stoutly.

She sniffed. "Is that a Redvayne vintage you're drinking?"

"I haven't read the bill of lading from the shipment we stole," he said, raising his cup in a toast, "but it could be."

"So *you* are the brigands who haunt the roads?"

"Oh, there are others," he replied with a laugh. "But how else could we survive here? No one gets hurt as long as they cooperate."

Being a trader herself, Lo frowned at this, but she could hardly blame them.

"Do you have any milk?" she asked. "For Thistle?"

"Ah, I'm afraid not. But I have meat in the larder."

Culach rose, the cat winding through his ankles.

"Don't let him clean you out," Lo called after them.

Her eyes grew heavy, but she couldn't drift off yet. Not until she had his promise.

"So you'll help me?" Lo asked when they returned. Thistle was waddling a bit. He stretched out on the carpet and rolled to one side.

"You remind me of your mother," Culach muttered. "Relentless."

"Castelio will not see Orlaith until we retrieve her son. He must still travel back across the mountains to Aquitan. This isn't her duchy anyway. It is Duc Caino Scalici's. By the time he finds out, you will be long gone."

Culach only grunted, but she could tell he was coming around. They reminisced for a while. Lo gave him the latest news from Nocturne and Solis. He seemed glad that the truce forged among the four clans was holding.

"Do you want help with this wraith?" he asked.

She hesitated. It was a tempting offer, but what if Lucius reappeared? The mortifex was obviously not threatened by *her*. He knew he was stronger. But how might he react when faced by a force of living, full-blooded daēvas? If she was right in her guess and Lucius was a Vatra, he had died in the midst of a bloody war against the other clans. What grudges might he hold?

The truth was, Lucius could incinerate them all in a heartbeat if he chose — and Lo wouldn't risk it.

"Thank you, but I'm sure Castelio and I can manage a single wraith. I will reveal my power if I must. We'll be parting ways soon enough." She should have been glad at the thought and found she was not. "It's settled then. I will snatch a few hours rest and depart."

Culach was silent for a moment. "Mina and I are having a baby. She's not far along yet, but . . ."

"That's wonderful news!"

He looked happy. "Yes, it is. I think she'll sympathize with allowing you both to leave if it means saving this mortal child, even if he is Orlaith's son. But I must speak to her first. If I make a decision for both of us, she will serve me my manhood on a platter."

"No more babies," Lo said sadly.

He snorted. "I will ask the Marakai about your wind ship. And I'll fetch you myself when it is ready. How long do you plan to be gone?"

"Two or three days, that's all." Lo thought for a moment. "I don't suppose you have any horses? We cannot allow the wraith to get ahead of us."

"No horses." Culach smiled. "But I have something better."

CHAPTER 21

Cas knelt among the rocks at the edge of the stream and upended the bucket over his head.

"Feck, that's cold," he gasped.

After a sleepless night waiting for someone to slit his throat, he was feeling every ache and bruise this morning. The woman, Mina, refused to say much other that Delilah would be treated well. Then she'd untied his hands, given him food, and let him roll up in his blankets inside one of the houses.

Half the brigands seemed to be women, including his guard. She was short and dark-skinned and wore a leather vest that exposed sinewy arms covered in tattoos of sea monsters. A many-tentacled kraken and other aquatic beasts he'd never heard of. The brigands spoke his tongue but with strange accents like Delilah's.

After a few hours, the guard had roused him and said they would be free to leave. The abrupt reversal of fortune made him even more paranoid. He'd asked why, which earned an amused grin. *The lady you travel with is known to us.* The guard had returned the rest of his belongings and waved him from the stone hut. When he asked for the nearest stream, she handed him a bucket and pointed the way. She'd faded into the trees, but no doubt she was close by, spying on him—

"They would have warmed some water for you. I had a hot bath."

He shook wet hair from his face and glanced over a shoulder. *The mysterious lady herself.*

"Do you make it a habit of creeping up on naked men?" he asked.

"You *are* wearing pants."

Delilah looked clean, though shadows lurked beneath her eyes. So she hadn't slept well, either. The presence of so many women in the camp had reassured him, but he still felt a powerful surge of relief to see her unharmed.

"Do you mind tossing me my cami?" he asked.

"What's a cami?"

He squeezed water from his hair. "My camicia." She looked clueless. Cas pointed. "*That.*"

Delilah handed it to him. "I call it a shirt."

He snorted. "Shirt? Sounds like . . . never mind." He tugged it over his head and tied the lacings. "So you know these brigands?"

"They're not brigands." Her voice was dry. "They're only hiding here because *your* people hate and fear outsiders."

The dart found its mark. "Yonders," he muttered.

"Pardon?"

"That's what they used to call me in Swanton. It's a village I lived in before I became a Quietus." Cas pulled on his boots. "Longest three years of my life. So . . . are they really letting us go?"

"Yes. That's what I came to tell you. Their leader is a merchant from Solis. They came on ships, hoping to trade, and were treated in the most hostile fashion. So they've been lying low until they're able to leave again."

"That's quite the lucky chance," he said, watching her expression closely. "That you happen to know them."

"Not as much as you might think. The Merchants' Guild in Samarqand pays taxes to my uncle, the king. The wealthiest traders are often at court. I have known Culach Kafsnjor since I was a little girl. Everyone thought he was dead. He was surprised to see me, as well."

Her story was ludicrous. Not the "greeted in hostile fashion" part — *that* Cas could well believe — but the rest of it. These people looked like seafarers, aye, but more of the piratical variety.

Delilah eyed him guilelessly, then turned to study the tools of his trade. He'd laid them out to assess what he had left. The pack was disarranged — they'd obviously searched his things — but nothing appeared to be missing.

"May I?" she asked, crouching down.

"Go ahead." He strapped on the wide leather braces that contained pouches to stash the various items he was required to carry. *At all times, without exception*.

Cas considered pressing her further, but every minute he stayed in this camp, the wraith was getting farther ahead. Better to let it lie for now, until he was well away.

"Kaethe's Tears," he said, as she examined the vials. "They come from the source of the Forkings River. There's a shrine to Bel. The priests add their blessing."

He was down to seven vials, each more precious than iron. Delilah passed them over and Cas tucked them into his braces.

"So you have only two gods. Bel and Kaethe."

He nodded. "The Sun Lord and the Drowned Woman. It is said they were married once, until they fell out with each other. He grew jealous that her powers were not limited to half the world." He gave her a quick grin. "Still, most people find it prudent to honor them both."

"There are dozens of gods where I come from," she said wryly. "The Greeks have one pantheon, the Persians another. Then there are the—" She cut off abruptly. "Well, many others. Oh, look at these!"

She picked up his interlocking knives. Nimble fingers clicked them together, then broke them apart again. "How clever. They fit into a single sheathe."

He scooped up the pouch of iron coins and tied them to a loop on his breeches.

"And this?" She held out the last pouch.

"Nails," he said with a laugh. "They were my first defensive weapon. I've found it hard to give them up."

"But they work?"

"As long as they're pure iron." Cas tied the pouch to another loop.

She handed him his knives. "How did you become a Quietus, Castelio?"

He tied his hair back. "I'll tell you, if you tell me who you were looking for in Tjanjin."

It was the wrong thing to say. The friendliness seeped out of her face like a cloud covering the sun. "You put that fisherman up to collecting the reward. I thought you already knew the answer."

Her icy tone irritated him. "You know I don't. I already told you, Lucius gave me that information."

Her face went even stormier. She said nothing.

"Then you can guard your secrets, my lady," he said lightly, hoisting his pack. "And I'll guard mine. Will you be staying with your *friends*? You have no obligation to continue."

"I've come this far," she muttered. "I intend to see the boy safe."

They walked back to the cluster of houses in tense silence. Delilah made a cursory introduction of their ringleader, the supposed merchant. Culach Kafsnjor was huge and scarred and, apparently, blind. He neither looked nor sounded like any trader Cas had ever seen.

Delilah wandered off to fetch her cat, which perched on a stool surrounded by a group of the pirates. They had laid various offerings on the ground. Plundered jewelry and morsels of food. Thistle stared into the middle distance as they whispered among themselves. What the feck?

"You're headed to the border?" Culach Kafsnjor asked.

His tone was cool, the roving green eyes downright wintry.

"That's right," Cas replied. "Ah, milord."

Whoever this hulking man was, better to stay on his good side.

"It's a full day's walk to Nox from here."

His heart sank. "I fear the wraith will beat us then."

"We will bring you ourselves," Culach replied brusquely. "You'll be there in an hour."

An hour? Cas's spirits lifted. The man must have his own wind ship. Though if he did, why had he and his companions stayed here, marooned in this remote, rugged valley? None of it made sense.

"How?" Delilah demanded, hurrying up with Thistle padding behind.

Cas got the feeling she'd asked this question before and been rebuffed.

"You'll see," Culach replied cagily.

The brigand tugged his hood up and headed toward the far side of the vale. Cas marveled at his knowledge of the terrain. The ground was rocky and uneven, but he didn't miss a step. A faint path was visible, the scraggly grass trampled down. They climbed the hill to a summit overlooking the next valley. A long, low stone building stood there, with three dark doorways. Cas caught the pungent scent of animal dung.

"The mounts are inside," Culach said.

Delilah frowned. "I thought you didn't have horses."

He smiled. "Like I said, these are better."

Mina emerged from one of the openings, her hand on the bridle of an enormous creature that looked like a cross between a bird and a lizard. Red-gold feathers rose to a stiff crest along its back. It had a long, serpentine neck and wickedly curved beak. Cas goggled, then took a hasty step back when it hissed at him.

"Abbadax!" Delilah exclaimed. "How stupid of me. I should have guessed."

Cas turned to her. "You have seen these things before?"

"They're native to my land." Her face was bright with excitement. "I have never flown on one, though."

Flown on one. His eagerness faded. "Are they safe?"

That merited an evil laugh from Culach. "Ragnhildur would disembowel you in a heartbeat at my command," he said, chuckling. "One snap from her beak and she'd pop your head right off like a grape—"

"Culach," Delilah said warningly.

He cleared his throat. "If you're asking whether you'll fall to your death, the answer is no." He sounded almost regretful. "We use harnesses. The feathers are sharp as razors, so watch your hands."

Cas was not reaching out to pet the abbadax. In fact, he had taken another step back. It cocked its head, peering at him with malignant curiosity.

For Enrigo, he reminded himself.

Mina led a second mount from the stables. This one had aquamarine feathers and silvery scales along its legs, which were tipped with bladelike claws. In short order, both abbadax were fitted with saddles and harnesses. Cas was somewhat mollified to learn that he wasn't expected to ride it alone. Mina would go with him, Culach with Delilah.

Mounting was tricky. Culach showed him the precise spot on the wing where he could put his weight, then guided his hand to the double saddle. "When you swing up, try not to lose your balls on her crest," the pirate-king cautioned. "Believe me, it's happened before." A grin. "Though not to me, of course."

Cas vaulted so high above its back he nearly went over the other side. He grabbed the bridle, heart thumping, and managed to right himself before he tumbled onto the left wing. It emitted an annoyed screech but calmed at soothing murmurs from Culach.

"Well done," Delilah said with an encouraging nod. "Now I'll give it a try."

She swung gracefully into the saddle like she'd done it a thousand times before. The abbadax gave a friendly trill. So she got the nice one. It figured, he thought sourly.

"Come, Thistle," she said, patting her knee.

The cat looked reluctant. His ears flattened as he regarded the beast. Then, with a low, disapproving growl, he sprang like a panther to its back. Her harness had been adapted to carry a third, smaller passenger. Thistle tolerated the bindings with ill humor, nipping at her hands.

"Don't," she muttered, sucking on a finger. "A short journey only, friend, I promise."

"Your cat lives up to its name," Cas remarked.

Thistle shot him a flat stare that increased his unease. It was a cat. An odd one, aye, but still . . . it couldn't understand. *Could it?*

Cas cinched into his own harness. His knees felt watery. As a boy, he'd enjoyed climbing trees and hills, but they were attached to the fecking ground. After the wind ship crashed, he'd vowed never to venture into the skies again if he could help it. And here he was—

Mina gave a sharp whistle. The abbadax waddled like an ungainly, oversized waterfowl toward the edge of the cliff, slowly picking up speed. Much too slowly for comfort. His gut clenched. Then a gulf of open air before them, a great spring from the back legs, and they were gliding like eagles across the valley. . .

No, not gliding like eagles. Plummeting like stones.

A yelp escaped him. The wings unfurled with an audible snap, gave a series of mighty beats, and their death spiral reversed. Wind rushed in his ears, tugged his hair loose of its ribbon. Mina gave another series of whistles. The abbadax tipped to the side, angling northward. He slipped a few inches before the harness caught him.

The first minutes were . . . not pleasant. Every time they changed course, he was far too aware that only a flimsy webbing of weathered ropes lay between him and a thousand paces of nothing. At least on board the ship, he could retreat from the rail. This was like being tied to the top of the mast.

But the harness held, he learned to anticipate the shifts, and after a while, his grip loosened a little. Not enough to wave back at Delilah as she passed, but at least he stopped feeling certain that each breath would be his last. Gradually, the sky darkened until he could no longer see the ground. Just a black ocean strewn with stars and two of the moons — bright yellow Selene and her white, coin-sized sister, Hecate. They hung low over the horizon, both descending. Artemis, the enormous moon also called the Traveler, had not yet risen.

Cas did a swift calculation and groaned inwardly. It was as he'd feared.

The rest of the journey passed in a blur. Then the abbadax entered a long, shallow dive. A scattering of lights appeared below. *Nox*. The last village in Alessia.

They alit at a crossroads a short distance from the outskirts. He dismounted gingerly, stiff and windblown. Culach and Delilah had already landed and were speaking together out of earshot.

"What did you think of your first ride?" Mina handed him his pack. Her cheeks were pink, her hair as wild as he imagined his own must look.

"I will never forget it, my lady," he replied honestly. "And I hope never to repeat it."

She laughed, then grew serious. "Watch over her, Quietus. She is like a daughter to me and I would be unhappy if anything happened to her." Dark eyes took his measure.

"I will do my best," he promised, glancing at the sky. "But I'm afraid we must hurry."

Mina sighed. "She spurned our aid. I hope she knows what she's doing."

He frowned. "Aid? She never mentioned—"

But then Delilah was coming over, Culach already back in the saddle, and Mina left him to bid her goodbye. A quick embrace, a whispered word, and the pair of abbadax launched into that funny, awkward gait up the road. Cas watched them lift off and flap toward the mountains.

"What's the plan?" Delilah asked, walking up with her pack over one shoulder. "Do you think we made it in time?"

Like Mina, she was flushed, her hair a bird's nest. Her blue eyes were soft and slightly glazed from the trip. He stared, unwillingly, at the little cleft in her lip. Bel help him, she looked like she'd just roused from bed after a long night of—

"I'm summoning Lucius." He turned away, hoping she didn't catch the reluctance in his voice. He still hadn't told her what the mortifex nearly did. "I wish we didn't need him, but true night is coming. That is when the wraith will try to cross the river."

"True night?"

"When all three moons are hidden. It doesn't happen often. Once every three lunar cycles."

She nodded in understanding. "Back home, we call it the lacuna. It means a pause."

Depending on the cycle, true night might last for seconds or hours. It was the time when the dead were at the height of their powers. When decent folk huddled in their homes with the doors and windows locked tight.

"This was planned carefully," he said, as the cat strolled over, winding between her legs. "Wraiths hide inside living bodies. That allowed it to cross the rivers west of the mountains. But the soldier it possessed died at the border. That will weaken it. The wraith needs the protection of true night to cross the final bridge at Nox."

"And it will be much stronger." She looked troubled but not afraid.

"Aye. Which means we need the mortifex." He drew one of his blades. "I must ask you to move away and turn your back, my lady. This has to be done in private."

She didn't budge. "Why? How does it work?"

"I speak his true name. It is a closely held secret."

"And? Surely that's not all."

"I must draw a nine-pointed star," he admitted. "In blood."

Her sharp gaze went to his bandaged hand. "Is that how you brought Lucius to Tjanjin?"

"Aye. It was the first time I've ever done it."

Delilah bit her lip, thinking. "So you make a sort of gate."

He hadn't thought of it that way before. "I suppose it's similar."

"Fascinating. And he must obey you?"

Cas gave her a rueful smile. "Sadly, no. I do not wear the menotte. But he will be forced to appear."

"Then you could have done this before. When Lucius left us in the forest."

He saw no way to deny it. "I could have . . ."

"Yet you chose not to. Why?"

"Because I was weary of his company," Cas snapped. "What does it matter?"

"No need to get testy," she murmured. "I just want to know how things work."

He glanced over her shoulder. Selene floated two hands above the horizon. Hecate was a mere sliver through the trees. "We're almost out of time. Please."

She sighed and walked a short distance away, turning her back.

Cas pushed up a sleeve and pressed the blade to his arm. How he loathed being forced to call on Lucius. But if he failed here, the last chance could slip through his fingers.

"Kaethe, grant me your blessing—"

"That won't be necessary," a voice rasped from the darkness.

He stayed the blade before it drew blood. Lucius stalked toward him, his eyes pinpoints of flame in the darkness. The cat hissed and shot off.

"Kind of you to join us," Cas said.

"You might have tried calling the normal way first. I was right over there." The mortifex pointed down the road. "Do you know what it feels like to be summoned? Let's see if I can describe it for you, Quietus. Like having a fishhook pierce your soul and—"

"I don't care what it feels like." Cas sheathed the knife. "You left me no choice."

"I'll admit, I wasn't expecting you so soon," Lucius replied. He sounded annoyed. "How did you manage it?"

So he'd just arrived. Or he was pretending he didn't see the abbadax land.

"You have your secrets," Delilah said, approaching them. "We have ours."

It was essentially the same thing Cas said to her back at the camp. They shared a quick look of amusement, quarrel forgotten.

Lucius bowed to her, sweeping his cloak back with a flourish. "As you say, khamoun. But there is no time to waste." He gazed at the skies. "True night will soon be upon us."

There was an eager note in his voice. And he looked hale. Color warmed his cheeks and Cas felt no chill in his presence. The gash on his forehead was gone.

"Who," he demanded softly, "did you kill?"

Delilah had spotted her cat; she was trying to persuade it to return and wasn't listening.

Lucius pressed a hand to his doublet. "You wound me. Why do you assume I killed someone?"

"It's obvious."

His expression hardened. "I did what I needed to. The river will stop me, too. I could not risk losing the heir."

Cas liked Enrigo. He would make a decent Duc someday. Not like most of the nobles, who viewed their vassals in much the same way as they viewed their hounds and horses. But the number of souls sent through the Veil to retrieve him kept climbing.

His shook his head in disgust. "How do you want to play this?"

The mortifex eyed him appraisingly. "I suppose you might be useful. We'll trap it at the middle of the bridge over running water. It will be the weakest there."

"Enrigo must be kept safe," he warned. "Our only task is to get him back, even if it means the wraith escapes."

"I leave that part to you. Come, Nox isn't far."

Lucius strode away in the same direction he'd appeared from — the eastern branch of the crossroads. Cas and Delilah shouldered their packs again and followed, Thistle prowling some distance behind. The mortifex produced a wavering flame to light the way. Like most of the roads Cas traveled, it was hard-packed earth with deep ruts from the passage of wagons.

They passed cultivated fields and orchards. Then, a rusty iron gate. Cas recognized it at once. The village lichyard.

It was very dark, but Selene was still high enough to illuminate the rounded humps of headstones, jutting like teeth from the ground. An unnatural chill came though the bars. That would worsen when the moons set, covering the lichyard with sparkling frost. But even now, the temperature difference was enough to conjure a thin mist that hung about a pace above the grassy earth.

Delilah stopped walking and gripped his arm. "Is that . . .?"

A solitary shadow hunched next to one of the graves. Its back was turned so the face wasn't visible, but Cas made out pale hands in the gloom. One rested on the headstone. The other scrabbled weakly at the dirt. He heard the faint scritch of its nails. Otherwise, the figure didn't move. Didn't seem to notice them at all.

"Aye," he said softly. "Newly dead, I reckon. There's no glow yet. If they rise within the first three days, they can retake their old body. After that, they're spirits like you saw at Midgate."

He hesitated, a hand falling to his knives. Lucius strode back.

"There's no time, Quietus," he snapped. "Deal with it later."

Cas hated to leave it loose, but the mortifex was right. He slid the knives back into their sheath.

"Will it trouble us?" Delilah whispered with a small wince, rubbing her arm as though it pained her.

"They're usually drawn to those who wronged them or those they loved. And the iron gate will hold it." He frowned. "Are you all right?"

She tore her gaze from the ghoul. "Yes. It's just . . . sad, isn't it?"

"Aye," he agreed. "Until they come for you."

The scratching faded as they hurried on down the road. He looked back once. It was too dark to tell if the ghoul had moved. Yet he had the strong sense of being watched.

They soon found the village. Candlelight glowed in the cracks of the shutters, but its residents all huddled inside, no doubt clutching whatever charms they could afford. Like Swanton, the bigger houses had horseshoes nailed above the door, the humbler ones woven knots of reeds or willows, both of which were associated with the Drowned Woman.

A dog barked as they passed, quickly silenced by its master. After that, the only sound was wind chimes tinkling in the darkness.

The bridge lay at the far side of town. Cas had never been all the way to the border between Alessia and Nyons. He heard the restless melody of the river before it came into view, a sound he always found reassuring. Then he rounded a sharp curve and saw the bridge itself. A slender stone span that arched over the surging whitewater. A gatehouse loomed on the near bank.

"Is there someone inside?" he asked Lucius, halting in the shelter of the trees.

The mortifex gave a thin smile. "Not anymore."

So that was who he fed on. Well, it could have been worse.

Cas realized that he was growing accustomed to the creature's habits. Like the proverbial frog in a cookpot who fails to notice the gradually boiling water until it's too late. But true night was coming. And what would Lucius become then?

"I suppose you want me to take the center," he said.

"That would be preferable," the mortifex replied dryly. "I will lie in wait on this side. When it crosses the bridge, I will appear and prevent it from backtracking. As soon as you have Enrigo, I will burn it. The wraith will be forced to abandon its vessel and run back to the Courtenays."

Lucius's gaze fixed on the hills, where Selene was slowly sinking.

"And what will I do?" Delilah asked.

Lucius shrugged. "Wait out of sight somewhere?"

She gave him her haughty khamoun look. "I think not. I will take the other side of the bridge, in case it breaks through."

One of Lucius's brows lifted. "I have no objection."

All the more reason for me to stop it at the middle, Cas thought. Her charm of protection made him feel better, but he didn't care to see her die again.

That led to other troubling thoughts — ones that had kept him awake the previous night. What if he hadn't pulled her body up before they crashed? The ship had left a swathe of destruction through the forest. Would she have revived with horrendous wounds?

Or if Lucius had had his way and drained her of blood? What then?

She claimed she hadn't tested the limits of the talisman. He hoped she never did.

They walked together to the bridge. It looked ancient, the stone pitted and cracked. But traces of ornate engravings remained. Flowers and vines, even the laurel wreath of Bel. This surprised him greatly.

"It dates to before the Sundering," Lucius said, following his gaze. "When the sun rose and set on these lands."

There was an odd, wistful note in his voice. Cas watched him leap down the bank and hide himself in the stone supports. They stashed their packs beneath an overhang. As he and Delilah ventured onto the bridge, he noticed other dedications to Bel, just visible in the fading moonlight. A python wrapped around a lyre. A bow and quiver of arrows.

"Those are the symbols of Apollo," Delilah said, trailing a finger along the carvings. "I have seen them in Delphi. Yet you call him Bel—"

Cas pressed a finger to his lips. He glanced at the sliver of moon. She nodded and took his sleeve, leaning close. Even in the dark, he could see the deep blue of her eyes.

"Take this," he whispered, pressing one of his iron knives into her palm.

"I have been trained to fight," she whispered, testing the balance with an expert grip. "You worry about the boy. I will stop the wraith."

"They are very fast," he warned.

A flash of teeth. "So am I."

And then she was gone, running lightly to the far side of the bridge.

Chapter 22

Thistle found her moments after Lo reached the far side.

"I will be your eyes," he said. "When the lacuna comes."

She crouched down at his side, concealed against the supports.

"That would be welcome," she whispered. "Even I cannot see in pitch darkness."

She could still make out Castelio's silhouette, pressed out of sight where the arch of the bridge dipped down again. In the sky above, the last silvery wedge of Hecate vanished. Wisps of cloud crossed the face of Selene, the brightest moon, their edges lit with gold. Slowly, slowly, she sank behind the mountains. The lights of Nox glimmered in the distance, but they were faint sparks between the trees. Lo settled against the low stone wall, holding the iron knife loosely in her right hand.

She was glad Culach hadn't argued too hard about staying — especially since her hunch about Lucius returning had proven correct. He *must* have seen them land on the abbadax, yet he pretended ignorance. Perhaps he wanted to stay far away from his living cousins.

The river rushed below, the only sound as Selene departed and true night fell. Within seconds, a deep, total darkness descended like a curtain drawn across the land. She felt the shift in her bones. A sudden ceding of power from light and warmth to their polar opposites.

Back home, she had never feared the lacuna. It was merely an astronomical curiosity. But here in Aveline, where life and death teetered on a knife edge, true night had a palpable weight and strangeness. Like the pressure in your ears when you swim up from a great depth, or the uncanny sensation of glimpsing the profile of someone you know well and realizing a moment later, when they turn to face you, that it's a perfect stranger.

The silence felt heavy and charged. She groped for Thistle, burying her fingers in his fur. His body tensed, and she heard the distant clop of hooves. They slowed at the approach to the bridge. The wraith seemed wary this time, having been tricked at the border. It paused at the far side.

She closed her useless eyes, allowing her other senses to take over. Nothing for a long moment. Then the soft grate of hooves on stone. The slight vibration as it began to cross. Very faint, the muffled whimper of a child.

The clouds parted, allowing a hint of weak starlight. She opened her eyes wide, straining, and perceived a shadow, darker than the others, at the center of the bridge. The suggestion of a hood, turning to and fro. A quick, rasping sound she couldn't place at first.

Her heart beat so swiftly she feared the wraith would hear it. If it got past Castelio, she had to be ready. The muscles of her thighs knotted, ready to spring, when the rider growled and she realized what the sound was.

Snuffling.

It lurched forward. A shape rose up, and the hooded shadow toppled to the side. She burst from hiding as flames erupted on the Nox side of the bridge. They blinded her, but only for an instant. Castelio had hold of the wraith's leg, but it still gripped the reins and drew its own bonewood blade, which it used to parry his iron knife. The horse was dancing and neighing wildly. It nearly kicked Castelio in the head before Lo darted forward and grabbed the bridle. She held it steady long enough for him to drag the wraith from the saddle. A writhing bundle was tied across the horse's back. With a scream, the horse reared again, wrenching from her grip. It wheeled and galloped back across the bridge.

Straight into Lucius, who uttered a terse command that halted the terrified beast in its tracks. The flames withered and blackness fell again, even more solid in their absence. She could hear Castelio struggling blindly with the wraith. Someone smashed into her and sent her sprawling. She rolled and managed to keep her knife.

"Lucius!" she shouted. "I need light!"

"A moment," he called back. "I'm cutting the heir loose!"

She hovered at the edge of the fray, afraid to get too close and stab the wrong person — or get stabbed herself. At last, a small flame appeared, scarcely brighter than a single candle but enough to dispel the thick darkness. Two silhouettes, one tall, one much shorter, on the far side of the bridge told her that Lucius had freed Enrigo. The receding thunder of hooves told her the horse had had enough.

She spun back to the wraith, which moved like a striking serpent. Castelio was barely holding it at bay — probably because he'd given her one of his knives. She dodged a swipe from the wraith's dagger, slipped under its flailing arm, and hooked one foot behind its knee. With the creature off-balance, it was a simple matter to heft it up and over. The wraith didn't make a sound as it plunged over the edge. She heard a splash as it hit the river, then a guttural howl.

"Nicely done," Lucius called, striding forward with a flame cupped in one palm, the heir at his side. Enrigo's golden hair was rumpled, his face bright red. Tears of relief leaked from his eyes, which he rubbed at angrily.

"It's gone, see?" she said, leaning over the side.

The black waters had swallowed the soldier's body. She turned to Castelio with a fierce grin. He smiled, then staggered backward with a look of surprise, an arrow planted in his chest. She heard a sound like a swarm of angry hornets. Castelio sank to his knees as a second pierced his arm. Somehow, he had the presence of mind to grab Enrigo with his other hand and pull him down.

"Get the heir back to Nox!" Lucius yelled, running toward the source of the arrows on the Nyons side. One whizzed past his ear, another pierced his gut. With a growl, he snapped it off and threw it aside.

All of this occurred in the span of three seconds.

Lo dropped flat and crawled to Castelio. His teeth were gritted, but he sheltered Enrigo behind him. Blood leaked from the corner of his mouth. Soaked his camicia. She tore her eyes from the arrow embedded in his chest. A few more whizzed overhead. Then, boiling flames from the Nyons side.

"I'm getting you off this bridge," she said, striving for calm even as her own heart clawed at her ribcage.

Castelio shook his head. He blinked once, heavily. "Take . . . him."

"No," Enrigo said forcefully, pressing against the low wall. He was shaking, but he looked determined. "I won't leave you here, Cas!"

"You see?" Lo said. "Now hold still. I'll see to that arrow in your chest first. Lucius has bought us time."

The look he gave her was chilling. "There's nothing . . . you . . . can do." His lips were red. Bloody fingers groped for a pocket. "My coin . . ."

She batted his hand away, filled with sudden anger. "I'm going to break the arrow and pull it out," she said to Enrigo. "When I do, there will be a lot of blood. I need you to keep pressure on the hole. Can you do that?"

The boy stared at her for a moment, frozen. He had been through so much. But he seemed to find inner reserves of strength and managed a nod.

She rolled Castelio to his side. As she hoped, the arrowhead had gone straight through. She cut strips from her cloak and got them ready. Then she eased the leather braces from his shoulders.

"Don't," he muttered weakly, before she snapped the arrow off and pulled the ends from his chest and back. He screamed once, a wrenching sound, and passed out. Thick blood flowed immediately. She wound the strips around his chest as tightly as she could.

"Here," she said, taking Enrigo's hand and bringing it to the wound. "Press down as hard as you can. Don't let up."

He obeyed, turning his face away. It staunched the bleeding somewhat. Not enough. Lo snapped off the second arrow, which had gone through his biceps. He didn't even stir. She bound that one, too. Then she gripped Castelio under the arms. The arrow fire had ceased. A battle raged on the far shore, bursts of flame in not one but two locations. Sizzling fireballs streaked through the trees. Lucius was fighting another mortifex.

Every few seconds, flares and crashing booms echoed from the Nyons side. Lo kept her gaze fixed into the darkness as she hauled Castelio up the arching hump of the bridge and down the other side, Enrigo trying awkwardly to keep pace with one hand pressed against the wound. A trail of blood gleamed scarlet in the firelight behind them.

"It's not stopping!" Enrigo cried. "What do I do?"

She glanced down. Castelio's face looked white as marble.

"Let me see." She laid him down and unlaced the camicia with trembling fingers, then loosened the bandage. The arrow had entered high in his chest, smashing through his ribs. From the wet rasp of his breath, it had pierced a lung.

"My lady?" Enrigo ventured. Orange light flickered on the taut lines of his face. "Someone is coming."

Lo looked past him. A cluster of lanterns shone along the road. The people of Nox had emerged from their houses to help! She felt a surge of hope as they drew closer. But the lights were too cold, too faint to be lanterns. They drifted along in a steady gliding motion, not bobbing as they should have. Among them, she saw darker, shuffling shapes. Her left arm started to tingle.

Not villagers. The dead from the lichyard, spread out in a wide arc to block escape.

She spun back to the Nyons side. Lucius stood at the end of the bridge, blade out. It sliced through the air, streaming fire, and met the other mortifex's sword in a shower of molten sparks. His foe was wreathed in flame, just a dark outline. Lucius leapt to the narrow wall, cloak swirling, and spun to avoid a slash. A hot wind reeking of brimstone lifted her hair as they hammered at each other.

No way out on that side, either.

And it was still true night. Until Artemis rose, the dead could cross running water.

Panic bubbled up and she sought the Nexus. Instantly, her mind sharpened and her roiling emotions dulled. A mantle of calm settled across her shoulders as she assessed their options.

There was one way out, but only for Enrigo.

"Can you swim?" she asked him, distantly aware that her voice was cool, inhuman.

The boy gazed past her at the lumbering corpses, which had now reached the foot of the bridge. His face was rigid with fear, his eyes blank.

"You remind me of the prince of Samarqand," she said, as if they strolled together in his mother's vineyards. "He is about your age, but he seems older because he has been trained from the cradle to lead one day. I imagine it is the same with you, Your Grace."

Enrigo gave no sign of hearing. She took his chin and forced him to look at her.

"You have been very brave, and I'm certain you can do what I tell you. It will save Castelio."

A lie, but his eyes focused on her. "What, my lady?" he whispered, a tremor in his voice.

"I will lower you down from the bridge. Then I will drop you, and you will let the current take you downstream. Don't fight it. Float on your back and let it carry you, understand?"

He nodded again.

"Save your strength to swim to shore. We will find you, I promise."

"But—" He stared past her again.

"Yes, I know. I will slow them down."

She rifled through Castelio's weapons. The vials of Kaethe's Tears would be better to save for close quarters. She chose the pouch of nails and ran across the bridge toward Nox. The Nexus helped to dampen her own reaction to the dead. She felt their presence, but it didn't drain her strength.

The ones with physical bodies were faster than the specters and had already reached the entrance to the bridge. Tattered garments hung from their sunken frames. They smelled of earth and rot. When they saw her, a soft sigh went up like a breeze rustling dry leaves. She opened the pouch and shook out a line of iron nails across the bridge. The dead stopped beyond the barrier, arms reaching, muddy fingers snatching at the air. She ran back to Enrigo.

"Ready, Your Grace?" she asked.

Lo didn't wait for an answer. She hoisted him up to the low wall and took his hands.

"I will find you," she said. "I swear it."

The boy was terrified, yet he glanced at Castelio and hesitated. She knew then that he was nothing like his calculating mother or the other nobles she had met.

"I will stay and take care of him. That, too, I swear. He would want you to have this." She tucked a vial of Kaethe's Tears into his doublet. "Use that if you need it, but I don't think they can get to you in the river and Artemis will rise soon."

She hoped it was true.

"Hurry," she said. "I must check his wound again."

Enrigo clambered over the stone wall and she lowered him as far as she could. The drop was about twelve paces, the river flowing fast and deep below. She thought of the soldier's corpse, floating somewhere downstream. True night had summoned the dead from the lichyard. Might the soldier wash up on some sandbar . . . and rise again?

And what of the disembodied wraith? Had it returned to its masters? Or did it lurk in the dark, watching them?

Well, it was too late for doubts. Lo met Enrigo's frightened eyes as he dangled beneath her. "The gods carry you to safety," she whispered, and let go.

He landed in the river with a splash, flailed around for a moment, then righted himself. How small he looked amid the black expanse of water. The red light of the mortifexes' duel lit his face for an instant. Then the current whisked him away.

Lo hurried to Castelio's side. She feared he was already gone, but his eyes fluttered open.

"The heir is safe," she said, gripping his hand.

He gave the barest nod. "Please . . . my . . . iron coin. *Please.*"

The desperate plea in his voice cracked her reserve. She realized that he feared returning far more than he feared death. The Nexus slipped away in a tide of regret. She bitterly wished she had learned the ways of healing with the elements. But she'd never had a need for it.

Never had a need.

Cursing her stupidity, Lo tore the silver chain from her own neck and hung it around Castelio's, tucking the disk inside the torn camicia so it touched his clammy skin. It was the first time in her life she had ever taken it off. Her own cuts and scrapes grew more acute, but she hardly noticed.

A bubble of blood formed on his lips as he tried to speak. He looked up at her, but his eyes were dim and she knew he no longer saw her.

He's slipping away . . .

It was hard to find the Nexus again, amid her own rage and grief, with the dead on one side and the mortifexes' battle on the other. But the place of calm finally came, and she fed power into the talisman, drawing water from the river, earth from the stone, air from her own panting breath. Fire was no trouble. An inferno roared not thirty paces away.

Her talents were meager, but the talisman absorbed the threads, magnifying and refocusing them in a complex web of power. Castelio's back bowed, eyes rolling up to the whites. Then he collapsed, limp as a broken doll. Blood no longer welled from the hole in his chest. His heart had stopped.

Lo rocked back on her heels. *I killed him*, she thought numbly. *I refused his last wish, and then I killed him—*

Her head jerked around at a deep and terrible groan from the end of the bridge. More dead had arrived, rank upon rank. They jostled and pushed in a frenzy. One of their number had been shoved across the barrier. It thrashed on the nails, limbs jerking. Without hesitation, the ones behind flowed through the gap, stepping on its prone body.

She watched them come, mouths open and black tongues gabbling the same sounds, over and over.

Sarg eresh'kigal.

She shook her head, but somehow she understood what it meant.

Shadow soul.

The others took up the moaning cry.

Sarg eresh'kigal. Shadow soul. Shadow soul. Help us . . .

"Lucius!" she screamed.

But the Nyons side of the bridge had gone dark, save for the burning crowns of trees. There was no one left to answer.

She picked up a vial of Kaethe's Tears. Unstoppered it and held it in her hand, then poured it out. Her left arm was aflame, the band around her chest tightening, and again, the sense of another place, so close. A way out?

This time, she didn't resist.

Something unfurled inside her. Light burst through the widening cracks. An icy wind tore at her hair and cloak. The dead staggered, garments whipping like ragged pennants. Cold leached into her marrow, an absence of heat as total as the surface of the moons. Colors bled away. There was only darkness and the white torches of the trees, the spectral glow of the spirits.

Then the river began to rise. Black waves crashed against the bridge. A great whirlpool rushed around her. She clung to the stone wall as the current gripped her legs. Faster and faster it spun, pulling them all down into darkness. She sensed a fathomless void waiting beneath. Terror turned her bowels to water, but her heart did not race. No, each beat came slower than the last. A clock winding down.

The whirlpool sucked at her like the undertow on a frozen beach. Her sweaty fingers began to slip. Then she heard another sound above the screaming wind and hollow cries of the damned. A rhythmic pounding that called to her. She grabbed hold of it, squeezed her eyes shut and tried to close the door. Her body was numb, a wrung-out rag, but she listened to the music of the drum, counted and listened and thought of nothing else.

Very slowly, the downward pressure faded. The wind died.

When she dared to open her eyes again, the bridge was empty. Sparkling frost coated the stone around her. Of the dead, there was no sign. Just a scattering of iron nails. Artemis had risen above the trees, nearly full, her silver light playing on the wavelets below.

Lo tried to stand. Cramps buckled her legs. She shivered violently and crawled to Castelio. He was soaked in blood, eyes closed, one arm flung wide. She smoothed the hair back from his pale brow.

"I'm so tired," she whispered.

Then she collapsed with her cheek against his chest, lulled to sleep by the steady beat of his heart.

Chapter 23

Lo came to in an iron cage.

When she sat up and it began to swing, she realized that it hung from a thick tree limb ten paces above the ground. She licked dry lips. Tried to calm down. Someone had found them — most likely the Courtenays. It must have been their mortifex that Lucius was fighting.

The cage hung in a dim cavity formed from the interlocking branches of trees with white bark and red leaves. Faint starlight passed through the gaps, gleaming on the iron bars. She had no memory of coming here, but she did recall everything else that had happened.

I banished the dead, she thought in wonder. *And I saved Castelio . . . didn't I? Or was it all a dream?*

Her clothes were stiff with dried blood. *His* blood she confirmed, after giving all her bits a quick tryout and finding no serious injuries. But her protective talisman was missing.

Not a dream. It was too vivid. The attack by archers, dropping Enrigo into the river. The arrival of the dead. She had almost managed to banish *herself* along with them, but Castelio's heartbeat called her back.

Lo felt a flood of relief that he had survived. That they both had. But the memory of that chill black void made her resolve never to do it again.

Whatever the hell *it* was.

Her mother had strange power. Apparently, she did, too. It had saved her life — and nearly taken it.

"Lo's luck," she muttered.

Her left arm was tingling again. She sought the Nexus and began to plot.

Apparently, the Ducissas of Nyons thought they'd caught another mortifex. But iron had no effect on her, nor would a cage hold her. She stood up and tested her legs. She felt thirsty but reasonably strong and rested. So she had been here for several hours at least, and they hadn't bothered to leave a guard. *Careless.*

A thread of earth and the heavy padlock clicked. She eased the cage door open, sat at the edge and swung down, dropping to a mossy floor. Clumps of mushrooms glowed an unearthly green in the darkness, sprouting within the gnarled tree roots like will o' the wisps. She walked along the intertwined branches that formed the walls, seeking a hidden lever. She found nothing. But if someone had locked her in the cage, there had to be a way out.

Then she had an idea. Her father often worked with living wood. He'd go into the cedar glades outside Susa and return with a beautiful flute or a new comb for her mother. Gifts from the trees. It was a trick of the Danai clan, his people. They were forest daēvas, attuned to every living thing within their borders. It was, he'd said with a wink, a matter of asking nicely.

She laid a hand on the nearest branch and opened her heart to the spirit that dwelt within.

Its skin was rough and gnarled, cool beneath her fingers. She tried to convey her humble need to pass but soon realized the tree had no use for words. It was an ancient thing and wise in ways far beyond mortal understanding. The ways of the deep, rich earth and nourishing rain. Of the moonlight and starlight, and how to sustain itself and its children on very little. Its roots twined with its neighbor, and its neighbor's neighbor, on and on, passing what was needed back and forth, aiding each other when one weakened.

Her own awareness flew along these lines of communication, cooperation, and memory. With a shock, she realized that it had known a time of sunlight, far in the distant past when it was young, although its sense of time was different. After the Sundering, the tree had starved and nearly died, until someone's hand shaped it anew.

Shaped it with magic.

The sheer complexity of such an endeavor stunned her. It was not simply *this* tree but entire forests that had been altered to use the moons as they once had the sun. Insects evolved, and the birds that ate them. Nature reborn, taught to thrive in a land that by all rights should be cold and barren. It was the same on the dark side of Nocturne, but she'd never really thought about how the daēvas managed it.

Without necromancy, this would all be gone.

The thought unsettled her.

"Thank you," she whispered. "For sharing yourself with me."

She could snap the branches, force a way through, yet she could not bring herself to do it. But then, with a rustle of foliage, the tree shifted, limbs rising and spreading to present a narrow gap.

Lo slid through. It closed behind her.

She stood in a long tunnel of arching trees, these bearing trefoil leaves of lustrous gold. Clusters of bats roosted in the dark branches overhead. They were rather sweet, with funny squashed faces and delicate membranous wings. A ripple went through them at the sudden movement. Lo happened to like bats, but she froze, understanding that they were, in fact, a warning system.

She found the Nexus again. Some were sleepy, others alert. None were especially clever, not in the sense of knowing that they were supposed to kick up a fuss if someone passed. But the wakeful ones were jittery, attuned to danger. She tried to project harmlessness as she walked slowly down the tunnel. Wings shivered, then wrapped tight again. The bats returned to their drowsy dreams of hunting insects. Of the sweet morsels of fruit their mistresses doled out.

She reached the end of the tunnel. It doglegged to the left. There were no more bats ahead. She blew out a soft breath.

"Thistle?" she whispered. "Are you about?"

Lo waited for a minute, but the cat didn't show. She didn't worry too much. He would turn up when he was needed. Although . . . he hadn't appeared on the bridge when she was in dire straits. That was most unlike him.

Well, she couldn't blame Thistle for steering clear. She sensed the power of death all around — and other things you wouldn't normally find in a noble's keep. Large albino toads that lurked in shallow pools, hopping off with a splash at her approach. Clouds of fluttering moths. Black bees droning among beds of trumpet-shaped black flowers.

She drew the shadows around her and crept forward, passing clearings bright with stars and squeezing between boulders that led to other arching tunnels. Every now and then, she paused to listen, using air currents to amplify sound. Quite distant, the soft whisk of slippers on stone. The eerie laugh of a screech owl. An indistinct scraping sound, like a rasp.

And a faint groan. It came once and fell silent.

Castelio?

She moved toward the sound, following a tall hedge with vicious thorns. It curved around; light flickered ahead. Lo crept closer, hood raised, utterly silent.

A chamber larger than all the others, holding another iron cage, this one resting on the ground. Lucius lay within it, curled into a ball. His clothes were charred. What she could see of him looked badly burned. Lo felt sick.

She was about to approach the cage when she noticed another mortifex lounging in a pool of darkness behind a stone column. Red hair hung in a long braid down his back. He wore a doublet with the stooping Nightjar of Nyons.

"I'll ask again. Why did your mistress send you here?" The mortifex pushed off the pillar and strode forward, stopping well short of the iron cage. "Did you steal that child from Nox to feed on so you could cross the river?"

"Let me . . . see him," Lucius whispered. His voice was a broken rasp.

The mortifex snorted. "Someone threw him into the river. I suppose you discarded him when he was of no further use to you. He was nearly gone when we fished him out." Flames erupted around the cage. "You come here uninvited, with a Quietus and a sorceress who heals mortal wounds, yet I am supposed to believe your intentions are innocent?" He scowled. "Well, your assassination plot has failed. As soon as the other prisoners wake, I will have every detail of it."

Lo pulled back, so surprised she lost the Nexus.

They don't even know who they have. And they think I'm . . . what exactly?

But he said I healed a mortal wound. Castelio is alive, then. And still sleeping.

She thought hard and could find no reason for the mortifex to pretend ignorance about Enrigo Redvayne. Assassination plot? What the hells was going on?

She peeked around the hedge again. The flames had subsided, but the iron bars glowed red-hot. Lucius gave another groan, drawing tighter into himself.

Pity welled in her heart. She stared at his tormentor's back. Felt that door inside her starting to rattle on its hinges. Her mouth twisted into a grim line as she forced it shut.

Not again. Never again.

Instead, she used a flick of air to tickle the colony of bats dozing near her own cage. Lo heard them burst from their roosts in a startled cloud. The mortifex's head snapped around. It spun and stalked away from the cage.

Directly toward her.

She ran down the tunnel, diving into a crossing passage and

squeezing against the dense branches. She still stuck out like a sore thumb. If he turned that way, she was done.

But when he emerged an instant later, he took a different route, gaze straight ahead.

The instant he vanished, she hurried back to the cage. The metal was too hot to touch. Sweat broke across her brow just getting near it.

"Lucius!" she hissed.

His head turned, barely. She studied the padlock. It was tricky with all the heat, which changed the properties of the iron to something softer and less brittle. Again and again, she failed. Sweat stung her eyes, coursed in rivulets down her spine. Surely, the mortifex must have discovered her ruse by now.

Then she saw the answer. Cooling the entire cage was beyond her, but she could use a bit of water on the lock . . . It finally gave with a hard snap, dangling from one clasp.

"I can't go inside," she whispered, wiping her face with a sleeve. "You have to crawl closer. I'll pull you out."

His green eyes met hers, glazed with misery. "Leave me. Find Enrigo and go, if you can."

"We need your help!"

"I'm in no shape—"

"Dammit, Lucius! Stop feeling sorry for yourself and get moving! He'll be back any second."

Lucius winced and rolled over. He began to pull himself across the glowing iron bars. It was the most horrible thing she'd ever witnessed. His flesh burned, tried to heal, then burned again. He made not a sound, just dragged himself inch by inch, until she could stand it no longer and reached inside the cage to take his hands. They gripped hers with surprising strength. The hem of her cloak caught fire but she didn't let go. With a mighty heave, she hauled him from the cage as far as she dared, then dropped and rolled around until the flames were smothered.

Lucius lay on his back, panting. Scar tissue webbed his hands. The menotte around his wrist still glowed faintly.

"How do you heal faster?" She crouched at his side. "What can I do?"

"Nothing," he croaked.

"Surely there is a way. You did it before—"

His eyes flashed. "You cannot give me what I need," he said roughly.

She scowled. "Well, I won't leave you here."

His face turned away. "Why not?"

"Just get up!" She slid an arm under his shoulders and hoisted him to standing. "Maybe if we move farther away from the iron it will help."

Lucius gave a hollow laugh.

She took most of his weight. Together, they lumbered awkwardly across the chamber.

"And where are we going, my lady?" It was the barest whisper, yet she detected his old dry tone.

"Anywhere but here. I'll hide you somewhere, and then I'll . . ." She stopped, heart racing. "Never mind."

The mortifex strode down the tunnel, his face a mask of fury. A young woman kept pace at his side. Barefoot, tall and sturdy, with curling white hair, white eyebrows, and dark skin. A necklace of bones circled her neck. She wore a gauzy plum-colored gown that fluttered behind her. More bones rattled at her ankles and around her wrists.

The mortifex raised a fist, flames flaring from between his clenched fingers. Their eyes locked. Lo called up a wind to smother the inferno before he hurled it at her. It howled through the chamber, driving the flames higher. They raced across the ceiling, withering the leaves on their branches.

Hot ash stung her eyes. She had nothing left. Lo swayed on her feet. The mortifex raised his other fist, smiling now. She was back on the bridge of the *Wind-Witch*, facing down Lucius — and she knew how this would end.

Very badly.

Chapter 24

Enough, Mace!"

The mortifex closed his fist. The flames winked out. After a moment, Lo released her own meager power, panting. Working too much air always left her out of breath.

"I will not have my home destroyed for these wretches," the woman snapped.

"Caul Courtenay," Lucius whispered in Lo's ear. "Rumored to have quite a temper."

So he *did* know them, the liar.

"How did you escape the iron cage?" Caul demanded with a hard stare.

"Why did you bring us here?" Lo shot back. "We did nothing to you!"

Caul's face hardened. She plucked a small bone from her hair and tossed it to the floor. Whispered words of power Lo didn't understand but which raised the hair on her neck just the same.

The bone — she thought it might be a toe — grew longer and sprouted a joint, a second bone, then another joint. Quick as a blink, a skeletal creature began to rise up, unfurling limbs in all directions. It had no head, only a multitude of pincers and spidery appendages. With rapid, jerking movements, it scuttled toward her.

"I know you had nothing to do with stealing the Redvayne heir!" Lo cried, trying to backpedal with Lucius in her arms. "A wraith took him! Please hear me out, Your Grace!"

Another hissed word and the bone-monster halted, steps away, one leg tapping impatiently.

Caul Courtenay exchanged a long look with her mortifex. "Stealing the Redvayne heir?" she echoed. Then she burst out laughing. "That's quite a story."

"He was taken from his bed by wraiths who possessed Orlaith's soldiers," Lo said quickly. "They carried a dagger with *your* sigil engraved upon it."

She snorted. "How convenient. Yes, that is precisely what we would do if we wanted her precious child. We would be sure to announce that we had done it." She addressed her mortifex, Mace. "Return Lucius to his cage. He shall have company this time. And you will not let either of them out of your sight!"

The bone-creature hopped up and down in anticipation. Lucius sagged against Lo's shoulder, wheezing. She saw no way to fight them all and save him, too. The thought of him being returned to the cage nauseated her.

"Lock me up again if you must," she said. "But look at him! He could not light a candle in this state. If you treat him more gently, I'll answer all your questions."

Mace's lips thinned. "You'll answer them regardless."

The bone-creature sidled closer, mandibles clacking.

"I don't want to hurt you," Lo warned. "But I will if I have to."

She gathered her power. Sensed Mace gathering his. Lo was all too aware that she no longer wore the talisman of protection.

"I fear she speaks the truth, sister," a soft voice said from the darkness.

Caul turned. Chaos Courtenay was smaller and rounder than her twin, though she shared the same wild, white, curling hair. Her eyes and lips were traced with dark kohl. She entered the chamber with the aid of two silver canes. The menotte circled one wrist. Enrigo Redvayne was with her. He looked pale and drawn but unharmed. His eyes widened when he saw Lucius.

"The boy finally revived," Chaos said. "I assured him we mean him no harm. He told me the whole story." Her brows drew down. "Someone is behind this, and I mean to discover who."

"Please, Lady Chaos," Enrigo said softly, touching her sleeve. "Don't punish Lucius. He was always kind to me."

"That is truly Orlaith's son?" Caul asked in disbelief. She threw up her hands. "*Merde!*"

Chaos moved to the bone-beast. She propped a cane against one leg, gave it a fond pat, and whispered a word. Immediately, the process reversed, limbs drawing into themselves and folding up like a collapsed scaffolding, until only the single small bone remained.

"Would you give that back to Lady Caul?" she asked Enrigo.

He shut his gaping mouth, gingerly picked it up, and ran to her sister, who blew a speck of dust off and tucked it into her hair.

Chaos regarded Lucius. "Lock him up," she said. "But not in the cage. Kaethe's Sanctuary will do. He cannot escape that."

Caul looked disgruntled but gave a sour nod. Mace shrugged, hoisted Lucius over one broad shoulder, and carted him off. Lucius did not protest, so Lo assumed that Kaethe's Sanctuary would be a marginal improvement. With that small victory accomplished, she decided it was time to switch tactics.

"Thank you for showing mercy, Your Graces," she said, sweeping a low bow. "It's clear there has been a serious misunderstanding and I do not deny that we are at fault. I hope we can set matters to rights."

"So do I," Caul muttered.

"If I might ask, where is Castelio?"

"The reaper? Sleeping." Her gaze narrowed. "Someone healed him of a mortal injury. You, I assume?"

A mortal injury *your archer* inflicted, she thought, though she didn't voice this aloud.

"With the aid of a talisman," Lo agreed.

"This?" Caul drew the disk from her pocket.

"It was a gift. Can I have it back?"

"After we have spoken, perhaps," she replied coolly. "If I am satisfied with your answers."

Mace returned a moment later. "Lucius is confined," he reported.

"Would you take Enrigo to the kitchens and see he's fed?" Chaos asked.

The mortifex eyed Lo with a scowl. "I would prefer to remain at your side, my lady."

"We are not defenseless," she replied gently. "I don't think our guest intends any more trouble." Her piercing gaze turned to Lo.

"No, I swear it, Your Grace," she agreed hastily.

Mace sighed. "Very well. Come along, Master Redvayne."

Enrigo looked reluctant. Lo gave him an encouraging nod. "You must gather your strength," she said. "Then perhaps they will let us both see Castelio."

The boy didn't look at the hulking mortifex. "Fine," he muttered.

Even under such bizarre circumstances, his manners were not forgotten. No doubt they'd been ingrained from the time he could speak. Enrigo Redvayne bowed at the waist to each of the women in turn, his face grim. Then he swept off down the tunnel, leaving Mace to hurry after.

"Come, we will talk in the gardens." Chaos moved to the wall of dense branches. She made no sign, said nothing, but they parted for her as one might make way for an old friend. Lo went through next, then Lady Caul, whose burning gaze she could feel on her back.

The doorway led to a high, broad rampart, allowing her to see the place where she'd been brought as a captive for the first time. It was a castle of sorts, with the vague outlines of towers and domes, but made entirely from living trees. The lights of a large town glimmered below. She guessed it must be Mystral.

Lo inhaled air scented with strange, heady perfumes. A riotous garden bloomed on all sides, humming with swarms of the black bees. The rampart was edged with thick-stalked blooms resembling sunflowers but with a bruised purple hue, their faces angled to drink in the moonlight. Sable roses twined up a trellis. She saw columbine and iris, dahlia and hyacinth. Each and every one blending with the darkness save for glints of maroon and deep plum.

Chaos used her canes to maneuver down to a flat rock. Others sat in a circle. Lo joined her, mostly because her knees decided to give out, but Caul remained standing, hands on hips.

"How did you summon the wind?" she demanded. "And unlock the cage?"

Both fair questions. But Lo had expected the first one to be: *How did you suck an entire cemetery of yammering dead people down into a giant black drain on the bridge at Nox?*

Could these two notorious necromancers possibly have missed it?

"Because she is a daēva," Lady Chaos replied. "She works elemental magic."

Lady Caul blinked in surprise. "A living one?"

"It would seem so," her sister said dryly.

"Half daēva," Lo admitted. "On my father's side."

She stiffened as a spirit drifted toward them, trailing ghostly garments. Her left fingertips began to tingle.

"You have nothing to fear from the ancestors," Chaos said with a reassuring smile. "The dead are welcome at Mystral."

And that is when Lo knew for certain that the Courtenays did *not* know. Because the dead had more to fear from her than the other way around. She saw more spirits now, floating through the gardens. Some had clear outlines; others were faint wisps.

"They don't attack you?" she asked dubiously.

"The opposite. They watch over us. Guide and protect us."

Lo watched as the spirit drifted by, skin crawling. To her vast relief, it did not try to speak to her. "Things are different across the mountains," she muttered.

Even across the border with Alessia.

"That is because they have no respect for the dead in the Sun Courts!" Caul ground out. "They spurn true knowledge and care only for power—"

She turned at the clatter of hooves. Lo had seen many outrageous things in the last hour, but she still startled at the sight of . . . yes, unmistakably a *centaur*, a female one, with long grass-green hair and eyes like full moons. Her breasts were bare, and she wore a medallion between them. It bore a symbol — the Nightjar of Nyons.

Sometimes, Lo's parents would leave her at the Temple of the Moria Tree where the Maenads lived. They were fierce women who loved nothing more than to drink, fight, dance, and tell old stories about the gods. She'd first heard of the centaurs from one of them, an elder named Kallisto. Centaurs were said to be the offspring of King Ixion and a cloud nymph named Nephele. None existed anymore, of course. Their race had been wiped out in the Vatra wars.

"We searched the forest," the centaur said, dropping both their packs on the ground. "There are no others."

"Astris is the one who found you unconscious on the bridge and brought you here," Chaos said. "She also fished young Lord Redvayne out of the river. He was nearly at the rapids downstream."

Lo eyed the golden bow across her back. "And did Astris shoot the reaper?" she asked, anger simmering.

The Courtenays might not be behind the abduction, but they had tried to kill Castelio. Had inflicted unspeakable suffering on Lucius.

"It was not intentional," the centaur said stiffly. "I was aiming for the mortifex."

"And what had he done to deserve it?" she demanded, unable to stop herself. "Isn't the bridge neutral territory?"

"Lucius killed both our brothers at Hellgate," Caul spat. "And a score of others. If you call him friend—"

"We did not come to quarrel over old grudges, sister," Chaos interjected, though she looked unhappy.

"I didn't know that," Lo said, still angry.

"Did you know that Robert Redvayne was trying to sneak through the mountains to invade our land by a northern route, in violation of every treaty? That he lured our parents into a trap, murdered them in cold blood at a parley? Mace barely managed to turn the tide, rallying their loyal retainers."

Caul's heated gaze swept across Astrid, who watched gravely. "The centaurs. The loups-garou. Even the wee lutins. It was a vicious, bloody fight. If Mace had not driven the Redvayne soldiers back, I have no doubt they would have fallen upon Mystral and slit our throats, young as we were. Mace has been father and mother to us both, and if he saw fit to extract a small measure of revenge on a foe stupid enough to set foot across our borders, I will not deny it to him!"

She crossed her arms, bone bracelets rattling.

Lo knew well how elusive the truth could be, depending on who told the tale. It was a fluid thing, poured easily from one vessel to another, taking whatever shape the vintner chose. But Caul certainly seemed to believe this rendition of events.

"I am ignorant of Aveline's history," she said carefully. "As you must have guessed, I am not from this realm, but from the one across the White Sea. But I, too, lost my parents at a young age. I know how painful it is. You have my sympathy, Lady Caul."

The Ducissa looked dubious, but her sister leaned forward, one hand resting on a silver cane. "You lost your parents?" Chaos asked. "What were their names?"

"Nazafareen and Darius Dessarian."

The pair of necromancers exchanged a long, meaningful glance. Lo looked between them, heart pounding.

"You know of them?"

"Our own parents did," Chaos replied. "Knew them well."

"They hunted the restless dead," Caul added. "The tricksome ones."

"The dangerous ones," Chaos agreed. "On the Lady's behalf."

She fell silent, gaze turning inward.

"And?" Lo prompted eagerly. "Do you know where they are now?"

"I have spoken with the dead on this subject," she allowed. "There is a place they gather. A marketplace of sorts. I go there to pick up gossip."

Her expression was not promising. The garden faded. It was as if Lady Chaos sat at the end of a long, shrinking tunnel. "Tell me," Lo said, girding herself for the worst.

"They were hunting someone in particular."

"The king of the unbound," Caul said. She eyed Lo with pity, which made it even worse. Caul had hated her guts five minutes ago.

"Magnus the Merciless," Chaos clarified.

"Magnus . . . the *Merciless*?" Lo repeated. "Who is he?"

"There is a place outside the borders of the Dominion. It is beyond my sight. But I've heard rumors of it."

"A place where the free mortifexes dwell," Caul said, sinking down and wiggling her toes in the black grass.

"They should not have sought it out." Chaos sounded regretful.

"But if they haven't returned," her sister added, "they must have found it."

Lo looked between them, pulse racing. "How would I find this place?"

"It is impossible," Chaos said.

"But you just said they found it!"

"Or the hunters became the hunted," Caul put in, "and they were taken by force. That is more likely."

"We would help you if we could," Chaos finished, "but that is all we know. Truly, I am sorry to extinguish your hopes. Sometimes the truth is worse than not knowing."

Lo was silent for a minute. "No," she said, "not knowing is worse. Thank you."

"Now, we would ask *you* some questions," Caul said. "*Someone* ordered that knife to be dropped where it would be found. *Someone* has tried to laid the blame for this fiasco at our feet. *Someone*—"

She broke off as a shadow shuffled down the path. It reeked of char. The creature staggered into the moonlight and Lo reared back. It seemed to be made of *ash*. Or dust. Both maybe. Its edges blurred like boiling smoke.

The sisters exchanged a narrow glance.

"I fear I know whose wraith took Enrigo Redvayne," Chaos said with a note of exasperation.

"*Nathan*," Caul muttered through her teeth.

The ash-man sketched a clumsy bow. "Bonsoir, demoiselles," it croaked. "The Duc of Vendagni extends his warmest salutations—"

"*Sanglant garcion!*" Caul erupted, slapping the ground.

"And requests the pleasure of Lady Dessarian's company at Castle Cazal at her earliest convenience. He has a proposal of mutual benefit she will wish to hear."

"Tell your master," Caul growled, leaping to her feet, "that he'd better lower the drawbridge and find a dark hole to hide in—"

"Hush," Chaos chastened gently, "it's still talking."

" . . . vows to greet Lady Dessarian himself and discuss the bounty with regard to the two individuals she seeks, although he humbly requests that she come alone. If she does not, there might be unfortunate consequences."

"Oh, there'll be consequences," Caul said with a deep, rumbling laugh. "For your master!"

The ash-man swept another awkward bow. Its faceless lump of a head angled toward Lo.

"Miaou," it croaked, bringing a crumbling hand to its mouth in a parody of washing.

Lo went cold, then hot with fury. She leapt to her feet and seized it — or tried to. The creature fell apart in her hands, drifting into an ash heap across her boots. She stomped it in a rage.

The Ducissas of Nyons stared at her, brows knit in identical expressions of confusion.

"My cat," she said, utterly livid. "Nathan Ouvrard has my cat."

Chapter 25

Something brushed his cheek.

A whispery touch, but it dragged Cas to awareness. He opened his eyes and saw Artemis, her light spilling through a high, oddly shaped window. Dozens of shapes fluttered about his head. It took a moment to make out what they were.

Moths.

Brown ones whose markings looked like painted eyes, and golden ones that shone like faeries in the dark. Tiny ones with blood-red wings on one side and sky-blue wings on the other. Others with the spots of a leopard, large as dinner plates, with long, trailing tails.

He held still and the moths settled down again. Cas cautiously prodded the spongy substance beneath him. It felt like a giant toadstool. With a grunt of disgust, he slid onto a floor of moss, dragging a sheet with him. The next unwelcome discovery was that someone had taken his clothes. Every stitch. He shivered and scanned the gloom, searching for a way out.

He saw none.

The only gap was far above. What he had taken for walls were intertwined branches of some monstrous tree. How had he come here? He closed his eyes and saw red tongues of fire licking at a black sky. The flames gave no warmth. Instead, he shivered at the memory of bone-cracking cold.

Gripped by sudden terror he didn't entirely understand, he pressed a hand to his chest. Felt a puckered scar that wasn't there before. More memories crashed down. The arrow shattering his ribs. Delilah dragging him across the bridge. Begging her for the iron coin.

She'd refused him.

He had stood at Kaethe's threshold. Had *seen* the Drowned Woman beckoning from the other side, no longer hooded or cloaked in shadow. Her skin was blue-veined and white as bleached bone. Her eyes held mercy.

And Cas knew one thing for certain. The living did not look upon Kaethe's face.

He pressed a palm to his chest again, searching vainly for a heartbeat. The branches seemed to close in, bony arms reaching to embrace him.

He knew where he was now.

Mystral.

They brought me back. Brought me back to serve them forever and ever.

Horror wiped his mind blank. The moths fluttered about him, luminous in the darkness. His hand stole to the scar again. If he was dead, how had it healed? Cas fumbled to the stubbled juncture beneath his jaw, digging deep. At last he felt it, the steady throb of blood pumping through his veins. His relief was so overwhelming that he didn't notice he was no longer alone.

"Castelio!"

Delilah stood in a crooked doorway that definitely hadn't been there a moment ago. He just had time to wrap the sheet around his waist before she was leaning over him, her raven hair falling across his shoulder. "Lie down," she scolded. "You mustn't tax yourself."

Even in his bewildered state, he was far too aware of her hands on his bare skin.

"Where did you come from?" he croaked.

She glanced behind her. "Oh, that. The door's a bit tricky. You look better than I expected!" She held out a crystal chalice. "Lady Chaos gave me this elixir for you. She said you must drink it all."

"Lady Chaos?"

"I will explain everything. But you must drink that first."

Her tone held forced cheer. He gave her a searching look, and she nodded. "Go on."

The liquid was a murky gray. He held it up, examined the silt at the bottom, then gave it a swirl. Sniffed it.

"I can't promise it will taste good," Delilah said, "but she swore it would make you feel better."

Cas gave her a crooked smile and drank it down. It left a chalky residue on his tongue. He waited a moment. No stabbing pains in the belly. No frothing at the mouth or paralysis.

"Did it work?" she asked, watching him closely.

Warmth spread through him. Tension leached from his muscles.

"Not bad," he said, setting the chalice aside.

"Are you hungry?"

"Tell me what happened first." His mind felt sharper. "Where's Enrigo?"

"Well and safe."

"Safe? How can he be safe?" Cas lowered his voice. "Is this not the seat of the Courtenays?"

"Yes, but they didn't kidnap him. They think Nathan Ouvrard did."

"The Duc of Vendagni? But the dagger . . ."

"Was forged or stolen. I overheard their mortifex questioning Lucius. He had no idea why we were on that bridge, or who Enrigo was, either. I'm telling you, it wasn't the Courtenays that did this. They said they'll let him go. Let all of us go."

"Then who shot me?"

"That was an accident. Lucius was the target."

He shook his head. "I'm sorry, but none of this makes sense. Necromancy cannot heal the living, only animate the dead. And they stay that way." He gave her a hard look. "I remember enough. I should have died."

"You did take an arrow." She eyed the scar. "Through the lung, I think. And another in the arm."

He examined himself. A second faint scar marked his biceps. It was much smaller and he hadn't even noticed it.

"But I remembered my charm of protection before it was too late," she continued. "I put it around your neck and . . . well, the wound healed."

He blinked. "You lent me your talisman?"

"I was a fool not to think of it right away." She gave him a weak smile. "But there was a lot going on. I had to lower Enrigo from the bridge. It seemed safest to let him swim to safety. Anyway, the Ducissas found him and brought him here." She paused, glancing away.

"I remember Lucius fighting another mortifex," Cas said. "But why didn't you take Enrigo to Nox?"

She looked uncomfortable. "Yes, well, the dead came from the lichyard. They were blocking the way. I suppose true night made them bold. But I used your weapons to drive them off."

"And then?" he pressed.

"I'm afraid I fainted. I woke up here." She stood abruptly and walked to the door, returning a moment later with his pack and boots. "Your clothes were all bloody. If you're up to it, I'll wait outside while you change."

He stared at her, wondering who had undressed him.

"Right," he said.

When she was gone, he rummaged through the pack, glad to find his extra supplies of iron nails and Kaethe's Tears. The knives, too. He pulled on his last pair of breeches and laced up a clean cami, then sat and tugged on his boots. Could it be true that the Courtenays were innocent? He'd believe Enrigo was safe when he saw the boy himself.

She returned a minute later, balancing a jug and plate covered with a cloth. He drank some water to wash the taste of the elixir from his mouth, then twitched the cloth aside. Tiny speckled eggs, hard-boiled; plump dewberries; a wedge of cheese; and a dripping, wine-dark honeycomb. He realized he was starving and set to. Delilah sat on the mossy ground, legs drawn to her chest, watching him.

"Castelio?"

He glanced up from the egg he was shelling.

"I have a confession," she said in a subdued voice. "And an apology. I'm not royalty. Not even titled. I only said it so Orlaith would treat me better."

He popped the egg in his mouth, amused at this new, humble Delilah. "Aye, I know."

Her brow creased. "It was that obvious?"

"I've never met a noble who forgot the fact for a single moment. You did a fair job of it in Aquitan, but afterwards . . ." He shrugged. "You stopped bothering."

She gave a tentative smile. "You're not angry?"

"Why would I be? We stole your ship. You did what you had to."

Delilah let out a long breath. "The truth is that I'm looking for my parents. Eight years ago, they disappeared."

He studied her with a twist of guilt. "That's who you were looking for in Tjanjin?"

She nodded.

"And I got your hopes up." He set the plate down. "I'm so sorry. I had no idea. I assumed they were thieves. Someone who had done you wrong."

Her face was solemn. "I'll admit, I hated you for it at first. But you led me in the right direction. I have caught their trail."

Yet she didn't seem thrilled at this development.

"Here?" he asked in surprise.

"They were . . . like you, Castelio. They hunted restless souls who didn't want to cross the Cold Sea. That is why . . ." She cleared her throat. "Well, when you said you came through a gate to Tjanjin . . ."

He remembered the wind ship plummeting toward the waves. How she had lifted the bow seconds before they smashed into the frigid waters of the White Sea. Cas shuddered inwardly at how close he'd come to drowning. If he hadn't said the right thing to spark her interest . . . Pieces fell into place, but he still didn't grasp the full picture.

"Your parents were Quietuses? But I thought there were no risen dead where you come from."

"There aren't. They hunted beyond the Veil."

Hunting in the Dominion itself? It sounded unspeakably dangerous. No wonder they had disappeared.

"They had Kaethe's blessing for this?" he asked.

"I don't know. They never told me the truth. I only found out after they were gone."

He chewed a handful of berries, thinking. "How long did this go on for?"

"Years. Since I was born." She gave a little snort. "They claimed they were traveling abroad."

"Then the Drowned Woman must have agreed to it, else she would have set the Shepherds on them. Those are her whopping black hounds." He tore off a hunk of bread. "And you? Are you really a wind ship captain?"

"Yes," she said firmly. "I work for a trading outfit based in Samarqand. After they vanished, I was taken in by family friends. The owners of Falcon Couriers. *Wind-Witch* is part of their fleet." She looked rueful. "*Was* part of their fleet."

"How old were you when your parents went missing?"

"Twelve."

He felt a stab of sympathy — and kinship. "I was the same age when . . . my mother died. Many things changed for me, too."

She reached out and took his hand. "I'm sorry, Castelio. But there is more. A message came from Nathan Ouvrard about an hour ago." Her jaw set. "He has taken Thistle. I don't know how, but my cat would have turned up by now so I must believe it's true. He wants me to go to Vendagni. He says he has an offer for me."

Cas's heart sank. "And you mean to obey?"

"What choice do I have? Besides which, I want to know what his proposal is." Her expression grew even grimmer. "I wonder if he knows something about my parents."

He set the plate aside. "Let me go with you."

Her face softened. "Oh, Castelio. Thank you. But he said I must go alone."

Was that a hint of reluctance? He leapt on it to press his case.

"Which is exactly why you shouldn't."

"If I break the terms, he might harm Thistle." She shook her head. "They said you can leave whenever you feel strong enough. Take Enrigo back to Aquitan."

"But—"

"Do you want to see him?"

He sighed and brushed the last crumbs from his hands. "Aye."

Lo pulled him to his feet. "Then let's go."

They stepped into a corridor of intertwined branches thick with roosting bats. She pressed a finger to her lips and he used all his stalking skills not to rouse them. Moonbeams filtered through gaps above, shining on a mossy carpet underfoot. Wherever Hecate's silvery light fell, the leaves of the trees gleamed brighter.

The tunnel twisted and turned, grew even narrower. Goosebumps rose on his arms as they walked through a sudden cold spot. Cas knew the sensation well; it meant a spirit had just been there. He kept a hand on his knives, but shortly they were passing through an archway in a tall hedge. The cramped tunnel opened to a wide, star-strewn sky. The Courtenays awaited them in a terraced garden. Scarlet windflowers and pale anemones bloomed in profusion, along with foxglove, oleander, and castor bean. A knot in Cas's chest loosened as Enrigo ran up. The boy cast an adoring look at Delilah.

"She promised to fix you," he said. "And she did!"

Cas smiled and clasped his shoulder. Delilah made introductions. He was surprised to find the twins looked so different from each other. Lady Caul was tall and regal, with a mobile face that revealed every passing emotion. It was obvious that she disliked him on principle, though whether that was because he served Orlaith or because he was a despised reaper, Cas couldn't tell. Both, most likely. She accepted his bow with a curt nod, black eyes flashing.

Lady Chaos had some affliction to her legs and leaned on canes. A tiny gray elf owl, small enough to fit in Cas's palm, perched on her white hair like a tiara. Her expression was more thoughtful and guarded than her sister. They were both young, yet he sensed the aura of power swirling around them. Much stronger than the hedge necromancers he'd dealt with in Clovis.

"If you are fit to travel," Caul said curtly, "Mace will escort you to the border of Alessia. I trust you will tell your Ducissa the truth when you arrive in Aquitan."

"Of course he will, Lady Caul," Enrigo said stoutly. "I will, too." He faced the two sisters. At that moment, he looked far older than his eleven years. "My father died in battle with your parents. I was raised to despise you. I expect you were raised to hate me, too. You could have treated me roughly, but you did not. Even if Mother doubts me, the nobles of Clovis know I have no motive to lie to protect you. And I will not be swayed in my recital of the truth. You have my solemn oath."

The elf owl gave a low, breathy whistle. Chaos smiled. "Well spoken, Your Grace. And I know that one day, you will inherit the menotte as your birthright. Mace has been a guiding light to us both. I hope that Lucius will give you the same loyal guidance."

"So you're letting him go?" Enrigo asked, surprised.

Caul's full lips tightened a fraction. "Yes. Provided he never returns."

"Did you drink the strengthening elixir?" Chaos asked Cas.

Her tone was courteous. And he had never hated them as the Ducissa Orlaith did. The squabbles of the nobility meant little to him, and he'd never even met Duc Robert. What he did hear from old retainers who had known the man was not flattering.

"I did, Your Grace, thank you. An interesting concoction. White mandrake was the base, I think? Mixed with powdered belladonna, henbane, monkshood, and . . ." He thought for a moment. "The bitterness nearly covered it, but I detected a trace of wormwood."

Caul's brows drew down. Chaos nodded approval. "All correct. Though you missed the single crushed moonflower seed."

"Ah. That was the hint of blue raspberry." He held her large, kohl-lined eyes. "Each and every one a deadly toxin, yet combined in the right proportions, they have the opposite effect."

She gave him a slow smile. "I did not know reapers learned the poison path."

"They don't. My parents were woodwards."

Her delicate features lit up in genuine pleasure. "Were they? I understand there are few left in the Sun Courts now."

"That is true, Your Grace. And I'll admit, I was a lazy apprentice. But my mother made sure I learned the appearance of *those*, and the corresponding tastes and smells. The lessons stuck."

"So you knew all that and still drank it?" Delilah asked in amazement.

"If their ladyships had wanted me dead, I would be."

Caul barked a laugh at that, and he knew he'd won her over — at least partly.

"True enough," she boomed. "Then I assume you are well enough to leave immediately?"

He eyed Delilah. "Are you really going to Castle Cazal alone?"

She nodded. "I must."

He shook his head in frustration. "Does no one but me find this to be a bad idea?" He turned to Caul. "With all due respect, aren't you going to do something about the fact that Nathan Ouvrard almost started a war with the Sun Courts? On *your* behalf?"

Caul gave a disgusted growl. "I would like nothing better than to go deal with him myself, but we cannot. Not for a week, at least. The gathering of Litha begins tonight, when all three moons are full. It always follows true night."

"Litha?"

"I see you know nothing about Nyons," Chaos said. "We do not rule by decree, like your Ducissa. There are many factions here. The centaurs and loups-garou. The revered ancestors. Others. Litha is when they all gather. When bargains are made, grievances aired. We cannot miss it."

"Which Nathan knows full well!" Caul snapped.

"Would you at least hear my proposal?" he ventured.

"Castelio—" Delilah began.

"I will not go inside the castle. Just wait outside, well-hidden. But you have no idea what you're walking into. Doesn't it make sense to have someone to aid you if Nathan takes you prisoner? Or worse? Do not forget what he is!"

Cas broke off. Chaos and Caul were staring at him.

"Well, it's true," he said mutinously. "Ouvrard could kill her and make her one of his servants."

"I do not believe Nathan would do such a thing," Chaos murmured, though she looked worried. "He has always been a friend to us. I am still not sure—"

"It can be no one else behind this, sister," Caul interrupted, her tone subdued. "And Nathan loves to make mischief. I am sorry, but the reaper is right."

Delilah opened her mouth, then closed it again. She chewed her lip in silence for a moment. "It's not that I don't want your help. But how could this be done without him finding out?"

The Ducissas exchanged a look. "There might be a way," Caul said. "If you consent."

"But what about Enrigo?" Delilah asked. "Lucius is in poor shape."

"Where is he?" Cas asked.

He caught movement in the corner of his eye. Their mortifex,

Mace, stood in the shadows. At a nod from Lady Chaos, he stepped forward.

"I'll show you," he said.

THE SANCTUARY of Kaethe was in a marshy part of the lower grounds. Willows grew in abundance, their limbs bearded with trailing moss. They followed a path of hummocks to an island on which a large nine-pointed star had been inlaid with bones, white against the dark earth. Offerings lay along the bank: crowns of woven catkins, piles of painted river stones, nosegays of dried flowers. Mace climbed the largest willow and lounged in a crook of the trunk, one leg dangling, the other bent.

"Have fun," he said.

The water was stagnant and black. Cas leapt across a gap and walked to the edge of the star. Lucius paced its confines like a wounded lion. His rich clothes were charred. One leg dragged stiffly.

"Come to gawk?" he asked.

"No. To talk business." Cas quickly explained the situation. "We cannot let Delilah face Nathan Ouvrard alone."

The mortifex gave a wan smile. "She seems quite capable of taking care of herself."

"That's not the point. The necromancers of Vendagni are in a whole other league, which you well know."

Lucius nodded. "Then you take Enrigo back to Aquitan. I will accompany her."

Cas laughed. "I think not. You've already proven yourself untrustworthy."

Lucius feigned confusion.

"The blood," Cas reminded him.

"Oh, that." He waved a hand dismissively. "If you'll recall, I believed she was dead at the time. I do have standards."

"It was still wrong. But why would I expect you to understand that?"

Lucius seemed unruffled. "So what do you propose?"

"You take Enrigo back to Aquitan. I'll go with Delilah."

Lucius studied him. "What do I tell Orlaith?"

"The truth. That the Duc of Vendagni is suspected in the abduction of her son. He used wraiths, which puts the matter within my jurisdiction. By the oaths, I'm empowered to enforce the will of Kaethe throughout the borders of the old empire."

A dry chuckle. "That's putting a fine point on it. You are a Quietus of Clovis."

"And *you* are not my master. I go where I am needed."

"Her Grace needs you."

"Are you refusing?"

Lucius gave a slow exhale. "Will they really let me leave?"

"If you go straight to the border. Mace will escort you both. They want Enrigo returned to his mother. They want her to know the truth. That the Courtenays had nothing to do with this."

Surprise flitted across the mortifex's face. Then he shook his head. "I might be fit to travel through the darklands, but I am not strong enough to cross the rivers of the Boundary. You'll have to banish me back home."

Cas had expected this answer. "It has to be you. I won't feed you my blood. I've lost enough. But there's something else I can offer."

Lucius looked amused. "I know it isn't your life force itself. Not even for the sake of the lovely *khamoun*."

He realized then that Lucius had known the truth about her all along. Anger sparked at his lies, but Cas crushed it, adding to the seething pool of hatred for the mortifex.

"Not my life force," he agreed. "But there is another way you feed. *Fear*."

Lucius propped his chin on a hand. "I'm intrigued, Quietus," he said with a ghastly smile. "But I thought you had learned to control that particular emotion."

"I have. This is an old memory."

He watched Lucius closely, but the mortifex gave no sign that he knew what had happened at the farm all those years ago. Perhaps Orlaith had never told him.

"I hope it's something better than a childish fear of the dark," Lucius said. "Because to be honest, it will take more than a light repast to restore me."

"Do you want it or not?" Cas demanded roughly.

"Your worst terror?" The smirk died. A spark lit in his eyes. "How could I refuse?"

Lucius, Cas realized, hated him with equal fervor. He knew the mortifex's true name. It was not equivalent to wearing the menotte, but it represented power over him.

And now Lucius would know his own weakness.

"How is it done?" he asked.

Lucius stood, swaying slightly. Half his face was burned. He swept an arm in a grotesque parody of courtliness. "Step into my parlor," he said, "and I'll show you."

Cas glanced at the willow tree where Mace lounged on his branch, watching them both impassively. "Go in there," he said in a bored voice, "and you're on your own, reaper."

There was a decent chance that Lucius would kill him. The mortifex was weak but still dangerous. Perhaps even more so now. And Mace would never set foot inside the star even if he cared — which he obviously didn't. Yet if he walked away, let Delilah do this alone, he would never forgive himself.

Lucius arched a brow. It contorted the scars on his face in hideous fashion. "Having a change of heart?"

Cas sighed. "No."

He stepped across the bones.

Chapter 26

The triple moons shone bright and full overhead as Lucius swung into the saddle.

Lo watched Castelio help the young heir mount behind him. Enrigo looked eager to be heading home, but Castelio had fresh shadows beneath his eyes. And Lucius . . . well, he appeared much better than he had when she freed him from the cage. His skin was raw, but the worst burns had faded. Moonlight picked out threads of rich, gleaming copper in his hair. He sat the horse tall and proud, face expressionless, hands loosely clasping the reins.

Castelio had batted aside her questions about what occurred at the Sanctuary of Kaethe, but it was obvious he'd sacrificed some part of himself to lend Lucius strength. She felt guilty, and it put her off-balance. Clearly, he felt he owed her a debt and meant to repay it. At the same time, she was glad to have company. His company, in particular. She stifled a bleak chuckle at the ridiculousness of it. What could be more romantic than a visit to the castle of a dread necromancer?

"I'll see you in Aquitan," Castelio said to Enrigo. "Journey safely, Your Grace."

"And you," Enrigo replied. He looked at Lo with an encouraging smile. "I hope you get your cat back, my lady."

"So do I," she agreed, patting the horse's muzzle.

"Khamoun," Lucius said.

She looked up at him. What a tangle of feelings he inspired! Pity, fear — yes, still a healthy dose of that — anger for whatever he'd done to Castelio. Admiration, too, and curiosity. What sort of man had he been once? What life had he left behind? How did he die?

Lucius bent from the saddle. "I'm sorry," he whispered.

She gazed into his green eyes, made more luminous by the tiny flames of his pupils.

"For taking the ship?"

"That, too." He gave her a smile, the first of genuine warmth she'd ever seen. It transformed him. "Be well."

Then Lucius was wheeling the horse around, his tattered cloak swirling. He set off at a gallop down the road, Mace easily keeping pace behind them on foot.

"We will regret allowing that one to leave," Caul muttered.

"No one would believe we weren't involved if we didn't," Chaos replied. "Lucius is nothing more than the Redvaynes' puppet — do not forget that, sister. And Enrigo will be Duc when he comes of age, only a few short years from now. I would rather have him as a friend than an enemy."

"I don't mind the boy," Caul conceded grudgingly. "He behaved decently. His loathsome mother is a different story. She will find a way to use this against us, mark me."

Lo glanced at Castelio to gauge his reaction, but his gaze was turned inward.

"Your coach will be along in a moment," Chaos said. "But I have a gift for you first, reaper."

He blinked and looked up. It seemed an effort for him to focus. "Yes, my lady?"

She pressed a small bottle of green glass into his hand. "This is an antidote for the poisonous thorns that cover the north side of the castle. I gave Nathan the seedlings myself when we were children. Devil's mantle."

His eyes widened slightly. "I have heard of it."

"Then you know its properties. Nathan doesn't realize they can be counteracted. He usually keeps his bedroom window unlatched." She cleared her throat. "I happen to know that the Duc has a fondness for stargazing. If you do need to enter the keep, it is the leftmost window in the north spire."

He tucked the vial in his pack and bowed. The gesture was perfunctory, every movement weary. "Thank you, Lady."

To her surprise, Chaos moved forward with her canes and kissed Lo's cheeks. She smelled of herbs, rich layers of scent that tickled the nose.

"I hope you find the ones you seek," she said softly, pressing the silver disk of the talisman into Lo's palm. "You have friends here, if you need us."

Lo hung it around her neck. She fussed with the chain to cover the rush of confusion. She'd never get the image of Lucius crawling across that white-hot cage out of her head, nor Castelio gasping his last bloody breaths. The bone-spider Caul had unleashed was nothing compared to the rest of it.

But . . . maybe they did have good reason to hate Lucius. He was Orlaith's wolf, and an undeniably savage one.

"Thank you, Your Grace," she said.

The rhythmic clop of hooves announced the arrival of the coach. It was a beautiful conveyance, lustrous ebony with the stooping Nightjar of Nyons painted in silver on the doors and little spirit lamps on the roof. But the beasts that drew it . . . She had expected flesh and blood horses, like the one given to Lucius, but these were gleaming skeletons, with spectral manes and tails flickering in the darkness. Glowing red embers shone deep in the sockets of their long equine skulls.

"They will not tire," Chaos said. "And the denizens of the Nightwood know our sigil. None will trouble you on the way."

Lo's left hand tingled fiercely, but she knew how to counter that now. She slipped into the Nexus and the sensation faded.

"When you see Nathan," Caul said, baring white teeth, "tell him that I will be paying him a visit myself when Litha has concluded. Tell him . . ." She pondered for a moment. "Tell him that he would be well-advised to find a spell to preserve his manhood, diminutive though it might be, because I mean to make it into a stocking for Mace. His balls will provide material for the other—"

"Sister!" Chaos admonished.

"I will relay the message," Lo said solemnly.

"Good. He will try to bully you, but I hope that Nathan has met his match."

They shared a silent look of vengeance.

Then she was climbing into the luxurious burgundy velvet interior and stowing her pack on the floor, Castelio clambering after. Caul stuck her head in and rapped her knuckles on the floorboards.

"The hidden compartment lies below," she said. "The lever is beneath the seat."

Lo groped around and found it. With a soft click, the floor slid away, revealing a dark space below.

"Can you fit?" she asked Castelio.

He got on hands and knees and peered inside. "It'll be tight, but yes, I think so."

"There is another lever inside the compartment," Caul said. "You can escape at any time."

He looked unhappy. "Do I have to . . .?"

"Pass the journey in there?" She threw her head back and cackled. "No, reaper. It is a day's hard ride. You will know when the time comes."

Lady Caul withdrew and slapped the side of the carriage. "*Tecare adasel Cazal!*" she cried.

The bone-horses pawed at the stone, striking sparks with their hooves, then leapt forward down the winding road. Castelio leaned back against the padded seat, resting his head on his pack.

"You should get some sleep," Lo said.

He shook his head. "I don't want to."

"I know you won't tell me why," she ventured cautiously. "But it might help."

"Just old memories." He stared into space, rubbing his bandaged hand. "They'll pass."

She tugged the velvet curtain aside as they entered Mystral, the carriage springs jouncing on cobbled lanes. At first it was a blur of lamplight and pools of darkness, but then the bone-horses were forced to slow for the throngs clogging the town for Litha. It looked like an ordinary, prosperous town at first glance, built of warm amber stone with slate roofs and mullioned windows. But the roses that bloomed along the balconies were dark as dried blood, and snatches of wild music skirled through open doorways.

Her nose twitched as it caught currents of scented smoke; frankincense and cassia, jaggery and clove. The people wore all manner of dress and seemed to be from every land. A group of tough women who looked like sell-swords stood outside a tavern chatting with a hugely fat man in a turban and long tunic, his mustaches drooping to his chest.

Set back from the street, the inn had a grassy courtyard in which long, heavy-hewn tables covered with dozens of wavering candles had been set. A handsome youth in a purple doublet embraced a centaur, her moss-green hair spilling across his broad shoulders. Her sisters laughed and raised cups of gold, toasting the lovers in a strange tongue.

Yet mortals and centaurs were not the only denizens of Mystral. There were creatures that skulked on all fours through the shadows, then walked erect as beautiful, dark-haired sirens when they reached the light. Shapes glided above the rooftops, visible in silhouette when they passed one of the moons like a flitting cloud. Lo craned her neck out the window for a better look and realized with an unpleasant jolt that the street was not cobbled at all but paved with the smooth domes of skulls.

Everywhere, *everywhere*, were the shades of the dead, illuminating the revelry with their cold, spectral light. They drifted after the carriage like gulls in the wake of a fishing vessel. No one paid them any attention.

She glimpsed shops with wondrous objects displayed in the windows. Bronze armillary spheres showing the positions of the moons and other heavenly bodies. Silver cauldrons and glass skulls and magical artifacts she had no name for, many of which appeared to be made of yellowed bones. Herbalists sold smoldering joss sticks and bundles of dried plants in open-air stalls.

When she turned back to Castelio, she saw he had ceded the battle and fallen asleep. The Ducissas had provided a quilt. Lo tucked it around him, studying his face. The curve of his jaw, rough with stubble. The thick straight brows. Even unconscious, he had a guarded look.

Castelio feared coming back. Understandably; it couldn't be much fun. Besides which, he banished the dead for a living. But surely it was a choice. Not everyone rose from the grave, did they? Plenty of people did as they were told and crossed the Cold Sea. Otherwise Aveline would be overrun with spirits, and it wasn't quite that bad. Something must have happened to make him fear it so deeply.

It was a relief when they reached the outskirts and the coach gained speed, leaving the trailing dead behind. Her thoughts turned to Nathan Ouvrard. Lady Chaos had told her a bit about him. He was the thirty-ninth Duc of Vendagni and a direct descendant of Jaskin Cazal, who had invented the menottes and bound the first mortifex, known as Vigo. Not his true name, of course. Only Nathan knew that.

All in all, the Cazal-Ouvrards, including Nathan's dead parents, were infamous for their ruthlessness, cruelty, and mastery of the black arts. The young Duc, Chaos insisted, was a much milder version, but his raw power was undisputed. He lived alone, with Vigo and an assortment of undead servants for company.

Lo rolled out the map and located Castle Cazal. It sat in the far north of the duchy, nestled among the foothills of the Montagnes de Cauchemar, which Caul had helpfully translated as the Mountains of Nightmare. Remote and untouchable but with a temperate climate because Nathan despised the cold.

It was unlikely — though not impossible — that he had captured her parents. Chaos didn't think so, but Nathan had no qualms about abducting both Enrigo Redvayne and Thistle. *Why* he would do such a thing remained unclear.

She was not eager to use her newfound influence over the dead, but she would if she had to.

Eventually, she drifted off herself. They were deep in the Nightwood when she woke with a stiff neck and rumbling belly. The bone-steeds kept a steady, tireless pace. She couldn't see much through the windows, but she could smell the fir trees, a crisp, clean scent she always associated with the boreal forests of Nocturne. Every now and then, a spectral green glow appeared. At first she thought it was spirits, but then Lo realized the light came from clusters of giant phosphorescent mushrooms.

She was rooting in her pack for something to eat when Castelio stirred. He gave her a wan smile. His eyes looked clearer as he sat up and stretched.

"How do you feel?" she asked, taking a bite of seedy bread.

He tested the arm that had taken an arrow, rolling the shoulder. "Well enough. You?"

"I'm not sure," she admitted. "I have the answer I sought, but it's another dead end. Unless Nathan Ouvrard knows something more."

"You trust the Courtenays?" He found his water skin and took a long drink.

She hesitated. "Yes. They said their parents knew mine. And they are orphans. I cannot see them lying about this. There was nothing to gain. They didn't dangle more information. Didn't ask for anything."

"They might want to stop you from looking. If they are part of it."

The suggestion — while entirely reasonable — irked her. She'd chased phantoms for so long and wanted desperately to believe she'd been right to risk everything by coming here.

"You have a dim view of people, don't you?"

He shrugged. "I'm sorry, but in my experience, most are . . . not kind."

She set the bread aside, appetite gone. "Have you ever heard of a mortifex named Magnus the Merciless? He does not wear a menotte."

Castelio's brows lifted. "No."

"They said my parents were looking for him behind the Veil. And that they probably found him."

"Lucius might know."

"Damn, I should have spoken to him, but he left so quickly after . . ." She trailed off.

Castelio regarded her for a moment, the price he'd paid hanging between them.

"You asked me about becoming a Quietus," he said at last. "The first soul I ever banished was my mother. She was killed by a mortifex. An unbound one."

"Oh." Her heart went out to him. "I . . . I'm so sorry. You don't have to talk about it—"

"No, it's all right. It was eight years ago."

She frowned, thinking. "That's when my own parents vanished. Do you think it could be the same one they were looking for?"

"It's possible. The mortifex was never caught."

The hair rose on her arms. It was a bizarre coincidence. They lived on opposite sides of the world. Had never even imagined the other existed. Yet . . . they did have something else in common. Or someone, to be precise.

"I understand now why you despise Lucius," she said. "But . . . forgive me if it's too personal, but how exactly do you banish a spirit? How old were you the first time?"

"Twelve." He laid his head back, gazing at the ceiling. "What a

Quietus does . . . it's not just iron weapons and Kaethe's Tears. Those are for when our true talent fails."

"I'm not sure I understand."

He seemed to gather his thoughts. "Let's put it this way. There are four reasons people come back." He ticked them off on his fingers. "Jealousy, greed, thirst for revenge. And love that burns too hot to let go of."

Lo frowned. "How do you know that?"

"Because I see how they died. Not in pictures. I mean, I *feel* it. The last thing they experienced at the end. Sometimes the dead talk to me but not often. But I talk to them in tongues."

She went cold. Tongues. Is that what the dead on the bridge had been speaking?

"I reassure them," he continued. "Offer them mercy. And if they are willing, I become a vessel for whatever emotion is anchoring their spirit. There are physical sensations, too. The heat of a fever. The pain of a wound."

She stared at him. "That sounds *awful*."

"It can be," he replied matter-of-factly. "Drowning, that's my least favorite. Others don't mind it. The man who trained me as an apprentice said it was the regret that got to him the most." A hollow laugh. "They all have that, except for the kids."

She thought about this for a moment. The strength it would take to go on doing that, day after day. Reliving the worst moments of another person's life. It was hard to imagine.

"Is the talent inborn?" she asked.

Castelio gazed out the dark window. "Gui — he's the oldest Quietus I know — doesn't believe so. He says it's just a rare combination of character traits."

"Like what?"

"Empathy. A certain comfort with death. Self-reliance. It's a solitary profession, but I like that."

"Same for me," she admitted. "I crash so often that no one at the Abicari in Susa will fly with me anymore."

He barked a laugh. "So I'm not the first passenger you've ditched in the trees?"

"No one ever got killed, I swear." Her cheeks flushed. "Broken bones, yes. It's why I was put on solo trading runs." She cleared her throat. "So you try to send the dead on nicely, and if that doesn't work . . ."

He gave her that crooked smile. "They go the hard way."

"And where do you send them?"

"I'm not even sure. Hopefully, back to the Dominion where they belong. None have returned that I know of. But I've often wondered the same." His smile faded. "I hope they found peace in Kaethe's embrace."

"Everything has a soul, doesn't it?" she said quietly, thinking of the ancient trees at Mystral.

"Aye. Which is why I don't eat animals anymore. People think I'm mad, but I can't do it."

The last sentence blurred into a single musical stream. She shook her head. "You talk so fast, Castelio. Your accent . . . I like it, but sometimes I can hardly separate the words." She ate a wineberry. "What do I sound like?"

The corners of his eyes crinkled in amusement. "Slow."

"That's all?" she teased.

"And like you're gargling a mouthful of marbles."

She laughed and swatted his leg. Castelio grinned.

"How about sharing those berries, your ladyship?"

Lo spilled some into his bandaged hand. He threw one up and tried to catch it in his mouth. It bonked off his nose.

"Once more," he said with a wink. This time he caught it. They passed a few minutes tossing berries until the floor was a sticky mess.

"The Courtenays'll kill us," he muttered, trying to rub a berry stain from the velvet seat.

The carriage sped along the road with barely a sound. Darkness pressed around them, but the spirit-lamps cast a cozy glow inside the coach. She felt relaxed. For all his fierceness, Castelio was a gentle man at heart. And didn't she owe him the full truth? He was risking his life for her.

How they'd managed to get this far with her secret intact, she had no idea. If Lucius had told Castelio how he escaped from the cage . . . If the Courtenays had mentioned daēvas . . . If Castelio had asked any of a dozen questions, he would already have guessed.

But he'd gone straight to Lucius, and then he'd been too subdued to pay much attention or demand answers. She opened her mouth to confess the rest when he leaned forward.

"I was taught to fear your lands," he said, gaze searching. "From the time I was a little boy. My Ma said the fire demons killed everyone, stopped Bel's chariot in the sky so they could turn it all to desert. That their feckless cousins had started the war and left the mortals to die." He shook his head in wonder. "But you won, didn't you? Survived and rebuilt. Are the demons truly all dead?"

Her speech turned to ashes. She gave a nod. "All dead."

He looked relieved. "So the mortifexes are the last of them. Well, they're scary enough. Can't even imagine a live one."

He seemed to sense the shift of mood for he changed the subject. "Have I told you about my family? Filippa and Teo? We call her Lip, on account of how she'd stick her lower lip out to pout when she was little . . ."

Lo nodded, though she barely heard. When he asked about her parents, she said her father was a carpenter who made figurines of the Prophet Zarathustra and her mother ran their little shop. She had no idea when or why they had taken the commission to hunt in the Dominion. If he suspected she was lying, he was too tactful to show it.

"I think I'll rest a bit, Castelio," she said at last, feigning a yawn.

"Call me Cas. And I'll stay awake to keep watch. I'm not tired."

She gave a wan smile. "Then you must call me Lo. I never go by Delilah."

"Lo." He tried it out. How soft and sensual her name sounded on his lips. And what pretty lips they were— She ruthlessly crushed the train of thought. No ogling the Quietus. He'd run screaming if he knew what she was.

"It suits you," Cas said.

He tucked the coverlet around her and sat back, staring out the window.

She didn't expect to fall asleep, but she must have been more tired than she thought, for some time later she felt a hand on her arm and heard him whisper her name. Lo sat up and rubbed her eyes. The coach was climbing a steep hill. They'd left the Nightwood. All three moons were high, illuminating a landscape of barren black rock that stretched as far the eye could see. Then they topped a rise and Castle Cazal came into view.

Neither of them spoke for a minute.

"Is he serious?" she finally asked. "I mean . . . *come on*."

"Feckin' hells," Cas murmured.

The road ended at a chasm stretching for many leagues. Its depth was impossible to gauge because roiling fog filled the gulf from edge to edge, a reddish glow pulsing in its depths as though great forges burned below. A narrow span arched across this misty sea, terminating at a rugged plateau of gleaming black rock. The castle appeared to be carved from this prominence. It was a construction of needle-sharp spires and blank walls. A single spark of light gleamed high in one of the towers. From its pinnacle, a blood-red banner rippled languidly, displaying an azure hand with argent flames dancing above the fingertips.

"Cozy," Lo said. "Who would guess necromancers lived there?"

Cas gave an uneasy laugh. "Time for me to squeeze into the compartment."

"Lady Chaos told me it's used for smuggling." She glanced at him, then quickly away. "Love potions and such."

"And forbidden tools of necromancy," he said dryly. "There's a brisk black market in the Sun Courts. The Ducissa's been trying to shut it down for years."

She vented a tight breath. "Thank you for coming with me. I must admit, I'm glad I'm not alone."

His smile faded as he yanked the lever. A dark gap slid open. "So am I," he said, tossing his pack inside.

Cas kicked it down to the bottom of the compartment. He twisted around to his back and slid into the cramped space. It was scarcely bigger than a coffin. Their eyes met. "Two hours," he said.

"Two hours," she agreed.

That sleepy look came over him, but it was more akin to a predator lying prone in high grass, waiting for its chance to pounce.

"You close it," she said. "So I'm sure you can open it again."

He fumbled around, found the lever, and tested it twice. The mechanism worked perfectly.

"See you soon," she said. "One way or another."

He gave a brief nod and the panel slid shut.

"To the castle, please," Lo called through the window.

The carriage lurched forward. In an instant, the rocky crags fell away on both sides and were swallowed by fog. The rattling of the wheels grew muffled as the horses sped across the smooth surface of the bridge, as if they galloped over volcanic glass. Lo checked to make sure the talisman hung around her neck. Her shoulders tensed with anticipation.

Her first impression had been correct. The keep had no windows save for the single spire. Nathan's bedchamber? She studied the clear sky, strewn with stars, and knew for certain that Thistle was in trouble. If he were free, he would have found her by now. Nathan must be controlling his power, else a furious storm would be raging.

She could imagine Thistle's wrath when he did get loose. There would be chaos to pay.

As they approached the plateau, the sound of the carriage

wheels changed and grew louder. Caul's words popped into her head. *Tell your master that he'd better lower the drawbridge and find a dark hole to hide in . . .*

It had seemed an odd choice of words. Drawbridges were *raised* to defend—

At that instant, Lo heard the rusty screech of metal chains slithering loose, followed by a thump. She stuck her head out the window. The final stretch of the span behind had disappeared. It left a gap twenty paces wide, into which the hellish fog billowed.

So there would be no retreat. Not unless Nathan Ouvrard allowed it.

Then the coach was drawing to a halt before a pair of obsidian doors, guarded by a pair of leering granite gargoyles perched on the lintel. Lo had wondered if the Duc might send a skeletal footman, or at least another dust-servant, but no one came out to greet her. She opened the door and climbed down from the carriage.

"I suppose you don't need seeing to," she told the skeletal horses. "But I thank you for bringing me so far."

One tossed its head as though it understood, then stood placidly with its brother, the embers of its eyes dimming as if in repose. Still no one emerged, so she trudged up the thirteen narrow steps and banged the knocker. A Hand Sinister, naturally.

The sound echoed hollowly within the reaches of the castle. A moment later, a series of heavy locks disengaged. The doors swung wide. A hatchet-faced giant with flowing, waist-length white hair peered down at her. He wore red leathers and more jewelry than a rich Persian dowager. Emerald earrings, a diamond brooch, and a bracelet inset with rubies circled one thick wrist above the iron menotte. He had piercing light eyes and carried an ivory dagger at his waist, also encrusted with gems.

"Let me guess," Lo said. "You're Vigo."

"Welcome to Castle Cazal," he said with a bow. His voice was a deep, chilling rumble; what you might hear if an avalanche could talk. "Come, my master awaits."

Chapter 27

The inside was as inviting as she expected.

Reflective black stone, pointy gothic arches, meager torchlight that failed to illuminate the recesses of the cavernous ceiling. Lo followed the mortifex through a series of stark, identical halls. She had the unpleasant sensation of furtive movement every time they passed a crossing corridor, as though someone had just turned the corner. The atmosphere was oppressive. Silent except for their overlapping footfalls, but again, she had the impression of whispering voices at the edge of hearing; of rustling within the walls that ceased immediately every time she paused to listen.

She saw no drifting ghost lights, but that meant nothing. The castle must be full of them.

At last, Vigo flung open the doors to a long rectangular chamber with a dining table that could have seated twenty without bumping elbows. A massive hearth occupied the far end. Blue flames danced within it, about a pace above the ground.

The table had been laid with snowy linen and groaned beneath a dozen silver platters. At its head sat the Duc of Vendagni.

Nathan Ouvrard was tall and gangly, with a long, pale face

and shock of unruly black hair. Clad in matching black from his doublet to his boots, apparently the *de rigeur* look for necromancers. A velvet half-cape settled across his shoulders, clasped with the gold Hand Sinister of his house. His chair was shoved back, one foot propped on the table, which he hastily removed when she entered.

"Demoiselle!" he cried, leaping up with great energy and striding forward with a loose-limbed gait. "I am enchanted!"

Before she could say a word, he bent over her hand and brushed his lips to her knuckles.

"I know my invitation was unorthodox, but—"

She snatched her hand back. "Where," she asked in a low voice, "is my cat?"

Nathan made a regretful face. "You are angry. But I can assure you, he is perfectly content. I will return him as soon as we have completed our business."

"And what business is that?"

Nathan signaled to Vigo, who withdrew, closing the doors with a resounding thud behind him. The Duc pulled out a chair. "Will you not sit, demoiselle?"

"Oh, very well." She sank into the chair, which he smoothly slid beneath her.

"Wine?" Nathan held up a decanter.

"No, thank you."

"To the point, then." He hesitated. "Not a morsel? Vigo was cooking for hours—"

"I already ate."

He gave a windy sigh. "As you wish. First, I will confess that I know who you are. Delilah Dessarian, yes? Daughter of Darius and Nazafareen Dessarian?"

She kept her face smooth, though it wasn't easy. "Now you will say you know where they are."

"Ah, but I do." He poured them both cups of wine and sat. "How did you mean to find them, if I may ask? I assume that is why you came to Aveline."

She saw no reason to lie. "I planned to hire a hedge necromancer in Nyons."

Nathan's aquiline nose gave a scornful sniff. "*Amateurs.* A waste of money, demoiselle."

"What do you want? And why did you kidnap Enrigo Redvayne? The Courtenays are quite angry with you. In fact, Lady Caul—"

"Do not tell me. I am sure she issued the most dreadful threats. But I did it to protect them."

His cavalier attitude irritated her beyond belief. "Oh, that's rich!"

Nathan studied her for a moment. "You have your father's eyes," he said softly. "Such an exquisite blue."

Lo's fists clenched beneath the table. "So you claim to know him."

Nathan Ouvrard lifted a silver lid from one of the platters. She glimpsed a gray appendage covered with glistening suckers, each sporting a small, curved fang in the center, before he sighed and dropped the lid with a clatter. "That would be an exaggeration. But I have seen him. Your mother, too. She is missing a hand, yes?"

"Were *you* the source of Lucius's information?"

"Not directly. That is common knowledge in the shadowlands."

"And why should I believe you?"

"Because I will show you where they are." He leaned back. "Once we've reached an accord."

She half rose from her seat, looking around wildly. "They're here?"

Nathan shook his head. "Be at ease, demoiselle. It is not I who hold them captive."

She sank back down. "Well, I already know all that. Chaos said they were hunting a mortifex in the Dominion. Magnus the Merciless."

"And they found him." A lazy smile played on his lips. "But

only I know exactly where they are."

"Here we go," she growled. "Just spit it out. What are you after? My wind ship crashed, so I can't offer you that."

"I don't care about your ship." He rose and paced to the fireplace, holding his hands out to the hovering flames. "There's an object I desire."

The mysterious tone irritated her even more. "Then get it yourself."

"Sadly, I cannot. It is in the Sun Courts."

"So? You might wear black and prance around doing dark magic, but you're human, aren't you?"

Nathan scowled. "I do not *prance*." He raked a hand through his hair. It stuck up like the crest of a bird. "The point is that not a single Cazal-Ouvrard has looked upon Bel's face in a thousand years. I will *not* be the first."

She blinked in surprise. "You've never seen the sun?"

"Nor do I wish to." He gave an ostentatious shudder. "It sounds awful."

The whispering started again. Very soft. She tilted her head and it faded.

"What is this object?" she asked, eager to hear his terms and be gone.

"A family heirloom." Nathan leaned back against the hearth, ankles crossed. "An item of sentimental value only."

She snorted. "Right. And I suppose you'll exchange it for the location of my parents."

"Fair terms, I think."

"And why," Lo wondered, "should I think you'll keep your word?"

"I propose we make a blood pact."

She laughed heartily. "With you?"

He affected a hurt tone. "Why not?"

Her smile withered. "What is the object you seek? It must be something powerful."

"That, I'm afraid, is private."

"Do you plan to use it against the Courtenays?"

"What?" Now his outrage seemed genuine. "No!"

Lo toyed with her wine. "You seem bent on their destruction."

"The boy, you mean?"

She nodded.

"He was never in any danger." Nathan looked puzzled. Then he laughed aloud. "Oh, you haven't caught up yet."

Rustling. Like mice gnawing on a stack of paper close by. She studied the black walls, her own reflection thrown back in a murky blur.

"Caught up with what?" she asked distractedly.

"The abduction was arranged at his own mother's request." Nathan made a minute adjustment to his half-cape. "To give her an excuse to invade us."

"Oh, that makes perfect sense," Lo snapped.

"It would if you knew Orlaith. Duc Scalici has always stood in her way. But if the wicked necromancers took her only son, she would have a wedge to drive between us. Scalici dotes on the boy. It's the one thing that would turn him to her side."

He said this so matter-of-factly, she didn't dismiss the story out of hand. If it was true, Orlaith had sacrificed her own soldiers to Nathan's wraiths. Allowed those foul creatures to put her child in a *sack*. But Lo remembered the Ducissa's bitter hatred of Nyons. The woman might be capable of such a scheme. She'd seen rulers do worse to get what they wanted.

"I can understand *that*," Lo said. "But not why you would cooperate."

He waved a hand. "She would have found a way to start a war eventually. At least I knew what it was."

She shook her head. "No, that's flimsy logic. You framed the Courtenays!"

"At Orlaith's insistence. She is my distant cousin." Nathan smiled. "Oh, she hates me, too, but not quite as much as she hates Ladies Chaos and Caul. It was all arranged well in advance. But your sudden arrival complicated her plans. There was no way to call it off. She didn't expect you to offer your wind ship in pursuit. The plan was for Lucius to go alone. My wraiths would return the boy before they reached the border, safe and sound."

Lo thought back. Saw Orlaith on the dais, whispering with Lucius. Her reluctance to accept the *Wind-Witch*. What mother would hesitate if she believed her son was in danger? With a sinking feeling, she realized that Orlaith had been trapped, standing before the whole court. She could hardly continue to balk at the offer. So she had made sure to send her mortifex along, too.

And Lucius . . . *That's* why he left them in the forest. So he could meet the wraiths and make the exchange. It was why he'd seemed so annoyed when they appeared at Nox. The threads of the plot all wove neatly together — except for one thing.

"What about the hordes of dead that rose at the gate?" she demanded. "All the soldiers who died? Why sacrifice them if you never really wanted Enrigo?"

Nathan stared at her. A long, considering look. "That wasn't me, demoiselle. Even I cannot work such a powerful spell from afar. It had to be someone who was there." A pause. "Any idea of who might have done it?"

"You!" She snatched up her goblet and drank, slamming it down so hard wine slopped onto the white tablecloth.

Nathan sighed in a patronizing manner. "If you knew anything about necromancy, you would realize that what you are accusing me of is impossible."

Anger flushed her cheeks. Or maybe it was the wine. "So you are blameless in the entire affair?"

"From my perspective, yes. Once it was over, I intended to expose Orlaith for the fraud she is. No one would ever take her seriously again." His lips quirked. "You've heard the tale of the boy who cried wraith?"

"And why would anyone believe *you*?"

His face hardened. "Because I meant to take Lucius captive

and hand the child to Duc Caino Scalici. Given the right inducements, Lucius would corroborate my version of events. Which happens to be the truth."

She stood, bracing her palms on the table. "It still changes nothing. I will not be your errand girl unless I know what it is I'm retrieving."

His eyes darkened. "That is a shame, demoiselle. Not only for your beloved cat, but for the Quietus you brought with you. Ah, don't look so shocked. The good Ducissas did not betray you. But you think I don't know about their little smugglers' holes? Vigo will have caught him by now. A stupid profession, if you ask me. Why waste perfectly good souls by sending them back behind the Veil—"

He threw up a hand to shield himself, but he was an instant too slow. The goblet flew through the air, spraying an arc of wine across the tablecloth like a slashed artery, and nailed him straight between the eyes. He staggered back with a loud curse.

The whispers and gnawing rustles suddenly increased like a wave surging toward shore. Vague shadows moved in the onyx walls. Slithered along the buttresses high above. She whirled to run and cracked her kneecap on a toppled chair.

Blood trickled down Nathan's pale cheek. He cupped his hand and blew. Whispered something that sounded like *sha'etemmu*. A fine sparkling dust rose into the air. It thickened into tentacles of darkness that reached for her like some horrible squid.

Lo pelted to the doors, slamming them shut on the writhing smoke. She jammed the lock with earth and careened down the corridor, skidding around the first corner. A mighty boom echoed through the keep. It sounded like doors blowing from their hinges.

Well, she thought without much surprise, as she ran for her life through Nathan's castle, *it's all gone to hell now.*

Chapter 28

It was quiet inside the compartment. Hot as blazes, too. Cas listened to his own slow breathing. He counted to five hundred, then eight hundred. Sweat trickled into his eyes.

He'd promised to stay hidden and, despite the discomfort, could have managed it for two hours. Waiting around in unpleasant spaces was not a novelty. But he had a bad feeling that only increased with each passing minute. The little he knew of Nathan Ouvrard was unsavory.

Most necromancers understood just enough to summon and bind a hapless soul from which they could draw power. Sever that connection and they were rendered harmless. Oh, they spat and cursed, but they were only men — or women — and he would simply arrest them and drag them to the nearest garrison.

But Nathan Ouvrard was steeped in the black arts from infancy. Castle Cazal had been the seat of his family for a thousand years. Centuries of death magic lived in the bones of the place. The stories about the necromancers of Vendagni were almost too lurid to be believed, though Cas was starting to.

Try as he might, he could not envision a scenario in which Lo walked out of that keep with her cat. Or her life.

The debate ended at a thousand. He grasped the lever. It

jammed for a nerve-jangling moment; then the panel slid open. He gulped in fresh air. Silently eased himself out and reached for his pack. It was stuffed all the way at the bottom. His fingertips brushed the strap . . . Was that a faint noise? He cocked his head, listening. A boom inside the keep, like a distant door slamming.

He forced his shoulders deeper into the cramped space, grabbed the pack, and filled his pockets with supplies, which he should have done before. Lo had addled his wits.

And the sight of Nathan's nightmarish lair.

At least the blank walls meant no one was looking out a window. He dropped the pack inside, sealed the compartment, eased the coach door open. Cas was standing at the bottom of the steps, studying the wide gap in the bridge and deciding on his next move, when he heard the click of tumblers releasing at the front door. If there had been fewer locks, he would have been caught red-handed. But the Duc of Vendagni believed in security. Those precious few seconds bought him time to gallop into the darkness. He dove around a sharp corner, then took a cautious peek.

A huge mortifex — Vigo, presumably — stomped up to the coach, threw the door wide, and reached inside to throw the lever. So he knew about the compartment. From the Courtenays? Or from Lo? The thought made him sick with worry. She'd never give him up willingly.

Cas took off again, following the blank walls around flying buttresses and sweeping towers. Footfalls, coming his way, signaled that Vigo had finished searching the coach and now hunted him in the grounds. Which were utterly barren. No outbuildings. No convenient caves or crevasses. Not even a lousy locked door. Just the hulking mass of Castle Cazal, perched atop its high, sheer promontory.

When he reached the north side, he found it covered in Devil's mantle, as Lady Chaos had described. Glossy, dark green leaves resembling holly, with tiny white flowers that concealed wicked thorns. One prick and you were as good as lich-touched.

But there was no time to drink the antidote, no time to climb the tower. He could hear Vigo's rapid tread drawing closer.

Cas ran, circling around the black walls. Found himself back at the front door. Would Vigo search the compartment again? Probably. He scanned the facade, frantic. The game of cat and mouse would not last long. Then he saw a possibility. A long shot, but . . . He sprinted up the narrow steps and leapt for a narrow ledge of stone that ran crosswise along the exterior wall. Caught it with his fingertips and pulled, teeth gritted, just high enough to grip the taloned foot of a gargoyle. Another mighty heave and the toe of one boot caught the ledge. He hoisted himself up and crouched behind the outspread wings as Vigo stalked around the corner.

Cas watched from his lofty perch on the gargoyle as Vigo nearly ripped the door from the coach and rummaged violently inside. After a moment, the mortifex emerged and loped off to make another circuit of the castle, this one at a blurring sprint.

A minute later, Vigo returned, stone-faced, searched the carriage a *third* time, and finally went back inside the keep. Only when the doors had slammed shut again did Cas draw a deep, steadying breath.

Now he needed to find another way inside.

He uncorked the bottle Lady Chaos had given him. He took a slug, grimacing extravagantly. "Feck," he muttered. "It tastes like rancid horse piss." He pinched his nose shut and downed the bottle. A narrow ledge ran from the lintel to a buttress at the corner of the roof. He inched along it, cheek pressed to the stone. The wind picked up, whipping his hair. He tried not to look down. Prayed Vigo wouldn't return.

The ledge led to a narrow buttress, which he straddled and wiggled across to the north tower. High above, light spilled through a window. The only one he'd seen.

Cas buried his hands in the thick vines of Devil's mantle and started to climb. The thorns weren't terrible; he'd suffered worse picking blackberries. But he felt them sting his flesh. A moment of numbness that instantly faded. *Kaethe bless you, Lady Chaos.*

He was almost to the window when soft shuffling persuaded him to look down. Two shadows trudged along below, insubstantial but not glowing with spirit-light. He froze, gripping the vines, until they passed out of sight. They hadn't given up looking for him. Seconds later, he was at the casement. The window proved to be locked, but he worked his knife into the gap and eased the latch open.

Cas dropped inside the room, blades ready. No one was there, though he knew at a glance that he'd found Nathan's bedchamber. A large spyglass rested on a tripod next to the window. The room was filled with heavily carved furniture, the wood dark with age. A massive wardrobe. A canopy bed. A writing desk and chair. Matching brass lamps cast mellow light across the desk. He cautiously approached. It held a large chart, weighted down at the edges. The parchment looked fresh-made. It was inscribed with a great circle intersected by a profusion of lines and arrows and smaller circles, with scribbles in the margins. Cas recognized the three moons, each of a distinct size and color. Some kind of astrological projection.

There were no instruments of necromancy that he recognized. No grim family portraits on the walls. No tapestries of people being impaled by demons. It could have been the chamber of a rich noble at Aquitan.

He crept to the door and tried the knob. Locked. Perhaps there was a key somewhere. He returned to the desk and started going through the drawers. Ink and quills, a paring knife to sharpen them. Reams of vellum. A heavy signet ring with the Hand Sinister, and bricks of black wax. No key.

He tried the bottom drawer. This one was crammed with letters, all penned in the same elegant hand. Dozens. Each one started the same.

My dearest lady . . .

Cas frowned, trying to decipher the script. It was written with such an excess of flourishes that he could scarcely make it out, but certain words jumped out at him. "Your *something* lips that dost promise *something something* lie awake imagining your tender . . ."

He lowered the letter. Was Nathan Ouvrard *courting*?

Cas returned it to the pile. Whoever the lady was, he wished her luck. Then he saw the glint of metal, hiding in the back of the drawer.

An iron key.

"Keeping your mortifex out, eh?" he chuckled, heading for the door. "Too bad iron doesn't work on me."

He pressed his ear to the door. All quiet. Cas slid the key into the lock. He heard a soft click. Which was peculiar, since he hadn't turned it yet.

"Oh, fe—"

He looked down just as a trap door yawned open beneath his feet. In a heartbeat, the chamber whisked away and Cas was hurtling down a chute into darkness.

Chapter 29

Lo flew through the castle. She dashed up corkscrewing staircases with no rails, along echoing black corridors and rows of blank doors without knobs. Cold blue flames flickered in sconces set at distant intervals. They left deep pools of shadow between which anything might be waiting, but she didn't dare slow down.

At first, the sounds of pursuit came close behind. The hot breath wheezing in his lungs. The rapid click of his bootheels and occasional bout of swearing, interspersed with dire threats. But she was part daēva and Nathan was not, and soon she left him behind.

Him — not the spirits.

She sensed them trailing her. Never visible when she faced them directly, but from the corner of her eye . . . oh, yes. They lived in the walls. In the reflective darkness of whatever substance the castle was hewn from. They whispered and they followed, but they did not try to interfere with her.

At last she slowed to a brisk walk, taking her bearings. The situation was rather bad. Alone, she might be able to escape, but if Vigo had Castelio . . . And she wasn't leaving without her cat, either. Which left few options.

She thought she'd climbed fairly high, up into one of the spires perhaps, though it was impossible to tell. "Why are there no windows in this stupid place?" she muttered.

Lo almost kicked the wall in frustration but caught a flicker of movement and thought better of it. Everything looked the same! Nathan hardly even owned any furniture. What on earth did he do all day besides scheming and kidnapping people? Surely, there must be a normal room somewhere. A place she could catch her breath and—

"Oh," she said. "What's this, then?"

The corridor had spiraled around, dead-ending at an archway. Beyond lay yet another very large, gothic chamber of the sort the Cazal-Ouvrards seemed so fond of, but this one was full of *stuff*, like the nest of some crazed magpie. The near side had six trestle tables with ominous dark stains. She saw scraps of twisted metal, mortars and pestles, tongs and hammers, instruments of every description. Beyond, high rows of freestanding cabinets and shelves created a maze of narrow lanes that stretched into the gloom. She picked up a heavy mallet from one of the tables and ventured deeper into the room.

She walked slowly through the workshop. Bones and skulls and scraps of hair were mounded in heaps, some human, some not in the least. The air had a dry, musty smell. A fine layer of gritty white dust settled over everything. She touched a fingertip to it and sniffed, then promptly sneezed. In the heavy hush, it sounded like a cannon going off. She cringed and pinched her nose. Then she noticed something on the floor that made her heart tighten and expand at the same time.

Little paw prints.

"Thistle?" she whispered.

There was no answer. Not even from the spirits. She wondered uneasily if they were reluctant to enter Nathan's laboratory. She followed the faint marks. They wound in a sinuous line around and under the tables to the warren of shelves. These, too, held a hodgepodge of items. Scrolls and manuscripts, ghoulish figurines, and glowing jars in which little sparks bumped against the glass. They gave off just enough light to follow the paw prints.

Thistle was here, she thought. *But where is he now?*

The shelves bent and turned like the crooked alleys near the wharf at Tjanjin. The air grew heavy, charged with dark energies. Her nape prickled as she gripped the mallet, trying not to accidentally brush the shelves. The prints led out to a second space that must be the opposite side of the spire. It was empty except for three rows of thirteen ornate oval mirrors fixed to the curving black wall. Thirty-nine in total. The number rang a distant bell, but she couldn't remember from where.

Thistle's prints continued for a short distance and vanished.

She eyed the blank faces of the mirrors. The frames were ornate and made of a dull, dark metal she felt sure was iron. The silvery surfaces of the mirrors did not reflect the chamber beyond. Could they be . . . gates?

Her left hand had not stopped tingling for a single instant since she entered the keep, but it worsened as she gazed at the gallery.

"Right," she muttered. "Time to go."

Lo turned around as a patch of darkness shifted between two of the shelves. An ash-servant shambled out from the gap. It had empty gouges for eyes, but she felt them fix on her. The creature was much larger than the one who had carried the message. About eight feet tall with a small, misshapen lump of a head. Its form boiled like smoke, and the heavy tread of its steps set the jars rattling on their shelves.

She backed away, feinted right, tried to dart around it. The thing moved quicker than she expected, blocking her path. Then it raised its thick, ropy arms and lunged to embrace her. She swung the mallet. It passed straight through the ash-man, but the metal must have contained iron for it howled, a sound like someone choking on wet earth. Dust swirled, stinging her eyes.

She hurled the mallet, blindly, and heard a sound that chilled her blood.

Glass cracking.

Lo blinked away tears. Rubbed her eyes again. The ash-servant had collapsed into a pile. As she feared, one of the mirrors was broken. Dark shards lay on the ground.

"Now I've gone and done it," she muttered. "Ah, hells . . . "

She was about to crunch the glass under her boot heel when she saw the glimmer of an eye in the biggest fragment. A foxlike face and grinning mouth. Dread sloshed in her stomach. The blue flames illuminating the room flared bright. Her ears popped and then . . .

Then she was no longer alone.

A woman rose up from the glass, black eyes glittering. She wore a dark gown that floated in streaming shreds around her. A ghostly menotte circled one white wrist. Lo saw the resemblance immediately. Thick raven hair, a high forehead and aquiline nose. One of Nathan's ancestors.

The woman pursed her lips and blew. A bubble of darkness slipped from her mouth. It floated for a moment, then burst into a web of black threads. Before Lo could move, they wrapped her in a net of burning cold. She fought for breath, eyes bulging. Her fingers spasmed, but the rest of her was stuck fast, as if she'd tumbled into a pool of quicksand. The specter drifted closer, a spider come to inspect an unlucky fly.

"Thank you for releasing me, little one." Her voice scraped down Lo's spine like a sharpened fingernail. "It has been a long time since I tasted freedom."

Chill fire licked at the edges of the spirit. Its gaze was avid. Hungry. Lo's strength flowed away, sucked into those black threads, even as the specter grew more solid. The woman wore a blood-red ruby at her neck, held in place by a choker of what appeared to be human molars. Below it was a ragged gash that looked like it had been made by a claw or talon. Shiny black beetles poured from the wound, skittering down her dress. They formed a seething carpet underfoot.

The necromancer noticed her staring. "I summoned a daemon from the sixth plane," she said with a gust of wintry laughter. "The blood spell failed and it tore my throat out. But you are young and strong. Strong enough to bring me back . . ."

The black threads pulsed like arterial veins. Lo's vision tunneled. Her skull throbbed as though beaten by a giant hammer. It was risk using her own power — or die. She tried to open a portal to the shadow world of the dead, as she had done on the bridge at Nox. Pain ripped through her chest. She sensed light in the corner of her eye, but it slipped through her fingers like moonbeams when she tried to seize it.

An expression of ecstasy gripped the woman's face. Her lips grew red and full, her black hair lustrous. The terrible wound began to seal itself. Spurs of pale bone jutted from her forehead, like some strange amalgam of human and daemon. The tether holding Lo's soul to her body stretched to the finest thread — yet it did not snap. Anger sparked in the necromancer's eyes.

"How do you resist me?" she demanded.

Lo blinked through tears of agony. Resist? She was at the specter's mercy! But then she felt a hum of power, a cold spot between her breasts. The talisman of protection was fighting the onslaught of dark magic. Her mind cleared a little. Enough to wonder if perhaps it had another effect, as well. If she was wrong, she would die. But the specter would find it sooner or later anyway.

"I . . . I have a talisman," Lo gasped.

The cruel gaze sank to the disk hidden beneath her shirt. "Ah . . ." A hand reached out. The spirit grimaced in pain when her hand touched the silver. One hard yank and the chain snapped. She tossed it away.

"Much better," the necromancer purred. She smiled with small white teeth.

"Thank you," Lo whispered, as the light burst forth.

The woman's eyes narrowed, mouth gaping in a silent scream. The black threads binding Lo evaporated. She felt the current beating against her, trying to suck her down with the spirit, but this time she was ready. She planted her feet against the tide and sought the Nexus. Through the shrieking wind of the gate, she listened for the steady thump of her own heartbeat, holding to the sound like a lifeline.

Down, down, the spirit sank, pulled into the gate like muddy water down a drain, elongating and losing its human form until it was nothing but a gibbering lich. When the last scrap was gone, her ears popped again. The gate sealed. The wind died. She sank down, panting, hair a wild, tangled mess across her face.

It was the talisman that blocked her ability to dispose of the dead. Only when she'd taken it off to give to Castelio did her true power show itself. It was the first time she'd ever removed it. Which meant . . . well, the power might not be new at all. Just dormant.

When she'd caught her breath and stopped shaking, Lo gave a fierce, gleeful laugh. Bounded to her feet and blew the hair from her face. She'd won. Learned to control it. And someone else was in the shit now.

"Nathan Ouvrard!" she bellowed, striding to the wall.

It took some fiddling, but she managed to detach the next mirror from its bindings. She peered inside it, nose nearly touching the murky glass. "Anyone home?"

Something stirred in its depths. Very faint. Reluctant, one might say.

"There you are. Come on out!"

She hurled it to the ground. Glass shattered. The blue flames flared as she stepped back.

An old man this time. Sinewy and hairless as an egg. He wore an old-fashioned frock coat and hose. Velvet slippers with gold buckles. The same iron menotte shimmered around his bony wrist.

"What's your name, then?" she asked briskly.

His voice was the grate of a stone sarcophagus lid sliding open. "Valentin Cazal." He licked his lips. "But pray, demoiselle, listen to me—"

"Nice to meet you. Have a safe trip."

The door inside her blew wide. Valentin Cazal barely had time to protest before darkness opened at his feet like a trap door. Wind whipped through the chamber, rattling the black mirrors on the walls. Her heart thumped in her ears like a bass drum. She staggered over to a cabinet and clung to the ornate handles. It was easier to resist the tug of the current now, though she felt its immense power. Worse — an itch to cross over and see what waited there. But she had other business to attend to first.

"Where," she shouted, "is my cat, *Nathan*?"

The gate snapped shut. Her ears popped. Lo released her grip and stalked along the gallery.

"Who's next?" Her gaze swept the mirrors. Their inhabitants were stirring now. White faces flashed into view, then vanished. Furious whispering broke the silence.

Lo sauntered to the wall again, choosing the largest, most elaborate mirror, which also happened to be the first in line. She waited. Gradually, an outline appeared. It approached on all fours, as though crawling down a long tunnel. The figure was cloaked in darkness, yet she sensed its intelligence. Its awareness of her.

She had her hands on the frame when the sound of running feet made her turn.

"Stop!" Nathan skidded out from between the cabinets, disheveled and panting. He flung a hand up. "Don't touch that!"

She regarded him coldly. "So you do care."

She tried to wrench the mirror from the wall.

He swore angrily, and then darkness enveloped her. A battering force knocked her off her feet. She flew across the floor, slamming into one of the cabinets. It gave a creaking groan and toppled over. The glass jars inside shattered and sparks flitted out like fireflies. They dove at her in a swarm. Invisible fingers pinched her flesh. Yanked at her hair.

Pretty, pretty! A high-pitched voice cackled in her ear.

Lo swatted at the sparks as they buzzed around her, gibbering. Poking and prodding. Ugh! Was that a *tongue*? She couldn't see a bloody thing.

But she could hear Nathan's footsteps, drawing ever closer.

Chapter 30

The shaft angled steeply downward. It was pitch black inside, the stone slick as polished marble. Cas's hands skimmed along the walls, groping frantically for purchase, but he was going way too fast. It twisted left, then right, then left again. Grew even steeper.

He tucked his chin and cursed as it veered around yet another sharp bend, slamming him to the side. He tried not to think about what would happen if it ended at a blank wall. He'd be buried alive deep in the bowels of the castle with no way out. Legs broken, most likely.

Which struck him as exactly the sort of punishment a necromancer like Nathan Ouvrard would devise to punish trespassers.

He rocketed straight down now, gathering speed. The only sounds were his rapid breath and the swish of cloth sliding on stone. Then the chute veered upwards. Momentum carried him along like a pea shot from a hollow reed. After a few seconds, he crashed back down, scraped over a hump, and flew out of the chute. An instant of flailing weightlessness and he landed with a startled cry in a deep pool of what looked, tasted, and felt like blood.

It was thick and viscous. *Hot*.

Cas broke the surface, sputtering, and swam to the edge of the cistern. Hauled himself out and rolled to the side, gasping and shuddering in revulsion. He tasted hot, coppery salt on his tongue.

"Bel's flaming balls," he groaned weakly, spitting. "What the feck . . .?"

He tore his cami off, using it to scrub his face and hair. Spit some more and squeezed his eyes closed to wipe them clean. When he opened them, the cistern was clear. He stared for a moment, then crawled to the edge and cupped his palm, letting the substance flow through his fingers. It looked like plain water.

He glanced down. Still soaking wet but not with blood. Cas knew he didn't imagine it.

"*Feckin' hells*," he whispered, looking around.

The dark mouth of the chute sat about twelve paces above his head. Too far to reach, and impossible to ascend even if he could. It was impossible to say with any certainty how long he'd fallen, but it felt like a minute or two at least. On either side, curving black walls. They held sconces that cradled dancing blue flames with no visible source of fuel.

Whoever had built this place obviously had a way to access it besides the chute. Which meant a way out. He yanked his cami back on and checked his weapons. The interlocking knives were in their sheath, but four of his glass vials had cracked, their blessed Kaethe's Tears seeping away. One remained intact.

Cas knew they'd be hunting him. There was no way Nathan Ouvrard didn't know his little trap had snapped. Time to get moving.

He took out his iron coin, relieved to find it had survived the fall. Tossed it and snatched the coin from the air. When he opened his hand, the rosette was facing up. Left then.

He took off at a jog, listening for any sign that he wasn't alone. The passage curved around, then branched into three. He chose the middle. It went for a bit and branched. Right this time. The walls were featureless and shiny enough that he caught his own faint reflection as he passed. He used this at the curves, watching for movement ahead.

It was hot and stuffy in the tunnels. His clothes were almost dry when he came around a corner and found himself back at the cistern. It flickered redly for an instant. Cas stared at a single spreading ripple, as though something stirred beneath.

"Feck!" he muttered, backing away.

This time, he chose the left side of the first branch. Chose left every time. Walked for what seemed like leagues, nerves drawn tight as a bowstring, tensing at every flickering shadow cast by the blue flames.

It led him back to the cistern.

He stood, weary and discouraged, as a bubble broke the surface. Ripples, overlapping now, like a gentle rain. When the center suddenly erupted in a geyser of blood, he took off running again.

Right, left, straight. Did it even matter? The walls themselves were bleeding now. Weeping rivulets of dark crimson ichor. It pooled on the floor. Showed him his own overlapping boot prints. Oh yes, he'd taken this route before. There was no way out—

Cas bent over, hands braced on his knees. Screamed as something bumped his leg. He spun away, knives out, then slumped against the wall with a crazed laugh.

"You!" he exclaimed. "Just the one I was looking for."

Thistle regarded him with the inscrutable, slightly contemptuous serenity of his species. Glowing symbols circled the cat's neck like a collar. Whirling round and round. It dizzied him to look at.

With a flick of his tail, Thistle padded off down the corridor, skirting the puddles of blood. So the cat saw them, too. Glad he hadn't gone completely insane, Cas gathered his wits and followed. "Do you know the way out?" he asked softly.

It should have felt stupid, talking to a cat, but he was too grateful for the company to care. No response came — hardly surprising. But the cat waddled along without hesitation, appearing confident, which made one of them, so he shut up and followed.

Cas had felt certain he'd explored every single branch of Nathan's monstrous labyrinth, but he must have missed a turning, for the bloody footprints faded. It all looked the same, of course. He couldn't be sure. But they might, just *might* be someplace new.

His spirits lifted ever so slightly. And that was the precise moment that Vigo found them.

The cat had been walking with its tail straight up, the tip hooked into a slight curl. Cas knew cats since they often hung about the lichyards and never seemed bothered by the dead. He'd spent many a long night waiting for an angry specter to appear, watching them in their nocturnal ramblings or quarrels, and knew that a low, swishing tail signaled a confrontation, while a tail held erect meant a relaxed, friendly cat. He brought scraps of meat on these occasions, garnering their goodwill, and they had alerted him more than once to a sneaky corpse creeping up behind.

So when Thistle's tail puffed up, he had the vial of Kaethe's Tears unstoppered even before the hiss came.

Cas hurled it at the tall form that sprang around the corner. It struck the mortifex in the face, raising wisps of steam. Cas caught a flash of bubbling skin and skidded past. Vigo groped blindly, catching the back of his shirt with one hand. The other was pressed to his howling face. Cas felt cloth tear as he yanked free, and then he and the cat were both running in the opposite direction. Despite his hefty girth, Thistle moved like lightning. Cas found himself hard-pressed to keep up, but he wouldn't lose Lo's pet now.

Roars of enraged pursuit chased them through the tunnels. He got his knives ready, but they were all he had left; laughable against a mortifex. Vigo would use air magic to tear them from his hands at a distance, then rend his body limb from limb.

This spurred him on, faster than he'd ever run in his life.

Thistle was a leaping blur ahead. Cas kept his eyes fixed on the swirling runes of his collar. If there was an exit, he thought grimly, now would be the opportune moment to stumble across it.

Instead, he flailed around a corner and hit a dead end.

The cat was already padding back, tail low, head low, yellow eyes glowing like forge-fires.

"Oh, double feck," Cas growled.

He spun back around. There were no sconces in the blind alley. Only a faint bluish glow from the end. Vigo's taunting voice echoed town the tunnel.

"I hope you enjoyed the labyrinth of blood! No one's been down here for a while. We were running a little dry." A deep chuckle. "But every bit helps!"

His steps were slow and heavy now, prolonging the anticipation.

Cas whispered a prayer. His gaze fell to the scar across his palm. Parallel to it, the half-healed cut from summoning Lucius. His jaw clenched. It would be a mortifex in the end, wouldn't it?

Then his head tilted. Or maybe not.

He couldn't kill Vigo. Couldn't even hurt him. But he might be able to slow him down.

Cas ran a short way up the tunnel. The footsteps were close now.

"Where are you, little reaper? Cowering in the dark?" Another chuckle. "How'd you like to become a dust-servant? I'll grind up your bones and—"

Cas tuned him out. He slashed the blade across his palm, relishing the sting, and sketched his blood across the stone. *Kaethe, let him not carry a flame.*

Then he retreated and adopted an air of defiance. The cat was sitting on its haunches now, tail wrapped across its paws. He could have sworn it was smiling.

"You'll never take me, fex!" he shouted, brandishing the iron knives as Vigo strolled around the corner.

In life, he'd been a giant of a man. As thick and broad as Gui

Harcourt. His silhouette blocked the light, rendering his flaming irises in vivid relief.

"Ah, there you are." Vigo halted. He crouched down. "Come along, little cat. Come out of there."

The mortifex made a kissing sound. Thistle eyed him with disdain for a long moment, then found something fascinating to stare at high on the wall.

Vigo stood. "Fine," he snarled. "If your fur gets singed, it's none of my concern."

The mortifex raised a hand.

"Afraid to fight me?" Cas called out. "Of course you are. Your sort are always cowards."

"Fight you?" he sounded genuinely perplexed. "*You*?"

Cas tossed a knife into the air and caught it with a flourish. "That's right."

A hearty laugh. As expected, both blades tore from his grip and sailed down the tunnel. Vigo leaned to the side as they hurtled past.

"I was trying to be merciful," he said. "But if you want to do it the hard way . . ."

He strode forward six paces. Stopped dead. How Cas wished he could see his expression! Then a wavering light appeared, dancing above one sausage-sized finger. It lit the hollows of Vigo's face from below in a most unflattering fashion. He looked down in disbelief.

"What have you done?"

Cas smiled. "You're really a big, dumb *sanglant* bastard, aren't you?"

In swift increments, Vigo's incredulity shifted to towering fury. A pillar of white flame erupted inside the nine-pointed star. His roar seemed to shake the walls.

"You can't hold me for long, reaper!"

Which, Cas knew as he backed against the stone, blinded and roasting, was entirely true.

Chapter 31

Nathan Ouvrard sounded most incensed.

"You can't banish the living!" he shouted.

Lo had crawled through the maze of shelving and glass-fronted cabinets, and now crouched under one of his long worktables. She could hear him hunting her in the crooked lanes between the two chambers. The nasty little spirits from the jars had almost given her away, but then, by some miracle, her groping hands discovered the silver talisman the dead lady necromancer had torn from Lo's neck and hurled away. The spirits fled at once.

Which still left their master to contend with.

"I'll find you, demoiselle! Why don't you come out and make it easier for both of us?"

He had sealed the archway with a boiling wall of smoke-tentacles. No way out there.

A moment later Nathan appeared, looking wide-eyed and disheveled. She leapt up and unleashed a whip-crack of air. It snapped his head back. He touched a finger to his lower lip and regarded the blood, gaze darkening.

"Let us go," she said firmly. "And I won't—"

"*Rabum usemi ukkin*!" he cried, hurling a fistful of dust.

She expected more tentacles, but the glittery powder vanished.

Then a very terrible thing happened.

The floor rushed up to meet her. Strange ticklish things sprouted from her face. In a panic, she ran . . . well, to be accurate, *scurried* across the floor, tiny claws scrabbling at the stone. Nathan reached her in three strides. Then she was sailing upward, dangling upside down, limbs kicking. She feared . . . yes, he had her by the tail.

The world blurred as he strode back through the shelving and stopped in front of the gallery of mirrors, twisting her around so she could see her reflection. Pointy nose, whiskers, adorable pink paws. Her little heart nearly burst. She squeaked in outrage.

"If you'll promise to behave," he said icily, "I'll change you back."

She emitted another frantic squeak, hoping it sounded like agreement.

Nathan set her down — gently, it must be said. He sifted dust over her, like a baker flouring a table to roll out dough, and muttered another incantation.

Things pulled and stretched, rearranged. It was less a sense of growing larger and more of everything else *shrinking*. She scrambled back, trying to glare at him and inspect her newly restored body at the same time.

Nathan regarded her with narrow eyes. "I wondered about that trick you pulled back at Nox, but I wasn't sure. Now I am."

She brushed herself off. Tried vainly for a sense of dignity. "You . . . I hate you!"

"There are worse things than mice." He sounded amused. "I could have made you into anything I chose."

Her furious gaze flicked to the mirrors.

"I wouldn't recommend it," Nathan warned. Again, the appraising look. "Don't you want to know what you are?"

The words dampened her rage. *What you are.*

Lo gave the barest nod, holding his dark gaze.

Nathan's voice was solemn now, with no trace of mirth. "You, demoiselle," he said, "are what is called a shadow soul."

VIGO'S TEMPER tantrum showed no sign of abating.

He howled and raged, hurling invective and threatening dire retaliation when he got loose.

Which Cas judged would happen any second now.

Nine-pointed stars drawn in human blood were not made to stand the test of time. They were used for summoning and banishing. Briefly trapping, with an emphasis on the word *brief*.

Under normal circumstances, the star would be surrounded with soldiers bearing iron pikes and silver nets. A great whopping iron cage would be hoisted up with a winch and dropped over the captive mortifex, rendering it harmless. Then the whole thing would be deposited on a cart drawn by a team of draft horses, hauled to the nearest gate, and tossed inside.

Kaethe's sanctuary in Mistral used enchanted bones which made the star stronger, but even so, he guessed that it had only contained Lucius because he was a weak mess. Had he wanted out badly enough, he would have escaped eventually.

The problem was the blood. Kaethe's power held the star together for a little while, but it couldn't withstand the onslaught of a mortifex's fire. Even now, the blood was bubbling, flaking off in little bits that whisked away in whirls of sparks. The star was *shrinking*.

And the instant a gap appeared, even a tiny hairline fracture, the whole construction would collapse.

Unfortunately, the inferno also blocked their only escape route. Cas was sweating profusely and pondering this intractable problem when a demonic voice spoke.

You must banish him.

At first, he thought it was Vigo. But the mortifex was still waving his flaming fists, kicking the invisible barrier, yelling about eating Cas's entrails, or possibly making him eat his own entrails, it was hard to be sure—

He spun around, searching wildly for the source.

Are you so thick? It is the only way.

Bel save him, it was the cat. Cas stared dumbly. It all felt like a strange, terrible nightmare. Not even when he fought the damned had he heard such a sound as that voice. Like wind shrieking through a lonely lichyard while a multitude of tortured souls moaned beneath a full, gibbous moon—

"I can't," he managed.

Why not?

The cat's mouth didn't move. He wasn't sure if that made it better or worse. But the creature stared at him with unsettling intelligence.

Cas glanced at the star. One point was very thin now. Whisker-thin, you might say. He swallowed an awful laugh.

"I don't know his true name."

The cat's eyes narrowed. *What is Lucius's true name?*

He hesitated. Oh, what did secrets matter anymore? He was conversing with a cat!

"Claudius Quintus."

And mine is Shelithoth. Do you not see the pattern?

Pattern? "Feck," he muttered. "No!"

Another vexed lash of its tail. *The common name of a demon must be formed from the letters of its true name. I was named after a she-goat named Thistle, but it is no coincidence that Nazafareen chose it.*

Cas tried to focus, but the star was bubbling, Vigo's cries sounded more triumphant than angry now, and all he caught was the word *she-goat*.

"Can you get to the point?"

Vigo's true name will have those four letters. I suggest you start guessing.

Another demented laugh escaped him. "It could be anything!" He rubbed his forehead, trying to pluck the right answer out. "I banish you, Verigoth!"

The flames rose higher, but it was only Vigo redoubling his efforts, apparently sensing light at the end of the tunnel.

"Vogileth," he muttered. "Vegiloth. No, that sounds like vegetable broth . . . Ah, this is pointless!"

The demon-cat groomed its claws. *I believe it is also written on the inside of the menotte.*

"The inside? That does us no good."

Then we are done for.

He bit back another heartfelt *feck* and crawled closer. The cuff around Vigo's wrist was white hot. In one small piece of luck, the mortifex seemed blinded by his own flames and gave no indication that he saw Cas coming. He'd paused to gather himself for the final assault, arms at his sides. But gods, the heat . . . Like an iron foundry in the western desert of Rhun.

Cas squinted, eyes streaming. If the menotte around Vigo's wrist hadn't been white-hot, the task would have been impossible, but he perceived tiny marks glowing red against the molten metal. Not indecipherable runes. Ordinary letters.

Of course, they were backwards and upside down.

A quick glance told him the star was almost entirely eroded now, the perimeter so lash-fine he couldn't believe it did anything.

Keep still, he implored silently. *Just for a moment longer . . .*

The sharp angle of a V came into focus first. A smaller oval that might be *e* or *o*. *E*, he thought. The hook of an *r*. A dangly letter. *G* for certain. There had to be a *g*. Two *l*'s. Or was it an *i*, followed by *l*? Then five more letters in a tight row.

Shimmering waves of heat blurred the rest of the name. Cas inched closer. The unholy conflagration dried the sweat on his face. Wicked it straight from his pores. The mortifex's long white hair crackled and flowed in great tongues of flame. He held up his palms as if in supplication. Cracks shot outward from the center of the star, neatly bisecting the points.

Here it comes . . .

"Ver . . Vergil . . . Vergilious!" he gasped. "I banish you!"

The flames abruptly extinguished, darkness rushing in. Cas brought a shaking hand to his face. One eyebrow felt burned to stubble.

"Ah, no. . ." the mortifex exhaled wearily.

Cas's ears popped. Wind rushed through the tunnel. The hulking silhouette vanished. He sank down to the stone, breathing heavily. Even the rank air of the blood labyrinth felt like a fresh meadow breeze against his tender skin.

Well done, Quietus.

Thistle padded over and gave Cas an affectionate butt with his head.

He regarded the creature warily. "So you are a demon?"

By the strictest definition only, since I am alive. The proper term is ala. I summon the wind.

A few other things clicked into place. "That is how she flies the ship? With your power?"

A slow blink. *Yes.*

He smiled, stiffly, due to the dried salt coating his cheeks. "I will never tell another soul your true name, I swear it."

The cat rose, tail curved in a shepherd's crook. *You cannot summon me with it — nor banish me. I am both a cat and an ala, and I answer to no one.* Thistle butted his knee again. *But if you call me again one day, I may choose to answer.*

Cas pushed up to his feet. He felt a thousand years old. "The collar? Is that how Nathan Ouvrard trapped you?"

He sent Vigo. The tail began to switch. *When the wraith came, I slipped away into the dark on the Nyons side. Lucius summoned flames against it and I do not like fire. Vigo was waiting.*

"At the bridge?" Cas grunted. "Makes sense, if Nathan was the one who ordered Enrigo's kidnapping."

Thistle did not reply for a moment. His eyes were luminous in the dark, but the light was warmer than the chill fire of a mortifex's gaze. More akin to a warm yellow lantern. *Perhaps. Let us leave now, Quietus.*

"You know the way out?" Then he nodded. "Of course, it will be near to the place where we first met Vigo."

He retrieved his iron knives from the end of the passage. Then he followed the ala around the bend, hoping Lo was having better luck. She consorted with a demon . . . but Shelithoth's quick thinking had saved them both, and anything that hated a mortifex he counted as a friend.

Cas chuckled. All that wild speculation. And it turned out she *was* a normal woman after all.

Chapter 32

Shadow soul.

It was what the dead of Nox had called her. But Lo wasn't about to admit that to Nathan Ouvrard. He'd find a way to use it against her.

She snorted and got to her feet, ignoring his offered hand. "You just made that up, didn't you?"

Nathan's lip was still bleeding. He blotted it with a sleeve, unsmiling. "I will tell you the signs. Your left arm tingles and grows numb when you are near a gate, or close to the dead. Left because that is the heart side. You may experience pain. Difficulty breathing. Your mortal body is bluffing death. It wants to cross the Veil. To reunite with the half of your soul that is already in the Dominion—"

"Stop," she growled.

"You have the power to open and close a gate at whim. You speak tongues, the language of the dead. The dead will be drawn to you—" He broke off, head tilting as though he heard a faint noise. Shock crossed his face. "*Putain,*" he whispered to himself.

"What is it?"

Nathan stood motionless, his gaze distant. "The Quietus banished my mortifex," he said with a note of disbelief.

Warmth spread through her chest. "Good for him."

"I'll just summon Vigo back," Nathan said carelessly, crossing his arms, though he looked shaken. "Once we are finished here, demoiselle. As I was saying, your presence attracts the dead. Like the bridge at Nox. Like Midgate."

She wanted to deny it. But she remembered the way the spirits had pursued the wind ship. How she had sensed the wraiths who took Enrigo before she even saw them. A dozen other times.

Lo flexed her left fingers. They were tingling like mad at that very moment.

"How do you know all this?" she asked caustically. "Did you learn it in evil necromancy school?"

"My ancestor Jaskin Cazal was a shadow soul, too. I would introduce you, but I'm afraid he is quite mad. And stronger than you can imagine, even in death." Nathan's face hardened. "Had you succeeded in breaking the black mirror that holds him, you would have found yourself in deep trouble."

She glanced at the first mirror. The one she'd nearly wrested from the wall when Nathan burst in. Its depths were quiet now, but she remembered the creepy-crawling shadow. A chill crept over her.

"This makes no sense," she muttered. "And what did you mean about *half a soul*?"

Nathan shrugged. "Precisely what I said. Your essence is divided between the land of the living and that of the dead. Kaethe marked you as her own. Perhaps it is the reason your parents hunted on the Lady's behalf in the Dominion."

She heard Javid's voice as they sat in his office at the Abicari. *It was a bargain, Lo . . . Not my secret to tell . . .*

Blood pounded in her ears. "No! They would never do that to me!"

Nathan's brows lifted. "It is a gift, and a very fine one. Nine is the Drowned Woman's number. That is how many lives she allots a shadow soul." He studied her face. "Ah. Perhaps you've died already?"

Lo went even colder. Her gaze roamed the gallery. A few specters had drifted to the surface of their prisons, watching her intently, whispering to each other, but she barely saw them. She was mentally reviewing the last few years. The thing was . . . she didn't remember any of the crashes. Not past the moment of impact. Just waking up afterwards amid the wreckage, with nothing but a bruise or two. And the branching scars, of course.

"I've had . . . accidents, yes," she admitted. "But it was my talisman that saved me."

Nathan shook his head. His dark eyes seemed to see right through her. "There is no talisman that powerful."

"It brought back Castelio."

"The Quietus? From the brink, yes. But he wasn't dead, was he? Not yet. And you used your own power to magnify the talisman's properties."

"How do you know that?" she demanded. "You weren't . . . Dammit. The wraith?"

Nathan smiled. "Vigo. He saw the whole thing and reported back to me."

She shook her head in denial, casting about for some other explanation. Then it came to her. "Ha!" She stabbed a finger at him. "What about the menotte? A talisman that brings people back!"

"The cuff traps the spirit, but the body remains dead. Last I checked, you're alive." He studied her stricken expression. "How many times *have* you died?"

She tried to tally up the worst crashes. Say, two or three? Plus the lightning strikes. Twice right there. And don't forget the lich. Icy sweat coated her palms. She briskly rubbed them together.

"I . . . I don't know. It's impossible to say."

Nathan laughed at her consternation. "You *do* live dangerously, demoiselle."

"It's not funny." She scowled. "What if I've lost count? Is there a way to know?"

"Not that I'm aware of. But I will do some research in the library and see what I can find out."

"So . . . this could be my last life?"

A bizarre question. Until ten minutes ago, Lo had viewed her current existence as her *only life*. Did she believe him? The rest of it fit. And the tingling had started with Lucius — all the way back in Tjanjin. She doubted even Nathan Ouvrard could have hexed her from that far away.

Lo watched warily as he picked up a shard of black glass.

"Your last life?" Nathan repeated musingly. "It could be. In which case, I suggest you use it wisely. Now, I will show you your parents, if you wish it."

She blinked, still reeling, as fresh fear gripped her. If they were being held by a mortifex named Magnus the Merciless . . . well, it couldn't be good. But she'd come all this way. Better to know what she was dealing with.

"Yes," she said. "I do."

Nathan whispered an incantation. She peered into the shard of black mirror.

It was cloudy at first. Then the vague outline of a ship appeared, floating on a calm sea. Mist shrouded the mast, curling in shreds along the limp canvas. It parted to reveal a small woman sitting on the deck, drawing a whetstone along a short sword. *Nemesis*. Forged from iron, double-edged and with a leaf-shaped design called a *xiphos*. The view moved in, close enough to make out an inscription along the blade in Old Valkirin runes. Lo silently mouthed the translation.

No battle is won in bed.

It was the blade that had once belonged to Culach's mother, Ygraine. Lo had seen it a thousand times. And her own mother . . . well, she knew every laugh line, every freckle. The stubborn set of her mouth, which transformed into a warm smile at someone out of sight.

The angle shifted, pulled back. A gold cuff circled the stump of the woman's left wrist, and the man who now stooped at her side wore its match. Broad-shouldered and handsome, with crystalline blue eyes. He said something that made Lo's mother throw her head back and laugh. She set the blade aside and rubbed the stump of her arm, another familiar gesture. Her amber eyes danced with merriment.

Lo studied her father closely, seeking some sign of wrongness. Something out of place. His dark brown hair was windblown, stiff and curling from salt. He wore the same clothing he had the day he left. A simple white tunic, open at the throat, with brown trousers and scuffed boots.

Her breath caught when she saw the pink shell on a leather cord. She had made it for him as a gift. Hung it around his neck four days before they left for the last time.

No one besides her mother knew about that.

The image swam through a lens of salty tears. *Eight long years.* Pain and longing clenched her heart. She wiped her eyes with a sleeve as the mirror went dark again.

"I will help you find them," Nathan said in a surprisingly gentle tone. "But I must have the object in the Sun Courts first."

She stared into space, bereft and empty. "Are they behind the Veil?"

He hesitated. "Yes, but they are not dead. They don't belong there. And they cannot stay much longer else they *will* die."

A knot in her gut slowly unclenched. "They looked . . . happy."

"They are under a powerful enchantment," he said. "That is not true happiness."

"Where are they? What *is* that ship? Did Magnus put the enchantment on them?"

"Three excellent questions. By a happy chance, I know the answers to all of them, demoiselle." His smile evaporated. "And I will tell you once you return."

How she longed to slap that smug face! Her mother would have beaten the answers from him. Whacked him soundly with the flat of her blade and—

"If it makes you feel any better, I will tell you why I want this object." A dramatic pause. "It is the only thing that can stop Orlaith from invading and destroying the Moon Courts. She will not give up until we are all dead. And you might despise *me* but think of the Courtenays. Of the many night creatures that dwell in Nyons, and my own realm, as well. Do they not have a right to exist?"

Lo thought of the ancient trees. The centaurs. The shadowy things that crawled and flew. She met Nathan's dark eyes. "A weapon, then?"

He gazed at her frankly. "In the wrong hands, yes."

"And I'm supposed to believe *you're* the right hands? You, who just turned me into a *rat*?"

Nathan seemed unconcerned. "Better than Orlaith. Or the new Duc of Cavet. I hear he's a real tyrant."

She shook her head in irritation. "I'm guessing it's a talisman."

"Guess all you like." He rubbed his hands together. "Now for the terms of our blood pact—"

"Hold on. My parents made a bargain with someone like you. Look where it got them. How stupid do you think I am, Nathan?"

His eyes narrowed. "Then leave. I'll give you your cat back. Your Quietus too, if he's still alive."

"Just like that?"

"I'll find someone else." He looked around. "I won't even charge you for the damage."

The final manipulation.

"Tell me what it is," she coaxed. "In general terms."

His swollen lip curled. "No."

"Fine," she snapped. "I'm going. I'll find them myself."

She walked slowly to the maze of cabinets. Nathan did nothing to stop her. She picked a path through broken jars and reached the workshop. The billowing smoke was gone from the archway. No sign of any ash-servants. No spirits, either. She halted at the exit.

It was stupid. Utterly insane.

Lo had learned to feign confidence in sticky situations, but she was out of her depth. If only Thistle were here. He always gave sensible advice. And, as the offspring of a minor deity, he might know something about shadow souls.

But . . . had she really expected it to be easy? If she walked out of that castle, she would see the image from the mirror for the rest of her days. The last glimpse she ever had of her parents. No one else was even looking anymore. They'd run out of places *to* look.

A clever fraud could fake her mother's sword, could fake faces, even mannerisms, but the shell necklace she'd made for her father? No, she felt sure the image was real. The first solid lead she'd had in eight years.

Nathan could be lying about the enchantment. And the dying part. But if he wasn't . . .

She trudged back to the ancestral crypt. Nathan had found a broom and was sweeping up the glass with a morose expression. "Aunt Mathilde I could do without," he said, not looking at her. "But Valentin was good company. Quite the raconteur. I will miss him."

So that's what the Duc of Vendagni did all night. Passed the time conversing with his dead ancestors. It was sad, really.

"This oath," she called across the room. "What happens if one of us breaks it?"

His head lifted. Nathan gave her a sunny smile. "Instant death, of course. But allow me to remind you that it's a far bigger risk for me. *Mon dieu*, you must have a few lives left. I am the last of my line. There's no one to capture my soul and stick me in a black mirror."

She frowned. "Did you do that for . . . ?"

"My own parents? Naturally."

They stared at each other.

"Don't expect me to glance at the ones they live in," Nathan said. "I'm not that easy."

"Then maybe I should shatter them all."

"Try it." He leaned on the broom. "Perhaps I'll turn you into a spider this time. You can take any dark corner you like. I'll instruct my servants not to bother your web when they come in to dust."

She let out a sharp breath. "What if I can't find this object?"

"Then you're down one more life." He tossed the broom aside with a clatter, eyes bright. "But I know where it is, and I will tell you once we have sealed our bargain. Truly, it will be child's play to retrieve it."

"I still don't see why you can't—"

"I already explained that," he said impatiently.

"Why don't you walk me through it again? Because if it's as simple as you claim . . ."

Nathan's nostrils flared. He turned his back and struck a huffy pose. "You wouldn't understand."

She waited.

At last, he spun back, gesticulating. "I am a son of the Moon Courts. It is a matter of principle — of pride! — that I have never seen the sun. What if it blinds me? Destroys my magic?" Nathan began to stalk up and down. "Moonlight is like the finest gossamer. Delicate and ethereal. A cool phantom whose touch soothes the fevered brow."

He halted and stared at something beyond the walls of Castle Cazal. "But a . . . a ghastly flaming orb that *hangs there*, unmoving, its baleful eye glaring down—"

"Calm yourself, Nathan."

He raked a hand through his hair, causing it to stand on end. "Not even to retrieve my rightful inheritance am I willing to cross those mountains!" He exhaled sharply through his nose. "Vigo can't go for obvious reasons."

"I thought you planned to summon him back."

"I do. I refer to the sun. It would burn him—"

"Now you're lying again. Lucius *lives* in Clovis. That's what coaches and heavy cloaks are for."

"Fine. I don't trust Vigo with it."

"But you trust me? This is the part I'm having trouble with, blood pact or no."

He resumed his manic pacing. "Let's put it this way. I mistrust you less than anyone else. And even if you got the box open, which you won't, I know you can't use it."

"Why not?"

"Now we're venturing into the realm of what the object is. And that point is non-negotiable."

"My curiosity is piqued."

"When you return with it, I'll tell you."

They locked eyes.

"Is it something that will end the world?" she asked.

"No."

"You hesitated."

"No," he repeated firmly. "But it might save it."

"With you as the deathless, invincible king of everything?"

"No."

Lo sighed. "I must be mad. How much time do I get?"

"Hecate is new tonight. When she is full, I'll expect your return."

"Two and a half weeks. That might be cutting it close."

"I have confidence in you."

"I'm glad one of us does. These are my terms, and *they* are non-negotiable. One, my cat back, unharmed. Two, the Quietus, also unharmed. Your vow to give me the exact location where my parents are being held, as well as anything else I'll need to rescue them."

"Agreed."

"The first two demands will be satisfied immediately. The last upon my successful return. When I have satisfied *your* terms, I will be released from your service forever. No more errands, no more favors."

"Damn." His eyes gleamed. "I hoped you'd overlook that one."

"You swear that you are not using me to get to my parents, and they will be free, as well."

"I have no interest in them."

"Good." She thought for a moment. "That's all."

Nathan gave a crisp nod. "Here are mine. You will tell no one about this pact. You will make your best effort to find and secure the object henceforth known as 'The Box' and bring it back to me before Hecate rises above the spires of this keep. You will not attempt to open 'The Box.'"

"How large is this box?"

"Not very. Smaller than your cat. *Fichu*, he is a plump thing."

"I have to tell Thistle. He'll be accompanying me."

"The demonic familiar?" Nathan's brow creased as he considered this. "That is acceptable. But no one else."

He blew dust from his palm. A long scroll unrolled across the floor. It flopped to a halt across her boots. Lo sank to hands and knees, squinting at the fine print. She stabbed a finger down. "Not that clause." The ink vanished. "Definitely not *that* one." Another section faded.

"Who reads these things?' Nathan muttered. "They're so tedious—"

"No, and no." A mirthless laugh. "I write contracts for a living, Nathan, give me a little more credit."

Her lips moved as she waded through all the wherefores and herebys. He watched sourly as she amended it to her terms. The end result was much shorter.

"That'll do," she said at last. "Do we have to sign in blood?"

"*Bien sûr*. What is your device?"

"My device?"

"Your sigil."

"I don't have one."

"Then make one up," Nathan replied with a touch of impatience.

She came up blank. "What's a good device for a shadow soul?"

"How about a gate? I could add flames. Give it some panache."

"I'm not a mortifex."

"A simple circle then. Sign here, please."

Lo set aside her misgivings, of which she still had dozens, and pricked her finger with the pin of his Sinister Hand clasp. Nathan followed suit, sketching his sigil with a flourish. The scroll immediately shriveled to ash.

"I wanted a copy of that," she protested. "And . . . ow!"

She yanked up her sleeve. Nathan's device was branded on her inner arm. A baby-sized hand with little teardrop flames above the fingers. "That better not be permanent," she growled.

"It's not." He shrugged off his half-cape and rolled up his own sleeve. A black circle was burned into the alabaster flesh of his forearm. "See? I have one, too. They'll fade as the period of the bargain elapses. Helps keep track of the time."

"I think I'll manage," she said, "considering that I'll die if I'm late."

He plucked another large shard of black mirror from the swept-up pile and blew on it. At the sight of his pursed lips, Lo took a hasty step back. But the mirror only shimmered and divided in half, its jagged edges softening to a pair of twin ovals, each the size of her palm. Nathan's slender figure tapped each in turn. She blinked and silver frames encased the dark mirrors. Nathan handed her one.

"We can use these to communicate. Only a shard from the same mirror will work, so no one can listen in."

"Like Orlaith? Or Lucius?"

"Precisely. I'll inform the Ducissa that you're dead." He seemed to find this funny.

"But . . . Castelio will know I'm not."

"Then you must persuade him to keep your secret."

Lo frowned. "I won't ask him to lie. Just say I went home."

"On the wind ship the other daēvas have repaired for you?" he asked innocently.

She gave him a disgusted look. "Is there anything you *don't* know?"

"A great deal," he replied. "How to find poor Valentin, for one. Do you have any idea which level of the Dominion you sent him to?"

She swallowed. "There are levels?"

"*Mon dieu.*" He clucked his tongue. "You are like a child playing with a box of tinder in a granary. But I have no time to teach you. Use your power sparingly. Such gifts often come with a hidden price." Nathan eyed her seriously. "I know as much as I do about shadow souls because I have spoken with Jaskin on a handful of occasions. He seldom appears. When he does, it is difficult to glean what is true and what is insane ranting. But I will try my best to discover what I can. We have an extensive collection of grimoires here. While you are gone, I will do some research. Perhaps I will have more answers when you return."

He glanced across the chamber. "The Quietus is coming. Do not forget your oath, demoiselle. He can know nothing of this."

She bit her lip. "I won't speak of our pact. But I have to tell him about Orlaith."

"Do you care so little for him?"

"No! That is . . . he deserves the truth."

"Ah, the truth." Nathan slung the half-cape around his shoulders. "And who do you think he will believe? Me or his beloved Ducissa?"

Lo didn't reply.

"He will go straight to Her Grace and repeat my baseless accusations against her. As a warning, of course. And how long do you imagine he'll live after he does?"

Lo saw immediately that he was right. It left a sour taste in her mouth.

"So she gets away with this deception?"

Nathan looked amused. "*Bien sûr.*"

His ancestors had grown bolder. A dozen watched their exchange from the mirrors. Now, a woman with elaborately piled hair tittered behind her hand, leaning over to hiss something at her neighbor, who gave a loud guffaw.

"That does not sit well with me," Lo said, trying to ignore them.

"Orlaith won't be a problem for much longer. Not if you succeed. Now listen closely. The Box is made of cold iron. When a flame is held to the lid, you will see my device. It is in the possession of the Sons of Bel at their temple in Prydwen. There is a reliquary beneath—" Nathan bit off an oath. "Ah!" he exclaimed with false cheer. "You have found us!"

"Thistle!" Lo cried, running forward.

The cat slunk into the room, gray fur on end, eyes blazing.

"Remove that at once," she snapped at Nathan.

A collar of sorts circled his neck. Glowing runes that flowed around and around, the symbols blurring in sparks of white light.

"But of course," Nathan murmured. He snapped his fingers. The collar vanished.

Had there been windows in the keep, Lo felt sure they all would have rattled violently. Even through the thick walls, she heard the crack and boom of thunder outside, like an angry Titan stomping across the bridge. Thistle's tail switched back and forth. His shadow grew monstrous, stretching across the chamber and settling across the Duc like a storm cloud.

Nathan covered a yawn. "I can put it back, you know," he said. "Now be a good little kitty and sheathe your claws, eh?"

Thistle stared for a long moment. Then he made a loud *harking* noise. Nathan's pale brow furrowed. "What is he . . .?"

The cat hunched over, coughing grotesquely, and finally ejected an enormous hairball. It flew across the room and bounced off Nathan's left foot. The Duc took a step back, nose wrinkling.

"Touché," he muttered.

Thistle began to wash his paws. Lo looked around. "But where is—"

Castelio stepped around the end of the toppled cabinet. He

raised a hand and she saw the skin was red. Burned and bloody. She ran over and threw her arms around him, not caring what Nathan thought. He staggered a little, then hugged her back. He felt sturdy and warm and very nice.

"Let me see you," she said, pulling away. "Oh, your eyebrows are singed! How bad is it?"

"Not too bad," he said, taking in the shattered mirrors and broken glass. "You?"

She thought about her brief stint as a rat. "Yeah, not too bad."

Nathan cleared his throat. "Demoiselle was most forceful in her desire to leave my castle," he said, feigning an aggrieved tone. "She wrought great damage to my atelier. But I am willing to forgive her if you both leave at once."

Castelio eyed him warily. "And the cat? He comes, too, or no deal."

Lo felt great affection for him at that moment.

Nathan flicked his fingers dismissively. "Please, take him away. I would rather have mice than . . . whatever *that* is." His gaze settled on the damp gray lump.

A shuffling in the darkness announced the arrival of two ash-servants. Nathan snapped into motion, barking commands. One took the broom and started sweeping. The other shambled off to raise up the drawbridge.

"I regret any misunderstandings," he said in a subdued tone, as he shooed them down a steep, crooked staircase that was concealed behind a clacking bone-curtain in one corner of the atelier. "I so rarely entertain guests at Castle Cazal. No doubt my, er, social graces have grown rusty." A pause at the bottom. A blinding smile. "Sure you won't stay for dinner?"

"No, thank you," Lo said quickly.

Castelio gave him a murderous glare.

Nathan sighed. "I understand. Another time, then." He pressed his palms to the front doors and flung them open, then practically shoved his visitors down the steps. The coach awaited, the bone-steeds pawing at the ground. It was raining buckets.

"Give cousin Orlaith my warmest regards!" he called.

Lo ran hunched over through the downpour and climbed in with Thistle. Cas flopped into the seat across from her. The Duc of Vendagni stood beneath the shelter of his gargoyles, waving. A great lance of lightning ripped across the sky, followed instantly by a cannonade of thunder. It almost drowned out his final words.

"Have a safe journey, demoiselle!"

She glanced out the window as the coach pulled away, meeting Nathan Ouvrard's dark, measuring gaze. The ridiculous persona he'd adopted was gone, his pale face grave and thoughtful. He turned away and was swallowed by the keep.

That, she thought — as if she needed any more reminders — *is a very dangerous man.*

Chapter 33

Lo was silent as they crossed the misty chasm, staring out the window with a distracted expression. Thistle curled up next to her, tail draped across his nose. Heavy rain lashed the carriage windows. Cas found a first-aid kit in his pack and saw to his hand. The cut was shallow and clean — he kept his knives well-sharpened — but both palms were becoming a mass of scar tissue. The ghost of a smile touched his lips. He was starting to look like Gui Harcourt.

"That went better than I expected," Cas said finally. "Why do you think he let us go?"

Lo met his eyes, but only for an instant. "I think Lady Caul was right. Nathan likes to play games. He claimed he knew where my parents are, but it was the same thing the Ducissas of Nyons told me. That they were hunting an unbound mortifex."

"So you learned nothing new?"

She shook her head. "I'm afraid not. But I did get my cat back. Thanks to you."

"I didn't really do much." He kept his voice measured. "Ouvrard must have wanted something."

"Oh, he was curious about the *Wind-Witch*, like everyone else." She finally looked at him. "When I told him it crashed, he seemed to lose interest in me." She seemed to realize how pathetically weak this sounded, because her cheeks flushed a little. "He denied having anything to do with Enrigo. I suppose it's impossible to prove one way or the other. How did your eyebrows get singed? And how did you banish Vigo?"

The last few sentences came out in a flustered rush. *You used to be a better liar*, he thought.

"Oh, we had an encounter in Ouvrard's blood labyrinth."

She blanched. "His . . . are you joking?"

"Not in the least. The walls really do bleed. As for Vigo . . ." He winked. "An old Quietus trick. No trouble at all, really." He stretched his legs out, leaning back on his pack. "So what are your plans now?"

Again, she looked away. "My friends, the ones you met, they found a way to cross the White Sea. They said they would take me home with them. Is that . . ." She glanced back, anxious now. "Would you be in trouble if you . . ."

"Let you go?" He stared at her, quietly simmering. "I did not come along to hold you captive, Delilah."

"I didn't mean that. Not at all!"

"You're a free woman. I don't blame you for leaving. It's my fault you came in the first place."

She nodded gratefully. "Thank you."

He almost warned her not to trust Nathan Ouvrard, but why bother? She would deny any involvement. But he'd overheard the last thing Nathan said to her. It wasn't on purpose. He'd simply followed the cat. Heard voices ahead. Perhaps he *had* hung back for a moment, but only to assess the situation before blundering into it.

Clearly, they had struck some sort of deal. And she didn't trust him enough to take him into her confidence.

Cas gazed out the opposite window. Her face when she ran up and hugged him . . . He'd thought that maybe . . . but then she'd lapsed into silence and fed him a cartload of horseshit. Nathan wasn't the only one who liked to play games.

When he turned back, her eyes were closed, chin nodding to her chest. She looked young and alone and very far from home. His anger quenched, remorse taking its place. Nathan was obviously using her. The thing she wanted above all else was to find her parents. That was the weak spot he must be exploiting.

He considered confronting her. Demanding the truth. But she was stubborn. He doubted he could shift her course, and then they would part on unpleasant terms.

Prydwen. The irony was that he longed to go there himself. To hear Lippa laugh, see Teo's mischievous smile. To make sure Da was keeping his promise to stay out of the taverns.

But his oaths came first. He'd already stretched them considerably by coming to Vendagni.

Delilah is smart and capable, he reminded himself. *I just wish she trusted me.*

She seemed exhausted, sleeping most of the way to Nox. He rested, too, though it was more fitful. They were both subdued for the last hour, sharing the remainder of the food in silence.

The bone-horses pulled up on the Nyons side of the bridge. Astris, the green-haired centaur, stood in the river up to her withers, drinking from a skin. She trotted up the bank as they disembarked from the coach.

"So you're still alive," she said, raising the skin in a toast. Her cheeks were flushed, her eyes bright as the full moons.

Cas eyed the bow slung across her back. "Are you here to take us back to Mystral?" he asked warily.

A neighing laugh. "You're missing a fine bacchanal, mortal. As am I — so I'm grateful you've arrived to end my sentry duty. But no, you are both free to cross the border." Her gaze tracked a flitting shadow. "I see you got the cat back."

"Nathan Ouvrard was . . . no trouble, really," Lo said. "You may tell the Courtenays that we thank them again for their aid."

Astris gave a brusque nod. She drank again, then offered Cas the skin. "I'm sorry I shot you, reaper. It was by mistake."

He took a glug of wine. It tasted both fruity and sour, with hints of mint and winter melon. Warmth spread through him. "If you were aiming for Lucius . . . well, no hard feelings." He handed the skin to Lo, who tipped it back.

"Was it Nathan who kidnapped the boy?" Astris asked with a hard glint in her eye. Her tail flicked, shedding droplets of water.

"I assume so," Cas replied. "But he did not confess to it."

He didn't look at Lo, nor she at him.

"My ladies will have the truth from him," Astris said in a tone that promised retribution. "As soon as Litha is over." She grimaced. "And I will miss it myself if I tarry any longer. Fare thee well."

The centaur spoke a friendly command to the bone-steeds. Then she set off at a gallop, the coach speeding up the road behind. Cas turned to study the bridge. The stone supports were charred black where Lucius and Mace had fought, the earth scorched for fifty paces around. He could still smell the sulfurous stench.

"I hardly remember it," he admitted.

Lo surveyed the skeletal trees, her face taut. "I have never seen the like," she said. "It's a wonder either of them survived." She turned to him with a wan smile. "But without the light of their duel, I could not have saved you, so for that I am grateful."

They crossed the bridge on foot. A chill pricked him as he passed the spot where he'd taken the arrows. But under the bright moonlight, with the lights of Nox ahead and moonlight playing on the swift-flowing river, it seemed less sinister and more a decaying relic from a bygone era.

Lo paused to examine the symbols of the sun god carved into the stone. A python coiled around a lyre. A quiver and bow. "What are the Sons of Bel like?" she asked.

The question didn't surprise him, since he had overheard Nathan Ouvrard mention their temple in Prydwen, but he kept his tone casual. *Help her, if you can.*

"It depends on where you are," he replied. "Bel has many aspects. In Clovis and Galatia, he is the patron of music and the arts. Also of war. In the old days, the priests armed themselves like soldiers and often attacked Kaethe's convents. By the grace of the Drowned Woman, that's mostly over now."

They reached the end of the bridge. The guardhouse on the Nox side remained empty; Cas wondered what Lucius would tell Caino Scalici. Probably that the wraith had killed the man; there were no witnesses either way. But he knew Lucius had done it. The mortifex had as much as admitted it—

"And in Cavet?" Lo prompted as they started down the dirt road for Nox.

Cas shook off his dark thoughts, grasping for the thread of their conversation. *The sun god*. "They worship him differently."

"How?"

He cleared his throat. "The main temple is in Prydwen, though you will find smaller shrines in all the major towns. To the Cavetti, Bel is the god of prosperity and, ah . . . the physical expression of love."

"Money and sex, you mean."

He laughed. "Aye. It's said the Sons of Bel are richer than the Duc himself. They practice sacred prostitution. Only the prettiest boys are chosen to join their ranks."

"And what makes it sacred?" she asked with a crooked grin.

"Anyone can come to the temple to, ah, worship Bel, men and women both, with none turned away. They do not pay for the pleasure of the young men's company directly—"

"But generous donations are strongly encouraged?"

He gave a wry nod. "It is nothing like Aquitan. The heat is extreme, for one thing. Most of the city is underground, though the rich can afford cooled houses in the air and light. Prydwen is a city of great contrasts . . . and much debauchery. By the primmer standards of my own duchy, at any rate."

"Sounds a bit like Delphi. That, too, is in the sunlands. It used to be ruled by tyrants, and then some corrupt archons, but now a popular assembly called the Ecclesia is in charge. They make communal decisions."

He frowned. "And the nobles allow it?"

"There are none. In Susa and Samarqand, yes."

She looked a bit nostalgic as she thought of the land she'd left behind. But he was still trying to imagine this place called Delphi.

"No nobles?" he echoed. The idea rocked him.

"Nor kings or queens, either. The call it *demokratia*. The right of all citizens to vote on matters that affect their future."

"Feck," he muttered. "Pardon, but it actually works?"

"Most of the time." She smiled and stopped walking. Cas realized that they'd reached the village.

"How will you find your friends?" he asked.

"Culach said he would look for me at the same crossroads where we landed. Or rather, his abbadax Ragnhildur would look for me." Lo tipped her face to the sky, scanning the clouds. "I imagine he is quite worried by now."

Again, Cas sensed far more to the story, but he'd already decided not to press her about it. Lo was only doing what she thought she had to. And she needed any friends she could get.

"I'll walk you there," he offered. "Make sure you find him."

She hesitated, then smiled. "I'd like that."

His thoughts drifted to words unspoken as they passed through Nox. The village was no longer locked up tight. Rushlights burned along the main street. The clatter of a loom came from an open window, and children's laughter. He smelled baking bread and woodsmoke, saw washing flapping from clotheslines and goodwives chatting across backyard fences. Others bustled in and out of the chandlery, carrying beeswax tapers and soap. The clang of a hammer and odor of fresh manure told him a farrier was working nearby. Cas made a mental note to ask the man about buying a horse.

Lo sped up as they walked past the lichyard, rubbing her arms as if she felt a chill. Cas scanned the graves; the crouched, scrabbling figure was gone, and he saw no sign of any other risen. When they reached the crossroads, she turned to him. They both spoke at once, then fell into an awkward silence.

"You first," she said.

He shook his head. "No, you."

She drew a long breath, seeming to choose her words with great care. "I lied to you in the coach. Again. And since you're not stupid, quite the opposite, I expect you've figured that out."

"You don't have to explain—"

"No, I do." A hint of the old khamoun surfaced as she lifted her chin. "You risked your life for me, and I've repaid you poorly." She paused. "I cannot tell you all that transpired with Nathan. I . . . I *can't*. But I want you to know that I consider you a friend, and I hope you can find a way to think . . . the same of me, despite everything."

"I do, Lo," he said gently.

She glanced down. Thistle was twining between his legs. "A rub!" she exclaimed with a laugh. "I think he has forgiven you."

"He is an uncommonly clever cat," Cas replied with an answering smile.

They eyed each other, and he thought that much was conveyed in that look without any words passing between them.

"Be careful," he said at last. "Don't put too much trust in people you've just met." A quick grin. "Excluding myself, of course."

She regarded him solemnly. "I wish—"

But he would never learn what Lo wished, because swift wingbeats sounded above the trees. In one graceful movement, she stepped up close and threw her arms around his neck, pulling him close. Planted a lingering kiss on his jaw. When she pulled away, her eyes were sad.

"Farewell, Castelio zah Nerides," she whispered.

Before he could reply, she was running into the darkness. He watched the abbadax land and Culach Kafsnjor pull her up to the saddle. Lo buckled her harness, holding the cat in her arms. They spoke for a moment, but it was too soft to make out. Then the abbadax gave an ungainly, waddling run. The muscles of its back legs bunched. It soared into the air, a black shadow crossing the moons, and turned west toward the mountains.

Cas watched until it vanished, his heart and mind consumed with unfamiliar turmoil. For a moment, he wished he had never met her. Not once had he regretted his oaths. The life of a Quietus suited him perfectly. The more he dealt with the risen and their endless, petty hungers, the less he liked people in general — and the dead were saints compared to most of the living he encountered. Men who beat their children and animals with equal indifference. Nobles who saw those beneath them as less than human, pawns to be killed in war or worked to death in the fields and mines.

Delilah wasn't like that. She was strong and passionate and kind and, he couldn't deny it, beautiful in a way that dried his mouth and made his own solitary existence feel even colder and emptier. But that was what he had chosen, and he was bound to it as surely as if he wore a menotte. The dead had not stopped returning. One by one, his fellow Quietuses were falling, and the number of new recruits was at an all-time low.

"I hope you find what you're looking for," he said softly, gazing at the dark line of the mountains.

Cas turned and strode back to Nox to find a horse.

Chapter 34

Lo gazed out over the valley, a fresh breeze tugging at her cloak. The *Wind-Witch* rested on a lattice of scaffolding near the abbadax stable. Her ship looked, if not quite brand new, definitely sky-worthy. The holes in the hull had been patched, the sails mended, and a sturdy mast of white pine set in place of the one that had snapped. Coils of hempen rope waited on the deck. The daēvas had even salvaged some of her cargo. Not the fragile clay amphorae she'd picked up in Delphi, but the spice crates and bolts of raw silk. They had filled her water barrels and restocked the galley with enough supplies for a month.

"The Marakai did an admirable job," she said to Culach. "I am in their debt. And yours."

Culach, she learned, had spent the last two days scouring the area around Nox from the air until Ragnhildur's sharp eyes finally spotted her. Lo wished she'd had a few more minutes with Cas. It had been a long time since she'd enjoyed someone's company so much. But she was also relieved their goodbye had been cut short. It was hard enough already, made worse by her many lies.

Lo's lips tightened. Which included keeping the truth from him about Orlaith. The vile woman had risked his life, risked her *own son's* life, just to get revenge on a pair of young women she'd never even met, and who had nothing to do with—

"Delilah?"

She looked over, abashed. "Sorry. Wool-gathering. What did you say?"

Culach smiled. "That everyone was glad to help. Your parents are heroes. The second Vatra war . . ."

"I know what they did." She wrapped her arms around herself. "But I am not them."

He laid a big hand on her shoulder. "That is true," he said gently. "But you *have* inherited all their worst traits."

Lo laughed.

"Stubbornness that would shock a mule," he continued. "Courage that can easily be mistaken for a death wish. A flimsy grasp of reality, and misplaced optimism that everything—"

"Will turn out well in the end," his wife Mina interrupted. She cast an amused look at Lo, then made a face at Culach, crossing her eyes and thrusting her tongue from the corner of her mouth. "Which I am certain it will, my love," she added serenely.

"Is she doing it again?" he demanded.

"Er . . ." Lo hedged.

Mina pressed a finger to her lips, eyes bright with suppressed merriment.

Culach sighed. His hand lashed out, unerringly finding her long braid. He gave it a gentle tug. "Mocking blind men?" The outrage in his voice was belied by a grin. "Really?"

"I think you're faking," she said, wrapping an arm around his waist. "One day I'll prove it."

Lo watched them, so in love and at ease with each other. Her parents had been the same. *Were* the same. At least whatever spell Magnus the Merciless had cast seemed . . . oddly benevolent.

She wondered what they were doing on that ship. Why he held them captive rather than killing them.

"We leave tonight, as well," Culach was saying. "I can't believe you're chasing after some fortune-teller in Cavet. They're all fakes."

"Perhaps," she said. "But this one is supposed to be the real thing."

"*I've* never heard of her."

"Because you don't concern yourself with mortal affairs," she replied innocently. "Isn't that what you said, uncle?"

Culach grunted. "So it's *uncle* now, is it? Well, I'm not keeping it a secret that you're here. Nicodemus will want to know. Meb, naturally. And Victor, of course."

She let out a groan. "My grandfather doesn't even think I should be allowed to fly wind ships. He treats me like a four-year-old! Do you have to tell him?"

Culach rubbed his chin. "If I do not, and he finds out that I know where his beloved granddaughter went, he will declare war on the Valkirin nation as a whole. He will find some young fools to follow him, as he always does, and then he'll stumble over a dusty old talisman with unholy power that escalates the whole affair into a maelstrom of blood. It's happened before."

She scoffed. "Victor wouldn't . . . well, yes, he probably would." She threw her hands up. "Fine. If the whole world is to know my business, then I'll ask you to stop in Samarqand and tell Javid and Katsu why I'm late with the shipment. Tell them I promise to get it to them eventually. And I'll pay for the losses from my wages."

Culach made a wry face. "I'm sure they'll be thrilled merely to know you're alive. I doubt they care about the money."

"You don't know Javid," she said, though Culach was right. "He would be insulted to hear someone accuse him of such a thing."

"Which part?" Mina asked. "That was a confusing exchange."

"Not caring about the money," Lo replied with a fond chuckle. "I have never known a man so committed to haggling a price down to the last daric."

Mina rose up on her tiptoes and whispered in Culach's ear.

"Ah yes, I almost forgot. You can pay the charlatan with this." He pressed a heavy, clinking purse into Lo's hand. "It's ill-gotten gains anyway, and I won't need foreign currency in Nocturne." A grin. "I intend to mooch off my distant relations."

Lo untied the drawstring and saw the glint of coin.

"The gold ones are called chariots and coronets. The silver are ferries," Mina explained. "Exchange rate is about twenty to one, though I imagine it depends on the duchy. The copper coins are called pyres in the west, sangettes in the east. It means 'small blood' in the necromancers' tongue."

Lo spilled a few coins into her palm. The gold had symbols of Bel, the silver of Kaethe. The little pyres were minted with a dancing flame. Simple enough to keep straight. "Thank you." She returned them to the pouch. "This will keep me for a while, if prices aren't too high in Prydwen. So you *do* know something about the mortals."

"I am the quartermaster of these castaways," Mina replied with a smile. "The one they send to buy and barter. I don't know much about Prydwen, I have never gone so far, but I did hear whispers that the old Duc might have been poisoned by his son."

"The new Duc?" Lo guessed.

"His name is Vaszoly Marcel. Just steer clear of the palace."

"I plan to," Lo replied honestly, hoping the Sons of Bel didn't mix prostitution and politics.

She bent to stroke Thistle's tail. He had been prowling restlessly around the ship. Heavy clouds darkened the sky. The wind picked up, smelling of rain.

"It's going to pour in a moment," Culach said, tipping his face to the approaching storm.

"I'd best be off then. Hang on." She joined the other daēvas gathered on the hilltop, a mix of Vatra fire-workers and Marakai seafarers. They clasped hands and wished each other safe journeys.

"I'm glad you're going home," she said as she rejoined Mina and Culach.

Aveline was no place for her kind, she thought. Although . . .

Nathan Ouvrard had known about the daēva settlement and done nothing to interfere with them. And the Courtenays were friends with her parents. Not *everyone* was hostile.

"As you should be, too—" Culach began with a scowl, before Mina jabbed his ribs.

"You have no right to tell her what to do, my love. If it were me that had gone missing—"

"I'd be praising the gods?"

"No, you big blond ape, you'd do anything in your power to get me back."

He gave a fierce growl. "True enough." Culach turned back to Lo. "When you are done consulting with the quack seer, please come home. I will help you continue the search."

"As will I," Mina added stoutly. "I am the eyes — and brains. He is the brawn."

"We make a fine pair, eh?" Culach said.

She hugged them both, then scrambled up the ladder and prepared for takeoff. The rough scrape of rope against her calloused palm, the snap of the mainsheet as it zipped up the mast . . . ah, how she had missed her ship!

Four of the Marakai released the hull from its bindings. Thistle sprang up to the deck in a single bound. Lightning forked in his eyes. A strong gust came, the timbers creaked, and they were sliding off the rails and launching into the storm. She found the Nexus, guiding the air currents so the ship swung around in a long arc. Lo gave a last wave to the tiny figures below as the vessel passed overhead. When it pointed due west, she tied off the boom and ducked down into her cabin.

Her new friends had seen to the structural integrity, but they were not maidservants. Her cabin was a mess. She tidied up her papers, righted the wardrobe and jammed her clothes back inside, made up her bunk. Then she went to the galley and brewed a pot of tea.

"Did you know I was a shadow soul?" she asked Thistle, blowing on the cracked mug.

"I did not," the cat replied, mildly offended. "I would have told you. Give me a biscuit."

Lo found a tin and gave him three. "Have you heard of them?"

A slow blink. "No."

"Nathan said I get nine lives." She grinned. "Like a cat." Her smile faded. "But I have used up a number of them already. I must be more careful. So go easy on the weather, eh?"

Thistle crunched loudly on the biscuit, breaking it into ever smaller pieces. Lo took out her mirror of black glass. She jogged down the companionway back to her cabin, wrapped it up in a blanket, and shoved it deep into the wardrobe. That should keep him from spying. Then she returned to the galley, which sat at the other end of the ship — well out of earshot.

"We have two and a half weeks to find '*Ze Box*,'" she said, lowering her voice to approximate Nathan's. "What a load of . . . He's mad if he thinks I'm handing it over. A powerful talisman of unknown purpose that belonged to his nefarious ancestors? I mean, come on."

Thistle regarded her gravely. "And the blood pact?"

"Says only that I must deliver it to Castle Cazal before Hecate sets behind the spires. Not that I must place it in his greedy little paws." She gave an evil smile. "An oversight he will come to regret."

Lo unrolled her map and found Prydwen. It was deep in the west, along the same meridian as the desert in Solis called the Kiln. The sun would be stuck at high noon there. She had visited Pompeii, the Vatra capital, many times and knew how scorching the heat was. Nathan's reluctance was understandable. Though she doubted it would be as easy as he claimed.

"He said it was at the Temple of Bel. In some reliquary." She sipped her tea. "I hope that's enough to narrow it down."

"Do you think it was wise?" Thistle asked, his golden eyes studying her closely.

"The pact? *Wise*? No, but it's done now." She pulled up her sleeve and regarded Nathan's brand. Did it already look a little bit . . . fainter?

"I do not refer to the diabolical bargain. I refer to the Quietus."

"Oh! *That.* He needs it more than I do, Thistle." She frowned. "His Ducissa is a snake."

The cat resumed crunching on his biscuits. Lo finished her tea. Rain beat against the portholes as she tipped her chair back and rested one bootheel on the edge of the table.

Be safe, Castelio, she thought with a twinge. *I hope . . . you do not forget me.*

Chapter 35

Cas rode hard through the Duskwood, pausing once to rest his mount and catch an hour of sleep. At the border, he was greeted with cheers by the Redvayne garrison. Lucius had passed through with Enrigo two days before. The soldiers gave Cas a bowl of barley soup and a fresh horse. He learned that the moment the *Wind-Witch* took off, the dead stopped pouring through the gate. It had been quiet since.

From there, he crossed the Darkwatch River by ferry and rode into the Boundary. He had always avoided the lands around his old home. It was too painful. But this time he deliberately took a route that led past familiar haunts. Old swimming holes where he would laze the day away watching kingfishers and herons. The open meadows where red-winged blackbirds built their nests in the high grasses and kestrels hunted on the wing. He was pleased to find the massive beaver dam at Solway's Pond was still there, with a new generation adding to its watery, domed halls.

At last, he reached the farm. Young ash trees had sprouted through the roof of the house. The barn had collapsed, its charred hulk smothered in vines. His mother's herb and vegetable garden was entirely given over to weeds, the edges of it blurring into thick brambles. Teo's rusting wagon sat in the yard. So did the table where they had eaten that last supper with Gui. The boards were warped from rain, covered in green lichen.

He stood for a moment, the cool mountain breeze lifting his hair.

Part of him regretted coming. He did not wish to remember it this way.

How many times had people told him that after he dispatched someone dear to them? Even when they didn't say it, he could see it in their eyes. The awful knowledge that the shuffling, vengeful spirit would be imprinted in their minds forever, eclipsing everything the person had been before.

Cas closed his eyes. For a moment, he heard Teo's excited shouts as he found a fat raccoon pillaging the grain trough, his mother's scolding laughter as Lip escaped the washtub and ran naked across the yard. Remembered the kind steadiness of his father, who seldom smiled but always had words of wisdom and encouragement. Now they were all scattered like ashes in the wind.

He opened his eyes and turned to the river. No, not all.

His mother's grave was unmarked, but he knew where to find it. Cas mounted his horse and rode to the biggest willow on the east bank of the Forkings. It had been a young tree when they buried her there. Willows didn't live much longer than men. Forty or fifty years at most. He was glad to see it still thrived, curtained green boughs trailing in the current.

He knelt at the roots and laid a bouquet of wild yellow roses on the low mound.

"I found these in your garden," he said, throat tight. "I'm sorry I haven't come to visit you." He glanced at the nearby stone landing. "They burned the ferry. It's no excuse, I know, but I . . . I couldn't do it." He laid a palm on the damp earth. "Lippa is a scribe now. You'd be so proud of her. Da and Teo are well, too." He hoped it was true. "I am a Quietus. Maybe you know that. I don't know where you are now, or if you can hear me. Probably not. But I miss you, Ma. Every single day."

Tears came, and he let them flow. It felt like a purging. One he had denied himself for far too long. He had an urge to leave some final gift, something meaningful. Cas reached in his pocket for the iron coin. Pulled it out and frowned.

The object in his hand was roughly the same size, but made of silver, not iron. A moon on one side, a sun on the other. It hung from a broken chain.

He stared at it in wonder. Lo's talisman. She must have slipped it into his pocket when they said goodbye. Shock ran through him that she would gift such a wondrous thing. She hadn't told him because she knew he would refuse it.

A slow smile spread across his face. "You were right, I cannot accept it. Which means I'll have to find a way to return it to you myself."

He stood and brushed the dirt from his hands, returning the talisman to his pocket. The wind picked up, blowing from the north and driving dark clouds before it. He would have to ride hard to reach the next ferry crossing before the storm hit. The one north of Swanton would be the closest.

"Goodbye, Ma," he said, his heart both heavy and lighter at the same time. "May Kaethe's blessing be upon you always."

The willow branches swayed. With a squawk, a great raven erupted from its hidden perch, black wings beating as it headed upriver. A sign? He sketched a nine-pointed star, nape tingling.

The horse had been nibbling at whatever it could find along the bank. It stared across the river, flanks twitching. Cas stroked its velvety muzzle. Then he swung up to the saddle and galloped into the twilight.

Chapter 36

Lucius woke in thick, choking darkness, the scrape of his own screams raw in his throat.

He lay there for a moment, fingers gripping the silken sheets. He had dreamt not of his own fiery death. That was long centuries in the past and held no terrors anymore. No, it was the same nightmare that always plagued him when he was weak.

The things his unbound kin would do to him if he ever fell into their hands.

When his soul was first trapped in the menotte, he had given up names. True names. And that was only a small part of it. Some still hated him for what he had done before he died, when he was a general called Claudius Quintus. Betraying his own mad king, Gaius. Leading his legion in open revolt. Leading them all to their deaths, himself included.

Lucius sat up, shaking away the cobwebs of memory. He snapped his fingers and a wavering flame appeared. The light revealed hands shiny and twisted with scar tissue.

"Better than I expected," he muttered, kicking the sheets away and climbing stiffly to his feet.

He recalled riding the last few leagues to Aquitan, the sun finding every crevice in his thick cloak. Reaching Orlaith's estate in a fog of agony. Nearly falling from his horse with the boy in his arms. He must have been insensible after that, but her servants had carried him inside, whisked him down to the lightless chambers deep beneath the manor that were his alone.

It was an irony of his undead state that he did not bleed but still felt pain and pleasure, still felt all the things he had as a living man. He had wanted that desperately once, not understanding what it meant until it was too late. The power of it, and the terrible weakness.

A day in the soothing, cooling black had restored him enough to get dressed, which he did with some haste. He could sense her coming.

Lucius lit more candles. Chose a camicia of the softest muslin, topped with a dark blue doublet and forest green breeches, which he tucked into gleaming black boots. Next, the cloak of blue woad, clasped with the gold phoenix of House Redvayne. He regarded himself impassively in the gilt standing mirror. Well, let her see what he'd sacrificed for her child. It might make her more pliable.

"Come in, Your Grace," he said, an instant before she knocked.

The door eased open. Orlaith stood at the threshold, all pale skin and golden hair. She often failed to cover it in his presence lately, when they met in private. A sign of familiarity he was all too happy to exploit.

Lucius swept a bow. Her blue eyes widened. He felt a stab of pity come through the menotte, which amused him greatly. The late Duc had understood the talisman's properties far better than his wife. He tried his best to conceal his emotions and sometimes succeeded, though not always. Orlaith, on the other hand, was utterly transparent.

The Duc should have warned her before going off to war, but he was arrogant and didn't expect to lose as badly as he did. Mace had disposed of him with a quick thrust to the gut; Lucius had come to his aid, but it took a while since he was fighting on the other side of the field. Where he had suggested the Duc send him, of course.

"Thank you for bringing me back my son," Orlaith said, her gaze skipping around the room, anywhere but him.

She was tied in knots today. Anger, guilt, frustration, relief. They poured into the corner of his mind where he kept her like a dog on a leash — though he was all too aware the analogy applied equally to himself. But Lucius had been playing this game for a very long time. She thought him cold and emotionless. He was neither. He simply knew how to partition it all away behind a wall she had no hope of breaching.

"I am glad it ended well," he said. "It was fortunate the Courtenays did not hold a grudge."

"The Courtenays!" Her lip curled. Fury poured through the menotte. "Enrigo is convinced they had nothing to do it. He has already told everyone how gently they treated him!"

Lucius stared at her. "But they did not take him, my lady."

"*I* know that!" she erupted. "But my son wasn't supposed to! And Nathan just told me the khamoun is gone, slipped through our fingers, thanks to his interference. He claims he wanted to meet her. The *demoiselle* from a strange land. For all I know, he's holding her hostage."

So that's why Orlaith came. To vent her rage to the one person who knew about her little scheme. She entered his bedchamber and began to pace. It was a habit that never failed to irritate him. Lucius watched her stride up and down, dark skirts swishing on the carpet.

"You spoke to Nathan?" he asked cautiously.

"Through the black mirror. The man is impossible! He didn't even apologize for the mess he made of all our carefully laid plans." She stopped dead, breast heaving. "He laughed at me!"

"How rude," Lucius murmured.

He had known the whole thing was doomed from the moment Delilah Dessarian offered her ship in pursuit. Knew it well before that. He did not remind Orlaith that he'd suggested she call off the harebrained conspiracy the moment they arrived from Tjanjin. She had refused to listen, too blinded by her hatred of the Courtenays. Mortal folly knew no bounds.

"I tried to question Nathan further, but he pretended the mirror had grown cloudy and he couldn't hear me," Orlaith muttered. "I know he was lying."

Lucius turned away and poured a cup of wine to cover his smile. He could picture it all too vividly. Nathan squinting and repeating *"Allo? Allo?"* while Orlaith went apoplectic.

Well, that's what she gets for dicing with the Duc of Vendagni, he thought, swallowing a mouthful of Redvayne claret. At least their wine was decent.

"What about the wind ship?" Orlaith demanded.

He set the goblet down on a heavy claw-foot table. "Smashed to pieces in the mountains."

"Can it be repaired?"

"I doubt it, Your Grace."

"This is a disaster," she snapped.

"I'm sorry. I did my best to salvage the situation." He sighed. "But it got out of hand on the bridge at Nox."

Her head snapped up. "I don't blame you, Lucius. You're the only one I trust."

Now *that* was a sad statement.

He inclined his head. "Thank you, my lady. What about the Quietus?"

Her face grew solemn. "He is like a son to me." The irony of this seemed lost on her. "Nathan swore that he let him go."

"Does Castelio know the truth?"

"Nathan claims not." His blue eyes grew a shade colder. "But I'm not sure I believe him."

"Then I suggest you send me to intercept the Quietus before he arrives."

Her hands knit together. "I don't want to . . ."

"Kill him?" Lucius finished. "And what if he does suspect that you had a hand in it?"

Castelio zah Nerides. The only living soul besides Orlaith who knew his true name.

Another, far worse error — and one he could only fault himself for.

Lucius had proposed the trip to Tjanjin. Had agreed to the summoning. But that was before he learned that Delilah did not, in fact, wield the same power as her mother. He'd hoped to be a free man now, though what he might do with that freedom, he didn't know. Live in the darklands somewhere. Mystral would be perfect if Mace and the Courtenays didn't hate him so much.

How, he wondered wearily, have I managed to amass so many enemies and so few friends?

Delilah . . . she had been a friend to him. Had saved him from the cage with nothing to gain by it. Only to lose.

"Lucius?"

He blinked. "My lady?"

Orlaith was staring at him, pale and determined. "I wish to speak with him."

"Castelio?" he asked, confused.

"No. My husband. He will advise me on which course to take."

He nodded slowly. "Of course."

"Now, Lucius." She swallowed. "I have been waiting for you to rouse. Robert must be told."

They walked in silence through the low tunnels in this most ancient part of the manor. Orlaith had come to him using an old passage that connected their bedchambers via a cramped set of stairs. A direct, secret link between master and slave that dated back to the first Duc, who didn't want half the court to know every time he met with his mortifex.

But it was a different path they took now.

As they walked in silence beneath the low, vaulted ceiling, he thought of the day Orlaith had taken over the menotte. Her husband lay in his bed, dying a miserable, lingering death from ill humors in the wound to his hefty gut. He could not speak, and Lucius had allowed all the hatred he'd so carefully concealed over the years to flow in an icy torrent through the cuff. At the last, Robert had stared not at his pregnant wife but at Lucius, knowing that he bequeathed her a poisoned apple but unable to do anything about it.

When he finally breathed his last, the nuns came and locked the menotte to Orlaith's wrist. She was heavy with child and had been far nicer than her husband, so Lucius accepted his new mistress gracefully, kneeling at her feet and pledging his undying loyalty. Literally.

He was impressed with how well she handled herself, though she was mad with grief — why, he couldn't imagine. Robert treated her like chattel.

"Can't you heal him?" she had asked, tears streaming down her red, puffy face.

It was not the first time he'd heard this request. "Healing is not within my power, Your Grace."

In fact, his power was its exact opposite.

Still, she came to him that night, weeping inconsolably. Begging him to use his magic to preserve the body so that her unborn child might look upon its father's face. Sensing a golden opportunity, Lucius had offered to do better. In her desperation, Orlaith agreed to it.

He paused now at a heavy oaken door. Beyond lay the convent's old wine cellar. She smoothed her flaxen hair. Pinched her wan cheeks for color and adjusted her skirts. "I'm ready."

Lucius withdrew a brass key from his pocket and unlocked the door. Beyond lay a black void.

"Light," Orlaith commanded, a quaver in her voice.

More candles burst into flame. Fine white tapers of beeswax, some in puddles of melted wax from the last time they had come here. The air was cool and damp, smelling of mildew. He went first, as he always did, leading the way past empty racks and barrels. The Redvaynes' extensive collection was housed elsewhere, had been for hundreds of years since a season of unusually heavy rain caused the cellar to flood.

Lucius paused at another door, unlocked it with a second key. Orlaith held one of the candles. Her hand was not steady, and it cast a wavering light that made the shadows flutter like dark wings.

"Your Grace," he said solemnly to the chamber's occupant, bending a knee.

Duc Robert Redvayne lurched to his feet. He staggered forward, as far as the heavy iron chains would allow, baring his teeth.

"It is I, my love!"

Lucius stepped aside as Orlaith brushed past him with the bright, shining eyes of a madwoman. For she *was* insane. Lucius felt quite certain of that.

"*Sosenan tar damar*," the Duc rasped. "*Elierim te tepiri!*"

She stared at her husband, transfixed. "What does he say, Lucius?"

In tongues, the language of the dead, Robert had cursed her for bringing him back and warned her that the mortifex was a deceitful worm. It was the usual greeting.

"That you look as radiant as the moment he first saw you," Lucius improvised. "And that he longs for the day when he can return to your loving arms."

Her gaze misted. "As do I, my husband."

The Duc had been two days' gone when they stole his body from the family crypt and removed the iron coin from his tongue — fresh enough that Lucius's necromantic spell anchored his soul within his own corpse. He had used a few drops of Orlaith's blood, which was especially potent since she carried Robert's child. It was meant to be a temporary solution, while he searched for a spell powerful enough to bring the Duc back as he was before — a spell that Lucius knew did not exist.

Generally speaking, he had little interest in necromancy. Most of them were cheap conjurers — Nathan Ouvrard excluded, obviously. And the Courtenays. But one couldn't live in Aquitan for a thousand years without picking things up here and there. Previous Redvaynes had also dabbled in the black arts, though like Orlaith they pretended moral outrage when rivals did the same.

He had done his best to preserve the Duc, as she'd requested, but Lucius was no expert. Over the last eight years, Robert had grown rather tough and leathery looking. He still had his hair and most of his teeth, which was a victory of sorts, but the rest had a ghoulish aspect. Not that it seemed to put his widow off in the least. She viewed him as a martyr to the cause.

"*Abonite dapim uleni barog, ni tatan nar,*" the Duc growled, rattling his chains.

For the love of all that is holy, release me, you fucking bitch!

"I fear His Grace is most wroth that his revenge against the Courtenays was thwarted," Lucius said, brow furrowing. "He already knows everything."

Robert glared at him with reddened eyes, then sank against the wall.

"*Adasel uleni barog,*" he whispered. "*Adasel.*"

Please let me go. Please.

Lucius regarded him without a shred of pity. The thirty-fourth Duc of Clovis had fathered bastards on the servants, ordered his vassals whipped without mercy when they displeased him, had even murdered his first wife by shoving her down a flight of steps in a drunken rage. Orlaith was twenty years younger than him when he married her, and very beautiful, but the Duc was already tiring of her by the time her belly started to swell. Really, Lucius had done her a favor.

But she still heeded Robert's advice, which was most convenient.

"What shall we do?" she asked, addressing her husband.

"I will ask him." Lucius regarded the Duc solemnly. "*Sepi ahem mel reta ciri nirup tasave nel. Subiwet mie beni vex ohire dorah.*"

I'm sorry to inform you that your widow is bedding half the court. Frankly, I'm starting to doubt the boy is even yours.

The Duc gnashed his teeth again, one sinewy hand slashing the air. It was an amusing game, eliciting an emotion to match what he supposedly said. But yes, anger was best for this exchange.

"*Hatanen imi rira yetoto nen ite ehar*," Robert snarled. "*Umalage dieru gatit*!"

A pox upon their cocks, and may her faithless twat wither and fall off!

Lucius nodded thoughtfully. "He agrees that the first priority is to discover if the Quietus plans to betray us."

Orlaith turned to him, her eyes glazed and distant. "Castelio has known loss, too, Lucius. Terrible loss."

"I assume you refer to his mother."

"He told you about that?"

I saw it, Lucius thought. "Yes, my lady."

"I don't want to silence him," she said, voice faint. "But . . ."

The infamous *but*.

I didn't mean to push the stupid wench so hard, but she made me angry.

I hate to raise taxes on people so poor they barely have a pot to piss in, but I really need the money for this war I'm about to start.

I would have saved your husband, but my horse threw me and I despised the sanglant bastard, so I took my sweet time about getting up.

"Find out what he knows," Orlaith said, hands clasped white-knuckled at her waist. She stared straight ahead, not looking at him. "Then do what you must. I trust your judgment, Lucius. Now, tell Robert. See if he agrees."

Lucius spoke in tongues, promising to castrate Orlaith's multitude of lovers if the Duc behaved like a gentleman. Alive, Robert had never been a brilliant tactician. Now, he possessed little more than a degree of low cunning. He shambled to his feet and swept a clumsy bow. Orlaith suddenly stepped forward and took his hand, pressing it to her lips.

"We should leave, my lady," Lucius said hastily, taking her arm and pulling her to the door.

Robert was a ghoul, and they were not to be trusted. Not in close proximity.

"Farewell, my dearest," she called over his shoulder as he locked the door behind them. "I shall return soon! With happier tidings, I hope!"

Lucius strode for the door, the candles extinguishing in his wake. Orlaith hurried to keep pace.

"I'll need blood," he said when they reached the outer corridor. "As it stands, I am too weak to leave the manor."

She gave a terse nod. "I saved one for you. He's meant for the gallows. You'll find him in the death cells."

How fitting.

"Then I will depart at once," he said.

She seemed like she might say more. He felt her reluctance. If she rescinded the direct order, he would have no choice but to obey.

"I hope . . . I hope you both return," she said, then turned and walked away, her back straight.

How quickly she rationalized the murder of her loyal Quietus.

Lucius shook his head, then headed for the dungeons. It had all gone well, just as he hoped, but the victory was nothing to the hunger that seized him as he drew closer. It obliterated everything else. The Quietus's fear, while enjoyable, was not especially sustaining. More of a light snack than a five-course supper.

And he *did* feel like warmed-over shite.

The clamor of the dungeons sounded well before he reached their torchlit depths. Men cursing and boasting and complaining. Farts and groans. It always reminded him that there were worse duties in the Redvayne manor than his own. The guards shot to their feet and thumped fists to their chests as he approached. Clearly, he was expected.

"Milord," they muttered in unison, avoiding his eyes.

"You have something for me," he said softly, trying to keep the mindless craving from his voice.

Lucius assumed he failed when they both turned the color of milky curds.

"Last cell on the right," the lumpy headed one muttered, tossing him a ring of keys. "Milord."

He wasn't but didn't bother to correct the man. He had authority and the Ducissa's ear. He wore fine clothes. And his very existence inspired a healthy dose of fear.

A noble in a nutshell.

Lucius stalked down the row of cells, whose sorry occupants shrank back into the darkest corners as he passed. Sighs of relief rustled like dry leaves behind him. He stopped at the last one and drew his hood up.

"I've come to hear your sins," he said in a kindly tone.

The man inside was lying on a bed of matted straw. He was big and strong. Lucius could smell his unwashed stink, and also the hot pulse of blood coursing through his veins. His nostrils flared slightly. The prisoner turned his head with a scowl.

"They sent a Son of Bel?"

Lucius smothered a laugh. "Yes, brother."

His brow lowered. "Well, fuck off."

"Don't you want to enter the golden halls of the sun god with a clear conscience?"

A ripping snort. "My conscience is clear, priest. The cunt had it coming. *Begged* for it."

Orlaith did know his tastes, he had to give her that.

Lucius unlocked the cell. The prisoner sat up, ham hock fists balling. His hair was wild, his red beard tangled and crusty with the foul pottage they served in the dungeon. The chill hit the man then. He rubbed his arms distractedly, too angry to recognize what it meant.

"Didn't I just tell you to fuck—"

The protests cut off as Lucius let his hood fall back. His eyes went round.

"Oh," was all he had a chance to utter before Lucius fell upon him, the sharp bonewood dagger slicing his artery, freeing the red ocean inside. He drank and drank, wallowed in the rush of sensation, of warm, salty life. Heat built within him, stoking fires long dormant, and when his victim's heart stopped, his own began to beat. To carry that same life through his veins.

The ecstasy of it was like nothing else. To step across the Veil again, from darkness into light.

In a dim corner of his mind, he sensed Orlaith. There was no way to keep this from her. It overwhelmed every defense. He felt her revulsion and yes, her excitement, too. It spilled through the menotte. Anger pulled him back to his senses. He dropped the dead man, breathing heavily. Brutally severed the connection in the cuff.

Lucius left the cell door standing open, the key dangling in the lock. He did not speak to the guards on his way out, nor they to him. In fact, the dungeons had gone so quiet, he heard the soft scurry of an enterprising rat as it ventured into the blood-soaked straw behind him.

He stopped in his rooms to bathe. Studied himself again in the mirror. The rapist or murderer or whatever he'd been — likely both, if he was due for the gallows — hadn't languished in the dungeons for long, not long enough to break him. He'd been strong and healthy to bursting. A veritable feast.

"I have not aged a day," he whispered to his reflection in wonder. "Not on the outside."

Claudius Quintus had been thirty when he died. Not bad to look at, or so he liked to think. Lovers had often complimented his green eyes.

It made him ache a little to see that man again, but the gift would not last long. And he had rivers to cross.

Lucius dressed and strode through the manor, ignoring the startled glances of the servants. Pulse quickening — and what a lovely feeling that was — he went straight to the front doors, threw them wide, and sauntered down the steps. Tipped his ruddy, unblemished face to the low sun, relishing the warmth on his skin.

He did not believe that Delilah Dessarian had left Aveline. Nor did he think Nathan would have much success holding her hostage. She was bent upon finding her parents and not a woman to be put off course. Nathan, naturally, had his own agenda. He always did.

Lucius wanted to know what that might be, and Castelio was the one person who might be able to answer his questions. Whether the Quietus lived afterwards . . . Well, that would depend upon what they were.

Lucius snagged a page who was trying valiantly to slip away unseen.

"Fetch my horse." He tossed the boy two copper pyres.

"Milord!" The boy snatched the coins from the air. He ducked his head and took off at a run for the stables.

One way or another, Castelio would lead him to Delilah. And Delilah would lead him to her mother. But the more immediate question was which crossing the Quietus would choose. Lucius considered it. There were several possibilities. If he guessed wrong, Castelio might beat him back to the manor, which would complicate things considerably.

He thought of Castelio's character. A decent, honorable man. Well, Claudius Quintus had been the same. It didn't work out so well for him.

But the traumatic memory the Quietus had unearthed would be long-lasting. He might even feel a need to pay respects. If so, it would place him at the nearest northern crossing to . . . what was that miserable village on the Forkings River called?

The nervous page returned, leading his mare. Lucius took the bridle and tossed the boy a silver ferry.

Ah, yes. *Swanton.*

ROGUE & REVENANT

THE FOURTH EMPIRE BOOK #2

Never make a blood pact with the most notorious necromancer in Aveline.

Especially if he wants you to steal a magic box that once belonged to his insane, demon-binding ancestor.

It just won't end well.

But Lo will risk everything to find her parents... even it means a fool's bargain with Nathan Ouvrard.

The quest leads to the scorching city of Prydwen, where a revolt is brewing against the tyrannical new Duc. Cas and Lucius are hot on her trail — along with a host of unsavory enemies. And Nathan's promise that his heirloom will be simple to retrieve turns out to be as empty as his social calendar.

What's inside the box? Will it save the world, as he claims? Or destroy it?

And if Lo returns to Castle Cazal a single minute late, just how painful will her death be?

Bien sûr... A hope in hell is still better than none at all.

About the Author

Kat Ross worked as a journalist at the United Nations for ten years before happily falling back into what she likes best: making stuff up. She loves myths, monsters, magic, and doomsday scenarios. Join her newsletter and get a free book, plus exclusive news, deals and discounts.

www.katrossbooks.com
kat@katrossbooks.com

facebook.com/KatRossAuthor
instagram.com/katross2014
pinterest.com/katrosswriter
bookbub.com/authors/kat-ross

Also by Kat Ross

The Fourth Empire Series

Savage Skies

Rogue & Revenant

The Fourth Element Trilogy

The Midnight Sea

Blood of the Prophet

Queen of Chaos

The Fourth Talisman Series

Nocturne

Solis

Monstrum

Nemesis

Inferno

The Nightmarked Series

City of Storms

City of Wolves

City of Keys

City of Dawn

The Lingua Magika Trilogy

A Feast of Phantoms

All Down But Nine

Devil of the North

Gaslamp Gothic Collection

The Daemoniac

The Thirteenth Gate

A Bad Breed

The Necromancer's Bride

Dead Ringer

Balthazar's Bane

The Scarlet Thread

The Beast of Loch Ness

Acknowledgments

A huge thanks as always to Carol Edholm, Laura Pilli, and Leonie Henderson for their insights and guidance. To the marvelous team at Acorn, my brilliant, inspiring, and generous publishing family. To Anna-Lena Spies for her gorgeous cover art. And to Mom and Nick, who keep me laughing.

Printed in Great Britain
by Amazon

41680897R00189